WEAPON OF CHOICE

Also by Patricia Gussin

FICTION
Shadow of Death
Twisted Justice
The Test
And Then There Was One

NONFICTION
What's Next . . . For You?
(With Robert Gussin)

WEAPON OF CHOICE
A NOVEL

PATRICIA GUSSIN

Oceanview Publishing

LONGBOAT KEY, FLORIDA

ISBN: 978-1-60809-051-8

Published in the United States of America by Oceanview Publishing, Longboat Key, Florida
www.oceanviewpub.com

10 9 8 7 6 5 4 3 2 1

PRINTED IN THE UNITED STATES OF AMERICA

This book is dedicated to my fabulous parents
who gave so much so generously.

Joseph E. Plese (1904–1989)
and
Gerarda Farrell Plese (1916–2006)

ACKNOWLEDGMENTS

I would like to acknowledge three scientific pioneers who unknowingly contributed to *Weapon of Choice.*

The first is Louis Pasteur (1822–1895), a French chemist whose experiments supported the germ theory of disease. He is best known for inventing a method to kill harmful bacteria in milk, a process now called pasteurization. He is regarded as one of the three fathers of microbiology, together with Ferdinand Cohn and Robert Koch.

The second is Joseph Lister (1827–1912), a British surgeon and a pioneer of antiseptic surgery and sterile technique. He is considered "the father of modern antisepsis."

I can't claim to have known either of these gentlemen, but I did know the third of these prominent scientists: Dr. Grace Eldering (1900–1988). Dr. Eldering with Dr. Pearl Kendrick, developed the first successful whooping cough (pertussis) vaccine in 1938. During the previous decade, whooping cough caused an average of six thousand American deaths annually—mostly children under the age of five. The vaccine virtually eliminated fatalities. She was the director of the Department of Health's Western Michigan Division Laboratory in Grand Rapids, Michigan, from 1951 until her retirement in 1969. My lucky break—she hired me as a bacteriology technician right out of high school, encouraged me through college and medical school, and modeled an incredible work ethic. I am thankful for her friendship and join all parents in gratitude for her efforts to prevent deaths due to whooping cough.

Thanks to the terrific folks at Oceanview Publishing: Frank Troncale, David Ivester, Susan Greger, Susan Hayes, George Foster, Joanne Savage, Kirsten Barger, and Cheryl Melnick. And a special thanks to my editor, Ellen Count. I am so fortunate to have such a spectacular team.

And a huge thanks—with hugs—to my husband, Bob Gussin, who reads everything first, makes my life a dream-come-true, and who happens to be an author and a gourmet cook and a vintner. How fantastic is that?

CHAPTER ONE

"This is Dr. Nelson." Laura had just reached over to switch off the bedside lamp when her phone rang.

"Duncan Kellerman. Sorry to call so late, Laura, but can you see a patient, please."

"Of course. First thing in the morning."

"Could you see him tonight?"

"What's the urgency?" Worn out after a weekend in Orlando chaperoning her son's baseball team, she'd nodded off before the end of the eleven o'clock news.

"I have a thirty-two-year-old white male, febrile, with worsening respiratory distress. Bilateral pulmonary infiltrates—"

"Pneumonia," Laura remarked. Pneumonia was Kellerman's own specialty, so why would he be calling her, a surgeon?

"Undoubtedly. But he has a right hemothorax. We put in a chest tube, drained off the fluid, and found suspicious nodules. Radiology thinks he needs a biopsy to see what's growing in there. Would you come in and check him out? Name's Matthew Mercer."

Laura sat up in bed. Despite her fatigue, she managed to focus.

"I have him on antibiotics," Kellerman persisted, "broad spectrum, including methicillin, but those nodules— "

"I'll be there in fifteen minutes," she sighed.

Laura sank back on her pillow. She disliked leaving her kids alone, even though Natalie and Nicole were seventeen and Patrick was fifteen. Dilemmas of a single mother immersed in a surgical career. Whenever Laura did go out at night, her housekeeper,

Marcy Whitman, always came from the apartment over the garage to stay in the house; just tonight, Marcy was visiting her sister in St. Petersburg, not to return until morning.

At least the hospital was close. Tampa City Hospital stood on Davis Island just over the bridge connecting Davis Island from Tampa proper, less than a five-minute drive for her. On her way out, Laura said good night to her twin daughters, checked in on her sleeping son, and grabbed an apple from the bowl on the kitchen counter.

Laura found Matthew Mercer in a private room on the fifth floor. On a cabinet just outside the door, she saw a supply of paper gowns, a box of rubber gloves, masks, and a plastic bag to collect the refuse. Good, the hospital's infectious disease protocol had been activated. Laura donned the protective gear and stepped inside to find her chief surgical resident adjusting the patient's chest tube connection.

"You put in the tube, Michelle?" Laura asked.

"Yes, Dr. Nelson." Michelle Wallace looked too young to be inserting tubes into chests, but if patients reacted skeptically to her youthful appearance, her energy and good humor won them over. She reminded Laura of herself at Michelle's stage. Right down to Michelle's longish blonde hair, now tucked up inside the surgical cap, and green eyes almost the color of her own. But Michelle was single; when Laura was a resident, she'd had five kids.

"Sorry Dr. Kellerman dragged you in so late at night, but this patient's condition is deteriorating fast," Michelle said quietly. "And he is so young—"

As Michelle held up the patient's chest x-ray to the light box, Laura planted her stethoscope on his chest and listened. Then she straightened up and draped the instrument around her neck. "Mr. Mercer," she began, "I'm Dr. Nelson, the chief of surgery at Tampa City, and I'm a thoracic surgeon."

How much of what she said could he make out with an oxygen mask covering his mouth and nose, and the constant bang of the positive pressure machine?

He flicked his eyes, nodded.

She assessed the patient's physical appearance. Curly auburn hair with clumps sticking to his damp forehead. Thin to the point of emaciation. Lung cancer jumped to the top of her differential diagnosis. She took a moment to examine the x-ray. Definitely bilateral pneumonia. But too often she'd found tumors lurking behind the infected lung tissue, hidden from sight on the x-ray. But in someone as young as thirty-two?

"Did Dr. Kellerman tell you that he recommends a biopsy of your lungs?"

A slight nod. His eyelids rose, panic flashed across the blue eyes.

"I know you can't talk with the oxygen running, but as soon as I finish my examination, I'll take the mask off so we can discuss our next steps. All right?"

Matthew Mercer nodded again. Despite the oxygen, his breathing was ragged and his color grayish. High-risk patient. Not too high risk for a biopsy, she hoped. And what were those raised purplish blotches on his face and neck? When she turned down the sheet to examine his chest and abdomen, something clicked, a suspicion. Red-purple lesions, some coalescing into plaques that marred his lower abdomen. Folding the sheet still lower, she saw how the lesions extended down both legs in an irregular pattern. When she checked his genitalia, she found more of the same purplish papules.

Laura pointed to one of the spots. "Michelle, did Dr. Kellerman go over this finding with you on rounds? Did he order a dermatology consult?"

"No, no one talked about these sores." Michelle paused, correcting her terminology. "These *lesions*."

Then probably no one's made the diagnosis. Yet. Laura had to check one more site: the patient's mouth. She removed his oxygen mask. Ready with a tongue blade from the bedside canister, she asked him to open his mouth. Indeed, angry-looking, raised lesions peppered his gum line: some of them covered with white cheesy material she knew was a fungal infection, candidiasis.

Medical school professors love to teach, but Laura held back.

She had to be sure before she shared her clinical impression. Her presumptive diagnosis: Kaposi sarcoma—KSHV/HHV-8 infection. If this was Kaposi sarcoma, then there was a reasonable possibility that this patient had AIDS. As far as she knew, AIDS had not yet hit Tampa, and she was afraid that the diagnosis would throw the hospital staff into a panic.

Four years earlier, the medical literature had reported an epidemic of Kaposi sarcoma in the homosexual population. The Centers for Disease Control and Prevention, the CDC, named it GRID for "gay-related immune deficiency," but now a retrovirus, HIV-1, had been isolated, and the outbreak was called acquired immunodeficiency syndrome—AIDS.

She'd been following the controversy swirling around the discovery of the virus: Dr. Robert Gallo at the National Cancer Institute claimed to have isolated the retrovirus HTLV-II; researchers at the Pasteur Institute in France claimed to have isolated the same virus. Still a running battle, but politics, legal battles, patents, none of that had been Laura's concern. Except now, faced with an actual patient, she realized how little she—or anyone—knew about this aggressive virus that had now moved into the heterosexual population. And even pediatric patients. Wasn't there recently a little boy, a hemophiliac, who'd been kicked out of school after the school found out he'd acquired the virus in a blood transfusion? Rock Hudson had died of AIDS just last month.

Now, as Laura stared into this patient's mouth, she was even more thankful that the Tampa City Hospital infectious disease nurse had initiated the isolation protocol. In addition to Kaposi sarcoma, the patient most likely had a staph infection and who knew what other bugs would grow out of the cultures. Laura's biopsy would likely reveal even worse pathology. Kellerman should have suspected this, but had said nothing. She wondered why? Had he missed the presumptive diagnosis of AIDS? Or was he trying to hide from it? Avoidance and denial, common defense mechanisms.

"Mr. Mercer," Laura said, "we need to get you into the operating room so we can find out what's causing all the fluid in your lungs. We see some spots in your lungs, too, and we need to know what they are. Could be an infection or a tumor. We need to know, so we can treat you properly. Are you okay with this? We'll need your written consent."

"No surgery! I have an infection," he objected. "A staph infection, I heard the other doctor say. There are drugs to treat that."

"Yes, that's true," Laura said, "but you're not responding. We may identify other organisms."

"Like what?" he asked.

"Like tuberculosis, fungal infections, Pneumocystis or—" Laura didn't want to get too technical.

"I don't mean to be difficult," Mercer's voice came in a raspy wheeze, "but my father, my biological father—he didn't really raise me—is a doctor, Doctor Victor Worth. He's a scientist at the National Institutes of Health. Would you call him? Tell him what you've found, ask for his opinion? I'll go with what he says."

Laura agreed. And she would call, but what she most wanted to do was to go home and sleep, so in the morning she'd be fresh. She'd open up this young man's chest to find out what bad stuff lurked inside.

"Mr. Mercer, first may I ask, have you ever been diagnosed with any serious infectious disease? Either bacterial or viral? Tuberculosis?"

He hesitated, shook his head, and reached for the oxygen mask. Laura helped him situate it, then checked the settings on the positive pressure machine.

At the nursing station, Laura stopped to phone Matthew Mercer's biological father. Mercer and Worth? Different last names. *What was that all about?*

A male voice answered on the first ring.

"Victor Worth?"

"Yes, this is Dr. Worth."

Laura introduced herself as Matthew's doctor, keeping her voice neutral as she detailed a dark medical picture, noted that conventional antibiotics were not working, and told him what she wanted to do. She held back her presumptive AIDS diagnosis, not sure what she could legally share, concerned about patient confidentiality. She waited for Worth's answer.

A lung biopsy was indicated, he conceded. He was not a medical doctor, he informed her. With a Ph.D. in microbiology from Georgetown University, he had made an entire career of antimicrobial research at the National Institute of Allergy and Infectious Diseases—the NIAID—a division of the National Institutes of Health.

The man had an inflated self-image, Laura decided—but never mind. He'd agreed to her treatment plan. He seemed genuinely concerned about Matthew and promised to fly to Tampa the next day.

Worth did have one request that he insisted Laura pursue—an investigational drug trial. A clinical study was underway, he explained, at Keystone Pharma, a pharmaceutical company in Philadelphia. The drug was ticokellin for the treatment of drug-resistant staph. Could she contact a Dr. Norman Kantor at the pharmaceutical firm—and get that drug for Matthew? Worth told her that he used to work with Dr. Kantor, who may have retired, but who would vouch for him and convince his successor to provide the drug immediately under a compassionate IND—investigational new drug application. Worth offered to personally transport the drug, but he reiterated that the request must come from her, Mercer's treating physician. At this time of night she wasn't ready to explain that she was the surgeon and that Kellerman was Mercer's primary physician.

What about a drug to treat the HIV virus? Laura thought as she terminated the call. *Not likely in Matthew Mercer's lifetime.*

Before leaving the hospital, Laura booked the first operating room slot. Her chief of surgery rank did come with privileges. She would place the call to Keystone Pharma the next morning. On her way out, she looked in on Matthew. Still struggling to breathe, he nodded his assent as she told him she'd phoned Worth and they'd talked. Matthew was first on the operating room schedule tomorrow—seven o'clock.

CHAPTER TWO

At five thirty a.m., Laura arrived at Tampa City Hospital. She'd left notes in the kitchen for her kids. They were perfectly capable of making their own breakfast and getting off to school, but still, she felt guilty about leaving them last night and again this morning. Marcy Whitman, her housekeeper of fourteen years, would be back before noon, and all would be well in the Nelson household. Laura hoped. With twin seventeen-year-old daughters, you never knew for certain. One day you thought you did know, but the next day brought surprises, not always pleasant ones, like the birth control pills that had fallen out of Nicole's purse last week.

Laura spent most of her professional time in Tampa City Hospital on Davis Island, but she also had an office and a research lab on the main campus of the University of South Florida Medical School. After graduating from medical school in Detroit and finishing her thoracic surgical residency in Tampa, she'd pioneered lung volume reduction surgery, considered experimental then, but now moving into the mainstream. And, a year ago, the University of South Florida Medical School named her head of the surgical department. She appreciated the title Chief of Surgery, but not the administrative burdens that came with it.

Laura's research labs were located at the medical school complex in Tampa on Fowler Avenue, where she and her research fellows did experimental surgery. She dedicated Tuesdays and Thursdays to research, and usually operated at Tampa City Hospital on

Mondays and Wednesdays. When all was said and done, Laura's schedule was erratic.

Her Tampa City Hospital office was dark and empty when Laura arrived, paper cup of coffee in hand. A stack of charts awaited her signature, as did today's hospital staff meeting agenda. As usual, she would present the surgical stats for the hospital: number of procedures, length of hospital stay, morbidity and mortality rates, wound infection rates, any quality control issues. Should she share Matthew Mercer's presumptive diagnosis of AIDS with the hospital staff?

If she was right and her new patient had the HIV virus, there'd be a steep learning curve as the hospital coped with confusion and chaos—all while trying to prevent transmission to healthcare workers. She'd decided to wait for the biopsy result, to know for sure.

HIV, as an infectious disease, would come under the purview of the internal medicine service. But as chief of surgery, she needed to do everything she could to protect the operating room personnel from contamination, as well as patients in the recovery room and on the surgical floor. She had to do that now, this morning, before she raised what could be a premature alarm.

With a presumptive diagnosis of HIV, the issues were complex. Not much was known about the retrovirus, how it spread, what precautions should be taken, not even how to definitively diagnose it. A test had been recently patented, intended to test the blood supply, but was not yet commercially available. And, she'd read in the lay press about certain problems swirling around the issue of confidentiality. Because HIV was associated with homosexuality, afflicted patients clamored for anonymity. Was it even legal to chart the diagnosis? Activists already were challenging everything about the controversial HIV virus. Laura could be heading into a public health and a public relations nightmare.

A few sips of coffee and she felt her brain function again. When she felt perplexed, Laura resorted to lists. Write down your priorities. What really *must* happen today, what can wait?

6:00: call her friend, Dr. Stacy Jones, at her CDC office in Atlanta. With a Master's in Public Health and an M.D. degree and working in the hub of cutting-edge research at the Centers for Disease Control and Prevention, Stacy would be as up-to-date as anyone on both the science and politics of HIV. She needed Stacy's advice.

6:15: call the O.R. nurse-supervisor to request that she personally supervise every detail of infection control in the operating suites that morning.

6:30: call home, in case the kids overslept.

6:31: check Matthew Mercer's vital signs, labs, blood gases, x-rays, meds, and the patient himself before they wheel him into the operating room.

6:45: scrub in for the procedure and reassure herself that every member of the team is properly gowned, gloved, and masked.

6:55: brief the anesthesiologist and the surgical team, emphasize infection control—a valid concern, because the patient had an infection not responding to antibiotics, probably due to a resistant strain of staph.

She had agreed to call that pharmaceutical company. If they had a new, better drug for resistant staph, now would be the time to get it to this patient, but she cringed at the thought of the administrative quagmire. Laura had been an investigator in experimental drug trials in the past—bronchodilators, anti-inflammatories, and an antibiotic—and she knew perfectly well how the massive paperwork would sabotage her schedule. Moreover, she knew that no one at the company would pick up the phone before eight o'clock. By then she'd be exploring Mercer's lungs. The Keystone Pharma call would have to wait.

Between now and 6:30: sign as many charts as possible to make the paperwork go away.

Noon: chief of staff meeting, mandatory—unless life-and-death kept her confined to the O.R.

How long would this morning's procedure take? Not long. Get in, drain the fluid, biopsy whatever was in there, culture everything, and get out as fast as possible. On a surgical risk scale of one to ten, this patient was a nine. If he wasn't so young, she'd put him at a ten. Losing him on the table would not be good for her statistics, but the only way they could help him was to get into his lungs and find out what lurked there.

1:00 or 1:30: if her look inside Mercer's chest and the micro and histology results more or less confirmed AIDS, she'd meet with her counterpart, the chief of medicine, and Kellerman, the infectious disease specialist. How to proceed with Mercer would be their decision. Maybe she could persuade one of them to call Keystone Pharma about the new drug; if not, she would, as promised.

2:00: lung reduction procedure

5:00: lung biopsy, suspected carcinoma, complicated by beryllium toxicity

6:00: dictate surgical notes

6:30: round with residents—critical patients, only

7:30: home for dinner, go over Patrick's and the twins' homework; call Mike at Notre Dame, she'd missed his call yesterday from South Bend, but she had caught up with Kevin at the University of Michigan in Ann Arbor. Both would be home on Thanksgiving, only four days away.

Patrick's baseball game: She'd have to miss it—but she had spent almost the whole weekend with his team.

CHAPTER THREE

Victor Worth had not slept at all after hearing from that woman doctor last night. Matthew, his son, dominated his thoughts. Victor only had learned of Matthew's existence a month ago, but in that short time Victor's life had turned around. No longer was he the self-focused individualist, caring for no one, convinced that no one gave a damn about him. Until that letter arrived from Cindy, Matthew's mother, Victor had never had reason to consider how being a father could affect him—could dramatically change his life. How could he? Matthew, flesh of his flesh—a reality Victor had dismissed as impossible. If he'd only known in time about Matthew, his son's life would have been so different.

Cindy Mercer, a shy, unassuming girl, could not be expected to raise a manly son. Bereft of a male role model, Matthew had turned gay. Victor didn't blame Cindy, but neither did he blame himself. He hadn't even received her letter, introducing him to Matthew, until after her death. But he couldn't help wondering what he'd have done had he known at the time, during the blackest moments of his life, that Cindy was pregnant? Back then he'd had to use every iota of his emotional and physical reserves to battle testicular cancer.

The arrival of the posthumous letter transformed his life, shook him to his core. According to Cindy, he had a son. Now thirty-two years old. The birth year coincided with Victor's only sexual relationship ever—in his senior year at the University of Virginia, with a student nurse named Cindy Mercer. In her letter, Cindy explained openly, yet sensitively, that their son was a homosexual, a sweet, vulnerable young man who was ill. She'd pleaded with Victor to help his son.

With uncharacteristic impulsiveness, surprising even himself, Victor had traveled to Clearwater, Florida, to meet the boy. One glance had been enough. Victor felt an immediate surge of love and compassion for the thin young man with the curly auburn hair and the most amazing blue eyes. But thanks to Victor's medical background, one look also made him suspect that his son was a victim of the disease known as AIDS.

Infectious diseases—though not viruses, per se—had been his life's work. Right out of his Ph.D. program at Georgetown, he'd started at the NIH, working first with staphylococcal organisms and then with pathogenic fungi. His government research position gave him access to the top resources in the D.C. area capable of treating AIDS. He planned to head back to Clearwater over Thanksgiving weekend and convince Matthew to transfer to George Washington University Hospital. Victor could get him the best of care. But before Victor could make the preliminary arrangements, first he'd have to broach the subject of AIDs with Matthew—in effect, deliver a death sentence to his own son. Victor had never envisioned Matthew ending up in a Tampa hospital so soon.

The dire prognosis of AIDS notwithstanding, Victor vowed to do anything in his power to prolong Matthew's life, to give them some time together. *His son.* He still was in disbelief. And during the night after Dr. Nelson's call, Victor had charted his first step. Matthew's immune system, damaged by the HIV virus, struggled to stave off other organisms, one of which Dr. Nelson thought was a resistant staphylococcus. With Victor's connections, he could get his hands on a new, not yet commercially available, antibiotic against staph: ticokellin was the generic name.

CHAPTER FOUR

Laura adjusted the water temperature, about to start her surgical scrub, when the operating room clerk handed her the phone. "Eileen Donovan."

"Just in time. What's going on, Eileen?" Laura's secretary was one of her three "moms." Peg Whelan, her real mother; Marcy Whitman, her housekeeper; and Eileen, each in her early sixties. Laura knew she could hardly function without all three generous, smart women in her corner.

"You must have been in before dawn to sign all those charts, Laura. Good girl. Sorry your schedule got all botched. I know Marcy is away, so I double-checked on the kids. All three are on schedule. Med school dean's office left a reminder message: don't be late for the noon staff meeting. And I'm going to call and tell the kitchen to make sure they bring you a big salad."

"I'll eat whatever they serve. Just expedite those charts so Medical Records stops breathing down my neck. Seriously though, the case this morning has the potential to go bad in more ways than one. Did Dr. Stacy Jones at the CDC return my call? I left her a message early this morning."

"No. Do you want me to follow up? What's it about?"

"I'll tell you about it later. Will you check with my research lab—make certain the bovine pericardial tissue arrived?"

Laura stood in the operating room glare, scalpel poised to access the patient's lungs through a left lateral incision. Matthew Mercer already had been intubated and placed on a ventilator. Over the past seven hours, his status had deteriorated to acute respiratory distress syndrome. Her mission was to retrieve lung tissue that would establish the cause—without the patient dying on the table, or in the recovery room, or afterward in the ICU. Her medical colleagues' task would be to treat whatever she found in his lungs.

Without explanation and ignoring their gripes, Laura had insisted that the operating team, including the anesthesiologist on his perch behind a screen at the patient's head, be issued plastic face covers as a supplement to the masks they routinely wore.

"Ready, Laura," announced the experienced anesthesiologist. "Patient is as stable as he's ever going to be. I'd suggest getting in and out fast."

Laura usually let her chief resident start a case and continue as far as he or she was capable, often all the way through the case. At the end, she would let a junior resident or a medical student take over, under close supervision. But not today.

"I'll do this." She would run this case to minimize the hospital staff's involvement. If they were dealing with HIV, she couldn't be too cautious.

"Michelle, spread the ribs," she said, having made the incision through the intercostal space, exposing the thoracic cavity. "Use the retractors to hold it open."

To the fourth year med student standing across the table: "Maintain suction and get out as much of this fluid as possible. Note how purulent it is. I'm betting that it grows out staph and heaven knows what else."

Laura exposed the left lung, holding it in gloved hands, inspecting it. "An abscess," she announced, "—focal point for the infection. Get a drain ready, please." She had her usual team: Willa, scrub nurse; Cathy, circulation nurse. They'd worked together so long that they could communicate in a few curt phrases.

"We've also got diffuse interstitial infiltrates. Let's get all this cultured." She didn't know the medical student's name. "Sorry, you—could you hold the culture tubes and then hand them to the nurse, specifying their origin. If you don't know, ask me."

"Michelle, see—here, this bruised area. Much like the lesions on his face and the rest of his body. We'll need a biopsy of these. Willa, are we ready with the instruments and the specimen containers? We are going to have to stop the ventilator long enough to do the biopsies. I only want to stop it *once*. Is everything ready?"

"When you say go, Laura," said the anesthesiologist, "I'll halt the machine. But I'm having some problems holding pressure."

"Ready. Disconnect." Laura used an automatic linear stapling device to harvest the ten biopsy sites she wanted.

"Okay, reconnect! How much time?"

"Sixty-one seconds," a younger male voice said from beyond the drape separating the patient's head from the operative site. "That was fast." The anesthesiologist's resident and his medical student stood alert, their stance as Laura had requested. These were bright kids; they all knew this was an unusual case, just not how it was different.

"Let's drain that abscess, put in two chest tubes—and get him to recovery. Keep him in strict isolation until we get those cultures back."

"Will he be able to come off the ventilator right away?" the medical student across the table wanted to know.

"No," the anesthesiologist answered. "When you open up a patient with acute respiratory distress, they usually need mechanical ventilation for hours, sometimes days. Until you control whatever is causing the lung disease. Let's just hope that antibiotics will kick in for this one."

Laura inserted the chest tube herself, something she hadn't done in years with all the eager house staff surrounding her whenever she operated. The entire procedure had lasted a mere thirty minutes. Now she was sorry that she had pushed back her original nine o'clock case to late afternoon. Another late night.

"Michelle, will you get x-ray confirmation of the chest tube placement before the team leaves the room?"

"Sure, Dr. Nelson, and I'll go with the patient into the recovery room. Any relatives we need to talk to?"

Laura knew why Michelle asked. Laura always included her

residents when she reported the results of surgery to the patient's loved ones. She'd tell them, "This may be the most important responsibility we have—to inform them truthfully, in a sensitive and understandable way." Michelle had taken this direction to heart; she was fast becoming not only a skilled, but a compassionate, surgeon.

"His father should be in later today," Laura said. "Reminds me, I did promise him I'd try to get some experimental medication for his son."

"What med is that?" Michelle asked.

"An antibiotic for resistant staph. I wrote down the name. Nothing familiar to me. May I ask you to do some research on that? Look at Keystone Pharma. It's a new drug now in clinical trials. Let me know what you find. Before eleven thirty, if possible."

"You can get an unapproved drug?" Michelle asked.

"Not without an extraordinary administrative hassle, but I agreed to give it a try."

Laura reached for the clipboard with the phone number and name of the drug, wanting to fulfill her pledge to the father, but not holding out much hope that she'd prevail over regulatory bureaucracy.

"Dr. Laura Nelson, here," she said, "I'm calling Dr. Norman Kantor in your research department."

Laura waited, forced to listen interminably to insipid music. The operator came back: Dr. Kantor was no longer employed at Keystone Pharma.

"I'll talk to your head of research."

She was told to be more specific.

"Connect me to the director of infectious disease research." This time she heard a voice message. She left her name, phone number, and told the machine that it was urgent.

While she waited for the return call, she phoned the recovery room. Mercer had arrived. Isolation protocol in effect. On a ventilator. Condition: critical. Then she called the head of Pathology. The lung specimen biopsies would show Kaposi sarcoma, she told him, and suggested a methenamine silver stain for Pneumocystis carinii cysts on the lung infiltrate specimens. Prior culture results had documented staph, she said. Would Microbiology please include all known antibiotics in the sensitivity testing panel?

She expected him to blurt out "AIDS?" but he didn't. He merely sounded annoyed that a surgeon had any knowledge of cytology stains and sensitivity tests. She thanked him profusely for the extra tests.

Laura took a breath and reached into her drawer, extracting her beryllium lung toxicity file. In an incredibly weak moment, she'd agreed to testify in a case against a metal machining plant about an hour away in Manatee County. The company used beryllium as a hardening agent in alloys. Beryllium is element number four on the element table, and because of its low density and atomic mass, valuable to many industries, particularly aerospace. Problem is, when inhaled, beryllium is corrosive to tissues, and when it leaks into the environment, well, that's not exactly beneficial, either. Whatever had possessed her to get involved? As if her schedule weren't off the charts already. Now she had to prep for what promised to be a vicious cross-examination by the defense.

Not able to concentrate, Laura decided to abandon beryllium—she'd just polish off the article she had cowritten for the *New England Journal of Medicine* on her real research love, lung reduction surgery.

At ten thirty, Stacy Jones called from the CDC. Laura briefed her friend on Mercer's case.

"Laura, I believe you're looking at full-blown AIDS. Your patient's prognosis is dismal. Send me a blood sample, and I'll get some tests done. We've got Gallo's test kit, the one the FDA is evaluating, and we'll look at the patient's T-cells and CD4 count. But with Kaposi and P. carinii, the prognosis can't be good."

"I hope I didn't send him over the edge, opening him up."

"You had to get the tissue, right? Make sure that in addition to those staph antibiotics, you get him on Bactrim. It's the drug of choice, intravenous is your only option. Another thing, this AIDS situation is moving so fast that I doubt your local infectious disease specialist will be up-to-date, so keep me in the loop."

"Doctor Stacy, I can't believe you used to be *my* protegé. How the tables have turned! When I advised you to go to Harvard, little did I imagine that you'd end up a hotshot public health expert."

Laura was proud. How many years had it been since she'd met Stacy, then a high school freshman in inner city Detroit? An easy calculation. Eighteen years. From the year she herself had entered University Medical School in Detroit. 1967, the year of the Detroit riots that decimated Detroit and nearly devastated her life, as well. So much bad fallout had come from those riots, but precious little good; Stacy Jones was an example of the good.

"You already know you need to put some stringent public health precautions in place," Stacy said. "I'll fax you our recommendations. This disease is such a political hot potato that the limits of confidentiality are a science in their own right: what can be disclosed about HIV and what can't. Your patient can have syphilis or gonorrhea or genital herpes and you can flag his chart; with HIV you have to keep secrets. Crazy, but that's how it's coming down. We have Dr. Koop, Reagan's surgeon general, to thank for that."

Laura could not suppress a chuckle. She, a Grand Rapids Republican; Stacy, a Detroit Democrat. Some things never change.

Stacy had the last, affectionate word. "You're my guardian angel, Laura, always will be."

Laura hung up the phone, envisioning the dynamic about to play out: thirty-two-year-old Stacy Jones, an African American, handing down instructions to Kellerman, Tampa's sixty-five-year-old prima donna senior infectious disease authority.

"Dr. L." Eileen looked in. "Michelle Wallace is here. She has the report you requested."

"Send her in, please." Laura had forgotten that she had asked her chief resident to research that new drug.

Michelle glanced around Laura's office, taking in all the family photos. Laura's colleagues at the university and the hospital knew she had several kids, but for the most part, she'd kept her life compartmentalized. Career. Kids. Focus on one. Or the other. Fully. In real time. Do not take your career problems home. Do not take your kid problems to work. Usually, an effective policy. Not always.

"You have such attractive kids," Michelle gazed at Laura as if she were supernatural. "I just don't think I could do it all."

Laura was always taken aback when female medical students considered career and kids incompatible. She'd had two little boys before she even started med school. For the moment, she stifled the career counseling impulse, took Michelle's packet, and began perusing the pages. "So Keystone Pharma has a drug that outperforms methicillin and vancomycin. They've started phase three."

"Yes," Michelle said, "They've completed phase two trials, so we know the drug is effective. Now they're enrolling more patients to make sure that it's safe."

"And is it?"

"The study is double-blind, so no one knows. Unless the code has to be broken for some reason."

Laura was impressed. This girl knew her stuff, and Laura liked to give praise when praise was due.

"Excellent, Michelle, and I appreciate the fine job you did in the O.R. today."

"I'm worried about the patient, Dr. Nelson."

"Why don't you go check on him in the recovery area? Then check with Pathology, see what they've found. Just be sure to follow isolation protocol."

"Oh," Michelle said on her way out the door, "did you know that the CEO of Keystone Pharma got the Nobel Peace Prize this year?"

Indeed. Paul Parnell. Keystone Pharma was respected among pharmaceutical firms for good science, good medical community relations, and generous philanthropy. But their research director had not returned her call.

CHAPTER FIVE

"No personal calls in the lab, isn't that the rule?" Charles Scarlett addressed Stacy Jones as soon as she put down the phone. "Who were you talking to?" Charles knew he sounded pissy, but he could care less.

On his way to the lab that morning, the boss had waylaid him in the hallway. Hadn't even invited him into his office to inform him that Dr. Stacy Jones was being promoted to director, Experimental Staph Section. Just like the CDC—hell, the entire government for that matter. Promote women. Promote blacks. They got a double whammy with Jones, who was both a woman and black. "Colored," his parents would call her.

"Not a personal call," Jones said, turning back her attention to her stack of petri dish cultures. "A friend in Tampa has a patient with probable HIV. Not that I'm an expert, but—"

"We're supposed to go through channels," Charles said, "before we get involved." He didn't know whether Jones had been told about her promotion yet, and he wanted to get in his jibes, petty as they were, before she technically became his boss. Even when that happened, she wouldn't be able to touch him. By the end of the week, he'll have requested a transfer to anywhere she wasn't.

Jones seemed to ignore him. "Tampa isn't San Francisco or D.C. or New York City," she said, inspecting a plate under a scanning microscope. The exotic staph organisms that the lab handled were potentially lethal and access to their Center for Disease Control P3 Lab was restricted to scientists with doctoral degrees and intensive training in antimicrobial technique. "My friend Dr. Nelson doesn't know whether her hospital ever has had a case. Well, you heard what I told her. Anything you'd have added?"

Charles had to tread lightly. He couldn't quite say, *Put the poor bastard out of his misery and cremate the remains.* Public correctness had been his watchword ever since Dr. Pierce had recruited him into The Order two years ago in Arlington. He had to remain non-confrontational even when The Order had openly advocated putting AIDS victims in "cities of refuge."

Not waiting for his reply, Jones continued from under the stainless steel containment hood. He could just make out what she said. "Something interesting going on with our flesh-eating AZ3510 series. Remember the fulminate growth we saw two days ago? Two days ago, I recultured the plate, and today there's nothing. It must have burned itself out. Nothing left for antibiotic sensitivities, and I really wanted to try the paralexins series we got in from Keystone Pharma." Jones recapped the petri dish and withdrew her head from under the protective hood. "That culture's so virulent, burned itself out before I could replate it. Can you move these, please, from a forty-eight-hour to a twenty-four-hour schedule?"

You black bitch. Trying to tell me how to run the lab? The two of them had M.D. degrees, but he also had a Ph.D. in genetics from Emory, and she had a master's in Public Health from Harvard. A Ph.D. trumps a M.P.H. any day, but no, not here at the CDC. His father's words reverberated in Charles's head whenever he faced Stacy Jones: "Because you are white, *you* will always tell *them* what to do, no matter what."

The lab phone rang and Jones picked it up. "Sure," she said. "Lunch? That'd be fine."

That would be the call, Charles thought. Stacy Jones, of African descent, a woman of color, about to be promoted ahead of him, a white male, of European descent, Southern aristocracy. At first he'd felt shame, then he thought about his Aryan Nation brothers in The Order. They talked and talked about something radical. A catalyst. Could this injustice be what they needed to fire them up? One of their own, passed over for a colored woman. Isn't this what The

Order had been warning the members about all this time? The Order had to do something to protect the future of white children. *Something radical.*

Jones looked up at the wall clock. "I'll put these cultures away," she announced. "Stan Proctor asked me out to lunch. Imagine. Can you lock up the lab, Charles, when you leave?"

His grimace was so taut that he had to consciously unlatch his jaws. Jones ordering him around enraged him—but what had she said just before that? About the AZ3510 culture? Ultravirulent? Flesh-eating?

The introverted, wimpy, overweight offspring of a charming Southern socialite and a stalwart white supremacist lawyer, recognized the kernel of an opportunity. With just a little clandestine effort, Charles would have something special to share with The Order when the cell met next Wednesday night. This time he would have their attention.

CHAPTER SIX

For his trip to Philly and after that to Clearwater, Victor Worth chose a camel-colored cashmere jacket, a pale green shirt, a multicolored striped tie, and tan wool slacks. In his breast pocket, he'd packed an extra monogrammed handkerchief. He wanted to look important when he presented himself to the big pharmaceutical company. Once he got to Florida later that day, he'd be overdressed, but he reasoned that wool would not wrinkle on the train ride from D.C. to Philadelphia.

Victor had never considered himself an emotional man. But ever since he'd learned about Matthew in Cindy's letter, just a month ago, he felt the yearning—unquestioning, with nothing held back—for a close father-son relationship. He knew it sounded trite, but a son brought meaning into his life. He and Matthew were a family. Even thinking the words *son* and *family* could bring tears to Victor's eyes.

The minute he was settled on the Metroliner from D.C. to Philly, Victor pulled out the letter handwritten on light-gray stationery from his all-but-forgotten college girlfriend.

Victor, I have no way to know if you ever discovered this: you have a son.

No, he had not.

Matthew, a wonderful young man with your cobalt-blue eyes and your curly auburn hair. He's thirty-two years old now. A college biology teacher, at least he was.

Here the paper was marked by what probably were tearstains, blurring the blue ink.

> *When I was told by my doctor six months ago that I have advanced ovarian cancer, Matthew left San Francisco and came to Clearwater to take care of me. He stayed with me through all my pain and anguish. What will happen to him now?*
>
> *Victor, I am begging you. Will you take him into your heart? Your life? He has no one. No other family. And his friends—I don't know how to tell you. Our son, Matthew, is gay.*

Victor had to admit that this revelation hit him hard. He had a son, but he was homosexual?

> *And although I'm a nurse, I don't know for sure, but I'm worried that he's ill, quite ill.*
>
> *When you receive this, I will already have passed. Matthew will be alone. I've never burdened you, but I am desperate. I have nowhere else to turn. You are an important scientist, not married—I do know that.*

That shocked Victor. He had never tried to find out what had happened to his girlfriend, the student nurse, Cindy. After he'd been emasculated, his testicles removed because of the cancer, he'd never looked back. Sex and women and love belonged to the past.

> *Please, dearest Victor, could you help him deal with losing me, help him get settled. He'll have my house in Clearwater, but not much else. Please, Victor, help him. Please.*

Victor was still overcome by his reaction, which was immediate and intense. His son, straight or gay, was his son. All he could think of was "flesh of my flesh." Where had that come from? The Bible?

And now the fear of losing Matthew frightened Victor to the point of panic. He would do anything to keep Matthew alive. He had underestimated the stage of Matthew's illness. He'd planned to convince his son during Thanksgiving weekend to move from the medical backwaters of Florida to D.C. with its sophisticated resources.

Last time he'd seen his son in Clearwater, two weeks ago,

Matthew had a hacking cough and a low-grade fever, but Victor needed to get back to D.C. so he'd left him. Each of the two times he'd seen Matthew, Victor had no choice but to leave Florida after a brief couple of days. He could not be away from the D.C. vicinity for more than seventy-two hours. Ever. But now, in retrospect, he realized he should have paid more attention to the purplish blotches on Matthew's face that his son had found so embarrassing.

Having spent his whole career in infectious disease research—the first nine on staphylococcus bacteria and the last nine on the cryptococcus fungus—Victor knew that Matthew was a victim of the HIV virus. Never in his career had he worked in virology research, but for the last few years, the entire infectious disease community had been focused in one way or another on HIV. Recently, even his own cryptococcus research had focused on opportunistic fungal infections in HIV-positive patients.

No one had a cure for HIV/AIDS, though experts recommended AZT—zidovudine—in high doses. Nor was there a cure for Kaposi sarcoma, which Victor knew was the cause of the blemishes that Matthew thought were merely cosmetic. But there was a new cure for invasive staph infections, and that female doctor in Tampa emphasized that Matthew had a staph infection. That cure had come out of Victor's lab at the NIAID division of the National Institutes of Health.

The drug that resulted from his own research was being tested now in clinical trials by Keystone Pharma. Right now, at this very moment, some fortunate stranger suffering with virulent staph was getting an infusion of his drug, ticokellin. Matthew would have ticokellin by the end of the day. And that was why Victor was headed to Philadelphia on his way to Tampa to see his son.

When the train arrived at 30th Street Station, Victor picked up his rental car and drove north out of Philadelphia toward Montgomery County. Fifty minutes later, he rushed through the glass doors of Keystone Pharma headquarters.

"Dr. Norman Kantor, please," he told the receptionist.

"I'm sorry, sir, Dr. Kantor has retired," the black female replied. Name tag: Marie. Pleasant smile.

Victor thought he'd heard that on the professional grapevine, but Norman had never bothered to inform him directly.

"Then I'll see his replacement."

"Without an appointment, sir, I don't believe that will be possible. But I will be glad to check with his assistant. Your name?"

Victor also gave his title at the NIH. He and Dr. Kantor had been colleagues he stressed—worked on related research subjects.

Marie dialed, explained into her headset. She smiled at Victor, "Dr. Minn will see you, sir. He's our director of research."

A diminutive man in an oversized white lab coat appeared without delay. "Fred Minn," he said, offering his hand to Victor. "We can talk in the conference room."

Victor followed the white lab coat. They entered a space about the size of a coatroom, to the left of the glass entrance doors. He'd expected to be ushered into the director's office, offered a tour of the labs—the same courtesies he would show a visiting colleague. So far, Victor hadn't even gotten past security.

"I'm afraid that I'm having a very busy day, Dr. Worth. I don't believe we had an appointment. So, what can I do for you?"

You can give me a supply of ticokellin, he wanted to say, but he knew these industry scientists were political animals, so he methodically presented his case for a compassionate IND for Matthew. He peppered his request with tidbits of cutting-edge scientific insight about the virulence and resistance of Staph aureus. Victor was not some nobody off the street.

Dr. Minn listened politely, apparently impressed with Victor's research acumen, until Victor concluded.

"Not possible," he answered.

Victor felt his face get hot—which meant his cheeks also were turning red. "I invented the prototype for that drug at the NIH. Norman Kantor as much as stole it from me. I demand that I leave with it!" Victor started to get up, not sure of his options. How could he convince this bureaucrat?

"Calm down, Dr. Worth." Minn gestured with his hands for Victor to sit down. "A few minutes ago, I had a similar conversation with Dr. Nelson in Tampa about the patient."

So she had called. Victor sat back down.

"I told Dr. Nelson the same thing I'm telling you. Not good news for you. Not good news for Keystone Pharma."

Victor felt his body slump into the chair and the blood drain from his face.

"This morning, we made the decision to stop the ticokellin clinical trials. Our CEO is meeting with financial analysts on Wall Street right now. By this afternoon, it'll be public knowledge. A third case of aplastic anemia has been reported in the clinical trials. As a researcher yourself, you'll understand."

"Ticokellin?" He paused briefly. "You used the butyl analog, didn't you?"

"Matter of fact, we did," Minn's eyebrows shot up. "Why do you ask?"

"Why do I ask?" Victor's voice rose. Kantor obviously had commercialized the wrong chemical analog. When his boss was leaving the NIH for a job in the pharma industry, Victor had argued with him. The butyl analog had a higher potential for toxicity. Granted, it was cheaper to synthesize the butyl analog and scale up to commercial quantities, but at the risk of more side effects such as severe anemia. The bottom line here: the bastard had deliberately sabotaged a lifesaving antibiotic so his corporate employer could save lots of money on manufacturing costs. Didn't that make Kantor a murderer as surely as if he'd strangled all those potential patients with his own hands? Just as if he'd murdered Matthew with his own hands.

"Just give me a supply." Victor leaned closer to Dr. Minn. "Ticokellin showed efficacy in phase two, I'm willing to risk the chance of aplastic anemia. My son is immune compromised. He needs ticokellin. No paperwork, no record, no nothing. Just go into your lab and get me a twenty-one-day supply. That's all I ask. No one will ever know. I will carry it on the plane and administer it myself. I'll say nothing to Dr. Nelson or to anyone else. Please. I developed this drug. My son needs it. It's only fair. Just give me a supply. Please!"

"I'm sorry, Dr. Worth, I really am." Dr. Minn got up, leaving Victor alone in the tiny room. As Minn disappeared through the security turnstile, Victor started to weep. It had come to this. A man who never had wept about his cancer, not even the emasculation, crying like a baby. Marie asked if she could call someone. A friend? A family member? Then she brought him a box of tissues. His handkerchief, and the spare, both tear-soaked, Marie's fresh tissues wadded in his hand, Victor left for Tampa.

At the Philadelphia airport, Victor rushed to find a pay phone near the boarding gate. His seventh call to a network of mutual colleagues hit pay dirt. Norman Kantor and his wife, Naomi, had retired to Longboat Key, Florida, to a condo on the Gulf of Mexico. How nice for Norman. No problem getting Norman's phone number, it was listed.

Victor's watch said he had five minutes for a phone call before his plane left at two thirty p.m. Delta, nonstop to Tampa. Kantor was his last hope. A former vice president, Norman should have enough clout to prevail on the bureaucratic Minn. In fact, Victor was ready to bet that Kantor had squirreled away some of the drug. A common practice among researchers. One never knew when one might need the drug for personal reasons or for unsponsored research purposes. Not ethical, but—

Victor heard Naomi's voice on the Kantor message machine. Her voice was raspy as he'd remembered. "Leave a message. Norman or Naomi will call you back."

He asked that Norman call his office at NIH, leave a message where he could be reached. "As soon as possible, Norman, this is urgent!"

Victor still had time to call Tampa City Hospital for information about Matthew. The last time he'd been told that Matthew was in the recovery room, listed in critical condition. No, Dr. Laura Nelson was unavailable—in a meeting. They informed Victor that Matthew was now in the surgical ICU, still listed as critical. That's all the hospital could disclose. For more information, he'd have to talk to the patient's doctor. Victor clanged the receiver into its hook and sprinted to the gate. He was the last passenger to board his Delta flight.

CHAPTER SEVEN

The Tampa City Hospital CEO and the chiefs: Medicine, Pathology, Anesthesia, Pediatrics, OB-GYN, Psychiatry, and Surgery sat at a large rectangular table, draped with white linen and brightened with fresh flowers in the center. Waiters presented a plate to each doctor and took a drink order. Laura had a big salad placed in fronof her. All the others had a Reuben sandwich and French fries. Eileen had intervened, as Laura had known she would. Eileen and Laura, each five feet, five inches, each fluctuating between five and ten pounds overweight religiously counted their calories, kept track of their exercise time, and struggled in their own little weight watchers support group to lose those infuriating last few pounds.

Before the staff meeting, Laura had forewarned the chief of medicine and the hospital CEO about the AIDS patient in the facility. The hospital CEO, a businessman with medical savvy, asked Laura to brief the group on Matthew Mercer's diagnosis. The faces around the table—all men—turned somber and concerned as she presented the facts, as she understood them. They were facing the first case of AIDS at their hospital. Everyone was aware that for many months, the lay press and medical journals had been publishing dire, even inflammatory, scenarios peppered with words like "death sentence," "highly contagious," "no cure," even "God's punishment." So many issues were intertwined: medical, epidemiological, social, psychological, not to mention legal. Laura had made the diagnosis—identified the problem—but, she made very clear, the patient's definitive care belonged to Medicine, not Surgery.

Indeed she would see to the patient's surgical recovery, but the HIV diagnosis—whatever that might portend—was not her direct problem. Having made the diagnosis, she now passed the baton to Medicine. She concluded by strongly recommending that the Hillsborough County Health Department be notified and by telling them that she had a CDC contact whom she'd called for preliminary advice.

Dr. Kellerman waylaid Laura as she left the dining room, pressing his case that she assume primary care for Matthew Mercer. "You did the surgery," he persisted.

She didn't really blame him for trying to avoid the stress of a diagnosis so controversial in so many ways. "But I'm not the infectious disease expert," she repeated. "I did the biopsy. The frozen section was positive for Kaposi sarcoma, not really a sarcoma, as you know, but a hallmark for AIDS. And the pneumocystis stain was positive, another AIDS-defining finding."

Kellerman just shook his head. "I'd like to transfer the patient to your care."

"Duncan, I'll follow the patient for surgical complications, you know that. But this is a medical disease with multiple infectious organisms, not my bailiwick. The patient certainly won't tolerate another surgical procedure. Not for a long time." Never, Laura guessed. "Dr. Jones at the CDC said to feel free to call her if you want advice."

When Laura returned to the O.R., Mr. Kelly had been prepped. A wide incision would expose his lungs, allowing her to remove the hyperinflated, useless portions so that the healthier remaining tissue could perform properly. The cheerful seventy-year-old was one of her favorite patients. Short curly gray hair with hazel eyes that sparkled despite his constant stuggle for breath. She knew his equally affable wife would be in the waiting room, pacing, praying.

Lung reduction surgery was Laura's specialty, and she was a principal investigator in a clinical trial of the procedure coordinated by Washington University in St. Louis. Patients with severe respiratory distress secondary to emphysema in the upper lobes of the lung responded best. She couldn't offer a cure, but she hoped to deliver a better quality of life for the elderly gentleman; less shortness of breath, a more active lifestyle so he could enjoy his grandchildren.

Mr. Kelly's surgery went well, and Laura let the gangly male med student close the large midline chest incision. The procedure had taken two and a half hours, giving Laura just enough time to regroup before starting her five o'clock case.

A new team, the second shift, had Tom Mancini, the beryllium toxicity factory worker, ready. Michelle's on-call day had ended, but she asked whether she could scrub in, too, and Laura agreed.

"This case should go quickly," Laura said as soon as the patient had been anesthetized. "We just have to grab a biopsy of that lesion over there." She nodded at the x-ray tacked to the light box. "Right upper lobe. Shouldn't be hard to find. Speed is important here. The lungs are compromised by the toxicity."

Laura let Michelle make the intercostal incision, and once the lung was exposed, pointed out the cratered nodule. "One centimeter diameter," she said.

"Is the tumor part due to the beryllium damage?" Michelle asked.

"Yes. Inhalational exposure. I'm seeing a lot more of these cases, mostly from the Bradenton/Sarasota area."

"And," Michelle concluded, "lung cancer's related."

So Michelle had read up on this. Very good. Smart, as well as technically competent.

"Do we need a frozen section?" asked Michelle.

"No, we can wait on the path report. If it's carcinoma, he's not a candidate for a surgical cure. Too bad, he's a nice man, active in the community. And only fifty-four."

This time, Laura asked the junior resident to close the incision with the staple device as Michelle supervised.

The surgical teaching staff made rounds every day at six thirty p.m. All attending physicians and house staff who were not in the operating room or responding to an emergency gathered at the nursing station before proceeding room to room to discuss patients' status. Patients who were stable were passed by with a word or two, but patients with complications were discussed, a group consensus developed, and the house staff left to implement treatment decisions. Laura made clinical rounds a high priority. She easily could get so mired in the administrative minutiae of running the department, that she feared losing touch with what mattered most: the patients and the students.

When Laura joined the rounding physicians they were just approaching Matthew Mercer's room. She decided to intervene. "This patient is in strict isolation," Laura told the students and doctors. "No need for all of you to gown up. Why don't you move on, and Michelle, you come with me."

Laura grabbed a gown, capped her hair for the umpteenth time that day, put on the booties, a mask, and gloves. She pointed to the chart hanging on the wall outside the room. "Use gloves when handling the chart," she told Michelle. "Check the blood gases, CBC, kidney, liver, and electrolytes. I'll check the surgical site."

The patient was sedated. The ventilation settings had been decreased, Laura noted with satisfaction. The incision looked clean and dry. She checked the intravenous antibiotics: trimethoprim-sulfamethoxazole, methicillin, vancomycin—a reasonable cocktail. She wondered whether Dr. Kellerman had decided to take her advice and call Stacy at the CDC for advice. She doubted it. His pride would get in the way.

"I was reading about AIDS," Michelle said. "That's what Mr. Mercer has, right?"

Laura nodded. "Yes. Although I don't know how we are going to handle patient confidentiality issues. That's why I didn't review him with the rest of the group."

"Would this be the first AIDS case in Tampa?" Michelle asked.

"Maybe, but since the diagnosis is shrouded in confidentiality issues, how would we know? I can understand trying to protect patients from the stigma of an AIDS diagnosis, but I think the treatment team has a right to know. Anyway, I'm leaving that up to internal medicine and the administration. AIDS or not, we have him in strict isolation. That's about all we can do to protect ourselves and the other patients."

"But what about the nursing staff?" Michelle asked. "They're the ones who come into close contact with the body fluids. Are they careful enough?"

"I hope Dr. Kellerman decides to inform them," Laura said. "Now let's go check on the families."

After rounds, Laura talked to her patients' families. Her message to Kelly's wife: upbeat and positive. Her feedback to Marcini's wife and two sons: guarded and tentative.

"What about Mr. Mercer?" Michelle asked as they left the Mancini family.

"I should check whether his father made it to Tampa."

"I'm going home to get some sleep," Michelle sighed. "I'm on call the entire Thanksgiving weekend. I traded for Christmas off so I can go to Toledo to meet my boyfriend's family."

"Toledo? Really, I'm not sure whether that's a good trade-off. You run along, I'm going home to my kids."

Laura forgot all about Matthew Mercer's father arriving from Bethesda.

CHAPTER EIGHT

MONDAY, NOVEMBER 25

Seven fifteen p.m. Victor hoped he wasn't too late to catch Dr. Nelson. Matthew was listed in Intensive Care, but housed in a separate room, off to the side of the ICU main entrance. You couldn't miss the sign on his door: INFECTION CONTROL. DO NOT ENTER. In smaller type: VISITORS, REPORT TO THE NURSING STATION.

At the station, the desk clerk looked up from a stack of lab reports.

"I'm here to see Matthew Mercer and I'd like to speak to his doctor. Could you page Dr. Laura Nelson, please?"

"Visitors are restricted to relatives. Are you a relative of Mr. Mercer?" The female clerk reached into her files. "Mercer, Matthew." She chose a chart. "Let me see who's listed."

"Yes, I am a relative," Victor said. "I'm his father. I'm his only relative, so it's urgent that I be here for him." *I am the only person in the entire world that loves this boy. Nobody's going to stand in my way.*

"I don't see a father listed, but—" The clerk hesitated with the chart in her hand. Before she could decide what to do, an orderly pushed a gurney up in front of the nursing station between the desk and Victor.

"Excuse me," Victor said, starting to work his way around the impediment, but the patient on the gurney, apparently sedated, still managed to preempt administrative attention.

"Just a minute, sir," the clerk spoke to Victor but looked past him at the orderly. "We're really busy here. I have to see to this new patient. What procedure?"

"Five days post discharge for hip replacement," the orderly answered. "Admitting diagnosis: pulmonary embolus. Erratic ECG. No beds in the coronary care unit, so here we are."

"Ma'am?" Victor tried to divert the clerk's attention.

"You have to wait, sir, until I get this patient admitted." She accepted the newcomer's chart and shuffled pages.

Victor turned, walked the few steps to Matthew's door. From a supply of gowns, masks and paper booties and head caps neatly stacked at the entrance to the room, he grabbed the protective garments and wrestled the gown over his heavy cashmere jacket. If someone came in, they'd expect him to follow protocol. He stepped inside. He thought he was prepared, but when he saw Matthew, tubes coming from everywhere, unconscious, hooked up to a ventilator, Victor's heart plunged, tears stinging his eyes. Victor did not breathe until he saw the steady pattern on the ECG monitor.

Victor wondered whether the medical staff here had come up with the AIDS diagnosis. That sign on the door suggested that they had. They'd have to tell Matthew, and when they did, Victor needed to be right there with his son. Victor himself had intellectually, but not emotionally, accepted that Matthew would not live more than a couple of years. But Victor wanted to be a part of every remaining day of his life, to create some common history. He needed to get Matthew home—and soon. His son certainly could not die hooked up to machines in a hospital nine hundred miles from D.C.

CHAPTER NINE

When Laura walked through the door into her spacious kitchen, Marcy was putting meatloaf, Brussels sprouts, and sliced beefsteak tomatoes on the table. That salad at lunch was a long time ago and she was starved, but she also felt contaminated. Just how infectious was that HIV virus?

"Marcy, I'll explain later, but I have to jump in the shower." Laura set down her briefcase. "Do we have any antimicrobial soap?"

"Just hurry, Laura, I'll put the meat back in the oven and keep the vegetables warm. All we have is that brown stuff you keep in the medicine cabinet."

"Betadine." The stuff she used pre-op for incision sites. "Yuck."

In ten minutes Laura was back, scrubbed, her hair wet and pulled back at the nape of her neck. She called the kids while Marcy put the food back on the table.

"Hey, Ma, I almost hit the cycle today. Thrown out at second, tried to slide, but didn't make it." Patrick never failed to give her a play-by-play for any game she missed. Of that she was glad. With three sons, she'd made a point of learning the basics of their various sports. All three played all three guy sports, but each had his favorite. Mike, football. Kevin, basketball. And her baby, Patrick, baseball.

"That means you got a home run! Coach James must have been happy. Sorry I missed the game." She meant it. Patrick was good, so good that he thought his career as a pro catcher was a given. "But how's that science report coming along?"

"I've got two weeks. And it's not just a report, Mom, it's a project. I have to come up with something. Can't you find some experiment at the hospital so you can make a chart and a demonstration? Remember the one you did for Nicole—different kinds of sutures and staplers."

A pet peeve. High school science projects that a parent ends up doing. But yes, she had more or less done one for her four older kids. And, no, she couldn't let Patrick down.

"I'll give it some thought tonight," she said. "Where are the girls?"

"Just four of us tonight," Marcy said. "I let Natalie study at Collette's. Her father is a math teacher and Natalie has a trigonometry test tomorrow. They said she could have dinner there. Home by nine, I said."

"Makes sense," Laura said, getting up, going to the staircase and hollering, "Nicole, hurry up. Dinner."

Nicole came bounding down the stairs, headed for the table, but before sitting down, she kissed Laura on the cheek. "How was your day, Mom?"

So the pleasant Nicole decided to show up. Interested in *her* day? Seventeen-year-old girls are internally focused. *Their* day. *Their* night. *Their* clothes. *Their* hair. *Their* friends. Not much interested in their parents. Or in Laura's kids case, parent. Seventeen-year-old girls are naturally narcissistic, an age-appropriate phenomenon, Laura judged.

"My day was busy," Laura said. "I had—

"Oops, I forgot to tell you last night before you left for the hospital, Jennie called. She's having a party at her parents' beach house. You know, the one in Tarpon Springs. Her parents will be there, naturally. She invited me and Natalie."

"Natalie and me," Laura corrected. "And Nicole, you and I have to have our heart-to-heart conversation before I let you go anywhere."

"That's not fair." Nicole tossed her napkin on the table. "My life's important, too. You can't keep doing this to me!" She stood, flipped back her long blonde hair, and flashed overly mascaraed eyes. "Sorry, Mrs. Whitman, dinner looks really great, but I'm not hungry."

"Okay," Laura said, trying for calm. "I'll be up to talk to you later. I'd like to see your homework, too."

"I'm a senior in high school. I'm responsible for my own stuff. Give me a break." Nicole stomped up the stairs.

Patrick helped himself to a second healthy slice of meatloaf. "What's wrong with her?"

"She'll be okay," Marcy said. "I do think you should talk to her, Laura. Soon."

Laura raised her eyebrows. Marcy's instincts about the girls and what was going on in their heads often exceeded hers.

As Laura and Marcy cleared away the dishes, the phone rang. Patrick answered, paused a moment then announced, "For you, Mom—Doctor Nelson." He handed her the receiver.

"This is Dr. Nelson."

"Dr. Worth. Matthew's father."

Laura had meant to call him, but had let it slip.

"Yes," she interrupted. "I tried to get that experimental drug. The research director at Keystone Pharma said it was impossible, that there'd been side effects—"

Worth said he already knew that. He'd called, too. The company had botched the study or the drug; she couldn't hear him that well amid the background noise. He must be in an airport.

He asked about the surgery.

Even though he was a relative, could she convey the AIDS diagnosis? What could she tell him? She decided to end the call and defer the decision. "Dr. Worth, I'm having trouble hearing you. Call Mr. Mercer's attending physician, Dr. Duncan Kellerman." Rude, maybe, but it got her off the hook for now.

Natalie came home on time, hugged Laura, and started to unpack the contents of her bulging backpack on the kitchen table. The twins were in their last year at the Academy of the Holy Names, an all-girls Catholic high school. Both had been good students for their first three high school years, but Laura had started to worry about their grades this semester. Natalie struggled in math as well as in honors history. And for the first time, Nicole's literature teacher had asked for a conference with Laura—scheduled for next week. She'd gotten two successive Ds on assignments. And barely squeaked out a C on her midterm.

The natural place to look, Laura knew, was their social life. The twins always had been popular. Very pretty, honey-blonde hair, the color of hers, cornflower-blue eyes the exact shade of their father's; slim, with breasts that were "too small," they complained, but to their male admirers, probably appeared quite perfect. Neither girl cared much about athletics. For a while, Nicole had done gymnastics, back when she wanted to be a cheerleader, an activity she now disdained. Natalie, who usually followed in her sister's footsteps, had fallen in with an equestrian set of girlfriends in middle school and had taken up riding—until she broke her arm in a jumper fall. She never got back on a horse.

Going to a private school, the twins had friends all over Tampa, and for their seventeenth birthday, Laura had swallowed hard and bought them a four-year-old, green Chevy Impala. A joint gift. With Mike and Kevin at college, the girls having a car took a lot of pressure off her and Marcy, but she now wondered if the car—all that freedom—had triggered whatever was going on with them.

"Natalie, can you stay downstairs for a bit. I have to talk to your sister."

"No, Mom, I have to go up to our room. All my stuff is up there, and I have to get organized."

It looked to Laura that all Natalie's stuff was dumped on the table. Laura hesitated before replying.

"If you'd let one of us move into Mike and Kevin's room," Natalie continued, "we wouldn't have this problem. Why keep their room for them? They're never going to live here again. And Nicole and I are so crowded. Our room is even smaller than theirs, and Patrick has his own room. Not fair, Mom."

"They'll be home next weekend for Thanksgiving," was all

Laura could think of to say. So unlike Natalie, this attitude. "And if you have to work in your room—go ahead." She would find another time to talk to Nicole about last Saturday night.

Her daughters had been out with friends. They got in at midnight, their weekend curfew, and everything seemed okay. That is, until Nicole tripped on the landing, dropping her purse, spilling the contents. The plastic cover of a dial pack of Ortho birth control pills cracked when it hit the polished oak floor.

Had Laura overreacted? "What are these for?" she'd demanded, grabbing Nicole by the shoulders, shaking her, barely managing not to slap her. "Why do you need these? Are you having sexual intercourse?" she'd demanded.

A stunned stare from both girls, a long silence.

"Answer me, Nicole."

"Mom, calm down." Natalie jumped between them, pulling her away from Nicole. "Give her a chance to answer you. Get your hands off of her."

When Laura thought about it, this was the first time her sweet, respectful Natalie ever had spoken to her like that. Nicole? Another story.

"Okay, Nicole, you tell me," Laura stared at them both. She was angry beyond words, yet confused and overwhelmed by a feeling of hopelessness. How could she have prevented this? "What are these for if you're not having sex?"

"I'm not having sex," Nicole shouted. "Think what you want. So what if you don't trust me. I don't care. You're a control freak."

"Where did you get these?" Laura grabbed Nicole again.

"They're not mine," Nicole said. "Listen to me, *Mother*. I am not taking birth control pills. Guess why not? Because I'm not having sex. I don't even have a boyfriend I give a shit about. If you even knew me, you'd know that."

"Nicole, I asked you a question!" Laura couldn't help yelling.

Natalie had picked up the dial pack, and Laura grabbed it out of her hands. A prescription product. There should be a patient's name on it. There wasn't. The label had been ripped off.

"Lots of girls have these. Take them every day. Pass them

around. I do not know how they got in my purse." Nicole stood, hands on hips, staring at Laura. "Would you rather have me lie to you? Make something up? Would that make you happy?"

"Nicole's telling the truth," Natalie said. "I've never lied to you, Mom. I'd know if she was taking those pills, and she's not. I swear."

"Okay. Let's go into the kitchen. Make some tea like we always do when we have a problem. I guess you understand why I'm so upset, don't you?" Laura was facing Nicole.

"How am I supposed to feel? As usual, you believe Natalie and not me."

Laura put her arm around Nicole and led her into the kitchen. "Let's calm down, give us time to get over the shock of this—of what I just saw." She brushed her fingers over Nicole's cheek. "We'll have to talk more about this, Nicole. I just don't know what to think right now."

Sunday night, she'd been called out to see the AIDS patient and tonight she'd let Natalie preempt the time. She needed to clear the air with Nicole—but she also needed a feasible reason why Nicole had birth control pills in her purse. She needed to trust each of her daughters. If she couldn't, obviously, she was failing as a mother.

CHAPTER TEN

Nicole didn't say much the next morning, but she did show up in time for breakfast, in her uniform, looking like she'd spent plenty of time fixing her hair into an up-do with tendrils falling in an artsy pattern. Natalie, in the same uniform, looked demure, her skirt two inches longer than her sister's, hair shining, but with a simple side part. On the right. Since the girls were toddlers, Laura had chosen to part Natalie's hair on the right and Nicole's on the left. Over the years, the identical twins had tried to switch to confuse friends and relatives, but their hair was so trained that Laura, at least, could not be fooled.

All the Nelsons left together, Laura in her Oldsmobile station wagon and Nicole driving the Impala with Natalie in the passenger seat and Patrick in the backseat. They'd drop him off at Jesuit High on their way to Holy Names.

Laura decided to stop at Tampa City Hospital since it was on the way to her research labs about a half-hour drive from Davis Island into Tampa. Before starting her research day at the university, she'd page Michelle and check out her critical patients. Being chief resident meant that Michelle would be there before the crack of dawn.

Michelle met her outside Matthew Mercer's isolation room. They donned protective coverings and Michelle briefed Laura on Mercer's status. "Making some effort to breathe on his own, and his electrolytes have improved. Still pumping him full of antibiotics. We should have culture and sensitivity results later this morning.

He's on hourly blood gases and chemistries. So far kidney function is in the normal range."

"Not much more we can do," Laura said, as they pushed through the door. "Either he's going to rally, or he's not." Now how profound was that pronouncement, from the chief of surgery.

Their patient had a visitor, a man, probably in his late forties or early fifties, sat in the lone bedside chair. Auburn curls slipped out from under the paper cap that covered his head. Above the mask, cobalt-blue eyes rimmed in red betrayed exhaustion. When Laura and Michelle approached, he reached out his right hand, but let it fall when Laura put up her hands to signal *no contact*.

"I'm Dr. Nelson and this is Dr. Wallace," she said. "Are you Mr. Mercer's father?" She wondered again how much information she should give the man. He was an expert in infectious disease, had been rather pompous on the phone, and she had to leave for her research labs. He could debate antibiotic details with the medical docs if he wanted.

Before the visitor could respond, Laura turned and spoke directly to Michelle, "The medical service said something about trying to get that experimental drug, AZT. Did they?"

"Not in the chart, Dr. Nelson. But Infectious Disease did start acyclovir. Works in herpes, but probably not—this."

"Yes, I am Dr. Victor Worth," the visitor confirmed, "Matthew Mercer's father." Aggressive-sounding tone. "I spoke to you on the phone yesterday, Dr. Nelson."

"Yes. I'm sorry that didn't work out," Laura said. "The drug had side-effect issues." She still wondered why father and son had different last names.

"That drug was deliberately sabotaged," Worth said. When he started to shake his fist, Laura was glad that she'd decided not to share Mercer's medical details. He seemed emotionally unstable, and she had no time to deal with the cause of his angst.

"We're doing everything we can for Mr. Mercer," Laura said. "Now we have to get back to our rounds." She turned abruptly to leave the room.

Michelle followed her and hesitated before taking off her protective gown. "Do you want me to go back and talk to the father?" she asked.

"No," Laura said. "As long as his incision is clean, there's nothing more we can do. Remember, we're just consultants. It's up to the medical service to handle the infectious disease pathology and they have him on a potent cocktail of antibiotics."

Dr. Worth followed the surgeons, but only as far as the door. Laura heard Worth mumble something, but his remark was not loud enough for her to hear.

She turned to face him through the doorway, saw the frustration and helplessness so common to the faces of loved ones. "I'm sorry," she said, and meant it. She and her chief resident removed their gloves, gowns, caps, and booties.

Michelle reported that Laura's other patients were stable, giving Laura a few extra minutes before starting the drive to her labs. So Laura made her way to the administrative suite of offices of the hospital. Not bothering to knock, she went in to see her best friend, Roxanne Ruiz, director of nursing.

Roxanne was on the phone to Human Resources. "We're down thirty nurses, so yes, we will have to bring in contract personnel to get us through the winter months."

"Isn't admin fun?" Laura said when Roxanne had concluded her call. "Remember when we just operated on patients? No bureaucratic headaches." Roxanne had been Laura's scrub nurse back before they'd each moved on to loftier positions.

Roxanne grinned. "The price of success. But what are you doing here? Aren't you supposed to be at the university today?"

"I'm on my way. I wanted to drop by to brief you on that patient in the surgical ICU. The one we think has AIDS. Tricky diagnosis. We can document the Kaposi sarcoma and the pneumocystis, both hallmarks, but without a definitive test for HIV—"

"Just what we need on a holiday weekend." Roxanne sighed deeply. "My staffing problems are bad enough, now with the isolation protocol and the panic that'll hit when the inevitable rumors spread, get ready for a nightmare."

"That, and we have confidentiality of the diagnosis to worry about. You're right, Roxie, a nightmare. But not a surgical nightmare. One that comes under Duncan Kellerman's purview. Doesn't he tell anyone who will listen that he's God's gift to infectious disease."

"We both know that Kellerman is in over his head."

"That's why I called my friend Stacy Jones at the CDC. I told him to call her if he wants to get up to speed. If not—"

"Laura, Kellerman passed your friend's contact information on to me. My infectious disease nurse has already been in touch with Dr. Jones. And she's already been helpful. She's contacted the Director of the Hillsborough County Health Department so we all have the most up-to-date information on the HIV virus. God knows so many frightening rumors are flying around. Anyway, I know you're busy, but thanks for stopping by this morning, and a huge thanks for getting us access to the resources at the CDC."

Roxanne checked her watch, but Laura did not leave. "Roxie, there's something else."

"Uh-oh, I know that look. A cup of tea is in order, with a slice of my mother's homemade almond coffee cake. Let's take ten minutes."

Roxanne got up and went to the electric teakettle she kept on her file cabinet. Pouring a cup of tea for each of them and slicing a generous piece of cake, she returned. Laura sat across from her. They'd done this countless times over the past twelve years, in one or the other's offices.

"I've always had such a great relationship with all my kids," Laura said, "but something's changed. Not with the boys, they're okay, but with the girls. Even Natalie, but to a lesser degree than Nicole."

"Like what?" Roxanne asked.

Laura told her about the birth control pills. "She must be lying to me," she concluded.

"What if she's not?" Roxanne asked.

Laura had to admit that she hadn't given that option any credibility.

"Maybe Nicole's been a handful from time to time, but she's never lied to you, has she?"

"How would I know? I can't trust my judgment. That's what scares me."

"Why don't you give her the benefit of the doubt? Tell her you trust her. Then keep a good watch on the girls. Nicole doesn't even have a steady boyfriend, does she?"

"No."

"So probably she's not sleeping with anybody."

"When you put it that way, I guess I overreacted. Sometimes I just feel so overwhelmed. Three teenagers in the house. At least I don't worry about the two in college."

Roxanne grinned. "What you don't know—"

"Thanks, Roxie. Why do I always feel better just talking to you? I'll follow your advice—let this all blow over. With Thanksgiving coming up, there'll be lots of distractions."

"When are the others coming in?" Roxanne was referring to Laura's sister, who with her husband and seven-year-old son, was flying in from their Paris home, and to Laura's brother, Ted, a Jesuit, stationed at the General Curia in Rome.

"Janet tomorrow, Ted on Thursday. In time for dinner, if my mother's prayers are answered. Mike and Kevin will be home tomorrow night. Then we'll head to Mom and Dad's for the long weekend. I rented a condo on Anna Maria Island, so we'll probably all hang out on the beach."

"Your life always has been complicated, Laura. Louis and I just have my mom and the boys."

"Hey, give my best to Louis—I've got to get going. And say hi to Stacy if you talk to her before I do. If anyone can give us advice about our AIDS case, she can." Laura was up and out.

"Guess what," Roxanne called out, "I bet I know something that you don't."

"Well, speak up!" Laura turned as Roxanne cracked a smile.

"Breaking news from the CDC. Stacy got promoted to Section Chief or some big title like that. How about that for your mentee kid?"

"Fantastic. That girl is going to make a difference in so many lives."

But Laura's pride was mixed with shame. Stacy Jones would never know what had happened to Johnny. Stacy would never know that her friend and mentor had killed her brother eighteen years ago.

CHAPTER ELEVEN

Victor held Matthew's hand in his gloved one. Then he moved his chair closer so he could caress Matthew's forehead and cheeks, letting his fingers run over the purplish blemishes of Kaposi sarcoma. Matthew had been worried about his disfigured face. He'd tried using different types of concealer makeup, but that had only made the blotches more ghastly.

So far Victor had not broached the subject of AIDS with Matthew. Had Matthew, a science teacher, suspected that those purple lesions were a sign of Kaposi sarcoma? Not really "sarcoma" meaning cancer, but tumor cells that cluster in nodules and darkly colored papular blotches.

An infectious disease expert, Victor knew that the antibiotics dripping into Matthew's intravenous line were appropriate for Pneumocystis carinii, the bane of AIDS, and staph, and almost every other combination of bad bacteria. But nobody in this mediocre hospital would share Matthew's medical details. What organisms were growing? What did the antibiotic sensitivity panel show? Doctors in a D.C. hospital would handle HIV without all this fumbling. Nevertheless, Matthew's cheeks were a little pinker and his skin no longer so clammy. And he'd even started opening his eyes if only for a few seconds.

Victor never should have left Matthew alone in Florida. What had possessed him to go chasing off to Keystone Pharma? When he got the call that Dr. Nelson wanted to operate, Victor should have headed directly to Tampa, chartered a plane that night, and taken Matthew home.

Matthew, alone and surely terrified, giving consent to surgery with no one by his side. Well, that would never happen again. *Matthew, I'm here and I will never abandon you.*

Victor had always been accused of being defensive, guarded, overly suspicious. Maybe that was true, but now, for the first time, Victor had found a relationship based on total trust. He was all Matthew had. And he vowed not to let him down.

When a nurse showed up to suction Matthew's nasotracheal tube, Victor stood, leaned over Matthew close enough to confirm the stability of his vital signs on the monitor, and told the nurse he was going to the cafeteria for breakfast. He'd spent most of the night in the chair next to Matthew, except for the hour or so he'd dozed off on the sofa in the ICU waiting room. He'd brushed his teeth and tried to shave in the men's room, but he still wore the same clothes he'd traveled in, not wanting to leave Matthew's side long enough to book a hotel room.

Victor paid for his oatmeal, orange juice, and hot tea and found a table in the far corner, away from all those people in scrubs and white coats. A woman sat alone in the back, wearing a designer-looking outfit. As he approached, she stood and called out, "Victor Worth—is that you?" She looked to be in her sixties, trim, with highlighted hair.

"Naomi Kantor," he said, pausing. He remembered the pretentious woman whom he'd always disdained. His former boss's wife.

"What are you doing in Tampa? Come. Sit with me."

Victor carried his tray to the small square table and sat down opposite her bowl of fruit, English muffin, and carafe of coffee.

"Norman's here in the ICU," Naomi began. "He fell out of his sailboat, can you believe that? I'm so worried. He fractured his hip, and they did surgery, then he got blood clots. Well, you can imagine, I've been beside myself. Our twins both wanted to come down, but they're so busy with their jobs. Kyle's a dentist in Richmond and has two girls. Kara is a CPA in Philadelphia and she has two boys. Four grandchildren, total."

Right, Victor thought: *Two and two. And, I have one son, he wanted to say. And your bastard husband has all but murdered him.* But he kept silent.

"I feel so alone down here," she continued. Typical Naomi. The woman could not shut up. "You can't believe how glad I am to see you." She reached across the table to squeeze Victor's arm.

You wouldn't be touching me if you knew where I just came from.

"You do know that Norman retired last year. Now that I think of it, you weren't at the party." The woman could not shut up.

"Keystone Pharma went all out. A gala affair in the Commonwealth Club at the William Penn Inn. I guess that was too much, to expect you to come from Bethesda to Philadelphia."

Nice of you to let me make the decision. I wasn't invited.

"Then we moved to Longboat Key, it's a barrier island off Sarasota. Norman was out in Tampa Bay when he got hurt, and this is the closest hospital, so I'm stuck here."

"Norman has blood clots, you said?" Victor asked his first question.

"Oh yes, they're giving him heparin, but there've been bleeding complications. Something about getting the right dose. You can't believe how many times they take his blood in that ICU. The man's a pincushion. I can't stay very long, can't stand to watch, and the smell in there makes me woozy."

"Norman's here? In the ICU?"

"For now. Once his blood tests come back okay, they're going to move him into a private room. God knows we can afford it. You can't believe the options and all the stock Keystone gave him. You'd be astounded."

Naomi still had not asked anything about him. Like, why would Victor be in a hospital cafeteria in Tampa?

"I'd like to say hello to Norman." Norman, on his mind since Sunday night, now an apparition?

"Oh, he'd love that. They restrict visitors to family only, but I'm sure I can talk them into letting you see him. You can't believe how bored Norman is. They won't even let him make phone calls."

They deposited their eating utensils in the proper bins and

placed their empty trays on the belt, Victor accompanied Naomi to
the elevator, up to the seventh floor. He walked with her, unchal-
lenged, into the surgical ICU. Victor had never been in the main
ICU—Matthew's room was separate—with its own entrance. He
was surprised at the bustle of nurses and technicians and the cacophony of sounds. Victor's parents had tried to convince him to be
a real doctor, an M.D., but hospitals made him physically ill. Alone
in the isolation room with Matthew, Victor had managed, but now
as Naomi led him toward her husband's bed, he felt a wave of nau-
sea. He pulled out his handkerchief, now well used, and coughed
into it.

"Sir?" a nurse looked up. "Are you okay? If you have any infection, you shouldn't be in here. These patients are very ill."

"I'm fine," Victor said. "Allergies."

The nurse had already turned away to tweak a patient's IV line.

"Look who's here, Norman." Naomi's husband had been
asleep, but she had not seemed to notice, or to care.

Victor's one-time mentor—turned traitor—slowly opened his
eyes, looking about.

Trouble focusing? Victor hoped not. He needed Norman alert,
oriented, and motivated.

Norman ran his right hand—the one not tethered to an IV
board—through crew cut salt-and-pepper hair. "What do you need
now?" he growled. "Can't you people give me a moment's rest?"

Naomi stepped forward to adjust his pillow. "Victor Worth is
here, darling." She moved aside so Norman had an unobstructed
view of Victor, and vice versa.

"Sorry about your injury," Victor said as recognition dawned on
Norman.

"Victor? What are you doing here?"

"Right now, I've come to check in on you," Victor said. Could he
overcome his disgust and discuss his son with this ruthless traitor?

"Well, I'm just great right now." Norman faked a smile. "Got
some obscure clotting problem. Threw a pulmonary embolus. Went
into cardiac arrest. They can't get the blood thinners right. I had a
gastric bleed, one thing after another—"

"Darling," Naomi interrupted, "I heard the doctors talking. They are going to move you out of ICU in a couple of days once the main danger passes. Good news, right?"

"I want out of this place." Norman sighed. "But I could live with a private room, a television, and a phone—anything would be a step up from—*this*."

"What's going on in your life, Victor?" Naomi asked. "You still a bachelor?"

"Afraid so." Should he tell them about Matthew? No, of course not.

"Naomi, why don't you give us a few moments?" Norman asked. "Just move this goddamned pillow over toward me. Please."

"I'll stay, darling. I just came from the cafeteria—"

"I want to talk shop with Victor," Norman said. "Good-old-days stuff. You'll be bored. Go call the kids or something."

"Well, okay, Norman." To Victor, she said, "I'll catch you later." Her lips brushed his cheek. "You need a shave—and a change of clothes. I just can't believe running into you."

As Naomi withdrew, an alarm screeched. Nurses and doctors rushed to a bed across the room, and Victor swallowed a surge of bile.

No sooner had the commotion quieted down around the other bed than Norman challenged his unexpected visitor, "What are you really here for, Victor? I was your boss for fifteen years; I know it's something else. What's up?"

Victor blinked, tried to sort out his thoughts. Rationally, he knew that Matthew seemed to be improving without ticokellin. Still, Victor wanted it, was entitled to it. Ticokellin, though flawed, had been his invention. Not only had he discovered the new class of drugs from which Norman had selected the wrong analog for development, but he'd genetically engineered the most virulent and resistant of staphylococci bacteria so that he could thoroughly test the series of new chemicals.

Now, standing at Norman's bedside, Victor felt a wave of white-hot anger. He'd warned Norman not to take the cheapest analog to the clinic, but Norman had ignored him and now ticokellin was dead in the water. Keystone Pharma would have to start all over again with a safer analog, surely the one he'd earmarked in the first place.

"Norman, I'm not going to beat around the bush. You being here in the ICU, and I'm sorry that I have to ask, but I need some ticokellin. I have a friend—" Some protective instinct told him not to say son.

Norman tried to jerk his head up off the pillow, but his IVs and probably his fractured hip held him back. Victor heard the beep-beep of Norman's heart monitor get faster.

"You can't be serious, Victor."

"Norman, take a breath. Please—just hear me out."

"No use. Before you even start, I've got bad news. Keystone Pharma stopped the clinical trials. They weren't going to tell me, but I've got my contacts."

"Then use your contacts to get the ticokellin, Norman. I need that drug for my friend."

"What part of 'no,' don't you get? I can't get a goddamned drug that's been withdrawn. Victor, stop being so naïve. Haven't I always said you're too academic? You wouldn't last a day in industry."

A reminder to Victor that this was the prick who'd stood in the way of his getting a cushy job at Keystone Pharma, too.

"You must have some stashed away. If not—with your connections—you know you could get some. Just call somebody there. Somebody who used to work for you will have access."

"No way. When I retired, I retired. I'm not doing research on the side. I'm not even consulting. I'm golfing, and sailing—well, I was sailing."

"Back in the labs, you know, we always squirreled away drugs we were working on. Hell, I first learned that from you, so don't try to deny—"

Norman's color had faded to an ashen pallor. The heart rate monitor had not increased, but abnormal beeps were making Victor nervous. He was so close—he would get that ticokellin. He knew that Norman could get it.

"Forget it. Pharmaceutical companies are not like academic or government labs. Every milligram of every chemical is closely controlled. I'm telling you, Victor, I can't get it for you. The goddamned CEO, the guy who just got the Nobel Prize, Paul Parnell, couldn't get it for you. God couldn't get it for you. Forget it."

"Let's talk about something else. Did you hear that Naomi and I went to Stockholm with the Parnells when the old man got the prize? That was one grand event, the company plane, the works."

Victor squeezed his hands together so tightly that they felt numb. Had Norman always been this egotistical? Now, with Matthew so sick, just a room away, this bastard brags about his luxury travel and connections to the rich and famous. Norman had changed after he went to work for Keystone Pharma. He'd sold his soul, but he'd also sacrificed the life-saving drug series that Victor himself had discovered. And now, Matthew needs that drug and can't get it. Does Norman give a fuck? "Forget it," Norman's exact words. Victor would not forget it. He now saw the equation very clearly. Matthew deserves to live. Norman deserves to die. Victor took a deep breath. Retribution.

Without another word, Victor turned away from Norman and walked out of the ICU.

CHAPTER TWELVE

Charles Scarlett had no chauffeur—he wanted his comings and go-ings private. Charles's full-time housekeeper cleaned and cooked, his part-time gardener doubled as a handyman. No wife—never had had one. Parents were quite enough, and his were Atlanta so-cialites: his father, managing partner of the city's most prestigious law firm—founded by his own daddy; mother, a debutante from old money with Southern roots dating back before the Civil War.

Charles was an only child, precocious, but overweight even as a toddler, and from puberty, lacking in libido. Wealthy, aristocratic, educated, but genetics had failed him when it came to physical at-tributes. He'd ended up on the opposite end of the attractiveness scale from his parents: Rosabelle, a stunning beauty—never mind the fortune she'd invested in products and procedures; Charles Sr.—Chas—tall, lean, with a styled mane of silver hair, the epitome of the genteel politician, business tycoon, blue-blood lawyer. No wonder they were regularly featured in the society pages of the *At-lanta Constitution*.

But, despite their aura of ostentation and pretentiousness, both parents loved their son, protected him fiercely for all his shortcom-ings; only in absolute privacy would they allude to Charles's imper-fections. Only once had Charles accidentally penetrated this privacy, a memory that would haunt him forever.

Tonight he'd appeared dutifully at their home, as he always did for Tuesday dinner, a Scarlett family ritual with gourmet courses appearing on the candlelit table. He endured a full-court press interrogation by Mother. Uncomfortable enough, but not as bad as retiring with Father to the library, to smoke a foul-smelling cigar and to try to act as if they were good old buddies. Charles had to admit, he had nothing in common with either parent. Except for one particular passion: all three Scarletts were true patriots, pledged to support the fundamental principles of American civilization, liberty, justice, and national safety.

Charles had known with certainty that this Tuesday evening would not go well. And sure enough, as if on cue, Mother asked about his job. They'd find out soon enough, so he'd told them about Stacy Jones's promotion. Yes, he would now have a black woman, one year his junior, as his supervisor. This would bring shame on his parents, he knew, but what choice did he have until he transferred into another department?

Mother's hands flew immediately to her neck, and her face turned pale. For a moment no one spoke. Then Mother cleared her throat and said, "Charles, did you say that the colored woman in your department was going to be your *boss*? A colored person might be telling *you* what to do?"

Her hands dropped the monogrammed linen napkin and started fidgeting. Turning to Father, she said, "Chas, darling, you have to do something. Use your influence at the CDC. Our son has a medical degree and a Ph.D. from Emory University. Get this substandard person out of there. Fired, transferred, anything. I can't bear the thought of our own son ordered around by a colored person. Everything we've worked for, everything that my parents and yours stood for—the Scarletts' long history of patriotism and devotion to this country."

Charles had never mentioned to his parents that Stacy trained at Harvard. Not that Harvard was better than Emory—certainly not in their minds.

"Son," Scarlett senior said, "I don't know if I can get this turned around or not. You know what's going on. First Maynard Jackson, now Andrew Young. Black mayors in the city of Atlanta. That black man, Julian Bond, getting the Bill of Rights Award from the ACLU.

The law firm's always getting pressure to support one Negro cause or another. Maybe if I'd known about this woman's promotion before it happened, but we're dealing with the federal government. You said it's been announced?"

Charles had known how this news would go down. "Yes," he admitted, almost doubling over with the familiar, sinking burden of his parents' shame, "it has." He carried that weight every day, wore it like a mantle, but at times like these, it felt utterly crushing.

"Charles, you are a white person." His father seethed, his face turning beet red. "Non-white people must come under you. Automatically and always and in every circumstance. Do you recall nothing of the convention last year? Dr. Pierce recruited you, personally, to protect the world for white children."

Charles suddenly had the resolve to speak up to the old man. The time had come. He'd intended to keep quiet about the plan that he'd been formulating. But now that Stacy had been promoted over him, he found the nerve. *Yes, Father, I will do my part. You'll see.* "Father, I can't tell you what I'm doing for The Order." he said. "It's that secret, but I can promise you that what I do will make a difference. A major difference."

"A major difference? I don't think I can have that cigar with you tonight. I'm too riled up. A colored woman for a boss, now that is a major difference." He shoved back his chair. "Rosabelle, I'm going to bed."

Mother reverted to her placating role, "He's just upset, darling." She hesitated, not knowing whether to follow her seething husband upstairs or stay to comfort her injured son.

"I will not let him down, don't you worry." Charles stood at the door, not bothering to bestow upon his mother the obligatory kiss on the cheek.

"He's just upset, darling." She stood there in the foyer by the oversized floral arrangement.

Charles let himself out the paneled mahogany door and began the three-block walk through the elegant Buckhead neighborhood to his own home.

CHAPTER THIRTEEN

As the staff gathered for rounds, Laura noted that all eight beds in the surgical Intensive Care Unit were occupied this day before Thanksgiving. Unusual, since elective procedures were usually postponed right before a holiday. The charge nurse explained that the medical ICU was overloaded and they had to take the overflow.

"Too bad," Laura said. "We all need a break and that's not going to happen for you here."

Laura joined her chief resident, observing as Michelle adroitly organized the group of medical students, surgical residents, and attending surgeons. The rounding group went from bed to bed. A student presented a patient. The residents and attending physicians quizzed the student. Some questions were straightforward; some brutally obscure. Laura enjoyed the interplay of personalities and she knew the importance of a student's ability to respond under stress. If the interrogation ever got out of hand, she would step in to restore any lost dignity.

The first male student had begun. "This lung reduction patient is being weaned off the ventilator and is—"

"Excuse me, Mr.—" Laura inspected the student's name tag. "Mr. Riffy. Please begin again. Here's how you start, 'Mr. Kelly is a seventy-year-old gentleman, who—etcetera.'" She turned to Michelle. "You've got to brief them, Dr. Wallace. Our patients all have names."

Michelle half smiled. "Start again," she instructed Riffy.

Laura was gratified to see that Mr. Kelly was indeed doing well. She personally listened to his lungs, for which he awarded her a big smile.

They moved to a gynecological surgery patient, an E.R. nurse whom Laura knew, but not well. The next medical student presented the case, a hysterectomy, complicated by pulmonary emboli. Laura questioned her heparin dose, spoke briefly to the groggy woman, and the group moved on.

A younger woman with internal bleeding following a colectomy for ulcerative colitis; an elderly gent, sitting up in bed examining *them*—not a surgical patient, overflow from the medical service. Then Laura's patient, Tom Mancini. The students needed to know more about beryllium toxicity, but not today.

"Carcinoma," another medical student reported when Michelle asked about the pathology. The kid looked so glum that Laura thought he might shed tears. These are the good ones, the students who give a damn about their patients.

A patient transferred from the medical ward occupied the next bed and the surgical rounding group passed by without comment.

Another preppy-looking student presented the patient in the next bed. "Nineteen-year-old kid. Ran his motorcycle into an embankment. No helmet, no leg protection. Ruptured spleen, tear in the liver, fractured pelvis, compound fractures of both legs, a concussion."

Laura looked at the chart, "Trey Standish is fortunate to be alive." What was it about that name? A friend of one of her daughters? Then Laura remembered. The patient's name also was the last name of the owner of the company being sued for using beryllium. She was to testify in court against the elder Standish. Could this be the company owner's son? In the same room as Tom Mancini—a victim poisoned by that company's toxic operation?

"So we have Matthew Mercer left," Laura said as they finished rounds. Via the hospital grapevine, the surgical staff already knew Mercer's diagnosis and when Laura suggested that only she and Michelle gown up to enter the room, nobody objected. The attending surgeons drifted away toward their offices or the hospital clinic. Laura dismissed the students and house staff, wishing them a happy Thanksgiving.

Laura and Michelle spent only a moment in Mercer's room. Michelle quietly slipped back the sheet to expose the two-day-old chest incision. She acknowledged with a nod that it looked good. Then, both women left, not wanting to awaken the patient who seemed to be much improved.

Laura had anticipated a light day and arranged to turn over her patients to her backup thoracic surgeon, Dr. Ed Plant, as soon as she finished at the hospital. She should have plenty of time to make it to the airport to meet Kevin's five thirty flight from Detroit. She hadn't seen her eighteen-year-old son since early September when he'd left for the University of Michigan in Ann Arbor and she was on pins and needles to hear in person about his freshman experience. Talking to him on the phone every other day, she felt 99 percent sure he was handling the transition to college life well; still, she longed to hug him and hear all the details. If Kevin's flight was on time, they'd make the last few innings of Patrick's baseball game. Laura knew her excitement to see Kevin was more than matched by Patrick's at having his big brother in the bleachers.

Laura spent another two hours in a conference room connected to the boardroom interviewing candidates for the chief of anesthesia post. She'd volunteered for the task. The right chemistry between the surgery and anesthesia departments could make all the difference in an operating suite. Laura and the retiring chief had been blessed—and three interviews later, she still was worried about finding an anesthesiologist who truly could replace him.

Finally, Laura called Dr. Plant to let him know that she was checking out until Monday morning, turning her patients over to him. On her way out, she rushed by the nursing admin office to wave goodbye to Roxanne.

Kevin arrived on schedule and the two of them headed straight from Tampa International to Jesuit High's baseball field. Patrick's team won, but, with his older brother in the stands, he'd struck out twice.

On the way home, Laura relaxed as Patrick pumped his brother for college details—the parties and the sports action and the girl-friend front. Kevin made Ann Arbor sound like nirvana as he regaled them with U. of M. anecdotes. His recount took her breath away, and for a moment she withdrew within herself. Kevin looked and sounded so much like his father, Steve. She'd met her husband when she'd been a naïve freshman at the University of Michigan and he a sophomore journalism major. They were married the next year and before she graduated, they had two sons. Of all her kids, Kevin, with his athletic build, wavy blond hair, and blue eyes, looked the most like his father. Though Kevin most physically resembled his dad, Patrick was the one who missed Steve the most. He'd only been eight when Steve died, but her youngest son still hero worshiped his dad with an intensity that unnerved Laura.

Yes, it had been tough raising five kids on her own for the past seven years, but for now Laura had to get back into the moment and enjoy her sons' banter.

She dropped Kevin and Patrick at home before turning around to go back to the airport to meet Mike's flight from South Bend. First, a quick hi to Natalie and Nicole—both of whom seemed annoyed to see her. Once she'd collected Mike, all five would be home with her. And tomorrow, she'd see her sister and brother—in from Europe to join them for a welcome family reunion on Anna Maria Island, an hour's drive away.

CHAPTER FOURTEEN

Victor Worth considered himself a logical man, analytical, methodical. Characteristics that made him proud, but most important to him, he was a fair man. An honest man, a man with righteous motives. Sadly, there were few others who shared his brand of personal integrity. Certainly not Norman Kantor.

In the past Victor would have applied restraint. Yes, Norman had taken Victor's intellectual property and parlayed it into a position of influence at Keystone Pharma. A position so high up that when his boss, the CEO, won the Nobel Prize, Norman had accompanied him in a private jet to the ceremony in Stockholm. Victor had tried to get Norman to hire him at the company. And what had he done when Norman had refused? Nothing. Nothing but sulk. Did that make him a coward? A loser? But now the stakes were raised. Victor had a son. Norman had refused his son. Victor could actually feel his blood start to simmer. As he paced the confines of Matthew's isolation room, he felt it heat to a boil. A whitehot, raging fury. An alien phenomenon to him. Nothing passive or restrictive about it. Was this what being a parent was all about?

A doctor had once diagnosed Victor with a paranoid personality disorder. Not that he was psycho or anything, but he tended to be suspicious, worry too much about finding the hidden meaning in things people said, feeling like he always had to watch his back, be prepared for all threats. Maybe the doctor was right, but now the time had come when his paranoid personality was about to pay off.

Neither Norman, nor anybody else, knew that Victor had carried on their staphylococcal research after their program was shut down by the government's brilliant plan to scale back programs with bioterrorism potential. Norman would be impressed if he knew how far the deadly staphylococcal research had progressed in Victor's hands, in his basement lab. Research that was unauthorized and clandestine.

The NIH had terminated the staph research program right after Norman had left. But Victor had been prepared for just such a sequence of events. He'd had the foresight to develop his just-in-case scenario, the scenario he then continued toiling over in secret, and that now was about to climax as a deadly reality.

Even with little or no sleep for his second night on the sofa in the ICU visitor's waiting room, Victor awoke with clarity of vision. He had made his decision and he had to move fast. Wearing the same clothes since he'd left home in Bethesda, he kissed his sleeping son on the forehead, ignoring isolation precautions, and headed for the airport to catch the six a.m. flight out of Tampa. He would arrive at Washington National Airport just before ten o'clock.

He'd spent most of the sleepless night refining a checklist. All the steps he'd have to take to get his strain of staph cultures into a suitable broth media for transport. Plus, he'd have to be extra careful to leave no trace. If something went wrong, there must be no evidence pointing to him.

At home an hour after his plane touched down, Victor didn't stop to eat. He had to finish securely packing the staph in time for the three p.m. flight back to Tampa. Downstairs in his clandestine lab, he donned protective garments, fully covering himself in a jumpsuit, mask, booties, and cap, lest an errant staphylococci organism land on him. Amazing how simple it had been, he thought, to set up a bacteriology lab in his basement at home in Bethesda. Not a high-tech operation, just simply culturing the bugs in growth media, combining nature's own genetics, and perfecting his selection techniques to amplify the virulence of this gram-positive cocci. Using his new strains, he could then test them against all known antibiotics and he'd hypothesize new molecular entities to treat the resistance he was creating. He was very close to defining a strain resistant even to ticokellin and its analogs.

Why had he done this? What had been his endgame? Simply this: once he was ready, he'd figure a way to leverage his discovery of this new, resistant staph. Because of his particular research background, the pharmaceutical industry would tap him to discover the cure for his own engineered monster bacteria. He was already really close. A little more research and he'd have figured out the lifesaving antibiotic structure. Followed by the flight to Sweden for his own Nobel Prize.

But now Victor couldn't wait for this perfect scenario. He needed to punish Norman for depriving his son—a son whom Victor for thirty-two lonely years hadn't even known existed. And payback would happen on Thanksgiving Day. How ironic was that?

Did anyone at Victor's prestigious NIH employer so much as suspect he'd continued his staph research after he'd been transferred into mycology—without even the courtesy of consulting him in advance? Hardly. No one ever had inquired or even commented on the brilliance of his past NIH work on staph. No appreciation whatsoever. They'd given him no choice but to continue his cutting-edge research illicitly, literally underground.

Victor went about preparing his deadly samples, packing them securely in transport media, readying the portable incubator that fit securely in his carry-on, labeling his samples as various flavors of yogurt in the unlikely event that he was stopped by security. As he worked, he reflected on how drastically he had changed since finding out about Matthew. He would do anything for Matthew. Anything.

CHAPTER FIFTEEN

Natalie waited by the phone. She didn't know whether to be angry or scared. Trey hadn't called for two days in a row. On days when she couldn't sneak away to meet him, he always phoned between four and six. Before her mom got home. Natalie thought about her mom, trying to give her the benefit of the doubt. Naturally, any mother of a seventeen-year-old would not approve of her daughter having sex. And her mom didn't know that she'd been seeing Trey Standish ever since school started, three months ago.

Trey was everything in a boy that Natalie never thought she'd have. Even her sister, Nicole, who'd always landed any boy she wanted, drooled over Trey. If her mom saw him—and someday she would, since Natalie planned to marry Trey—she would complain that his hair was too long. The only feature about Trey that anyone could criticize. He had the blackest of eyes and the cutest curly eyelashes. She was five foot five, and Trey was six feet tall. Her long blonde hair contrasted with his coal-black hair. And when they were seen together, how could people not say, "Wow, that's a beautiful couple."

She and Trey had only one problem, and neither knew how to handle it. In time they figured that it would go away, but for now they kept their relationship secret from both her mom and his parents. Natalie felt powerless to interfere with her mother's business. Her mom was a rather well-known doctor, the chief of surgery at the city's main hospital. And her specialty was lung surgery, had been as long as Natalie could remember.

The issue and why it was causing a problem with Trey: Mom was going to be an expert witness in a trial against Trey's father's business, a factory that used beryllium to make parts that are used in lots of other industries, the space industry for instance and in x-ray machines. Natalie and Trey had spent hours in the library trying to understand how the factory used beryllium and why people accused the factory of disregarding health hazards to the workers there, but the issues were confusing. Natalie's honors chemistry course didn't help much—and Trey was majoring in business at nearby University of Tampa. An only child, he was expected to take over running the family business, but he joked that he didn't have a scientific gene in his body.

Natalie heard the front door open and she checked her watch: 7:55 p.m.

"So give me a hand." Nicole juggled two bags of groceries. With Mike and Kevin coming home from college, they needed to load up the cupboards and fridge.

"He hasn't called," Natalie said, accepting a bag of groceries in each arm.

"I don't know what to say," said Nicole. "You didn't have a fight or anything? Maybe he took something you said the wrong way?"

"No, Nicole, I told you about Monday night. It was perfect—everything."

"Let's get the rest of the stuff out of the car. Patrick's game will be over, and Mom expects us to put everything away. You know how she gets when Mike and Kevin come home, like they're crown princes and we're the hired help."

Nicole had always had a chip on her shoulders when it came to their two older brothers. But Natalie's take on Mom was that if she had any favorites it would be them. They argued about it a lot. Natalie always taking Laura's side. Nicole always dredging up how they—Natalie and Nicole—had been their father's favorites. They'd been ten years old when their dad died, and Natalie's memory of him was diametrically opposed to Nicole's. Regardless, their dad was dead, so what did it matter whose memory was accurate?

They had just arranged the cold stuff in the fridge when Laura arrived with Kevin and Patrick. Patrick went right upstairs to change out of his baseball uniform, and Kevin ran straight for Natalie and Nicole to grab them in a big bear hug. Kevin was not one to hold back on enthusiasm, emotion, opinion, or anything else. He had one of those loud voices that boomed and at just one year older than Natalie and Nicole, he'd always been their buddy. People called them "the triplets" because with wavy blond hair, Kevin looked so much like his sisters.

"Everything unpacked, girls?" Laura set down Kevin's book bag by the steps. "I've got to get going—back to the airport to get Mike. Kevin, you'll be okay?"

"You're leaving me with these two?" Kevin grinned. "Could be trouble." Reaching into his duffel, he pulled out two sweatshirts emblazoned with the University of Michigan's big *M*. "One maize; one blue. I want you wearing these when Mike gets here with his Notre Dame shit."

Nicole grabbed the yellow one, getting first pick, as usual.

Laura gave Kevin a fast hug, ignored Natalie and Nicole, and left for the airport.

Natalie had to make her move. "Nicole, I'm going over to his dorm. I have to check. I'll be back before Mom gets home, but if I'm not, you know what to tell her."

"Studying for a test at Collette's just won't fly," Nicole said. "You sure you want to do this?"

Natalie knew what Nicole was thinking. What if she found Trey with another girl? What if Trey had dumped her? What if he'd left for his parents' house without even calling her? He'd promised he'd see her one more time before going home for the holiday weekend. What if something had happened to him?

"What's the deal?" Kevin asked, devouring a Twinkie.

"Tell him, Nicole," Natalie said, grabbing the Impala keys off the hook. The twins and Kevin had no secrets. Still the Three Musketeers. "But not in front of Patrick."

Natalie arrived at Trey's dorm at eight thirty. The darkened campus seemed empty, most students on their way home for the holidays.

She'd be off with her family starting tomorrow morning, so Trey planned to wait until Thanksgiving morning before hopping on his new purple Kawasaki for the sixty-mile trip to his home in Sarasota. But Trey had not called. Not yesterday. Not today.

He lived in a quad on campus. A central area in the middle, a bedroom on each side shared by two. Trey's roommate was from Taiwan, so he wouldn't be going home for Thanksgiving.

Natalie parked the car, no problem with parallel parking tonight. Shivering, she pulled her new blue sweatshirt over her head, then hesitated for an instant to say a quick Hail Mary. Something had to be wrong. She loved Trey so much—what would she do if he'd left her for another girl?

Smoothing her hair and straightening her miniskirt, she approached the kid doing security. They recognized each other. His eyes flashed something like alarm and he started to get out of his chair. Wow. Did everyone but her know that she'd been dumped?

She could turn and run, but she struggled to say, "Trey Standish?"

"I know who you are, Natalie. But don't you know—?"

"Know what?" Natalie asked, beginning to shake, her heart slamming in her chest.

"Are you okay?" the kid asked. "Do you want to sit down?" He got up, moved his chair toward her, never taking his eyes off of her.

"What?" Did he have a new girlfriend? Had something happened at school, like he'd cheated or something? Was he hurt? He was always messing around with pickup sports. "Did something happen?"

"Sit down, Natalie. I know you and Trey had a thing going. Please, sit."

She did, her knees shaking so badly she had to steady them, pressing down hard with her elbows.

"There was an accident. Monday night. He was riding his motorcycle—"

"Is Trey hurt?" Natalie jumped up. "I have to go to him."

"He's in critical condition. A concussion, multiple fractures. No visitors, I heard. His roommate couldn't even get in, family members only. Geez, I hate to be the one to tell you. You and Trey had something special—"

Tears streamed from Natalie's eyes. Monday night. For two days she'd been getting more and more pissed because he hadn't called her. A concussion? Meaning he was still unconscious? She had to know. She had to see him. "What hospital?" she asked.

"Tampa City. Like I said, he's in the ICU, so—"

"My mother is the chief of surgery there. They have to let me in."

Before the security kid could answer, Natalie had jumped up and bolted for her car.

By the time she reached the hospital, visiting hours were over. She knew the ICU was on the seventh floor, but she didn't know the hospital layout well enough to find some back elevator. She had to pass directly by the information desk.

"Miss, may I help you?"

"No, I'm okay." she said.

"You can't go beyond the lobby," the older woman in a mint-green smock said.

"I...I need to see a patient," Natalie said. "I just found out—"

"Name?"

Should she tell the truth? How to get out of this trap?

"Trey Standish." Should she have she said she was looking for her mother on the surgical floor. If the nurses up there knew that she was Laura Nelson's daughter, they'd let her up for sure.

"Miss, Mr. Standish is in the ICU."

"I know that," Natalie said, biting her lip to keep from crying. "That's where I'm heading."

"Are you a relative?"

Should she say she was Trey's sister? No, the hospital would have a list of family members. Before Trey, Natalie had prided herself on never telling a lie. Nicole could lie nonstop, but not Natalie.

"A friend," she said.

"Sorry, miss. No nonfamily visitors. It's highlighted on the chart. They're very strict up there. Have to be. Maybe tomorrow, contact a family member. All I can tell you right now is that Mr. Standish's condition is critical."

As visitors continued to pour out the front door, Natalie stood halfway between the information desk and the elevator. She was shaking, tears pouring down her cheeks. "My mom," she tried once more. "I need to go up and see my mom. Dr. Laura Nelson, chief of surgery." Natalie fumbled inside her purse. "I have something to give her. It's important."

"Wait here." The woman's eyes narrowed, but she did pick up the phone. "Switchboard says that Dr. Nelson is checked out. Dr. Plant is covering her patients until Monday morning."

Natalie, turned toward the exit. The other departing visitors ignored her tears. She heard the woman at the information desk, "That girl is the spitting image of her mother."

CHAPTER SIXTEEN

As he did on most Wednesday nights, Charles Scarlett dismissed the household help once they'd finished in the library, making it comfortable for his guests, stocking the bar, setting out the array of food the two other members of his cell of The Order had come to expect.

When Will Banks was in residence, the help knew they were forbidden to go into the basement for any reason. Charles could take no chances: the Feds and about every law enforcement agency in the South were hunting Will. How surprised the FBI would be to unearth the contents of the basement in young Charles Scarlett's mansion.

In addition to Will, Charles had only one other guest on Wednesday evenings. Russell Robertson had no criminal record. He was a young husband and father, a professor of nuclear physics at Georgia Tech. All three men had been born in the same year, 1952, each was thirty-three. Last year, all had been summoned to a convention in Arlington, Virginia, and while there, personally recruited by a patriot, a friend of all three of their fathers, Dr. William Pierce. Ever since, they'd been a cell, soldiers on call for their cause, the Aryan Resistance Movement—The Order—dedicated to the salvation of the white race.

On leaving Arlington on that September day as chosen members of The Order, they all had been instilled with radical zeal. But for Charles, at least, that excitement had gradually dimmed over the past year; these days, The Order seemed to want from him only money and the use of his home as a safe house for Will.

Will, the munitions expert, had seen action all right. He had seen his own uncle gunned down in a forty-hour battle with the Feds, complete with helicopters and ground troops. After that showdown, Banks, like most in the vanguard, went underground as the FBI cracked down, made arrests—and yet more arrests when The Order's own yellow-bellied traitors turned informants. The Order's overt reign of terror had come to a halt a couple of months ago, after they gunned down a cop.

Charles's father didn't merely condone his son's induction into The Order, he actually had arranged it. Chas came from old-school Klan. He'd been a member and his father and father's father before him. Proud members.

When *Brown v. Board of Education* reared its ugly head, when the Klan was outlawed and went underground, Chas and his Southern chums founded the White Citizens' Council, opposed to racial integration, dedicated to protect the European-American heritage. When Charles Jr. was growing up, in the shadow of this organization, the "Uptown Klan" was for the privileged whites, "a white-collar Klan," "a country-club Klan." No shame, no stigma—a culturally acceptable way to promulgate racist practices. He remembered when he was a kid, roadside signs had proclaimed, "The White Citizens Council Welcomes You."

Well, things sure had changed. Over time, the White Citizens' Council had faded from the scene and Charles's father joined the new Council of Conservative Citizens, still advocating white supremacy and relying on the support of sitting members of the U.S. Congress. Charles himself had heard U.S. Senator Trent Lott address the group, so for sure their organization had clout. His father, though, doubted that the genteel flavor of white supremacy was enough. Charles Senior became convinced of the need for the violence perpetrated by the movement's most radical factions. So he threw his surreptitious support and that of his son to various Southern white supremacy groups: The Covenant, The Sword and the Arm of the Lord, Posse Comitatus, as well as to the most vicious bands of Aryan guerillas flush with money from robberies, equipped with weapons, code names, safe houses.

So now here was Charles hosting a safe house, playing hotelier. Is this why his father had introduced him to The Order? Was he testing him like he'd done when Charles was a kid? "What I cannot stomach, Rosabelle," he'd once heard his father say when he'd walked unnoticed into his parents' bedroom, "is a coward. Our son is a chicken-shit coward. You know it and I know it. And I pray to God every night he'll grow a backbone and show some leadership." Was Chas waiting for his son, for the first time in his cowardly life, finally to take a stand?

Charles, backing out of the room, had heard his mother mumble some reply, but whether she'd spoken up for him or sided with his father he'd never had a way to know. So by default, he bore the shame, nursing an obsession to prove to his father that he was indeed a patriot, that should he be tested, he would risk all for the cause. So far, he stagnated in the Aryan Resistance vanguard, proving nothing. But not for long. Tonight, he'd lay out a plan that would elevate him to the leadership that his father so craved for him.

The door chimes interrupted Charles's reverie. Russell Robertson had arrived. Charles breathed a sigh of relief. When Robertson had given some flimsy excuse for having missed the last cell meeting, Banks had gone off on a maniacal tear about allegiance to The Order. Tonight all three would be here: Banks with the necessary firepower; Roberts, nuclear access. And Charles, with flesh-eating bacteria.

CHAPTER SEVENTEEN

Thanksgiving morning or not, Laura woke as usual at five a.m. The house was quiet. Her kids were not morning people. The apple doesn't fall far from the tree: at their age she'd never have gotten out of bed a minute earlier than she had to. But later, a rigorous medical school schedule of a mom with young kids had altered her sleep patterns. For life.

Over a cup of coffee, she said a little prayer that all her plans would go perfectly today, for her mother's sake. The whole family of world citizens would come together. Her sister, Janet, who lived in Paris with her French husband and her Vietnamese adopted child; her brother Ted, a Jesuit stationed in Rome; and Laura and her five kids. They'd have dinner at Mom and Dad's on Anna Maria Island, about an hour by car from Tampa. And over the long week-end, everyone could hang out at the beach house Laura had rented on the lovely barrier island. She figured she'd leave about ten to get there in time to help Mom with the last minute dinner details.

After pouring her second cup of coffee, Laura's hand reached for the phone. *Just one call to the ICU.* "No," she said, aloud. Dr. Plant had her practice covered. Her family deserved her total focus today.

Patrick joined her in the kitchen, followed by Mike, and not long after, Kevin. As she went about making their breakfast, they chatted about school, sports, friends. The evolving meal—eggs, sausage, bacon, biscuits, pancakes, Belgian waffles—whatever they wanted—kept the boys in the kitchen talking, just as she'd hoped. Any minute, Laura would have to wake up the girls, but right now she floated happily on the currents of testosterone eddying around the kitchen.

At five after nine, Nicole came downstairs, still wearing her robe.

"You and Natalie better hurry," Laura said, "or you'll miss breakfast. I'd like to be on the road about ten."

"Mom," Nicole said, "Natalie is sick. Really sick. She was throwing up all night. I could hardly sleep."

"I'd better go check on her." Laura felt more annoyed than worried. Her perfect plans had not included a sick child.

Laura found Natalie lying on her back, propped up by pillows, and rocking her chest up and down as if she were in pain. She looked up at Laura, her eyes puffy and bloodshot.

"What's the matter, sweetie?" Laura asked. Was Natalie in so much pain that she'd been crying? "Where does it hurt?"

Natalie pointed to her abdomen, to the center, the umbilical area.

Laura had developed a knack for reading body temperatures with just the touch of her fingers on a forehead. The nurses joked about not needing a thermometer when Dr. Nelson was on-site. She brushed aside long strands of blonde hair and felt her daughter's brow. Normal. "Lie down flat, okay, so I can feel your belly?" She removed the pillows supporting Natalie.

"This might hurt a little, but do your best to relax. I'll just move my hand around and push. Palpate, we call it. Do your best to relax."

Laura placed her left hand over her right and carefully, slowly pushed down on Natalie's abdomen. No distention—good sign. She started at the right upper quadrant, over the liver and the gall bladder. As she pressed, she concentrated on Natalie's face. When you palpated an acute abdomen, the face said it all. She remembered that from her general surgical training, before she'd veered off into chest only.

"That hurt, Mom," Natalie said, but her body did not react, her face did not signal the type of pain that Laura would expect with an acute abdomen. She moved her hands across Natalie's abdomen, under the ribs. She stopped at the left upper quadrant, over the spleen. So far, the spleen on the left and the liver on the right both felt normal, not enlarged, not particularly tender.

When she moved down to the left lower quadrant, Natalie flinched. "There. That hurt bad."

Her next move would tell the tale, the right lower quadrant. If Natalie had an acute abdomen, odds would be on an inflamed appendix. Laura hesitated before pressing down, watching Natalie's face. Nothing. More pain on the left than the right. Not likely an appendix. Good. One last pressure: center abdomen. Where Natalie said she hurt the most.

In the background, Laura had heard the phone ring. She'd signed out for the weekend, so the hospital wouldn't call. One of these days she was going to order a separate line for the kids. Or was it already too late? Next year the twins would be off to college; one line would work fine for just her and Patrick.

"Mom, it's for you." Nicole yelled from the bottom of the stairs.

"Okay, I'll take it in my bedroom. Natalie, I'll be right back."

Laura picked up the phone on the nightstand. She breathed easier in her sanctuary. For the first five years after Steve died, she'd kept the room exactly as he'd left it. In his job as anchor on a Tampa news channel, he'd accumulated a wall of honor plaques, photos of himself with important people, that sort of thing. Then one day, about two years ago, on impulse, she'd assembled all his accolades on the dining room table, gathered the kids, and officiated as they selected their favorite mementos of their dad. She'd done that much for Steve. She'd preserved for the kids an almost devotional memory of him. But a deserved memory? Five kids. Five different answers to that question. With Steve's memorabilia decorating the kids' rooms, Laura's space became her own. She could indulge her taste for Laura Ashley designs, a favorite decadent indulgence.

"This is Laura Nelson."

"The ravishing doctor, I presume."

"Happy Thanksgiving, Tim."

"I'll be right there," he said.

"Pardon?" Laura never knew what to expect from her good friend, Tim Robinson, a pediatric heart surgeon. They had met when both were medical students in Detroit. They had a history, more or less. Now Tim was a prominent pediatric cardiac surgeon at Children's Hospital of Philadelphia. He'd been there for Laura in a professional and personal capacity seven years earlier, when Patrick underwent dangerous heart surgery at Tim's hospital. That year, they'd spent Thanksgiving together for the first time. Ever since then, she and Tim had carried on a long distance, now-and-then relationship.

"Laura, my dear, I'm on a stand-by flight to Tampa. I should get in by two thirty. I'll grab a car at the airport and drive to your parents' place. That is, if I'm still invited. You haven't replaced me, have you?"

"Tim, that's wonderful. Mom will be thrilled and the kids, too. There's just one thing—"

"Uh-oh. I *have* been replaced." The disappointment in his voice made Laura giggle. Their friendship was so weird. Close, but not intimate.

"No, nothing like that. You're still the one. It's Natalie. She woke up this morning with abdominal pain and vomiting. I was just doing an exam."

"But you know better—a mom is never objective. You're going to have to take her to the E.R. or call in one of your surgical buddies."

"I'm not sure. She doesn't have a temp and the pain is not localized."

"I've gotta hop on this plane, Laura. But tell you what, if there's any doubt about Natalie's abdomen, and you don't feel comfortable taking her to your mother's, you go ahead with the other kids. As soon as I get into Tampa, I'll drive over to your place. If you decide to leave Natalie, I'll check her. If she's okay, she can ride to your mom's with me. If not, I'll call you and I'll take her to the E.R. You're only an hour away. You can meet us and see what's what. She's probably got a viral gastritis and she'll be a lot better in a couple of hours. Make sense? Say yes, because my flight's boarding."

What about mom? Laura thought, torn between her mother's perfect holiday and her desire to stay with Natalie.

"Now would be a good time to say yes," Tim said. "I've got a history of taking good care of your kids."

"Yes," Laura said.

Back to Natalie. Nicole was sitting on her own bed, speaking in a voice too low for Laura to hear.

"Hey," Laura said, "that was Tim. He's on his way to Tampa."

"That's great." Nicole looked as if she meant it. "Football on the beach is going to be a blast. Tim, Uncle Ted, and us. And Uncle Dale, but being French, he's not too good. Mom, I think you should leave Natalie home. She's throwing up like crazy. Marcy will be home later tonight."

"Yeah, I'll be okay," Natalie said. "Marcy will be back from her sister's. Maybe Mike or Kevin could come and get me in a couple of days so I won't miss seeing Aunt Janet and Uncle Ted. Or I could drive down in our car. By then, I'm sure I'll be fine."

Laura didn't like the girls driving on their own except back and forth to school.

"We'll see," Laura said, resuming the bedside exam position, fingers to the center of Natalie's abdomen. She pushed gently at first, then harder; holding, then suddenly releasing the pressure. No rebound. Good. Whatever pain she was having did not require rapid surgical attention.

"Ouch," Natalie said, with a slight flinch.

"Okay, what's going on with your period? When did your last one start?" Laura noticed that Natalie glanced at Nicole. The girls had started menstruating five years ago and seemed always to be on the same schedule.

"Don't look at me. I just started mine and I'm not the one who's sick," Nicole said.

"I haven't started my period yet," Natalie said, "but it'll probably start soon."

"In that case, I think you may have Mittelschmerz," Laura decided.

"What's that?" Nicole said. "I hope it's not some kind of, you know, venereal disease?"

Laura expected at least a grin from Natalie, but instead, got a sudden flood of tears.

"Hey, she was just kidding," Laura said, propping Natalie up on the pillow again. "Mittelschmerz just causes painful ovulation. The pain can be pretty bad, but it's nothing serious."

"So, I'll be okay?" Natalie wiped her eyes with the corner of the sheet. "If only I could stop puking. I'm going to throw up again."

Natalie climbed out of bed and hurried for the bathroom across the hall.

"Grandma would be so upset," Nicole said, "if we missed Thanksgiving dinner. And now that Tim's coming—"

"Tim offered to stop by the house and check on Natalie if she's still feeling too sick for the trip. Then he'd drive her up, later."

"Perfect." Nicole's face brightened. "When's he supposed to get here?"

"About four hours," Laura said, "but I'm not sure I should leave her."

Natalie, still in her lavender pajamas, flopped back into bed.

Nicole jumped up. "Mom's got the perfect solution," she announced. "Tim's coming, right? So we can all go and leave you here to rest. And in about four hours Tim will be here."

"And Marcy will be back this evening," Laura repeated, smoothing Natalie's polka-dot sheets. "You sure that's okay, sweetie, or do you want me to stay here with you and let Mike drive the others to Anna Maria?"

Natalie gave the faintest of smiles. "I'll be just fine. You go ahead. If I try to go now, I'll just throw up all over the car. I probably do need rest. Tim's a doctor, if I get any worse, he'll know what to do."

Laura felt Natalie's forehead. Normal. Just to be by the book, she verified. Thermometer read 98.6.

CHAPTER EIGHTEEN

"Mercer, Matthew is off the critical list," reported the hospital information clerk.

Back in Tampa last night, Victor had gone straight to the hotel and called the ICU. He'd asked to speak to the nurse, found himself on hold for a long time, and then heard a harried-sounding voice say that, just today, Matthew had rallied.

"Is he awake?" Victor had asked. If so, he would drop everything and get to the hospital.

"No. He's sedated. Off the respirator, though."

Did she mean that Matthew had improved so much? Or had the doctors just given up? Once they figured he had AIDS, in their ignorance or even repugnance, would they just take him off the respirator to let him die?

"Should I come in to be with him?" he'd asked.

"Mr. Mercer is stable and he's quite comfortable. Leave your contact information, Dr. Worth," the nurse insisted. "I'll call you if anything changes, I'll be on until seven in the morning."

Encouraged by this report and knowing he desperately needed sleep, Victor chose to defer his hospital visit until first thing in the morning.

He'd checked his cultures and secured the tubes again inside his carry-on before climbing into the hotel bed, and setting the clock for six a.m. Exhausted as he was, he remained awake, tossing and flailing as he replayed in his mind the past month. Matthew's arrival in his life. His covert ticokellin research. His hospital visit to

Kantor. Everything churned in his head until he got up, snapped open his briefcase, and pulled out a pad of lined paper.

Had he forgotten anything important? Was his timing right? Would he be able to get close enough to Norman Kantor to infect him? Would the onset of infection be rapid enough? Would anybody see him administer the dose?

Was there any way the bacteria possibly could be traced back to him? Victor scrawled notes to himself. No question he was doing the right thing. The bastard had denied Matthew a lifesaving drug. He did not deserve to live.

At four a.m., still unable to sleep, Victor called the hospital again. He spoke to the same nurse, and she reported that Matthew had stayed off the ventilator, and was breathing comfortably on his own. Then Victor knelt at the bedside in his hotel room and prayed. Matthew believed in God—Cindy had raised him as a Catholic— but Victor didn't know any Catholic prayers except snippets of the Lord's Prayer. He repeated them over and over before he climbed into bed again and drifted off to sleep.

Victor woke to the noisy alarm clock. Thanksgiving Day. Retribution Day.

He got out of bed and, even before taking a shower, rechecked his cultures. They looked healthy, as well they should, in their nutritious broth now at room temperature. After replacing the glass tubes in his carry-on, he dressed in light-gray slacks and the new aquamarine-color shirt that Matthew had given him for his birthday. Before heading for the hospital, he went over the notes he'd made in the middle of the night. Holding the paper in his hands, he blinked once, then again, as a jolt of acid erupted from his stomach, burning the length of his esophagus. The omission in his plan was so blatant that it terrified him. Could he have been so fixated on harming Norman that he'd left Matthew vulnerable.

He needed to get Matthew out of that hospital before the lethal staph took hold. Picking up the hotel phone, he called information and within minutes was connected with a medevac provider. Yes, they had the resources to transport a patient such as he described.

He left out the HIV part of Matthew's condition. Yes, they'd meet him at Tampa City Hospital. Next Victor called the HIV specialist at George Washington University Hospital, a physician who had collaborated with the NIH on joint projects. Plans for Matthew's transfer were efficiently confirmed.

Arrangements made, Victor headed to Tampa, his cultures tucked away in the carry-on.

No matter how hard hospitals try to look cheery for the holidays, they never succeed. The struggle between life and death doesn't take breaks. The staff is cut to almost skeletal levels. The unlucky ones manning the floors just wanting to be home with their own families. Subpar morale—and service not peak, either. Victor hoped that the Thanksgiving staffing level would help him implement his scheme.

By the time Victor arrived at the seventh floor ICU desk, the nurse who had attended Matthew last had already left. The arriving nurse was getting ready to take report for the new shift, but she offered to check on Matthew first.

"Your son is doing well," she reported. "Still sleeping, and his blood gases off the ventilator are okay."

Before Victor could ask anything more, the clerk manning the desk announced, "We're ready for report." Turning to Victor, she said, "Why don't you wait inside the ICU, sir?"

Enter the ICU. Had he heard correctly? Access to the main ICU had been the weak link in his plan. The clerk who'd just come on duty was clueless of the fact that Matthew Mercer, the patient they were discussing, was in an isolation room, not in the main ICU.

Victor knew he would have to act before anyone noticed him. He thought he had maybe five minutes, maximum. No way he could have predicted exactly how he'd implement the inoculation phase, but he knew without a doubt that speed, precision, and safety were essential. The staph he'd cultured was so virulent that he could not risk even one organism straying from his target.

CHAPTER NINETEEN

Pounding on his bedroom door awakened Charles Scarlett on Thanksgiving morning.

"Wake the fuck up and let me in," Banks's voice shouted.

What the heck was he doing up at the crack of dawn? Banks usually slept until noon, especially after an all-nighter. And he never came out of his basement cave. Since nobody else lived in the house proper, Charles slept in the nude, never locking his bedroom door. Before he could throw on a pair of shorts, Banks was in the room. Not his usual lethargic self, but hands on hips, agitated, black eyes glaring, shoulder length hair a glossy auburn brown.

"You serious about that germ shit you talked about last night or you just blowing smoke up my ass?" he asked. Charles fumbled to tie the drawstrings of his old workout shorts.

He hadn't slept much, second-guessing himself. Could he uphold his oath to The Order? Could he carry out the plan that he'd proposed to Banks last night? Did he have the balls to walk into his high-security laboratory, cause a distraction or whatever, and walk out with a vial of a flesh-eating staphylococcus that could resist any antibiotic? Bacteria so deadly it was considered a potential bioweapon and was protected by armed guards, 360-degree cameras, and electronics to monitor sound and motion. Charles had security clearance and he knew the exact placement of every culture and every camera. And now, with Stacy Jones being *promoted*—how could he even accommodate to that word, that concept—he would be in control of the incubator system for the department. The Lord works in mysterious ways. Maybe that promotion was the key to unlock a momentous opportunity. But the bravado that had braced him when he'd presented his proposal last night, eluded him this morning as Will Banks got in his face, so close that Charles could smell his rank breath.

"Chuckie, I'm talking to you, not the fucking wall." Nobody but Banks ever called him "Chuckie" and then only to annoy him. "You gonna do this or not? I'm goin' in today. Meetin' with the leadership. You know what I'm talkin' about. These guys are the true patriots. I'm gonna tell them that you got the weapon they been lookin' for."

"Me?" Last night, Banks had seemed to like Robertson's nuclear material better than Charles's staph organisms.

"Yeah, you, dickhead. You better not be shittin' me about how those germs can kill."

Charles hated vulgar language. A Southern gentleman did not need to resort to such filth. "The cultures that I control are deadly, but Russell—"

"I don't give a fuck about Robertson and his shit. He was wafflin', couldn't commit. Besides, his radioactive nuclear goes missin', you got a real mess. I had to test him—he failed."

Charles wondered what that meant.

"You got your test tube of bacteria," Banks continued, "you let it out, you get yourself out, you are home free. Ain't that what you said, Chuckie? Ain't that what you were braggin' on last night?"

So Banks had been listening to his plan to exploit his research, to release his bioweapon to The Order.

"Hey, I just woke up, Will, I have to think this over, I mean—" What did he mean? Would he go through with this or not?

"No, Chuckie. You are called to action. Now. As of today, this cell is just you and me. Robertson's taken out."

Taken out? The guy had been equivocating last night, had been like that for the past few months, but taken out? Sweet Jesus. He had a wife and two kids. Taken out?

"God," Charles grappled with the reality of what he was about to pledge. "I guess I can do it. I have to make a definite plan for how to get the bacteria out of the lab. The strain is extremely potent. You have to replate it every eighteen hours or it will just die. Like I told you last night. It acts ultrafast. Infects. Kills. Dies out. Unless it's passed on to a fresh host before it dies out. I mean, that's what we think. The only reason we grew it in the first place was so if we ever need to, we could come up with antidotes to mutations in the real world. But this strain has never been in a human."

"Don't you worry about humans," Banks said. "That's gonna be decided by The Order. The leadership will pick the right guinea pigs for your mean-ass little bugs."

Charles had sunk back down on his plush king-size bed. So his time had come. He'd been selected for a job. This is what he'd wanted, but— "Russell?" Charles could not help but ask.

"Viewing is Friday night at Briarman Mortuary. You were such good Wednesday night buddies; you need to show your face. His missus will be expectin' you to show up, won't she?"

"God, Will, this is a lot—"

Banks took a step closer, anger flashing in his black eyes. "You tellin' me you gonna chicken out. Because if you do, you'll end where Robertson is. You hear me, Chuckie? We clear on that?"

Charles stood up, absorbing Russell Robertson's fate, stunned by Banks's unveiled threat.

"How will you let me know?" he asked. "Like, when do I need to produce it? Where?"

But maybe Charles wasn't scared. Maybe the shaky sensations traveling up and down his body signaled pure excitement. Isn't this what he'd wanted? A means to prove himself, finally?

"Today is Thanksgiving," Banks mused, "yeah, The Order's leadership will be meeting. I will be back with the plan. Tonight. Be ready. Lot of shit going down—time's short for The Order. Got to make a stand soon, real soon."

Charles remained sitting on the edge of the bed as Banks left. Not until he heard the roar of the Harley did he move. This was his chance. What he'd considered a demeaning assignment had turned to his advantage. He was the designated scientist in charge of the department cultures today. Except for the usual security personnel manning the cameras, he'd be alone in the incubator. Not a major problem to duplicate a culture line and secrete it until The Order says Go. Banks had said *soon*. Charles would be ready.

Charles had been surprised at first that The Order had chosen him, not Robertson. Charles and Robertson had not been friends; Charles had no friends. But Russell had been a decent type, respectful, a Southern gentleman. Charles had sensed that Robertson had lost his passion for The Order, and Banks had picked that up, too. For certain Banks was The Order's enforcer. And now Russell Robertson was dead.

Charles had no options. If he failed, he'd end up laid out at Briarman Mortuary. He wondered how his parents would feel. They might be ambivalent about whether he lived or died. But if he were dead, the manner of his death, death with honor or death as a coward, that would mean everything to them. For once, he would not disappoint them.

CHAPTER TWENTY

Laura sat in the back seat of the Oldsmobile wagon between Nicole and Patrick, letting Mike drive and Kevin ride shotgun. The four kids bantered as if the older boys never had gone away to college, but Laura felt uncomfortable. If she didn't have all five kids around her, she never felt quite right. She'd doubted she ever could shake the trauma of almost having lost her kids and her career seven years ago. But Steve, she had lost Steve. Now she questioned the wisdom of leaving Natalie behind. Her clinical instincts said Natalie did not have a surgical abdomen, yet the vomiting seemed excessive for a simple gastroenteritis.

"Mom?" Laura felt Nicole's elbow poke her in the ribs.

"What?" What had she missed?

"Mike said he wants to invite a friend from Notre Dame to come down over Christmas break."

"Nicole's already salivating," Kevin said. "Fresh meat—a Domer in the house."

Nicole reached over the seat to punch Kevin in the shoulder. Kevin swiveled, fists in the air, mock boxing mode. Just like old times, Nicole and Kevin going at it.

"What friend, Mike?" Laura said. "I must have zoned out. I'm really worried about Natalie."

How she missed life with all five kids at home. Would they ever be all together again; living together? Unlikely. She needed to reconcile herself to this. They'd finish college, maybe go to grad school, then move into their own places, get married, have their own kids.

"A guy in my dorm. I want to invite him down for New Year's." Mike made friends easily and used to fill her house with boisterous buddies. "His family lives in Grosse Point, near Detroit. Crappy weather there, so—"

"That'll suck," said Patrick. "Kev will have to move into my room."

"That's right, you spoiled little runt." Patrick actually was bigger than Kevin now, but to Mike and Kevin, he'd always be the baby.

Patrick started to reach over the seat to pummel Kevin, but Laura pulled him back. "Of course that would be okay, Mike. What's your friend's name?"

"Paul Monroe. Nice guy. Patrick, he'll kick your butt on the baseball field. His brother is Scott Monroe. He's with the Yankees."

"That'll be the day. I'll show—"

But Laura didn't hear the rest. Paul Monroe? Grosse Point? David's brother, Nick, had four sons. She knew their names: Scott, Jonathon, Paul, and Bobby. She'd seen pictures. She'd actually seen them, dressed in tan slacks and navy jackets, filing out of the church at David's funeral. Her son Mike had been seven years old, the same age as Paul, Nick's third son. And now they'd met at Notre Dame.

"Mom?" Nicole again, shaking her arm. "What's the matter with you? You're all sweaty." Laura wiped her hands on her shorts. "You're sick, too?"

"Must have caught it from Natalie," Kevin said. "I wondered what was wrong with her last night. Unlike you," he touched Nicole's shoulder, "she's not a moody one."

"Mom," Mike interrupted, "do you have a problem with me bringing Paul home?"

"Maybe his brother can get us spring training tickets for the Yankees?" Patrick fantasized. "Oh, man, would I like to meet Scott Monroe!"

The drive from Tampa to Anna Maria Island took sixty-five

minutes. Mike drove while the others clowned around. Laura closed her eyes, hoping that they'd assume she'd fallen asleep. Mike's innocent request had reopened a closed chapter in her life. Inside that chapter was an explosive, destructive secret.

Once Mike pulled the Oldsmobile into her parents' driveway, Laura had no more time for reflection. So much catching up to do. She rushed into her parents' two-story Key West-style home on Key Royale. Charming, just the sight made her smile. She'd see her sister whom she hadn't seen for a year, her brother-in-law, and French-speaking seven-year-old nephew; her little brother, now a Jesuit missionary doing a stint in Rome, and her proud parents.

Amid the chatter of the family reunion, the phone rang. Her mom answered, "It's Tim," she announced.

Laura jumped up from the chaise lounge on the patio to grab the phone. *Natalie.*

CHAPTER TWENTY-ONE

Victor Worth surveyed the surgical ICU: seven beds, arranged in a semicircle. Behind each bed stood an array of equipment and monitors that emitted a cacophony of random rhythmic chirps. Movable partitions separated the patients. These patients had practically no privacy, but that would hardly matter for Victor's maneuver. Most everyone in the unit looked either unconscious or asleep.

An empty, straight-back chair stood next to each bed. During shift changes, Victor knew, no visitors were allowed inside the ICU, they were asked to relocate to the waiting room until the nurses finished report. Lucky opportunity for him; the holiday staff deficit and the clerk's obvious desire to dismiss him from her desk lent him freedom of movement. He needed to appear as if he belonged there so as to not attract the attention of the four staff still in the room: a cleaning lady, mopping in the far corner, three aides clustered around a young boy's bed, one fussing with his catheter bag, the other two changing the sheets.

But any minute the ICU would be teeming with personnel. *Better move now.*

Trying to avoid drawing attention with sudden gestures, Victor made for the nearest bed and took inventory. Norman's bed had been moved across the room, as far as it could be from where he stood—and right next to the boy's bed where the three aides were working. He had to stall a bit.

Victor inched his way into the chair by the nearest bed; he would sit quietly as if he were the patient's loved one. The patient was unconscious and hooked up to a noisy ventilator. The cleaning lady mopped with her back to him; for now, no one was paying him any attention. But he'd have to wait longer.

"Don't forget the patient in isolation," he heard one of the aides say from across the room. "We still have him, and he takes three times as long as the others, what with putting on all that protective crap we have to wear."

"He's got some horrible disease," her coworker answered, "but now that he's awake and all, seems to be a nice guy." The aides chatted, still oblivious to Victor.

He stiffened. They were talking about Matthew. *So he was awake?* Victor almost bolted out the door, across the hall into Matthew's isolation room, but he did not move. His goal was retribution. His resolve had not weakened. Another few minutes. Just a few more minutes. Victor eased down in his chair.

After stuffing soiled sheets into a laundry bag, the two aides moved toward the door.

Then a realization jolted Victor so violently that he felt lightheaded. What if somehow, the lethal bacteria could be tracked to him? He'd been seen in the ICU talking to Norman. Would somebody make the connection? Norman Kantor and Victor Worth: former colleagues; lethal staphylococci. If he was implicated—Matthew had no one but him. Victor could not take the chance of getting caught. Not now.

Just as suddenly, a solution suggested itself. Instantly, Victor acted on it. He had no time to analyze, to weigh the pros and cons. To consider anyone other than Matthew. He needed to proceed. He patted the pouch of his leather bag. Plenty. Not only enough culture material to kill Norman, but enough to kill every patient in the ICU. Infecting multiple patients would give him cover, camouflage. But he had to act. Now.

Hunching, he reached into his pocket, removed a pair of rubber gloves, and pulled them on. The old man in the bed closest to him was not breathing on his own, either sedated or unconscious. He noted the name posted at the head of the bed: Bart Kelly. Physician: Dr. Nelson.

Victor calculated that the hospital would be so busy trying to figure out how their ICU became infected with such a deadly, resistant bacteria that nobody would remember him. Nobody would connect his history with that of Norman Kantor, the intended victim. By then, Matthew would be safe in D.C.

Gloves on, Victor reached into the culture transport pouch and deftly selected an impregnated swab from the secure carrier. He eased forward, inserted the saturated swab into the old man's nostrils, swiveled it, and for extra measure, wiped it around the exposed end of the tube coming out the man's nose. Done. Victor imagined himself looking like a concerned layman, just observing a patient.

He moved to the next patient, next bed. Still no one was paying him the slightest attention. He leaned over a middle-aged woman in a deep sleep—sedated, maybe—but he'd have to be careful. His gloved fingers pulled out a second swab and gently wiped it on the woman's cracked lips. She slept, and he applied as much pressure as he dared. The inoculum would be smaller, but surely enough to jump-start the noxious bacterium.

In the third bed, Victor found a younger woman. Tubes going everywhere, but the woman's eyes were open. Had she seen him with the swabs? Should he infect her—or just move on? Instant decision needed.

Victor moved to the next bed. The cleaning lady mopped, her back to him, oblivious. He knew he had to hurry before staff flooded the place. The old man in this bed mumbled incoherently, moving his lips, not awake, but not asleep either. Not as many tubes running into him. Victor decided to pass him by. Why, he didn't know.

Next, a man on a ventilator. Older. Eyes closed. Mancini, another Dr. Nelson patient. Victor pressed his third swab around the tube coming out of the patient's mouth, returning the used swab, as he'd done each time, to its secure holding container.

Now he was about ten feet from Norman Kantor's bed. How long had it taken him to process three patients? Only a minute or two, but it seemed like hours. After Norman, he'd get out.

Victor's heart rate accelerated as he moved to Norman's bedside. Hovering over his one-time mentor, Victor steadied his hand. How propitious. Norman would succumb to the very staphylococci he claimed to have conquered. Except the staph that would be painted around and inside his nasal mucous membrane was several generations more virulent and much more resistant to that flawed antibiotic Kantor had developed for Keystone Pharma. This staph would eat away at the insides. A painful but deserved reality for the old bastard who denied Matthew a chance to live.

Victor grinned as he proceeded with the inoculation. Norman's eyes were closed, his breathing regular with a light snore. Victor deftly inserted the swab into Norman's first nostril. Norman stirred; his eyes fluttered for an instant. Second nostril done. The bacterial load would be more than adequate, but he could not resist Norman's open mouth, so when he replaced the used swab, he reached in for another that he quickly inserted inside his cheek, pressing against Norman's gums to release the maximum bacterial load. Norman opened his eyes a slit, and a smile seemed to form as he recognized his former colleague. But the smile faded to a grimace as he fell back into slumber.

Inoculating Norman had taken only seconds. Victor looked around. The mopper was working herself out of the room, approaching the door, blocking his immediate exit. He should stop now. He'd infected his target, his primary mission accomplished.

The pathetic-looking boy in the bed next to Norman stirred and seemed to call out. Norman knew that he needed to get out of there, but he had to wait for the lady mopping the floor to move away from the door.

"Water," he thought the boy was trying to say, but his voice was too weak for Victor to be sure. Victor approached the bed, hoping to placate the kid. Like most of the ICU patients, he was hooked up to multiple tubes and instruments. But unlike the others, he was awake, eyes focused on Victor in an alert stare. What had this kid seen?

Victor heard a sudden buzz of conversation at the door of the room, and knew he had only an instant left. He drew out a fifth swab. Hastily, he forced open the kid's mouth and pressed the swab firmly against his perfect teeth, releasing millions of the deadly bacteria. If the kid had suspected him, he'd be dead by the time he'd recovered enough strength to make sense of whatever he'd seen.

Victor glanced up at the boy's name: Trey Standish. Then he turned away with not so much as a twinge of remorse. Moving slowly, methodically, just a concerned relative leaving the unit, he felt like the angel of death. He *was* the angel of death.

Finished with the report session, the nursing staff began to drift back toward their patients in the ICU.

As they passed Victor on his way to Matthew's room on Thanksgiving Day, the tiniest flash of guilt made him hesitate for a split second. Should he warn them? Tell them to defend themselves with protective garments, to use proper infectious-disease techniques? Of course, he could not. Victor ignored the nurses, as they approached the newly infected patients on Thanksgiving Day, handled contaminated endotracheal tubes and oral secretions, and then, probably without even washing their hands, moved on to the next patient.

Contamination and rapid spread. He had to get Matthew out of there. Now.

Victor approached the nursing station as if he'd just arrived. Again, he inquired about Matthew. This nurse, a woman with short gray hair and a commanding air, gave him her full attention. She set down the stack of charts she'd been carrying and looked him directly in the eye. "Are you a relative?"

"Father," Victor said.

"Okay." She grabbed Matthew's chart and headed to the isolation room. "I see you've been his only visitor." They'd arrived at Matthew's cubicle door, and the experienced nurse pointed out the fresh gowns and caps and slippers and masks that had to be worn inside.

"Taking him home today," Victor said.

The nurse stared, hands on ample hips.

"Not home, home," Victor clarified. "He's being transferred up north where they have more sophisticated medical care. Arrangements are being finalized and medevac will be here soon to take him."

"Nobody told me," she said, with a grimace. "We're understaffed today. Why today? Can't it wait?"

"Afraid not." Victor set down his bag, checking that the combination lock was set. Then he slipped on the sterile gown and tied it in back.

By this time tomorrow, this hospital will be under siege. And Matthew and I will be a thousand miles away.

"Well, since you're here, I might as well give you an update. Mostly good." The nurse recited some numbers: temperature curve, blood pressure, lab values, oxygen saturation. Victor listened intently. By the numbers, Matthew was getting better.

But as Victor approached Matthew's bed, he cringed. Matthew still looked very ill. The entire extent of his skin seemed covered with raised, purplish blotches. His eyes were closed and sunken into their sockets. How could this be better?

"Matthew?" Victor whispered, holding his breath as Matthew's eyes flicked open and a smile broke through the blotches.

"You're here?" Matthew said with a shy smile. "Thank you."

Victor was reminded of their first meeting. The day after Cindy's burial. They'd met at her house, now Matthew's, in Clearwater. Victor had had no idea what to expect from this son whom he'd never known existed. He could react with any emotion from hateful anger to passive indifference. But Matthew offered instant acceptance and blamelessness and gratitude. Father and son had talked for hours, unveiling to each other their hopes and fears. Matthew had been a good son to Cindy, and he'd offer Victor nothing less. Although Victor wondered if Matthew could ever come to call him "Dad" or "Father." He hoped the day would come.

"Matthew, I was here early yesterday, you were too sedated. But now you're doing so much better. I've made arrangements to take you to a hospital near my home in Bethesda where you'll get the best possible care and I can see you every day." Victor realized that he'd made tight fists with both of his hands, he was so intent on his mission.

"What do the doctors say?" Matthew asked. His voice was faint and scratchy, affected by the tube in his trachea for the past three days.

"I'm getting you out. This morning as soon as you sign the papers."

Matthew looked bewildered. He tried to lift his hand, tied to a board to support his IV line. "You think?"

"Medevac plane. Not to worry." Victor pointed to the IV bag. "All that stuff's going with you. Time to say goodbye, to Tampa City Hospital."

"What's wrong with me?"

Victor's eyes welled up at Matthew's feeble, abrasive voice. "Plenty of time to discuss that later," he told his son. "Now I'm going downstairs to the business office to get the paperwork started. Once I move the bureaucratic mountains and get you to George Washington Hospital, you'll be fine."

On his way out the door, Victor heard, "What did Dr. Nelson say about the biopsy results?"

CHAPTER TWENTY-TWO

The kitchen was too noisy, so Laura took the call in her parents' bedroom.

"Tim?" She knew her voice sounded strident. "Are you there? Is Natalie okay?"

"Everything's fine, Laura. I'm enjoying the abnormal quiet in your normally crazy house. About Marcy's chocolate chip cookies. Only two left. Those boys must have gobbled them all up. I brought you Tastykakes from Philadelphia. Looks like I'll have to break into them."

"Enough about your snack addiction; how's Natalie?"

"I assume she's just fine."

"Assume?

"Here's what she wrote: 'Dear Dr. Tim. After the family left, I started to feel better so I went over to a friend's. I'll be back before long. Don't worry—I'm fine.'"

"What? Natalie's gone? She was still vomiting when we left. I thought maybe you would have to take her to the E.R. I mean, I'm glad that she's okay, but she should have stayed home."

"Teenagers," said Tim. "Thank God I don't have kids."

"You could've been on your way here with her by now. Natalie knows how important getting together is for Grandma and Grandpa."

"You're an adults' doctor, Laura. I'm in pediatrics. Kids get sick fast. They get better fast. Natalie had one of those eighteen-hour gastrointestinal viruses. You'd better hope the whole family doesn't come down with it."

"As soon as she gets home, will you put her in the car and get over to my mom's?"

"Will, do, babe. How are the college boys? And how's my favorite, Patrick? And that sassy Nicole?"

"They're all fine. Going at each other as usual. But I love having them all together. So get here quickly with Natalie, okay?"

"Yes, ma'am. You did have one message. Hope you don't mind, your message light was blinking, thought maybe you wanted to tell me something. A Dr. Worth, calling about his son. Knew you weren't on call, but said he still needed to talk to you."

Whatever Mr. Worth needed, Ed Plant could handle when he made rounds.

"I'm pretty sure his son has AIDS," Laura said. "You have any experience with the HIV virus?"

"Unfortunately, yes. We're starting to see it in kids who've had transfusions. With the kind of heart surgery I do, most of my patients need blood—so they're at risk. I'm really scared about the epidemic potential. And the social implications are tough, too. Is your patient homosexual?"

"I don't know." But Laura's attention had drifted. Until this conversation with Tim, she had never even considered the implication, the possible risk of the HIV virus to her own family.

"Tim, what about Patrick? He had transfusions during his heart operation. Was the virus out there in the blood supply seven years ago? I can't believe I've never even thought about this before."

Her youngest son, at the age of seven, had undergone major surgery for a tumor in his heart. A benign tumor, she had to keep reminding herself. Patrick was fine now, with no cardiac restrictions. Just a scar all the way from his belly button to the top of his sternum—a scar he'd loved to show off when he was younger, but now kept hidden under his shirt.

"The best we know, it didn't show up on our radar screen until 1981. So I don't think we have to worry."

For a moment, Laura's attention shifted away from her family.

"But what about now? How can we prevent our patients from getting blood tainted with this deadly virus?"

"Blood tests. Maybe urine. Too early to know. Right now all the flack about patents on the test kit puts more emphasis on geopolitics than on diagnosis. Who cares if it was invented in the U.S. or France or Timbuktu?"

"I can't think about this anymore now, Tim, but thanks for being there for Natalie. Soon as you lay eyes on her, put her in that car, and get out here. You won't make dinner, but we'll save all the leftovers. Count on it."

"That'll be my motivation, babe. And to see you, of course."

Laura felt the smile spread over her face. Yes, it would be good to see Tim. Since Steve's death, he had been her only steady male confidante. She knew Tim wanted to take their relationship beyond trusted friendship.

CHAPTER TWENTY-THREE

Collette knew everything. About her and Trey, that they'd had sex, how in love they were, and about how they wanted only to be with each other. After everyone left for Grandma's, Natalie called her friend. Collette had cried with her when she found out about Trey's accident and his awful injury. Collette even knew about the medical and legal issue—Trey's father's factory using beryllium, the mineral that was supposed to cause lung disease in workers.

Neither Natalie nor Trey knew what the truth was: maybe beryllium did injure workers or maybe they were trying to rip off Trey's dad's business. Anyway, the two of them had made a pact not to dwell on this potential disaster and just keep their relationship from their parents to avoid any static. They'd kept their secret. But now with Trey in the ICU, if Natalie wanted to get in to see him, she'd have to tell his family she was his girlfriend. She would do anything to be with Trey, including face up to his family—and hers.

Natalie asked Collette to cover for her. In case her mother called, figuring that if Natalie wasn't home, of course she'd be at her best friend's—"tell her I'm feeling better, just not well enough to travel to my grandparents'. Say I'll be home tonight—say whatever you have to say." Collette would know how to handle her mother.

Then Natalie flung off her pajamas, showered, and dressed in what she considered her most demure dress. She found the keys to the Impala and headed for the hospital. She'd cried most of the night, off and on, and hadn't slept. Her eyes were red and puffy and she didn't take the time to tame her blonde, wavy hair. Nicole would never leave the house looking like such a freak. But though Nicole always had plenty of boyfriends, she'd never had one as awesome as Trey and she'd never been even close to being in love.

When Natalie arrived at the main entrance of the hospital, she bypassed the Information volunteer, walked straight to the elevator with a friendly wave. It was twelve thirty. Her mom and the kids had taken forever to leave and she had to get back before Tim became worried. That gave her an hour.

As she passed the ICU waiting room, she glanced inside to see if Trey's parents were in there. She didn't know the ICU rules, just that visitors were limited and couldn't stay long. She tried to remember all the stuff Mom told her that time a few months ago when she and Nicole had agreed to go along on rounds. Mom thought they should all become doctors. Natalie thought she might want to be one, but not a surgeon like her mother.

The sign on the ICU door said: VISITORS MUST BE 16 YEARS OLD. No problem, Natalie was seventeen. She stepped inside, and walked directly to Trey's bed. A man with jet-black, tousled hair sat slumped forward in the only bedside chair. A faint snore confirmed that he had drifted off to sleep. This must be Mr. Standish. How would he react to her?

Concerns about Mr. Standish vanished once she got a glimpse of Trey. Her knees buckled and she grabbed the metal headboard for support. She'd expected him to be all bandaged up, some sort of body cast, but he looked so gray and frail and lifeless. Not caring whether his father woke, Natalie leaned over and kissed Trey. His lips felt dry, almost shriveled, except for a tiny speck of frothy mucous. With her hand she brushed back strands of black hair from his forehead, which felt very hot.

As Natalie had expected, Trey was hooked up to lots of tubes and drains. Both legs were in casts and elevated. She thought his breathing seemed labored, but that machine beeped a steady beep. He had not responded to her kiss, but perhaps he was numb—she knew he would be getting pain meds. The doctors wouldn't just let him suffer.

"Excuse me?" she heard a baritone voice before seeing the flicker of movement as the man in the chair looked up.

Her lips were still hot from Trey's, and she brushed at an annoying particle stuck to her lower lip. Before responding, she reached for a tissue from the box on the bedside table, and swiped it away.

"I'm Natalie Nelson," she said, her voice sounding squeaky and her whole body starting to shake. "Trey's girlfriend. Are you his father?"

"Yes, I am. Before he drifted off, Trey had been calling out—"

"Mr. Standish," Natalie interrupted in a rush. "Is Trey going to be okay?"

"He has a fractured pelvis and two broken legs. They had to take out his spleen and fix a tear in his liver." The man sounded so weary, Natalie thought. Had he been here the whole time, since the accident?

"Now the nurses are worried about his temperature. Postoperative infection, they say, is quite common."

As tears started to flood Natalie's eyes, she grabbed a fistful of tissues. Trey's father stood and Natalie felt a strong arm encircle her. "Trey just has to be okay. I—" She stopped before she blurted out how much she loved him.

"Trey never mentioned that he had a girlfriend. I mean a girlfriend that seems to care about him as much as you do, Natalie."

"I have to be honest with you, Mr. Standish. He didn't say anything because of you and my mother."

"I don't understand."

Natalie looked at Trey. She thought his eyes fluttered when she spoke, but otherwise he was immobile. They did plan to tell their parents, eventually, about their decision to spend their lives together, to get married her first year of college, support themselves if need be. But they would keep the secret until after that lawsuit was settled one way or another.

"Trey and I agreed not to say anything. Our families have a conflict, which we're sure will pass with time."

"Natalie, what are you talking about?"

"My mom is a doctor, and she's testifying as an expert in the lawsuit against your company, so we—"

"That Nelson. You're her daughter?"

"Yes."

"You know, you look just like her. I saw her video deposition last week. She made some good points. But I would never let my business interfere with my son's happiness. I'm surprised Trey didn't realize that—"

"It's just that he has so much respect for you and for Mrs. Standish."

"As I hope that you have for your parents," he said.

Laura turned to face him, feeling an instinctive trust. "It's only my mother," she said. "My father's dead."

She then pulled away to touch Trey's cheek. "He's so hot," she murmured. "Maybe Mom can do something." Should she call her? She'd be so pissed that Natalie had faked an illness.

"Let me introduce you to Trey's mother," Mr. Standish said. "He's our only child so both of us have been here around the clock. She's in the visitors' lounge. I'll go get her."

Again, Natalie leaned over to kiss Trey, letting her long hair fall over his face. "I love you, Trey. Please, please get better. Please, Trey."

Her attention on Trey, Natalie never saw the cluster of medical staff gather across the room. She did register the nurse's anxious voice: "Dr. Plant is covering for Dr. Nelson. Call him STAT."

CHAPTER TWENTY-FOUR

Charles's badge got him onto the property, through building security, and into his lab. Because of the holiday, the building was almost deserted; he walked alone into his laboratory. What a break that on the very day The Order had called upon him, he had complete and exclusive access to what Will Banks called a "bioweapon." Usually aloof, he took a moment to speak to the two armed men who guarded the secure incubator, commiserating with them about having to work the holiday—somebody had to feed the cultures and that somebody was him.

Charles was a microbiologist and a geneticist. Though he had an M.D., he was well aware that he was no clinician. Neither was he a chemist or a toxicologist or a pharmacologist. His job description at CDC was specific: to genetically develop killer staphylococci. What happened after that was not his concern. Supposedly his fellow researchers used his cultures to develop new antibiotics that would work against new natural strains of staph that were sure to emerge. That, he assumed, was the official cover story. What the government—the United States Army Medical Research Institute for Infectious Diseases—USAMRIID—really wanted were instruments of bioterror. Although never yet used to attack humans, his little clusters of round bacteria would kill like the plague, only quicker and with more pain.

Naturally, he wondered where The Order would choose to deploy his bioweapon. Banks had said nothing about their choice of a target. When Charles had signed on as a soldier in The Order, he had sworn absolute obedience, total secrecy, and infinite allegiance. And Charles, if nothing else, was a man of his word. He'd been called a coward and wimp, but nobody could accuse him of ever breaking a pledge.

Charles moved about the incubator, a space lined with enclosed shelves housing petri dishes of culture plates on one side and cubicles, all equipped with stainless-steel laminar flow hoods, on the other side. He'd identified the exact cubbyhole where he would stash his set of duplicate culture plates. The temperature and humidity would be ideal, and now that Stacy was moving up, he'd have daily access—which meant he'd have to hold off on his request for a transfer to another department. Banks had hinted that they'd be put to use soon, within days. The sooner, the better. What he was doing may be technically easy, but risk was everywhere. He had only to glance at the sophisticated camera system and all the auditory and motion detectors scattered about. His obsessive personality helped him mentally map where each device was situated so he could evade each mechanical roving eye. At least he thought he could.

Could The Order have chosen a political target? Release the bacteria at a civil rights forum? Or were they planning to attack a hospital? One of the newly integrated schools? The possibilities were endless. Would The Order claim credit for the attack? Probably not. With so many members of The Order already in jail, the leadership might rather sit back and gloat privately.

But most importantly, would they consult him about where and how to release the staph? Would they want him to play a part? Or would they try to appropriate the cultures and send someone else to get the bacteria to the target? Charles had tried assiduously to explain to Banks—his sole contact from The Order—that the bacterial growth phase was ultraaggressive. If not precisely controlled, the culture would burn itself out before its prime—only tens of people would die rather than thousands. Well, maybe that was what The Order wanted. Charles did not know the endgame.

Charles emerged from the incubator. Mission accomplished. Duplicate cultures of flesh-eating staph safely hidden away.

CHAPTER TWENTY-FIVE

"What is it you don't understand?" Victor demanded. "My son is to be moved. *Now*. Medevac personnel have cleared him. George Washington University Hospital will admit him. Matthew has signed all the releases."

"I'm sorry, Dr. Worth," said a young female in Discharge, "I need a physician's approval. It's hospital policy."

"Doctors have pagers. Page a doctor. *Now*."

"I already did so, sir. Dr. Kellerman isn't answering his page, and since he's not signed out to another doctor, we have to wait for him to call in."

"I can't wait. Do you know how much a medevac transfer costs? Will the hospital pay for that?" Victor didn't give a damn how much the flight cost. Matthew had to be moved well out of range of that infected ICU. Now.

"I'll try again," the administrator said.

Victor's fingers drummed on her desk. He couldn't afford this delay. Even if Matthew was protected to the extent possible by the isolation protocol, the risk of exposure was increasing by the minute.

"Not picking up." The clerk frowned.

"Then call Dr. Nelson," Victor demanded. She'd at least tried to intervene to get ticokellin for Matthew.

The woman consulted her directory. "Dr. Plant is covering for Dr. Nelson. Let me put you in touch with Dr. Plant."

Victor already had called her home, had left an urgent message requesting a call back. So far, nothing.

The woman dialed a number, waited, and then handed over her phone.

All was in order for a transfer, Victor explained; he merely needed a signature.

The male doctor wished he could help, he said, but since he had not actually treated Matthew—

Every minute of this struggle escalated the odds that Matthew would come in contact with the bacteria that was, at this very moment, killing Norman and the others. Every minute.

"Dr. Nelson operated on him, and you are responsible for her patients." Victor felt his voice rise at least an octave. He must not sound as if he were losing control. "Okay," he said, "then put me in touch with Dr. Nelson." He added, "Please?"

"She's out of town with her family," Dr. Plant said. "I really don't think she'd—"

"Look," he said, "I'm a doctor. She and I have collaborated on this patient's care. She supports his transfer. She gave me her private number, in case something came up." Victor had the scrap of paper ready and read off the Tampa number.

"Well," Dr. Plant said, "I didn't realize—"

CHAPTER TWENTY-SIX

The Jones family didn't live in the inner city anymore, but in a two-story brick house, just inside the Detroit city limit near 8 Mile Road and Grand River Avenue. Stacy Jones, M.D., M.P.H., sat at the foot of her mom's Thanksgiving dinner table, riveting the attention of her three younger sisters. She was Harvard educated, and employed by the CDC. Federal benefits and job security—and miracle of miracles, she'd just been promoted to director, Experimental Staph Section. Not bad for a thirty-two-year-old black woman from the Detroit ghetto.

Stacy had paved the way for her sisters, and they respected and admired her. Sharon was a labor lawyer in the Detroit firm where she'd interned. Rachel, following in her mom's footsteps, a social worker in inner-city Detroit, and little sister, Katie, was in her third year of med school at the University of Michigan in nearby Ann Arbor. Stacy beamed at her sisters, and accepted congratulations on her promotion. When they'd finished the Thanksgiving prayer, she gazed with pride and love around the table of five women. Her sisters had not always looked up to her, she vividly recalled. Stacy had gone through a rough phase when she'd turned thirteen in 1967, the year both of her brothers were killed in the Detroit riots. Look where the Jones family was now. Accomplished. Together. Happy, if not complete.

Preparing the meal had been a team effort. Stacy had flown in from Atlanta last evening and her sisters all lived locally. Mom was alone now in the house, and the girls had been trying all morning to convince her to move into a townhouse in the suburbs. Lucy said she'd think about it.

"Or, you could move down to Atlanta with me," Stacy said. "No more shoveling snow."

The phone rang in the kitchen, and Lucy jumped up to get it.

"She never stops," Stacy said, "and she'll never leave Detroit." Her sisters nodded. Mom would never leave Anthony and Johnny though they had died eighteen years ago.

"For you, Dr. Jones," Mom said, nodding at Stacy, then looking at Katie. "Next we'll be calling you Dr. Jones, too."

"Guess I better take it." Stacy managed another couple of mouthfuls of stuffing. "Part of this promotion is being available for emergencies."

The caller was a Dr. Duncan Kellerman from Tampa. Why was he calling her? Then she recognized the name Laura had mentioned when she'd asked Stacy for advice about that AIDS patient she'd done the biopsy on. Laura had informed her that Kellerman was a good ole boy. Did that translate to jerk?

After introducing himself in a long-winded speech about his professional attainments, Kellerman said he had at least three "difficult bacterial" infections in their ICU. What could she tell him about bacteria that spiked fevers to 105 degrees, caused severe respiratory distress, and didn't seem to respond to appropriate antibiotics?

"Dr. Kellerman," Stacy interrupted, "I'm not a clinical consultant. I do experimental work for the CDC in Atlanta. I don't have a license to practice medicine in Florida."

"One of my colleagues gave me your name. Dr. Laura Nelson. Do you not know her? She said she'd asked you to help her out."

"Laura and I had talked about a suspected case of HIV virus. It sounded like full-blown AIDS, and I've spoken to your director of nursing, but—"

"No matter about that case, I've got three patients going bad. One is Dr. Nelson's patient—one of her lung reduction procedures.

We all know he's high risk, but there's a strapping nineteen-year-old boy who's going bad, too."

"Look, I'm a research scientist. You're an infectious disease specialist: get cultures and cover them with broad spectrum antibiotics until you get the sensitivities back."

"Look, missy, I have sick patients here. Laura Nelson left me your number the other day. When I called today, your associate, a Dr. Scarlett, said you were in Detroit and he gave me this number. I don't care if it's a holiday. I'd like some help here."

Missy? Did holiday intrusions from jerks like him go with the territory on her new job? If so, put me back in the lab.

"Here's what I'll do," Stacy said, "I'll call Dr. Nelson. Assess the situation." She hung up before he could say a word. But not until *I've polished off Mom's pumpkin pie.*

Lucy Jones could have fed the proverbial army, and that was, in reality, where she was heading after stuffing her four daughters with turkey embellished with her signature trimmings. To the Salvation Army, taking her traditional late-afternoon shift. As she prepared to leave, the girls cleaned up, chatting incessantly. When the last of the pots was put away, Katie headed to her boyfriend's mother's house. Sharon and Rachel, off to the feasts at their respective husbands' families. All three had invited their big sister along, but Stacy chose to stay at home, kick back, and reminisce.

Before she settled down, Stacy decided to tell Laura about Kellerman's call. Pausing to burp, she dialed Laura's parents' number. She'd probably catch Laura in the middle of dinner, but if she waited it'd be too late to do anything. Not that there'd be anything Stacy could do.

"Whelan residence." A stong male voice. Too young for Laura's dad and not a kid.

"Uh, hi, this is Stacy Jones, I'm looking for Laura Nelson."

"Oh, hi, I'm her son. Kevin. We haven't seen you for a long time, Dr. Stacy." Stacy remembered when she'd first met Kevin. She'd stepped in to take care of Laura's kids when Laura attended a medical meeting in Montreal. Kevin had been an adorable, tow-headed two-year-old. Could that have been sixteen years ago?

"So good to hear your voice, Kevin." Of Laura's kids, Kevin had always been her favorite. "Hey, I'm sorry to bother you on Thanksgiving, but is your mom around?"

"Yes and no," he said. "If I hurry, I can get her. She's about to leave. You know how it is, the hospital calls."

Stacy waited as Kevin yelled, "Tell Mom she's got a call."

She did know *how it is*. And that's one of the reasons she'd chosen research over clinical practice. How did Laura handle all this? Five kids, her research, her surgical practice, and the administrative crap that came with being chief of anything.

"It's Stacy Jones," he heard Kevin say.

"Stacy, are you clairvoyant? I was going to call you as soon as I got back to Tampa." Laura sounded winded and her voice a little shaky.

"What's up, girlfriend?"

"It's Natalie," Laura said. "I never should have left her—"

"Laura, slow down. What's going on?"

Laura told Stacy about the three recent phone calls. "One from Kellerman, the infectious disease guy I told you about. He reports a series of patients in the surgical ICU; febrile with rapidly developing pneumonia." Before Stacy could tell her that Kellerman had called her, too, Laura continued. "Second, Ed Plant, who is covering for me, who wouldn't bother me if it wasn't serious, thinks my lung reduction patient is probably not going to make it. The third call, Stacy, is why I'm leaving right now for Tampa. It's Natalie."

"Natalie? Where does she fit into all of this?" Stacy had pictured Laura surrounded by her five kids, her brother, sister, both parents.

"She complained of nonspecific abdominal pain this morning. I examined her, didn't think it was a surgical abdomen, and I let the girls talk me into letting Natalie stay home."

"She's home? Alone?"

"Yes. Not really. Remember my friend Tim Robinson? He's the pediatric surgeon in Philadelphia who operated on Patrick."

"Yes." Stacy did remember him and always thought that Laura had something romantic going on with bachelor Tim.

"He's with her, they were to drive out here today, but he called to say he was taking her to the E.R. Now Natalie's running a fever. I'm heading to Tampa right now. I don't know what's going on with her or with the ICU patients. I planned to call and get your advice. I'm worried, Stacy. Really worried that we may have some weird disease down here."

"I don't like the sound of this, Laura. There's no way I can do anything about it from here, but I can be on the first flight to Tampa in the morning."

"Thank you, Stacy. I hate to disrupt your holiday. Please tell Lucy that I'm sorry."

"You just drive carefully, Laura."

She had never managed to mention Kellerman's call and his veiled demand that Stacy come to Tampa.

Stacy glanced out the window. A few fluffy flakes of snow had started to fall, as predicted, although no accumulation was expected. Since moving to Atlanta, she'd learned to live quite well without snow.

CHAPTER TWENTY-SEVEN

Thursday, November 28
Thanksgiving Day

Polite, deferential, respectable: the creed of a well-bred Southern gentleman. Charles Scarlett's heritage and that of his father and his father's father before him. No crude language, not a trace of overt hostility. But just under the polished brass genteel surface, a rabid extremism had raged throughout his ancestral lineage. Did it burn within him, too? Did he believe in white supremacy? Really believe? Or did he embrace the cause to gain his father's respect? When he joined The Order, did he conceive of plotting the destruction of lives? Dream of personally releasing a bacterium that would prove lethal to many? How many, he did not know, could not know.

As he joined hands with his mother and father in prayers of thanksgiving, he contemplated the impact of his task for The Order. Is this how a suicide bomber feels before a mission? Not that his was a suicide mission, but Charles was too smart not to think that he might get caught, might rot in prison, or might even be executed. Chances were good the staph would be traced to his lab. Sooner or later.

"Son, did you know that the citizen swearing-in ceremony this week was the largest ever? Just think—"

"Wonder how many immigrants were white, if any," Mother interrupted.

Charles had been trying to predict The Order's target. A courthouse full of immigrants would make sense, but too late now for that. "We have to stop them," he said, offering a simple, predictable response before ladling thick brown gravy onto his mashed potatoes.

"Dear, will you carve the turkey?" Mother asked. "And let's discuss something pleasant."

"What would it take to elect officials who would send all of them back?" Dad went on as he brandished the carving knife. "Instead we give them our jobs. Let them go to our schools, eat with our children. Admit them to our hospitals. No, we have to freeze them out. Economically. Economic reprisal. Control the economics. Control the money. Control the politics. Fight back with economic reprisal."

Schools? Hospitals? Promising, Charles thought. Negro schools. Negro hospitals. Both logical targets for an attack. Apprehensively, he awaited Will Banks's report on today's meeting with The Order leadership. Charles was in; now that he was committed, he wanted the plan, his marching orders.

As he carved, his father yammered on about politics and economics. Neither of his parents realized that across their elegantly appointed dining room table sat the Angel of Death in his blue blazer and gray flannel trousers.

CHAPTER TWENTY-EIGHT

At five o'clock on Thanksgiving evening, the trim Medjet lifted off into cloudy Tampa skies. Once Victor had reached Dr. Nelson by phone at her parents', she'd called the doctor covering for her. Within the hour, Dr. Plant had signed the discharge papers. Victor suspected that the entire staff of Tampa City hospital was glad to get rid of their hush-hush HIV patient. Well, soon enough they'd have their hands full.

The jet plane interior was designed exactly like a hospital room. Two male paramedics tended to the patient and his hookups: two intravenous lines with antibiotics dripping in, a urinary catheter, a heart monitor, and oxygen flowing into the mask that covered his nose and mouth. To Victor's amazement and delight, Matthew had continued to rally. His color was better, his blue eyes brighter, and he'd taken sips of water.

Victor considered briefly whether his murderous revenge fit Norman Kantor's crime. No one could have foreseen that Matthew would respond to commercially available antibiotics, obviating the need for the investigational drug ticokellin. But suppose he hadn't responded?

And the other infected patients? Collateral damage, Victor told himself, but that seemed so cold. Didn't they have families, too? Especially that banged-up young boy. How would his father react as the staph liquefied and shut down his organs? But he was not that boy's father. He had his own son to worry about. He could not afford remorse, but he did wonder how long the kid would live. The infected would succumb soon, including Norman. The hospital would be in chaos. He needed to be out of there.

As he settled into the Medjet seat next to Matthew's gurney, Victor had an inspiration. Why hadn't he thought of this before? Keystone Pharma. Now that Norman Kantor was not only retired, but dead, wouldn't they need to recruit a research scientist with exactly Victor's expertise? Kantor had trained him. Once the lethality of the Tampa strain of staph became known, wouldn't Victor be the researcher they'd desperately need? He pictured the pretentious Dr. Minn begging him to step in and develop the right chemical antibiotic.

For now, Victor would focus on Matthew. Within three hours they'd be met by paramedics at Washington National Airport. An ambulance would take Matthew to George Washington University Hospital, where he'd be seen by qualified doctors. Doctors who know how to treat AIDS patients. Now his son would have the absolute best medical care, Victor would make sure of that.

But Victor had no choice now—before the plane landed, he'd have to tell Matthew that he had AIDS. Had Cindy ever discussed the possibility with him? She hadn't said so in her letter, so Victor doubted she had. But did Matthew have suspicions? What did the boy know about HIV? Having lived in San Francisco, probably enough. Whatever Matthew's reaction, Victor would swear to be at his side, to never abandon him no matter what might ensue.

To assure Matthew's comfort while they boarded the plane, he'd been sedated. As Victor watched the sedation wear off, the pilot announced cruising altitude and Matthew stirred, opened his eyes. With his free hand, he pushed aside the oxygen mask. Victor's breath caught as Matthew's dry lips parted in a shy smile.

"Where are we?" were his first words. "I know I'm in a plane, but where? Over what?"

"We're still over Florida somewhere. Hey, not sure you should take that mask off." Victor glanced at the paramedic now relaxing in a rear seat. The paramedic nodded okay.

"We need to talk," Matthew said. "About what's wrong with me and where you're taking me. You know, I don't even know what to call you. Victor? Dad? Father?" He grinned. "Pops?"

"Matthew, you are my son. Anyone can see the resemblance. But I don't deserve for you to call me your father. I was not a part of your life."

"Yes. We talked about all that, but it wasn't your fault. Mom never told you about me, but there's something else you need to know. I'm gay. There, I said it. Mom knew. But—"

"Yes, and I did know, son. No reason to let that come between us. I am your father and I want to be a part of your life."

Matthew's face relaxed, tears glistened.

Victor wasn't ready for this conversation, yet he knew he must continue. "But Matthew, you asked what's wrong with you."

"I have gay-man's disease, don't I?" The tears started flowing, Matthew's cardiac monitor picked up pace.

The paramedic returned to the gurney, reached for Matthew's wrist, and took his pulse.

"Please, would you give us some privacy?"

"Pulse is up. The oxygen mask should go back on."

"Yes," Victor told the paramedic. "I'll make sure."

The paramedic retreated to the rear of the plane, but remained standing, keeping his patient in sight.

"They don't call it that anymore, Matthew. They call it acquired human immunodeficiency syndrome." Victor leaned closer, keeping his voice low. "But yes, I think that is what you have. And we're going to a hospital in D.C. where they have all the resources to deal with it."

"AIDS," Matthew said, the tears starting to seep. "I knew guys in San Francisco who died from it. I know how bad it is." The cardiac monitor alarm sounded. Victor reached for a handful of tissues from a box attached to the wall. Dabbing the tears from Matthew's face, he replaced the oxygen mask over his nose and mouth, ending their conversation. Victor felt his heart might break as his muffled sobs blended with those of his son until the jet's wheels set down on the tarmac in D.C.

CHAPTER TWENTY-NINE

Thursday, November 28
Thanksgiving Day

Despite holiday traffic and extra highway police on the roads, Laura ignored the speed limit, passing every vehicle on Route 41 from Bradenton to Tampa. What could have gone so drastically wrong since she'd left home feeling mildly concerned about Natalie, but with her life on an otherwise even keel? Now, Natalie's symptoms alarmed Tim enough for him to rush her to the E.R? Three patients in her surgical ICU—or was it four?—had a strange infection. She'd been too upset to concentrate properly on what she'd heard. Her daughter needed her.

Laura headed straight from her reserved parking spot to the emergency room. The charge nurse stood, holding open the door. "This way, Dr. Nelson." Without another word, she ushered Laura into a small, but private examining room. Another chief of surgery perk.

"Natalie!" Her daughter lay on a gurney, looking pale but not in acute distress.

Tim sat in the lone chair at her side and rose as Laura approached. "Laura, I hope I didn't overreact, but when Natalie spiked a fever—"

"You did the right thing, Tim," Laura moved past him to her daughter. "Does she have an acute abdomen, or doesn't she? Appendicitis? Ovarian torsion? Do we have a diagnosis?" Natalie did have all the hallmarks of a surgical abdomen: abdominal pain, vomiting, and now a fever. Something had to be done, and quickly, Laura thought. Why had they not prepped her for surgery?

So far Natalie had not said a word.

"Laura, Natalie has to tell you something," Tim said, but stopped as Duncan Kellerman strode into the exam room.

Laura moved closer to Natalie as the three doctors crowded into the small space.

"Duncan. I just got here," she said. "Give me a minute to examine Natalie."

"Hi, sweetie," she said as she placed her hands on her daughter's belly, automatically palpating, probing. But not finding what she'd feared.

"Mom, that hurts, but I—"

What was wrong? This didn't feel like a surgical abdomen.

Kellerman spoke. "Thank God that you're here. All hell's breaking loose in the surgical ICU."

Laura ignored Kellerman to focus her professional attention on her daughter. "Natalie, tell me exactly how you feel. I'm so sorry that I left you this morning. I thought—"

"Laura," Kellerman's voice again, "now would be a good time to listen to what's happening in the hospital. I need you on the seventh floor."

"Duncan, I'm with my daughter."

"Mom, that's all right. I'm really okay. I'm sorry. I shouldn't have lied to you."

Natalie was not making sense. Lied? Sorry? About what? That she'd disrupted their Thanksgiving plans? So typical of Natalie, concerned about others, not about herself.

"We've got real problems, Laura," Kellerman insisted. "A bizarre infection of some sort."

"Laura," Tim said, "Natalie seems stable, so while we're waiting for her blood work, why don't you go with Dr. Kellerman. I'll stay here with Natalie."

Laura turned to Tim for a fraction of a second. Why would he support Kellerman's request?

Before responding, Laura stroked Natalie's forehead: only a slight fever, not over 101.

"I'm okay, Mom. Just hurry back. I have to tell you something important. It's about Trey Standish."

"Okay, Natalie, we need your CBC results before we decide what to do. I will be back very soon. You just rest here. Tim will stay with you."

"I didn't get a chance to tell her," Laura thought she heard Natalie say to Tim as she closed the exam room door. "She needs to know about Trey because—"

Trey Standish? Now that had made no sense. Standish? She tried to concentrate. Kellerman at her side, she headed for the seventh floor ICU.

"Your patient Bart Kelly is already dead," he told her. "Others are seriously ill with a virulent, contagious infection. Not responsive to antibiotics."

Laura willed Kellerman to shut up. She needed to focus on her daughter. She should not have left her, scared in the E.R., trying to share some secret. From the very beginning of her medical career, Laura had been faithful to her mantra: My first responsibility is my family. In any conflicting circumstance, I always will choose family over career. Including medical school, eighteen years and counting into her career, she'd never faced such a defining choice. Until just now.

On the elevator, Kellerman saw fit to lecture her. "The surgical ICU is your responsibility, and we waited for you to make major decisions that must be made."

The first thing Laura noticed was an ISOLATION sign posted near the ICU door. Beside it, another: HOSPITAL STAFF ONLY. ABSOLUTELY NO VISITORS. Okay. Good to take precautions. But no visitors was a bit drastic.

CHAPTER THIRTY

Charles had saved room for pecan pie and that special caramel cake that his mother always served on holidays. Only this year, he was disappointed. Mom's new diet, Dad's cholesterol. All the maid offered him with the coffee was some low-fat custardlike pudding that tasted like, well, the stuff didn't even have a taste. As soon as the servants cleared the table, Charles got up and left his parents' home. He'd overindulged on turkey, cranberry-walnut stuffing, potatoes, you name it.

Letting himself into the mansion, he went straight for the kitchen, took out a spoon from the drawer, and pulled a half gallon of Haagen-Dazs butter pecan out of the freezer. He ate right out of the carton. Nobody here to scold him. Then he heard steps coming from the basement.

"That you, Will?" he called. He hadn't expected Banks back until tomorrow. Had The Order already chosen the target?

"Yeah, Chuckie, where the fuck were you?" Banks stepped into the kitchen. "You got an important mission, you gotta stay on call. We're in combat mode, you can't go runnin' to Mama and Daddy's. Don't fuckin' care if it is Thanksgiving. That where you were?" He held out his hand for the carton of ice cream. "Give me that."

"What did The Order decide?" Charles asked. Just the question made him queasy, and he gladly surrendered the carton.

Banks grinned, dipped in with the same spoon, and swallowed a lump of the butter pecan ice cream. "Creamy. Only the best for

Chuckie. What, you didn't get enough to eat over there at the ancestral mansion?"

"Did The Order decide?" Charles repeated.

Will took another mouthful and grinned. "Indeed they did, Chuckie. Indeed they did, and you're the star player, my man."

Charles backed into the nearest kitchen chair and sat down. He had overeaten; his stomach felt uneasy.

"We're on, my man. You're gonna do the deed. I got all the details." Banks patted the right front pocket of his tattered jeans. "You're gonna release those bad ass germs and all we gotta do is stay out of the way and enjoy the show. I can hear the moans and groans and gnashing of teeth already. Those people are gonna die, my man. And it's not going to be pretty, is it?" Banks stooped and leaned over Charles so they were face to face. "That right, Chuckie? Not pretty?"

The Order had chosen Charles.

"Not pretty," the star player managed to reply.

CHAPTER THIRTY-ONE

During her training at Detroit City Hospital, Laura thought she'd seen every variety of pain and suffering, but never anything like this. When the door to the ICU swung open, she heard herself gasp. Yesterday, the unit's seven occupants were doing reasonably well, most drifting in a sedated state close to sleep, their monitors steadily blinking and beeping. Now, she faced sweat-soaked patients writhing on damp sheets, some shaking violently. Patients who'd been recovering twenty-four hours ago, should be getting better now, not worse.

The plague came to mind. The bubonic plague; scourge of the Middle Ages. Pulmonary failure followed by organ shutdown. Signs and symptoms: shortness of breath, shaking chills, raging fever that melted organs. Back then, antibiotics had not existed; they did now, thank God. She scanned the patients, their beds arranged in a semicircle facing a central nursing station. What she saw in the last bed made her steady herself against the closest supply cabinet. Bart Kelly, her carefully selected lung reduction patient, so chipper yesterday, lifeless, covered with a white sheet.

She felt a hand grip her shoulder. "Laura, thanks," Ed Plant said, "for coming back—glad you're here. I don't know what to make of this. They're deteriorating right before my eyes."

Her colleague's disarray stunned her. His red hair had lost its styled perfection; blood and body fluids stained his pressed white pants and starched lab coat. But his expression scared her the most. Amber eyes widened in terror, his face so white you could count each freckle.

She felt a tremor in his hand on her shoulder. "Let's take a moment," Laura said, indicating two vacant chairs behind the nursing station.

"I can't. I've got to get a chest tube into bed seven. He's a young kid. Take out the fluid. Radiology is shorthanded for the holiday and they can't get the on-call staff to answer their phones. So no portable x-rays. And he's too critical to take downstairs."

Laura looked to bed seven before something struck her as strange. Despite so many patients taking a turn for the worse, she saw only two nurses in the room. ICU standards called for a one-on-two ratio. Where were the other two? And where were the aides? The only other personnel on the floor was chief resident Michelle Wallace and she was inserting a central line into Mr. Mancini in bed five with no one even assisting her.

"Where is everybody?" Laura asked. "Not a good time for a coffee break."

"The staff is worried, Laura," Ed said. "Something frightening is happening, a virulent infection of some type. The AIDS patient we had here spooked everybody in the first place, and now they think we've got the next plague."

So she hadn't been the only one to invoke the specter of plague. And why wasn't Ed wearing protective clothing?

The remark about the AIDS patient made her ask about Matthew Mercer. "Didn't he leave, transfer up north?" Could this possibly have anything to do with him? Not much was known about the HIV virus. But he had improved enough to transfer via Medjet.

Ed lowered his body onto the hard-backed chair, never taking his eyes off bed seven. "Yeah, he left all right. This afternoon. The father raised hell. The staff's attention was diverted from other patients, trying to keep him placated. Sorry I let him call you, but we all wanted him out of here. Not the patient, so much, but *Doctor* Worth. Good riddance."

Laura noted the tremor in both of Ed's hands. She reached out casually for one, held it. Warm to the touch. *Good lord, what was happening here?*

"Are you all right?" She wanted to say, but didn't. Until she was sure that her daughter was okay, she'd have to leave the ICU in Ed's hands. Even if Ed was sick, she couldn't bring herself to suggest he go home. She needed him. She just wanted to get back to her daughter. *But what was going on here?* Something she couldn't fathom.

"Tell me what's happening, Ed. From the beginning. Since I signed out to you about five yesterday afternoon."

"Nothing in the evening. Matter of fact the whole night was calm. Unusually so. Not a single call from the nurses. I came in this morning, later than usual since it's a holiday. I planned to round about ten. The patients seemed okay, but I did note that Mr. Kelly had a low-grade temp. A hundred and one. I thought about calling in Kellerman but didn't want to upset his holiday so I decided to wait. I left orders for our ICU patients. Then I rounded on my other patients on the surgical floor. And those of my partners, as I'm covering the entire practice." He coughed, raspy, but superficial. "I could use a drink of water."

"Sure." Laura got up, went to the watercooler at the nursing station, returning with water in a paper cup.

"Thanks. Then I decided to come back to the ICU and check on your patient, Mr. Kelly." He nodded to the inert figure in Bed 1, then looked over at the chief resident. "Michelle's doing a great job, Laura. I told her to go home, but as you see, she's still here."

For the first time, Laura noted that Michelle and the nurses were gloved and gowned. Good. This whole unit was under strict isolation protocol. Shouldn't the entire hospital be?

"The minute I came through the door, the charge nurse hit me with it. Five of the seven patients in the ICU were spiking fevers." Ed's eyes moved across the room. "That kid in Bed 7 was a 105."

Laura looked around. "Where is the charge nurse?" she asked.

"Went home sick. No joke, she was sick. Shaking chills. God, I hope she doesn't have whatever's going around."

"Where's Kellerman?" Laura glanced around. "He insisted I come up here STAT and now he's disappeared." She didn't have much confidence that the infectious disease specialist would be able to handle this rapidly deteriorating situation. Thank goodness that Stacy had offered to come to Tampa in the morning. She wondered whether he'd talked to her about the AIDS patient as she'd suggested. As for Matthew Mercer, good thing his father had taken him out of here. A weird infection like this is just what he didn't need. Even in isolation, physically separated from the seven patients in the main room, there always was the risk of cross contamination. With an immune-compromised patient, just a small break in sterile procedure could result in rampant infection. Mercer was lucky that his bacterial infection had responded so well to antibiotics—contrary to the prediction of his expert father who'd pushed her so hard to get that investigational drug.

"You need to take a look at these patients, Laura. Maybe something will jump out at you. I am tired, low energy. Really feeling the stress of this day. Not a young resident anymore," he said, as Michelle approached them.

"Dr. Nelson, we are all so glad you're here."

"Michelle, give me a quick rundown, please," Laura said. "Ed, I know you're anxious to get to that chest tube."

Laura watched with concern as Ed rose slowly from the chair like an old man, using his arms to push up. A terrifying notion stopped her. *Did he have it, too? First the charge nurse who'd gone home with shaking chills? And now her colleague?*

First, Laura needed Michelle to brief her on the status of the seven patients inside this room.

Then she needed to call Roxanne; the director of nursing had to be updated on the severity of the raging infection-like phenomenon in the ICU. Roxanne would contact the ICU charge nurse who'd gone home, and she would monitor for signs of infection in the rest of the ICU nursing staff. Might as well ruin Roxanne's family dinner, too.

Then Laura could leave Ed Plant and Duncan Kellerman with the ICU, and she could devote her attention to Natalie. By tomorrow morning, Stacy Jones would be here, sharing all her high-pow-ered CDC expertise about this frightful outbreak. Laura looked around the ICU, bed by bed, feeling a shiver of alarm. *Would these patients be alive in the morning?*

"Okay, Michelle. Here we go. Start with Mr. Kelly: what hap-pened?"

CHAPTER THIRTY-TWO

Two paramedics in green scrubs met the Medjet when it touched down at Washington National Airport. Working in perfect synchrony, the men transported Matthew in a medically equipped van, Victor at his side, to George Washington University Hospital. The infectious disease staff greeted Matthew with warm smiles. The look of relief on Matthew's drawn face touched Victor. He knew by now that Matthew never took acts of human kindness for granted, always showed his gratitude.

Yes, Victor had been right to get Matthew out of Tampa. No hospital in the South could hold a candle to the advanced hospitals in the East, Victor was convinced. And for the treatment of HIV, the seven-hundred-bed George Washington University Hospital was second only to the San Francisco medical facilities that had built their AIDS expertise on treating victims for the past four years.

As soon as aides settled his son into a comfortable bed in a private room, Matthew had encouraged Victor to leave. "Have you slept at all?" he'd asked. "You look terribly tired. Go home. I'll be fine. And, thank you."

Truth was, Victor had not slept. His back and forth to Florida and the all-night preparation of his cultures had taken a toll. Nor would he get any sleep that night. Too much had to be done.

"Tomorrow," Matthew said, "I need to talk to you." His voice trembled and he turned his head away from Victor, "About what all this means."

*   *   *

Victor took a cab to his home in Bethesda, arriving in the dark of a moonless night. He'd left a few lights on in the house, to make it appear that someone was home. Now he questioned that decision. If someone looked inside, they'd see disarray. He'd come and gone so quickly, so urgently, yesterday, that he'd left clothes and papers lying around. Never Victor's style. His first instinct was to tidy up, but he knew he couldn't afford the energy now. Or the time. Anyway, who would be peering inside his house?

After he lowered the shades on all the first-floor windows, he hurried toward the basement. From outside, no one could see any of this secret part of his home. He pulled out a key to unlock the door leading down to the basement. The basement windows were blackened and secured by metal grates; the door leading downstairs always double locked. But what if, in his absence, there'd been an emergency, like a broken water pipe, or a fire, and the fire department had to gain entry? They'd simply have to chop through the door. Victor shuddered at the ramifications.

Entering his basement laboratory, Victor faced the same scene he'd left: pipettes, petri dishes, graduate cylinders, and beakers scattered about on the workbench. Everything was just as he'd left it last night in his hurried getaway. For the first time since he'd left Tampa, the reality of his deeds in the Intensive Care Unit crashed into his consciousness. For a moment, he felt faint and grasped the edge of the workbench to steady himself.

Yesterday, in this room, the plan had seemed so straightforward, so righteous. Punish Norman to avenge Matthew, but in less than twenty-four hours, Matthew was recovering—without ticokellin. Norman? Had he killed him? Had he killed others to cover up his tie to Norman? How many had he infected? Was it five, or six, or maybe four? He couldn't be sure. His staph, after all, had never been tested in humans. Maybe the test tube virulence wouldn't translate to violent infection in humans. Maybe a yet-to-be-discovered natural antibody would combat the bacteria.

He remembered feeling convinced that he'd done the right thing. Had he? Or had he done something terrible?

"Too tired to think," he said aloud. "Clean all this up. Dismantle the lab. Dissolve any trace of a staph organism."

Victor rubbed his aching neck, longing for a massage. But he had work to do that could not wait. So he started collecting the laboratory glassware. Everything would go into the autoclave to be sterilized. Tomorrow, first thing, he'd crush the glassware and haul off the shards to a landfill.

What about the cultures he'd nurtured in his basement lab for all those years? "Autoclave them all," he said aloud. Destroy every trace. Destroy his life's work. With clarity, almost mystical clarity, he now knew why he'd done what most people would consider crazy. Why had he kept his staph alive? He'd had an unrelenting, inner premonition that someday he'd need these cultures. And he had needed them to protect his son. When that need arose, he'd had the weapon and he'd used it to punish Norman.

Yes. But for Matthew's sake, he could not risk being caught. Victor was Matthew's only support.

Going to the walk-in incubator he'd installed in the far corner, Victor removed glass petri dish after glass petri dish. Using sterile technique, he placed them in the autoclave, set the temperature to Kill, and waited the required time. He repeated this procedure until all the cultures were dead. Every lethal trace of his bacteria—destroyed. Then he liquefied his supply of growth media, dumping the congealed mess down the drain and adding the empty container jars to the bin of glassware to be destroyed. He'd have to get rid of the equipment, too, but for that he'd need to rent a truck and make a trip to the dump. No time now. But with no trace of live bacteria, how suspicious would it be for a microbiologist to have some outdated laboratory instruments in his basement?

The sky had turned pinkish when Victor came upstairs from the basement. Ignoring the clutter everywhere on the first floor, he continued to the bedroom. He fell across his bed without undressing, too tired to worry about perhaps one infinitesimal, invisible staphylococcus having found its way onto his clothing.

CHAPTER THIRTY-THREE

Thursday, November 28
Thanksgiving Day

Will Banks had ranted about white supremacy for twenty minutes, his face redder and redder, his tone belligerent, his speech peppered with obscenities that Charles, himself, would avoid using.

Stop playing games with me, he wanted to scream at Banks. *Who do they want me to infect?*

Banks stopped pacing and sat on the brocade ottoman, leaning right in Charles's face. He bared tobacco-stained teeth in a snarl. "Gonna hit 'em Saturday."

Charles drew back involuntarily, eyes in a fixed stare. His pudgy body froze. "Not enough time—" he began.

Banks cut him off, his face within an inch of Charles's. "Saturday. Right here in Atlanta. Make it real easy for you. You're gonna take out a shitload of big shots. Ever heard of Julian Bond, Chuckie?"

"What—" Charles managed to clamp his mouth shut. Julian Bond, who'd just received the Bill of Rights Award from the American Civil Liberties Union of Georgia? Oh, he'd heard an earful about that from Dad. That and Bond's recent appearance in *Time* magazine. Bond definitely would be on The Order's hit list. But how to get to him?

"Payback time," Banks sat back with a grin. "No more of him polluting the airwaves with crap on that *America's Black Forum*. We're gonna teach those diversity people and the Southern Poverty folks a lesson. But they're never gonna see it comin', that's the beauty."

Charles's mind churned, trying to process what Banks was saying. He'd been trying to visualize the kind of target The Order would choose. Some crowd scene. But a celebrity target? No, he had not expected that.

"Remember when you said that you could put the bacteria in room-temperature liquid. That they could survive for a decent period of time, like several hours."

Charles nodded, still keeping still. *How was he going to do this?* A million questions swarmed.

"There's a party Saturday night at the Palace Hotel, Bond is gonna show up. And the swanky ballroom is gonna be full of black people plus white people kissin' up to black people."

"The Palace?" Charles asked. "What kind of a party?"

"Some kinda celebration or anniversary thing for a black bitch runnin' the *Atlanta Daily Reporter*—African American rag. Been in her family a long time, some kinda shit like that. The important point is the guest list. You're not gonna believe it, Chuckie—all the uppity-up black folks in Georgia will be there. You got Bond, he's buddies with the *Reporter* bitch. You got Young and you got Jackson."

Atlanta Mayor Andrew Young and the previous mayor, Maynard Jackson? Speechless, stiffening his neck to keep from cringing, Charles did his best not to look away from Banks.

Snickering, Banks pointed at Charles's face.

Must look stricken. He'd never been any good at poker.

"Gotcha, didn't I?" Banks leaned back, his laugh now a hearty roar.

Charles relaxed. "You sure did, you jerk. Almost gave me a heart attack, Will."

"That's not all," Banks ignored Charles and continued. "Their families will be with those fools. A family affair. Bitch from the *Reporter* has fifteen *grandchildren*. All gonna be there, my boy."

"I don't want to infect kids," Charles protested, "if that's what you're saying." He'd always had a soft spot for kids. Why, he'd never know. The only kids he knew were Russell Robertson's and them, just barely. He'd almost passed out that time when Russell's wife handed him a baby to hold. He didn't know what to do, but the baby had cooed and smiled, until it spit up stinky white crud. And now that baby had no father.

"Yeah, we got young and old. Ideal demographs, the leadership said."

"Demographics," corrected Charles, mechanically, not that he wanted to educate Will Banks. *What was the maniac going on about anyway?*

"Whoa, Will, I'm not following you." Charles had been gritting his teeth, as if that would stop the words spewing out of Banks's mouth. *"In the kitchen." "Cream puffs?" "Profiteroles?"* The words suffocated him, as if he were laying in a grave and each word another shovelful of dirt.

"It's your show, Chuckie." Banks shrugged. "I'm just the stage manager. You get the bacteria into that Palace Hotel kitchen and load it into those cream puff things."

"Impossible." Charles felt better, realizing that this idiot scheme could never work. Preposterous. Will Banks may be able to charge in with heavy weapons, but walking into a fancy hotel and—

"You got a better idea?" Banks snapped back. "See, The Order's got a guy inside. The top pastry chef. Been in a sleeper cell for a while, just like you; waitin' and waitin'. And this is his chance. He said it would work. It's a big party, he'll need an assistant. You come in—with your test tubes or whatever you keep them deadly germs in." Banks gestured with his index finger, as if scooping whipped cream, and pointed at Charles. "You just get those germs in the creamy filling of the cream puffs or profiteroles, whatever."

"But—"

"I know what you're going to say, not everybody's gonna eat one. True, but this pastry chef claims that this is the most popular dessert at Palace events, a famous delicacy, the hotel specialty. Don't worry, Chuckie, we'll get plenty of 'em. They won't be havin' any more fancy social events in white people's hotels for a long while."

Charles had joined The Order to prove himself in his father's eyes. So far, his job had consisted only of donating a good meeting place for their cell of three and a safe house for Banks when he was in town. Now, because of his own unreal stupidity, mouthing off about his killer staph, The Order had signed him up as a mass murderer.

Well, no. He could not do this. Sure, he hated all people of color, anybody who wasn't white, but this was way beyond him.

"Even if it did work," Charles said, "I'd never get away with it. They'd figure out that the strain came from the CDC. They'd circle back to me."

"Hey, Chuckie, this ain't an option. These here are your orders. Remember what happened to Russell. Wait till your old man finds out for sure that you're nothin' but a chicken-shit, a dead chicken-shit."

Charles felt a twinge and a heave in his guts. He needed to make it to the bathroom before he humiliated himself. Running down the hall, he knocked a lamp off the bookcase. Before he even reached the threshold, his stomach gave it up. Thanksgiving dinner spewed over the navy-blue flock of the wall covering, chewed up turkey and all the trimmings floated in ice cream streaks.

When he straightened up, he stumbled the last few steps to the bathroom, and yanked a couple of towels off the tub. He laid them on the floor, more or less covering his vomit. Sidestepping the mess, he bent over and removed his soiled shoes. Then, head bowed, he shuffled into the kitchen, rinsed his hands and face and took off his monogrammed dress shirt. Standing in his tee shirt, Charles turned to face Will.

CHAPTER THIRTY-FOUR

Natalie hated that older doctor for dragging Mom away from her. Why had Tim encouraged her to go? Nothing new. Ever since she could remember, the hospital was always paging Mom, even when she wasn't on call. What a joke. The hospital didn't care, they called her anyway.

"What's happening, Uncle Tim?" she asked. That's what they'd always called him. They only had one real uncle, a priest who lived in Rome. They called him Father Ted, not Uncle.

"The patients in the surgery ICU need your mother."

"Oh, my God!" Natalie tried to pull into a sitting position, tugging on her IV line, almost jerking it out. "Trey's in the ICU. Has something happened to Trey? Could that be why they wanted her up there?"

"I don't think so, Natalie," Tim said.

She'd told Uncle Tim all about Trey, the lawsuit, why she had kept the secret from her mother. But not that she and Trey were having sex, and not that Mom blamed Nicole for the birth control pills that she was about to start taking.

Don't think so. But, then it could be about Trey.

A nurse came to take her temperature, and Natalie shut up. She glared at Tim. Would he tell her the truth?

"Hundred and two. How do you feel, Natalie?"

Truth is, she hadn't even felt a twinge of abdominal pain, but she did have a headache, a throb in her head that seemed to keep pace with her heartbeat.

"The pain in my stomach is gone," Natalie said, "but could I have a Tylenol for my headache?"

"You have an NPO order," the nurse said.

"Nothing by mouth." Tim translated. "If you do need surgery, you can't eat or drink."

Natalie knew that perfectly well, having heard her mother give that order over the phone about a million times.

After the nurse left, Tim winked at her, "But you and I know—you don't need surgery. Right?"

"I need to tell Mom about Trey and how I lied to her about being sick. But she left before I could and now if she's up there with Trey. Uncle Tim, let me get dressed and go up there."

"Natalie—" Tim already was shaking his head.

How many times had she practiced telling her mother about her boyfriend? *Mom, meet Trey Standish. It's his dad that you're going to testify against.* Or, *Mom, those birth control pills that fell out of Nicole's purse—they were for me. I love Trey Standish. There's nothing you can do about it.*

"There are some terribly sick patients in the ICU. That's why they need your mother."

"Trey?"

"I don't know. Let's wait until your mother gets back."

She started to protest when a dark-haired, skinny woman about as old as her mother came into the room. She wore a blue smock and carried a plastic basket of tubes and needles.

"Need to do another blood test," she said. "Orders are a blood culture if your white count is high." The woman was already swabbing the crook of Natalie's arm with alcohol.

Natalie grimaced as the needle went in, accepting her punishment for faking stomach pain. But she would not leave this hospital until she saw Trey. Tim would help get her up there. Once the tube was full of blood and the needle out of her arm, she looked to him to repeat her appeal, but hesitated when her mother walked in the door. What was wrong? Natalie had never seen her mother look so awful, like she was scared to death.

Just after midnight, Laura returned to the E.R. She'd pick up Natalie's chart before going into the exam cubicle. A lab tech was packing up her kit after a blood draw. And Laura knew why. The decision as to whether to keep Natalie or let her go home depended on her white blood count, which was high. Blood cultures would be done and her daughter would have to be admitted for observation.

Thank God for Tim who'd been with her the whole time. What a great Thanksgiving for him. It's not as if he didn't have enough of hospitals.

"Mom," Natalie said, "you're back! Can you tell me about Trey?"

"Trey?" Could Natalie mean the boy in the ICU? The one Ed Plant was so worried about?

Before Natalie could respond, Laura said, "Honey, it looks like we're going to have to admit you to the hospital." Laura started to sit on the gurney next to Natalie then thought better of it. She'd just been in an ultracontaminated space. As much as she wanted to hold Natalie close, better to maintain a distance.

Natalie started to cry. Not an unexpected reaction to being stuck in the hospital, maybe facing surgery. Then she started to cough. Not good for a surgical candidate.

"That cough." Laura said as she moved in to kiss Natalie on the top of her head. "How long have you had that?" She turned to Tim, "Negative chest x-ray. But maybe we should get a repeat."

Tim walked over and took her daughter's chart out of Laura's hands. "Natalie has something to tell you," he said. "I need some coffee. See you in a bit."

"Okay. Good," Laura said, sitting in the chair that Tim had vacated. "Natalie, sweetie, I am so sorry that I had to go upstairs. We have an emergency in the hospital." Laura stopped. "But that's not the important thing. You are." She took Natalie's free hand, dismissing her concerns about having been in close proximity to the infection raging in the ICU. She'd protected herself with a gown and mask and gloves and rigorous hand washing.

Tears filled Natalie's red, puffy eyes and spilled over. She must have been so scared. "You're going to be okay," Laura reassured, moving in close to brush strands of hair off her forehead. It felt warm, but not hot. A hundred and two, she guessed. NPO, so they couldn't give her Tylenol.

"Stop. Mom, this is not about me!"

Laura almost bristled at the demanding tone.

Natalie's voice sounded raspy. "This is about my boyfriend."

With the surgery ICU erupting in some mysterious contagious nightmare, this might not be the time for a heart-to-heart mother-daughter talk about boyfriend stuff.

"Trey," Natalie continued, "he was in a real bad accident and he's here in the hospital. In the ICU. I know that's where you were. Now tell me about him. Take me to see him." Natalie's tears flowed down her cheeks. Stunned, Laura reached to grab the tissue box from the bedside table

"Mom, please—is Trey going be okay? I have to know. I'm sorry I never told you about him, but we were afraid that because of his father's business and you and the lawsuit—"

"Oh, no!" Laura's mouth had a mind of its own. "Trey Standish is your boyfriend, Natalie?" The young boy in the ICU struggling for his next breath, about to go on a ventilator until the antibiotics they were pumping into him could take effect.

Natalie reached for Laura's hand, gripping it, tugging on it. "I have to see him. Can you take me there now? Right now?"

Laura let Natalie pull her closer.

"I'm okay. Just put me in a wheelchair and take me there. I need to see him, Mom."

"Let's talk about this for a minute," Laura said. "I didn't know you had a boyfriend, sweetie."

"I just couldn't tell you because you're going against his father in court. And I know you're going to think this is not serious, but I love Trey and he loves me, too. He really does. And I need to see him." Natalie struggled to sit up, stretching her IV line, almost pulling it out. "Just help me get to the ICU."

"So you never told me because I'm testifying against his

father's company?" Laura wasn't sure exactly how she'd have reacted had Natalie been upfront. *What else don't I know about my
daughter? What else does either of my daughters feel but think she can't tell
me?* The birth control pills came to mind.

How old was I when I fell in love with Steve? Eighteen?

"And I wasn't sick this morning. I lied to you because I wanted
to stay home—so I could see Trey. I tried Wednesday night, but
they wouldn't let me into the ICU. Today I did get in and I talked
to his dad. Trey was in a terrible accident, Mom. On his motorcycle.
He looked awful. He was unconscious."

The news echoed in Laura's brain. "You got in?" she asked.
"Natalie, what do you mean?"

"When you left, I went to see Trey in the ICU. Mom, he's hurt
really bad. Can you help him? Can I go see him? You know everybody here. Can we go *now*?"

Laura had to figure out exactly what happened and when. That
boy Natalie was talking about was critically ill with whatever bacteria or virus was rampant in the ICU. Had her daughter had contact
with him? Physical contact?

"Natalie, I am not mad at you, okay? But I need to know about
you coming to the hospital to see—Trey. What time, exactly? I need
to know what you did there. Who saw you? And—" *Did you touch
him?* Laura did not ask. Sounded too harsh.

As she struggled to formulate her questions, Tim stepped back
into the room. With his help, they reconstructed Natalie's day, hour
by hour. When they had it all on paper, she explained as gently as
she could to Natalie that Trey was gravely ill, that because of the infection, absolutely no visitors, not even his family, could see him.
Then she explained to her inconsolable daughter that she would
have to be admitted to the hospital, too.

Tim left them, volunteering to work out arrangements for a private isolation room. Natalie shook with sobs, and Laura held her
close, her own anguish accentuated by her daughter's proximity to
whatever organism had invaded the ICU.

Natalie had kissed Trey Standish.

CHAPTER THIRTY-FIVE

Stacy Jones had booked a 7:15 a.m. flight out of Detroit, layover in Atlanta, then on to Tampa. She awoke to her travel alarm at 4:00 a.m. She thought she'd convinced her mother not to get up, but when she crossed the hall to the bathroom she heard Lucy moving around in the kitchen. Despite yesterday's gluttony, the idea of sausage, eggs, and biscuits made her ravenous. She already could smell her mom's coffee laced with cinnamon.

A quick shower, a hint of makeup, a hasty packing job, and Stacy descended the stairs, dragging her suitcase step by step. "Mom, I told you—" she started.

"Stacy, stop. I'm making all your favorites including that special spicy link sausage that you liked ever since you were a little girl."

Stacy felt a pang of guilt. No doubt, Mom had all of her favorite foods lined up for the weekend, not to mention the Thanksgiving extravaganza leftovers.

"I wish I didn't have to leave, but I couldn't turn Laura down after all she's done to help me."

"It's you doctors. Katie has to leave early, too. She's on her psychiatry rotation." Lucy turned from the stove. "I was hoping you'd have more time to spend with her."

"She's doing great, Mom. U. of M. was the right choice for her."

"Academically, she's fine. It's her boyfriend, Keith Franklin. Something's not right."

"They've been together since high school. Eight years. She ought to know him pretty well by now."

"Still—" Lucy said.

"Speaking of problems," Stacy wanted to segue out of relation-ship talk. At age thirty-two, she was not in one. "I haven't even of-ficially started my new job yet, and I expect I'm going to have some—problems, that is." Stacy poured herself a cup of coffee as Lucy pulled a tray of biscuits out of the oven.

"Got your favorite jam, too. Cherry, from Traverse City. Sorry, honey, you were saying?"

"Personnel trouble. My coworker, Charles Scarlett. Until re-cently he was my peer. Now he's going to report to me. He's from one of those old Southern lily-white families."

"Things have changed, people, too."

"Not this guy, Mom, I don't think. I wouldn't be surprised to find out his family has roots in the Klan."

"Well, you just show him who's boss, honey. It's 1985. Detroit and Atlanta have black mayors. I know it's different in the South, but everything Dr. King did, bless his soul, is paying off for us. Look at you and this promotion. Look at Sharon, hired right out of college by Detroit's biggest law firm. Rachel, a master's degree from Harvard, and little Katie almost finished with medical school. Who'd have thought that possible? If only Dad were here. He's the one that stressed education. And your—"

Stacy gulped down another sausage and checked her watch, "Mom, I really have to run." No time now to listen to her mother reminisce about the heartbreaking losses in their lives: Dad and Stacy's two older brothers.

Stacy had changed her departure date, so she had to stop at the ticket counter, but the lines were short. She'd arrived at the airport in plenty of time. Once on the plane she found it half empty, no Thanksgiving rush on Friday.

In Atlanta she had to change planes for another Delta flight to Tampa; she had enough time to call her lab. Someone should be there to assure her that all was under control, that she had no wor-ries other than chasing off to Tampa to see what was going on at

Laura's hospital. She looked forward to seeing Laura and wondered what was wrong with her daughter—which one of the twins? Stacy could never tell them apart despite their distinctly different personalities.

"CDC. Lab Fifty-Two." The male voice was familiar: Charles. Stacy wished she had reached one of the technicians. She disliked this man at a visceral level and she sensed that the feeling was mutual. Charles always had been civil, she had to admit; her problem was that he did not communicate with her. At issue was the color of her skin—a major obstacle when dealing with white supremacists, which he was. She'd seen the literature on his desk. Organizations that burned churches, set off bombs, condoned these acts of terrorism, and even assassinations. Targets of these hate crimes? Surprise. Blacks. Yes. And also Jews. Homosexuals, too? She wasn't sure. The good news: many of these bigots had been arrested across the South last year. Stacy wanted to believe that the white supremacists' reach had diminished. Or had they just gone underground?

"This is Stacy. Just checking in. How's everything, Charles?"

"Oh, I'm so glad you called in. Thanks." Charles normally didn't bother to thank anybody for anything. She waited for him to continue, reminded of how much she detested his Georgia drawl. "I didn't know what to do. I'm the only senior scientist on call for the weekend. And I have to go home. I am so sick I can hardly stand. Vomiting and diarrhea. Dehydrated, too. I made myself come in, thinking that maybe I'd feel better, but I'm feeling worse."

Stacy did think that Charles's voice sounded weaker than usual. His typical tone was petulant, right in line with his wimpy persona. "Okay," she said, pausing, as she debated what she should do. As far as she knew, he'd never called in sick. Why now? All these circumstances conspiring against her. This was what management was all about?

"Stacy, I don't have anybody to cover here. And the cultures need to be replated. I'll get through them today, but if I'm this sick, I will not be in tomorrow. I have a terrible fever. I don't know when I'll be okay to come back."

"Shoot. I got called into Tampa on a case or I'd come in." She didn't say that she was standing at that moment in the Atlanta airport. Priorities filtered through her mind: her job at the CDC laboratories; her promise to go to Tampa; her dedication to Laura.

"I have to go. Bad cramps. I just wanted you to know that I won't be able to come in at least for the rest of the weekend."

"Okay." Stacy repeated, then the phone on the other end went dead.

The CDC would be on skeleton staff, but someone in administration would be there to connect her to the technicians in the lab. Because the bacteria they worked on were so lethal, only a highly trained senior-level scientist was allowed inside the incubator or inside the level three PC labs during active biomatter transfer. But the techs would have access to the computer records. If they could confirm that Charles had actually replated the cultures, the bacteria would be good for another twenty-four hours. So if she flew to Tampa, took care of matters there, she could return tomorrow in time to replate the cultures again on schedule.

As she placed the call to the CDC, she wondered how tough it'd be to get a morning flight from Tampa to Atlanta. Delta ran several a day, but could she fly early enough to get her back in time? Worst-case scenario, if she couldn't schedule a flight, she could always rent a car for the eight-hour drive, but with the extra cops on holiday patrols, would have to watch her speed.

Over the airport's speaker system, she heard her flight being called. The CDC office clerk had picked up quickly, but she still was waiting to speak to one of the technicians.

"I just have a minute, so I'll be quick," she said when one of her favorite techs finally picked up. She explained what she needed them to do and asked if Charles had completed the series of replates.

"Yes, I know, he's sick." She cut him short. "Tell me about the cultures."

"Dr. Jones, yes, I have the computer printout. He took care of the cultures."

"I'll be in tomorrow to do the next plate transfers," Stacy said, "but it may be late—sometime between three and seven p.m. Can you make sure that I have a tech to help me get set up?"

"I'll stay, Dr. Jones," the tech said. "Me and the wife are expectin' another baby. I need the overtime."

CHAPTER THIRTY-SIX

Charles's boss—before they promoted Jones—had been influential in the creation of The American Biological Safety Association (ABSA). Out of that came the delineation of biological safety levels—BSL—designated BSL1 through BSL4. All federal agencies and university and private laboratories as well as hospitals and industrial complexes that handled pathological organisms now had a framework by which they could protect their workers and the public, as well. The BSL level assignments designate the most dangerous pathogens as four and the least as one, with two and three being intermediate. This classification correlates to the designations P1 through P4, for pathogen protection level, a shorthand understood by personnel at all levels in the field of microbiology.

The exotic staph organisms that Charles's lab handled were potentially lethal. All procedures in the BSL3 classified—P3 Lab— were conducted in laminar flow cabinets with containment hoods and HEPA air filters. Personnel wore full-body protective clothing and gas masks, and stringent protocols were in place and monitored vigorously. Ingress and egress through double doors with both human and electronic surveillance prohibited anyone not specifically authorized to be in any given lab. No exceptions.

Since Charles's laboratory grew bacteria deliberately engineered to resist every known antibiotic, access to it was restricted to scientists with doctoral degrees and intensive training in antimicrobial technique. When live cultures were exposed, only he and Jones could pass the biometric identification process and enter the double doors to the domain of their lab and incubator. Once they had worked with the cultures and stored them away, their techs could clean up and prep the lab for the next round of "hot" experiments. UV-CD lamps were left on when the lab was unoccupied to keep all surfaces sterile.

At the outset, Charles had not planned to screw up Stacy's holiday plans, but if he could make her miserable life even more miserable, that was a bonus. The option to simply not show up without notification meant their immediate supervisor would be called in on an emergency basis. No point in kicking up all that fuss. Besides, he liked Stan Proctor—had liked the man—before he'd promoted a Negro woman. Charles reporting to Stacy? Unthinkable. "Your race is your religion, son," his father had recently told him. "White Supremacy rules. Don't you ever forget it."

But now, Charles never would have to take orders from Stacy Jones. He'd never again set foot in the CDC lab. Maybe not even in Atlanta. Once the staph was released, the folks at Fort Detrick in Frederick, Maryland, would track it to his program at the CDC. Those folks at the Army Medical Research Institute of Infectious Diseases didn't mess around. The USAMRIID brass would go ballistic. Rumor was, the Fort Detrick hierarchy wanted to make the case that the CDC staph program is indistinguishable from bioterrorism and should pack it in. The CDC countered that their program was a vital hedge to protect the public if ever ultra-lethal or super-resistant staph strains showed up in the population. Except for USAMRIID, the CDC was the last agency to run such a program after the NIH Labs' resistant-staph program bit the dust in Bethesda a few years ago.

Charles didn't think they'd shut down his program, but he didn't know much about politics. That was his dad's department. Never mind. He had Will Banks's word for it: by tomorrow night, Charles would be out of the country. The Order, Banks claimed, had safe houses everywhere in the world. But where exactly would they send Charles tomorrow night? Will still hadn't told him. Would they tell his parents? Certainly they'd let his father know; Chas was a big deal in The Order. For a chilling instant, Charles thought of

Russell, laid out on a cold slab at the morgue. Sweet Jesus, he had to go to Russell's wake tonight as Will had directed.

Charles told himself to stop thinking about Russell. What good did it do—other than scare the heck out of him. He was committed now. He would not falter. He had the staph in the test tubes, in nourishing media. Now, all he had to do was store them at room temperature till it was time to transport them to the Palace Hotel kitchen—and then inoculate the cream puffs as instructed by the pastry chef. After that, Will Banks would take over the operation. Charles, The Order's all-time MVP, would be the hero of all his glory dreams.

One final look around the lab. A light over one of the containment hoods flickered, the negative pressure system hummed in the claustrophobic sterile room.

He'd chosen tubes of media to transport the bacteria, not the clumsy bulk of petri plates. While in the incubator, he'd secured the specimens he'd secreted yesterday. Turning his back to the security cameras, he expertly transferred the inoculum from petri dishes to his transfer tubes. Sterile technique. No nervousness whatsoever. He did this every day. It was his craft.

Satisfied, he replaced the contaminated petri plates in their hiding place and simply walked out of the secure zone, tubes tucked into a pouch strapped to his waist. *Too close to his testicles?* That thought amused him. Good thing he wasn't smuggling out radioactive material. But the grin faded when he thought of Russell. Only a few days ago Russell with his background in nuclear technology had been his competition. But The Order had picked him. Satisfied? he asked himself.

Putting on his best hangdog, sick look, Charles shuffled toward the office he and Stacy Jones had shared. He answered the ringing phone. Stacy. How considerate of her to call at this moment. He was about to leave her a message. Faking hoarseness, he told her that he was not feeling well, that he would not be in tomorrow, and he hung up the phone.

For the benefit of any unseen witness, he made a show of bolting for the men's room. There he hid out in the stall for a while, and artfully mussed his hair a bit more before returning to his office. After he'd safely nestled the culture tubes in the padded section of his briefcase, Charles collected the few mementos from the lone shelf behind his desk. Coughing and fake sneezing for the security cameras, he made his way down the long hallway lined with locked office doors and out of the building.

CHAPTER THIRTY-SEVEN

On one hand, Emma Goode was honored—who wouldn't be?—the newspaper had planned an extravagant party in her name in the grand ballroom of the Palace Hotel. On the other hand, she felt a bit used. The sixty-nine-year-old black woman, born in the Deep South in 1916, picked up the cream-colored, engraved vellum invitation, still not quite believing that she was the honoree. Tomorrow night. *The Atlanta Daily Reporter*, the newspaper founded by her father, was making her their poster child. The society section of the *Atlanta Constitution*, the mainstream Atlanta newspaper, lay on the table, her photo on the front page. Medium-brown skin, nose sprinkled with freckles, hair streaked with gray and pulled back in a bun. In the photo, she stood at the door of the *Reporter*'s new building, in the trim, coral silk business suit that accentuated the slim figure, hardly changed since her wedding day forty-three years ago.

Emma and her husband, Edward, each had put in almost fifty years at the *Atlanta Daily Reporter*. As it turned out, each would retire at the same age. But for Edward, seventy had come twelve years ago. Emma could have chosen to retire with him, but she'd been only fifty-seven then, and at the peak of her journalism career. The city was a hotbed of racial tension and the *Atlanta Daily Reporter* was the voice of the Negro—about Negroes for Negroes.

For the first nine years of his retirement, Edward puttered cheerfully around their large house in an upscale, but segregated neighborhood. He'd busied himself with the grandchildren and taken up household chores. He looked after their finances, even became a gourmet cook. Then gradually he had started to slide—but she'd missed the clues. He just seemed more and more listless, and then one day, three years ago, he simply did not wake up in the morning. He'd been seventy-nine years old. She remembered both of her sisters advising her way back when, not to marry a man twelve years older—she'd just end up a widow. They were right, but she would not have missed a day with Edward. Life without him would have been no life at all.

Emma had not succumbed to depression, but Edward's loss did seem to sap her physical energy and drain her emotional reserve. Their seven children helped sustain her, along with the challenges of her job and her pride, always, in her family's newspaper.

The party tomorrow night may be in her name, but it really was the celebration of her beloved newspaper. And that was fine. She was turning seventy—after fifty years, she could retire gracefully. She couldn't really remember not working at the paper. She'd started during high school, spending summers in the Circulation Department. During college she worked evenings and summers in Accounting. Then with a journalism degree from Atlanta University, she launched into reporting, and finally, editing, the news. First her mother, and then one of her sisters, cared for her children when she went back to work after each of seven pregnancies.

The *Atlanta Daily Reporter* always was the centerpiece of dinner table conversation. Each of her kids worked part-time at the paper during their teens, and three stayed on for a career—her oldest daughter, vice president of operations; oldest son, financial vice president; another son, public relations manager. Newspaper publishing was in the Goode family blood, past and future. But enough reminiscing, Emma thought. She had to get the spare bedrooms ready. Make up the bunks for the kids and check the fridge, make a grocery shopping list and what had she forgotten?

CHAPTER THIRTY-EIGHT

Stacy headed straight for Davis Island and Tampa City Hospital from the airport. She intended to page Laura as soon as she arrived, before calling Dr. Kellerman. She hadn't been in her job long enough to know whether she should have responded to Kellerman's demand for CDC input or not. Kellerman had insisted that Tampa City had a virulent staph outbreak, and Stacy had not wanted to bother her boss on a holiday weekend to get administrative clearance. Anyway about it, seeing her friend Laura in Tampa over a holiday weekend would give her the perfect cover if she was violating some government protocol by chasing to Tampa on the whim of a community doctor.

She never had visited Laura at the sprawling Tampa City Medical complex, the main teaching hospital of the Tampa Bay area. The hospital's island setting did not fit with the public health segment of Stacy's training. Not with the city smack in the middle of hurricane territory, not with the endless list of possible bridge catastrophes that could cut off the city's main hospital from the population.

Not her problem now. Her problem was to find Laura and Kellerman, evaluate the infectious disease phenomenon here, and get back to the CDC to take care of her cultures since Charles was too ill, or so he claimed. If the culprit here was a staph, the right antibiotic cocktail should work. Stacy thought about nature and antibiotic resistance. Too much indiscriminate use of powerful antibiotics seemed to dare Mother Nature to develop yet more resistant organisms. Stacy's work was like a chess game with Mother Nature: predict her opponent's next move and have an antidote ready. Mother Nature was the ultimate winner; Stacy knew that any victory could only be fleeting.

Developing bad bugs to preempt Mother Nature's evolution was controversial, too, obviously. But, God forbid, America's enemies should launch a biological warfare attack, CDC management wanted to be ahead of the curve with antibiotic solutions to potential biological threats. A few years ago, the Fed bosses had gone paranoid about lab security, and the government terminated the CDC-NIH collaborative project. No question that her CDC research program was under close scrutiny by the army's biological researchers in Maryland at USAMRIID's top-secret facility.

She remembered that Keystone Pharma had hired a prominent scientist from the NIH several years ago. Norman Kantor. They wanted his promising drug discovery, ticokellin, for commercial drug development by the company. But recent disturbing news; Keystone Pharma had pulled the drug out of clinical studies because of side effects. Too bad. But not even ticokellin would work against the cultures in her lab.

When Stacy's cab pulled up to the front door of Tampa City Hospital, she decided to go to the information desk, introduce herself, and have Laura Nelson paged. But on the way to the circular desk in the center of the lobby, she was approached by an attractive man in fresh scrubs, looking to be in his forties.

"Dr. Jones?" he asked.

"Hello," she said, looking straight into the man's blue eyes. Reddish hair on the long side, white skin with freckles, tall, maybe six feet.

"I'm Tim Robinson, a friend of Laura's," he said. "I've heard a lot about you over the years. Laura will so glad to see you. Please, come with me."

"Tim Robinson?" Stacy couldn't restrain a grin. "'Dr. Tim.' That's what the kids call you. Laura's annual Thanksgiving guest from Philadelphia. See, I know about you, too."

"Thing are bad here," Tim said right off.

"Natalie?" Stacy asked, keeping up as Tim headed toward the bank of elevators.

"Natalie's admitted, but—"

Stacy interrupted Tim, "That infectious disease guy, Dr. Kellerman, pretty much demanded I come down here. What's going on?"

Tim held the elevator door, they stepped inside, and he pushed the third floor button. "We'll meet Laura in Natalie's room. She's seventeen, so they put her on the pediatric floor."

"Seventeen. Hard to believe. Did Laura tell you that I babysat for them once when they were toddlers?" Stacy felt an icy prickle run the length of her spine. That night had ended in disaster. She had ended up in the hospital with a concussion and a dislocated shoulder.

Tim seemed to scrutinize her. "Our Laura did not share that memory with me," he said.

Stacy had always speculated about Laura's relationship with Tim. Now as she followed him off the elevator, she imagined them as a couple. Steve had been dead for seven years, and didn't Laura deserve to have someone in her life? *And a man in my life would be nice, too.*

"Stacy, I'm so glad you're here." Laura stood at the door to Natalie's room, gowned, her hair pushed up into a paper cap. Stacy wanted to hug Laura. But, Stacy recognized the isolation setup.

She grabbed a gown from the shelf. "Where's Natalie?" She threw on the gown over her pantsuit.

"Down for an x-ray," Laura said. "I was going to Radiology to be with her, but now that you're here—"

"I'll find Natalie and stay with her," Tim said. "You take care of business here."

"Laura, tell me everything." Stacy was now gloved, wearing booties and a cap as well as the gown.

They went into Natalie's private room, Stacy noting the inappropriate décor for a seventeen-year-old: clowns and cartoon characters.

"Thanks so much for coming." Laura led Stacy to two vinyl-covered chairs in the corner of the room. "I've never faced anything like this. Patients in the ICU dying of a virulent infectious disease, a staphylococcus, resistant to all antibiotics, including methicillin, oxacillin, and vancomycin."

"That's what Dr. Kellerman told me," Stacy said. "But what about Natalie? Tell me what's happening with your daughter, and then we'll focus on the ICU." No way to make a connection, but Stacy could appreciate the tug of war between Laura's dedication to her daughter and to her patients.

"It turns out, Natalie has a boyfriend in the ICU. Yesterday morning she faked abdominal pain so I'd let her stay home. I knew as soon as Tim got into Tampa, he would check on her. But before he got to my house, she'd left to go to see the boy in the ICU."

Stacy drew a deep breath as Laura continued, "Now he's one of the sick ones. Natalie came in close contact. His name is Trey."

So the two are epidemiologically related. Not good at all.

Laura's eyes brimmed with tears. "And now she's febrile with a high white count. Stacy, patients are dying up there. What if Natalie—"

"Slow down, Laura." Stacy needed Laura focused and logical. "You said that Natalie was inside the ICU. What was the nature of her contact with the patient?"

"I just don't know. She met the boy's father, she told me that, but Trey was her boyfriend. She said she kissed him. She went there before there was any evidence of an epidemic."

Stacy gritted her teeth at the public health implications of the word "epidemic."

"I'll need details," Stacy said, shifting full gear into infectious disease control mode. "When exactly did each patient begin exhibiting signs of infection? Every symptom—nurses' notes are usually the most reliable." Stacy stood up now. "I'll need all this data charted by fifteen minute intervals. I need every health care worker who was in that room identified, and probably quarantined. Same with every visitor—to the best of our ability. We need triple infectious disease precautions. But I'm getting ahead of myself. Let's go to the ICU now."

"I should be here when Natalie gets back." Laura remained in her chair, twisting one plastic-gloved hand with another.

"Laura, we do need to get on top of this infection. Your daughter's life may hang in the balance if the staph in your ICU proves truly antibiotic resistant."

Stacy watched the color drain from Laura's face. Then she nodded and got up. Both women took off their protective layers, and Laura led Stacy to the elevator that would take them to the ICU.

An older white man in green scrubs and a long white coat met them at the elevator on the seventh floor.

"The pediatric floor called to say that you were on your way up, Laura." The man eyed Stacy. "I was on my way home to get some sleep, but they said the doctor was here from the CDC."

Stacy read the name tag sewn on his coat. Duncan Kellerman, M.D. She didn't wait for introductions by Laura. "Dr. Kellerman, I'm Dr. Jones from the CDC. Dr. Nelson has given me a preliminary briefing, but I need every detail of what's happened in this unit."

Stacy had seen it before and she'd see it again. The look: a black woman, telling me what to do?

"You're Dr. Jones?"

"Stacy is a microbiologist at the CDC, the world's foremost expert in antibiotic resistant staph," Laura said. "She's given us a list of precautions we must put in place if we're going to stop this epidemic."

World's expert? Laura was exaggerating. One of them, maybe. There were others, her boss, Stan Proctor. The boys at USAMRIID. Norman Kantor formerly of the NIH, recently retired from Keystone Pharma, and his former associate, Victor Worth, relegated to fungus research after the staph program at the NIH had been terminated. One of the first things on her to-do list was to see if she could recruit Norman Kantor out of retirement as a consultant.

"Laura, Dr. Jones, I'm exhausted. I'm going home for a couple of hours. I can't function without some sleep. I'm a lot older than either of you."

"Dr. Kellerman, we're on a tight schedule. So let's proceed, before you go anywhere."

"No, way, young lady," Kellerman said, his tone resentful. "I may have called you, but not to take over. I'm in charge here, and I'll—"

She had to shove this organization into gear before it self-destructed. She faced him down, "How many patients did you tell me have fallen ill to this infection, Dr. Kellerman? And how fast are they deteriorating? And, yes, you called me. I'm here and I know what I'm doing."

Stacy didn't know exactly what she was doing, but who did in an emerging situation like this? Little comfort, but she was as well equipped to deal with this as anybody she could think of, other than her boss, of course, and she'd have to get him on the case immediately.

"So young and..." Kellerman hesitated. "How can you have any experience?"

And so nonwhite is what Kellerman did not quite say. "I have expertise, Dr. Kellerman, so unless the hospital trustees ask me to stand down—" Stacy was winging it now. *Hospital trustees?*

"Duncan, I have a personal interest in this," Laura said. "I just found out that my daughter was in the ICU yesterday when all this was starting. Now she's febrile with a high white count."

"My God, Laura, how could that have happened?"

Stacy thought she detected genuine sympathy in Kellerman's tone.

"She was visiting her boyfriend, the Standish boy."

"Oh my, he's one of the sickest," Kellerman said. "I just spoke to his parents, tried to prepare them for worst."

"Let's get started," Stacy said. "I want to see the patients; I want you and the ICU head nurse to take me through every detail of every patient's course. Then, I'll get to the labs to see the cultures and the sensitivity results; meet with your infectious disease nurse and the director of nursing to go over infectious disease protocols. I'll call my boss, maybe conference in experts at the CDC."

"Duncan, can you show Stacy the patients?" Laura asked. "I'm going to admin to get the board of directors involved. They'll need to hear Stacy's recommendations and get this hospital locked down. And then I'm going to see Natalie. I'd appreciate it, Duncan, if you could check on her after you're finished with Stacy."

"Laura, let's get your computer staff here, too," Stacy said. "I'll need them to input data to the CDC system."

Stacy, already back in sterile garb, waited as Kellerman pulled booties over his shoes.

"I'll gladly see your daughter," Kellerman said. "Will you ask one of the nurses to call and tell my wife not to expect me home?"

If the CDC imposes a quarantine, none of us will be expected home.

CHAPTER THIRTY-NINE

In the safety of his BMW sedan, Charles looked at the test tubes he had protected in strips of bubble wrap and placed in a Styrofoam six-pack case with a flip-up handle. He debated transporting them in the spacious trunk, but with no means to secure them there, he decided to stow them on the floor of the passenger seat. God protect him from a crash. If anything disrupted the tubes and exposed their contents, he'd be dead. And so would anybody else who came in contact with his microorganisms.

Charles rarely bothered to park in his garage—temperate Atlanta weather wasn't rough on the car. He'd pull up to the semicircular portico leading to the front door and park there, the lord of the manor. But today, he fumbled for the remote, opened the garage door, and waited for the door to close behind him before he got out of the car. He couldn't risk a neighbor or anyone else observing him with the package. Silly. What were the odds of someone thinking, *Charles has toxic staphylococci in that little cooler.* Nevertheless, he proceeded stealthily.

No one would be here, in his own home, to challenge him. He hesitated, clutching the small, insulated box, before opening the door leading from the garage to his kitchen. What if the CDC had cameras in places that he did not know? He answered his own question: they'd have swarmed him already.

Will Banks sat at the kitchen table, a rifle leaning against his knee, a plate of sugar cookies and a glass of milk in front of him. Will had always kept his own food in the basement, and he stayed

.

out of the rooms on the first floor and the upstairs rooms, for that matter.

"Chuckie?" Banks set down the glass of milk to lay his hand on the butt of the rifle. "Mission accomplished?"

Charles glanced about for a safe place to set down the case, where it would be undisturbed.

"That's the shit? You got enough bad bacteria in that little box to kill off a roomful of degenerates? Here, let me see what you got?" He started to get up.

Charles stepped back, extending one arm in a back-off gesture.

"Don't even think about it. I told you how lethal these cultures are. Just the tiniest leak here, the most infinitesimal inoculum could—would—kill you and me. So, sit back down. Please."

"Yeah? You sure this stuff works?" Banks dropped back into the chair, his hand returning to the rifle.

"I told you. I'm an expert in this particular infectious organism. This staph doesn't need an open cut. It'll attack intact skin and mucous membranes. So anybody it touches will become ill and most likely die. But first, they will infect others. It'll be a chain reaction." *Where could he safely store the cultures until tomorrow night?* While he wanted the cultures as far from his person as possible, he had to have them close to feel certain that nobody else could mess with them.

"The Order only cares about the guests tomorrow night. You told me that anybody who eats the special dessert cream puff thing will catch the disease. Right? And you said that they'd have boils on their skin. Just like the plague in the Bible—where all the Egyptians get boils before Moses gets the Israelites to the Promised Land."

Charles didn't know if Banks had his Bible right or not, but yes, the victims would have skin lesions. "Here's what will happen. The staph will penetrate into the mucous membranes of the mouth, no problem there. It will spread rapidly through the blood to the rest of the body. Yes, the skin will be affected by a condition described as 'flesh-eating' or 'toxic epidermal necrolysis.'"

"Flesh-eating. Yeah, that's what I promised The Order. They loved flesh-eating. That's the thing that pushed them to a yes vote."

Charles had never seen a case of toxic epidermal necrolysis, a dire condition more likely associated with streptococcal rather than staphylococcal bacteria. But he had seen pictures in full color. Not only skin, but fascia and adipose tissue and muscle dissolving down to the bone, you'd have nothing left but a semi-liquid slimy residue of lysed cells. And all that as organ after organ shuts down: lungs, kidneys, the liver, the heart, the inner part of the brain that controls respiration and circulation. Life itself.

What am I about to unleash?

Charles had earned a medical degree along with his Ph.D. in microbiology, but his focus always had been research. He had no interest in clinical medicine and had elected not to complete the year of internship training required by the state to practice medicine in Georgia. Maybe he should have. Maybe he'd have a better appreciation of what he was about to do. And maybe he, not Stacy Jones, with her M.D., M.P.H., and her fellowship certifying her as an infectious disease specialist, would be director of the Experimental Staph Section. And maybe he wouldn't have been compelled to pitch his idea to The Order.

But pitch he had. The Order endorsed his mission. He was on.

"Here's how it's going down, Chuckie." Banks took a gulp of milk then pulled his wallet out of his pocket. He removed a plastic card and handed it to Charles. "Logistics. Take this ID, go to the Palace Hotel, ask for the assistant manager. She'll be expecting you. Tell her you're the pastry chef dude, to see the head pastry chef. Name's Lonnie Collins."

Charles stared at Will's hand with the plastic card. He was in no rush for it. Louisiana driver's license in the name of Bernard Boyle. Photo looked a lot like him. Same dirty-blond hair. Brown eyes in a pudgy face, no smile. Charles wanted Banks to eat the photo of the unattractive Bernard, cheap tan polo shirt and all.

"What do I know about cooking or baking?" Charles protested. He pinched the corner of the license like a dirty tissue between

thumb and index finger. "No way I can pose as a chef of anything."
Could this be his way out? Truly, there was no way he could pass as
a chef. Maybe it wasn't too late. No one ever would have reason to
know he'd taken the staph. He could kill the cultures with nothing
but boiling water.

"No worries, Chuckie. Lonnie already told the management he
needs help—big event tomorrow night. He has your "résumé."
He'll interview you personally. Now," Banks picked up his rifle and
the plate of cookies, "all you gotta do is just protect those little
bugs. You'll work out the final details with Lonnie." He was gone to
his basement lair.

Charles gingerly carried the Styrofoam cooler upstairs to his
room, wedged it behind his shoe rack, and left immediately for the
Palace Hotel. Just follow the plan. Was this what the military was
like? Blind obedience, no thought to ethics or morality or conse-
quences.

When Charles arrived at the Palace, he followed Will's instructions,
unsure whether he was pleased or distraught that the plan proceeded
just as Banks had laid out.

The attractive assistant manager was overjoyed that he'd shown
up. She hadn't even asked for his ID, the Louisiana driver's license
for a Bernard Boyle. "Lonnie Collins has been driving me crazy,"
she said. "His main assistant didn't come in yesterday, and we have
a huge event tomorrow. In case you haven't heard, our profiterole is
our signature dessert. People come from all over the world to eat
those fluffy creations. I must admit a weakness for them myself."

Don't snatch one tomorrow night, lady.

The engaging young woman reached for the phone, dialed the
kitchen, and having delivered her message, chitchatted with Charles about Thanksgiving.

A large-boned, crew cut blond man interrupted. "Mr. Boyle," the
man said, not waiting for an introduction, "follow me to my office."

Nothing more until Charles was seated across the desk from his
potential boss. "Okay, no bullshit," the man who must be Lonnie
Collins said. "I know why you're here. You're ready to poison to-

morrow night's guests. Mostly black people. Some whites. Too bad, but they shouldn't be mixing socially. I'm told that you'll inject a super bacteria into my famous profiteroles. Man, I really hate that idea. People come to dine here because of my profiteroles. But what choice do I have. They got my daughter."

"What?" Charles asked. "What does your daughter have to do with this?"

"You're dealing with The Order, man. I don't know how you got into it, but I got initiated when my daughter was in high school and whoosh, the schools got integrated. Listen, I got nothing personal against black people or brown or yellow. I just don't want any of 'em pollutin' white kids' schools. No reason they should. Let them have their own schools."

"Your daughter?" Charles asked again.

"Yeah, I joined The Order for her. To try to protect her. Now she's eighteen, going off to college next year. Emory. Full scholarship. She's a competitive swimmer."

"Great school," Charles said. "My alma mater."

"Like I said, The Order does not screw around. I stopped going to their events a couple of years ago. Too damn radical for my taste."

Charles noted how Lonnie kept glancing at the door, which he'd taken care to lock. His right foot tapped a nervous pattern on the tile floor.

Radical? Yes, killing off a few hundred people with a super-potent bacteria qualifies as radical. "I hear you," Charles said.

"But The Order still has me in their database. I get a visit from one of 'em—day before Thanksgiving. I'm home with my wife. Son of a bitch tells me what they got in mind. I said, okay, I'll think about it. 'By the way,' he said, 'we have Diana.' My daughter! 'The choice is yours,' he said."

"You're saying they kidnapped your daughter?"

"Yes. The guy showed me one of those Polaroid shots, still damp. Just a few minutes after I'd heard the doorbell, and Diana said not to bother, she'll get it. She was still in her bathrobe. A neighbor, I figured, or one of her friends. Someone's always coming by. My wife was cooking. I'm still reading the paper, finishing my coffee. The doorbell rang again and now I go to open it. This man from The Order pushes right past me. I showed him into my study; my wife is not a fan of The Order. That's when he laid it out. First, the picture of my daughter—in her bathrobe, no shoes, a gag stuck in her mouth, pinned by a large man against a white van parked in the driveway. She looked so scared, man. I'm out of my mind. Whatever The Order asks, I'm ready. No ifs, ands, or buts. Just do it. Well, Mr. Boyle, it's all yours. So let's talk business, man."

As simple as that. An abduction of a child. Charles thought of Russell, lying in a casket, mourned by a wife and kids. He glanced down at his attire, a dark suit, conservative tie, starched white shirt. After this "interview" he'd be expressing his condolences to Russell's wife. He hoped the kids wouldn't be there.

"I see," Charles said. And he did. Lonnie Collins had no choice. The Order wouldn't think twice about Diana Collins's life.

"You're a single man?" Lonnie asked.

"I am," Charles said. Did being single make him more expendable?

"The guy from The Order said that you might come under suspicion. If so, you would have to get away from Atlanta. You good with that?"

Charles had given this a lot of thought. Factor into his decision what had happened to Russell, factor in the safe houses that Banks had promised. Would he turn his back on a mansion and destroy his career. Considering his miserable personal life, his unacceptable new boss, and his parents' pride when they'd find out about his service to The Order, Charles knew what he had to do.

"I'll handle it," Charles said.

Both men would toe the line. Do The Order's work, like two good soldiers.

"Let's do a tour of the kitchen," Lonnie Collins said. "You'll need the lay of the land."

"I can't cook or bake." As soon as he said the words, Charles realized how foolish he sounded.

CHAPTER FORTY

Emma Goode heard herself say, "I need my beauty rest." She never napped, but today the notion had its appeal. The day after Thanksgiving, the day before her party extravaganza.

Her eldest granddaughter had helped her choose the jewelry she'd wear with her Gianni Versace gown tomorrow night. "Okay, Grandma, but don't forget I'm taking you to see *The Nutcracker* at the Fox Theatre tonight. I still remember you took me to see it the first time when I was six. I wanted to be a ballerina. Too bad that didn't work out."

"That would have been delightful, Karen, but going to medical school at Emory isn't a bad second."

"Seriously, you know I really want to be a doctor."

"I am proud of you, child. I had always hoped one of my children would go to medical school, especially your mother, but no, they either went into the family business or became lawyers." Emma rolled her eyes as she always did when the subject was lawyers. She'd had her share of them. The good and the bad.

"You get some rest, Grandma. I promised Mom I'd go with her to get some last-minute accessories for my sisters. Dressing five girls for a big party has its challenges. Too many prima donnas, Dad always says."

"And expensive." Emma couldn't forget the money it cost to keep her seven kids in clothes. Two girls, followed by two boys, then two more girls, and one last boy. And now, she had fifteen grandchildren. All here in Atlanta to celebrate her seventieth birth-day, and her retirement after almost fifty years at *The Atlanta Daily Reporter* tomorrow. No wonder she could do with a nap.

As she sat on the side of the bed and shed her shoes, she glanced at her portrait wall. Fourteen of her grandchildren, each one photographed at the age of four. Such a cute age, just before they start losing their front teeth. Old enough to cooperate. Young enough so their innocence still shines through. The tradition had begun with Karen, who's now twenty-one; number fourteen is that bundle-of-energy, Wyatt—about to be five next month. Not yet represented on the wall was Emeril, who'd just recently turned the magic four but still resembled a "terrible two."

I am so blessed, Emma thought, her eyes closing for just ten min-utes.

CHAPTER FORTY-ONE

When Victor arrived the next morning at George Washington University Hospital, he'd been almost giddy with relief to find Matthew sitting up, eating from a tray of regular hospital food. Color had returned to Matthew's face, and he had either shaved himself or someone had done it for him. The purplish blotches on his face even seemed to have faded during the night. Matthew still was connected to an intravenous line, but he no longer was on oxygen. He smiled at his dad.

For the second night in a row, Victor had not slept. After destroying the last culture in his collection and assuring himself that his basement was sterile, he'd contemplated sleep. But he needed to see his son. So he showered, changed into clean clothes, and drove to the hospital. And now, rewarded with Matthew's smile, he was glad he'd come. Matthew needed him and Victor would not fail him.

But his elation soon gave way to the realization that he and his son still needed to talk more about the HIV virus and AIDS—Matthew's illness. How there was no cure, no treatment. Matthew surely would rather hear it from his father, a Ph.D. microbiologist, instead of from a stranger. But, Matthew still would hear the truth as a death sentence. How could Victor sugarcoat that?

Victor settled into the bedside chair and encouraged Matthew to talk about growing up in Florida, how he loved the indigenous plants: palms, the ferns, the lilies, even the scrub palmettos. Victor hadn't summoned the nerve to bring up the AIDS subject; Matthew had not asked.

Mid-morning, while a nurse took Matthew's vital signs, Victor nodded off.

Matthew said, "Father, go home. You look like you're about to collapse. Matter of fact, you look worse than me. Please go home, sleep. You've done so much for me. It hurts me to see you so tired."

Father.

Matthew was right. Victor was too exhausted even to think. He did need a few hours of sleep. He and Matthew had so much to talk about, but they could wait until he had more emotional and physical stamina. Maybe later in the day.

Victor gently kissed Matthew's forehead. No more fever, no more clamminess. His son had rallied, valiantly fighting the virus that ultimately would claim his life. *But before then, I promise you the best life, the most comfort I can give you.*

On the way out of the unit, Victor stopped at the nursing station to make sure that they had his contact information. He was surprised to see Matthew's primary doctor working on charts.

The lanky, deeply tanned physician looked up and smiled. "Dr. Worth, I was hoping to have a word with you. Your son is doing extremely well."

"That's great."

"So well, that I hoped you'd consider home care. He'll have to be on IV antibiotics for another two weeks, but his lungs have cleared up. As you see, he's no longer on oxygen. And—"

"Yes, yes. I can manage the intravenous." Victor assumed that Matthew would agree to live with him in Bethesda, but they'd not discussed it.

"Just don't try to do it yourself. You know what they say about treating relatives," the doctor said. "If you could get a daily nursing service to come in, I'd consider discharging him on Monday. Other than that, Mr. Mercer has no restrictions. His staph infection responded beautifully to the methicillin, I must say. And Bactrim handled the pneumocystis. I wish all my patients showed such a good response. That Dr. Nelson in Tampa did an admirable job. If she hadn't done that biopsy and nailed the diagnosis, your son might not be alive today. But you do know that Mr. Mercer will need ongoing care for—"

"AIDS. Yes, I know," said Victor. "I'll make sure he gets the best."

Victor should have stopped at that, but he could not keep himself from asking, "About the staph infection. So it wasn't antibiotic resistant at all?"

"No, just the run-of-the-mill staph. You can see how well he responded to the antibiotic cocktail. If only we had a cure for the HIV virus—"

All I wanted was revenge on Norman. But then to cover up, I infected a roomful of patients. And Matthew had never even needed ticokellin in the first place! Can anyone in Tampa connect me to those ICU patients? No— because I've destroyed the cultures. My entire life's work, trashed. But to protect my son. I had to protect my son.

"But, Dr. Worth, sir," the younger doctor said, "you have to take care of yourself, too. You look exhausted."

"I'll be back to see my son later today," he said.

Will I have time to take my discarded glassware to the landfill? To get the microbiology equipment out of my basement? Too drained to answer his own questions, Victor left the hospital.

CHAPTER FORTY-TWO

The patients in these beds were Laura's responsibility. How could this have happened? In a daze, a trance almost, Laura stood and looked at bed after bed. "Yersinia pestis" stuck in her mind. The plague organism—the Black Death—killed almost half of Europe's population in the Middle Ages, or was it the Renaissance? She wasn't sure. A pandemic. Is that what she was facing now? Rapid onset. Highly lethal. Swiftly spreading. Carried by rats? Fleas? But there were no rats and no fleas in her ICU. Forget yersinia; the lab's early culture results showed a staphylococcus. A staph highly resistant to all antibiotics.

On the way to the seventh floor, Laura and Stacy had agreed that Stacy would impress upon her boss the seriousness of the situation and then start intensive isolation procedures, relying on public health protocols. Stacy was at the nursing station now, calling the CDC. Laura would take charge of patient care. Why, she wondered, was the ICU so eerily quiet. Seven beds—one empty as her beloved patient Bart Kelly was dead. Six patients, but only one nurse and no doctors? And only one clerk at the desk? How could that be? More like four nurses and as many aides would be minimum in addition to the usual complement of residents and medical students. A holiday weekend, yes, but the hospital must have adequate on-call coverage. This was unacceptable.

Laura headed for the lone clerk, a dark-skinned woman whom Laura did not know. Unusual. She must have been called in from another floor. At least she was protected: cap, mask, gloves, full-length gown. Laura noticed an apple sitting alongside a stack of lab reports. "Don't eat that," she said, "and, where is everybody?"

"Don't know," the clerk drawled, "I've never worked the ICU before."

Laura asked, "Has anybody called for more nurses and paged the on-call medical and surgical residents?"

"I tried the nursing office, Dr. Nelson," the woman said. "They said they would send more help, but—"

"But?" Laura prompted.

"Everybody's scared. The word's out that there's a bad disease in here and that it's spreading fast. I'm worried, too."

"We can't leave our patients," Laura said. "Just make certain that you and everybody else follows strict isolation procedures. And don't forget to get rid of that apple. Nothing should go near your mouth."

The clerk looked stricken, her pupils dilating.

"Soon, a stricter isolation process will be set up for anyone entering or leaving the ICU." At least, Laura hoped that Stacy had the clout to get a state-of-the-art isolation program up and going.

The clerk wrinkled her brow, skepticism in her eyes.

"Thank you for staying," Laura said. "Now, will you track down the director of nursing, the head of medical education, and the chief of staff. Wherever they are, find them. I need to speak with them directly. Meantime, I'm going to check out the patients."

"Yes, doctor," the clerk said, sounding far from optimistic. "I'll do my best."

Laura walked by Bed 1: empty, stripped to the mattress. Bart Kelly, one of her favorite patients, so vulnerable, so trusting, now dead. She still had to speak to his wife. *Not now. You have to compartmentalize. Focus on the six patients in this room.* But she had little success compartmentalizing Natalie. And someone else stuck in the back of her mind—the ICU patient with AIDS, Matthew Mercer. Amazing that he'd rallied sufficiently to be transported up north. How? Not ticokellin. Dr. Worth, Matthew's father, had tried to commandeer ticokellin from Keystone Pharma. The drug company had refused him. A side effect, she couldn't remember what side effect, had made them stop clinical trials. But suppose they were briefed on the situation at Tampa City Hospital, would they reconsider? Ask Stacy—anything about staphylococcal research was her expertise. Good bet this Dr. Worth from the NIH was in Stacy's Rolodex; probably the Keystone Pharma research doctors, too. Stacy worked for the federal government, could she convince the FDA to intervene? Would ticokellin cure the six patients? And, if Natalie—

As soon as she checked on the six ICU patients, she'd ask Stacy to call Keystone Pharma. In the meantime, where are the surgical residents? Why hadn't Michelle called them in to cover this extraordinary emergency?

Laura approached Bed 2. Hooked up to a ventilator, the nurse who'd had a hysterectomy looked moribund. Gray skin tone. Bloated, comatose. Toxic shock syndrome.

The solitary nurse working in the ICU was busy suctioning the patient in the farthest bed across the unit, and Laura had not wanted to distract her. The middle-aged, overweight R.N. tried for a gruff persona, but Laura knew she was as compassionate as they came. The nurse was working on Trey Standish. She would keep her promise to Natalie. She rerouted her path toward Bed 7.

"Dr. Nelson!"

Laura couldn't ignore the urgent tone in the clerk's voice.

"The E.R. needs you. STAT."

Before turning to face the clerk, Laura paused to observe the boy. Gray color, maximum ventilator setting, going into shock. Natalie was in love with this boy? Had actually visited him here in the ICU. For a moment, nothing else penetrated. Had Natalie been exposed to whatever this was?

"Dr. Nelson, Roxanne Ruiz needs you. I was trying to reach her like you wanted, but she called here. She said to come to the E.R. It's urgent."

Following procedure, Laura removed her protective clothing,

then stepped outside the ICU, into the hallway. She found Stacy in a heated discussion with Duncan Kellerman. At least the infectious disease specialist hadn't abandoned them.

"On my way to the E.R. STAT call," Laura explained, "but, Stacy, I have to talk to you about getting ticokellin."

"Already contacted Keystone Pharma," Stacy said, "and the FDA. Will know more in an hour or so."

Laura should have realized that Stacy would think of ticokellin. They'd discussed it just a couple of days ago, in relation to Matthew Mercer.

Taking the elevator down to the lobby, Laura headed for the E.R. Along with the surgical ICU, the E.R. came under her direct supervision. She needed to talk to Roxanne about getting more nurses in the ICU, but instead of returning Laura's call, Roxanne had summoned her to the E.R. STAT. Why?

Roxanne met her just inside the doctors' entrance, "Laura," she said, "we have two patients down here presenting with a fast onset, rapidly accelerating febrile illness. They're both delirious, with tachycardia and dyspnea. We need to admit them. I'm opening up an infectious disease ICU."

Laura nodded. Did Natalie belong there, too? She needed to check on her daughter. "Agreed. Good idea," she said, assuming that Roxanne wanted only her approval.

"Both of these patients are on staff here," Roxanne continued. "Both assigned to the surgical ICU."

"My God," Laura said. "This is an epidemic."

"One is on our housekeeping staff. She was on duty yesterday, assigned to the ICU. The other is your chief resident, Michelle Wallace. She collapsed just inside the ladies' room door in the residents' on-call room."

"Oh Roxanne, what's happening? Michelle? I had been wondering why she hadn't called in more residents. Poor Michelle." Laura turned toward Roxanne. "And what can we do about getting more nurses and support staff? I have a roomful of critical patients but I have only one nurse. Roxanne, we have to get help there. If you add an extra ICU, we'll need even more extra staff. Can you do that?"

"My office is calling in every staff nurse and every temp. But I'm getting one excuse after another. The grapevine here is on fire. Avoidance is the operative principle. Maybe Stacy could give us some key points we can use to convince staff we're using the proper procedures to contain this bacteria. We need her to get the CDC down here ASAP. Send us as many infectious disease specialists as they can. I don't have to tell you that Kellerman is in way over his head."

"Stacy mentioned that maybe we'd need a lockdown: Nobody comes in. Nobody leaves. We'll need to have adequate staff in here before we lock down. Roxie, we have to care for these patients. Let's close the E.R. to all but suspected cases of this rampant infection."

"I'll start on that right away," Roxanne said.

"I need to convince Medical to call in all the medical interns and residents. And meantime," Laura went on, "we have to redirect all noninfected patients and all obstetrics to other hospitals. I'm going to cancel all surgical cases across the board. Even before the CDC makes a recommendation."

"Do you want to see Michelle now?" Roxanne asked. "And the cleaning lady?"

"Yes."

As she made her way through the emergency room, Laura sensed the underlying current of dread. Word spreads fast in a hospital. By now the on-duty staff would be talking among themselves about the virulent, resistant bacteria in the ICU patients. And they'd be scared. Naturally enough.

"Not good." Dan Marsh, the E.R. charge nurse, a stocky man with a military-style crew cut, met them as they approached an examining room roped off from the others. Michelle and an older lady, presumably on the housekeeping staff, lay on gurneys on opposite sides of the small room, both hooked up to monitors, both with intravenous lines.

"We've kept them isolated from the other patients," Dan explained. "Both have high temps, dyspnea, mottled rash, painful limbs."

Michelle had looked exhausted but still energetic on Wednesday's rounds, just forty-eight hours ago. Now she was strapped on the gurney, making writhing motions, her eyes closed, moaning something unintelligible. Michelle's blonde hair was lusterless, her skin marred by splotches of pale red and grayish tones.

Dan handed Laura the chart. Twenty-eight years old. Vital signs: temp 104, pulse 126, BP 90/70. Mental status: confused, thrashing in apparent pain.

"Is she getting antibiotics?" Laura bent to inspect the labels attached to the bag of intravenous fluids.

"From the minute we got blood cultures," Dan reassured her. "The internal medicine resident ordered them. Broad spectrum including methicillin and vancomycin," he added without being prompted. "Same with Mrs. Miller, here."

He then led her across the small room, a cubicle, really.

"Mrs. Miller is a longtime employee. She cleaned the E.R. back in the day. Age sixty, former smoker; now presenting with a high fever and escalating respiratory distress. She's restless, on the verge of combative. We drew blood cultures, got the usual labs. Blood gases ordered. Portable lung x-ray shows dense bilateral infiltrates."

"Was she working in the ICU Thursday?" Laura asked. Everything had seemed fine on Wednesday; somehow the unit must have got contaminated on Thanksgiving Day.

"Yes. She put in a full day. Had the rest of the long weekend off. Started to get sick during the night. She lives alone—a neighbor stopped by—"

As for Michelle, she'd worked in that ICU all day long yesterday, doing postsurgical checks. And Natalie, Laura realized, had been inside that ICU, at least for a short period of time.

Laura looked from one patient to the other. The older woman's breathing was ragged, but then age and a smoking history would make her lungs more susceptible. Yet Michelle looked more anxious, her mental status worse that Mrs. Miller's.

"Get me out of here," the woman grunted, her eyes unfocused, her free arm flailing. "I know you. You're Dr. Nelson. I gotta tell you somethin'. Get me out of here. I'm burnin' up."

"Now, Bunnie, calm down," Dan urged.

Laura recognized the name "Bunnie." She'd heard it bantered around the ICU, but she'd never bothered to make the acquaintance of this particular member of the housekeeping staff. For shame.

"Bunnie," she said, careful not to come in physical contact with the woman until she was wearing protective gear, "what is it you wanted to tell me?" Was Bunny suffering from delirium or was she mentally competent?

Bunnie's attention seemed to drift. Laura didn't have much time, but the woman seemed to want to communicate something.

"Bunnie? What is it?" Laura leaned as close as she could while preventing contact.

"Saw a man." Bunnie's words were garbled, but that's what it sounded like. "Doin' sumthin' to the patients." The later part came out more clearly.

"Yes," Laura prompted. "Doing what, Bunnie?"

"Don't know. Just leanin' over. Like he was feedin' them or sumthin'."

"Who was this man?" Laura asked. *What was this all about?*

"Don' know. A doctor, maybe."

"Lots of doctors in the ICU, do you know him?"

"Musta been new."

From across the room, Laura and Dan heard a loud moan. They rushed to Michelle's side. She had managed to slip out of a restraint and yank out her IV, upending the pole. Her plastic bag of IV fluid had hit the tile floor and blood was dripping onto it.

"We're setting up an alternative ICU," Laura said. "Let's transport these two up there now. Admit to Dr. Kellerman's service. I'll call him, get the orders. Then would you help Roxanne Ruiz to get this E.R. locked down to all but patients like these." She looked from Bunnie to Michelle. How many more would there be?

As Dan called for help to restrain Michelle, Laura left for the pediatric floor, making one stop at the ICU for a quick update. She needed to see Natalie. To make sure her daughter's condition had not worsened. What could she do to help her daughter, to help her resident? She was powerless against this lethal microbe. With all her surgical skills, she had no weapon to bring to bear on a microscopic organism that was proving resistant to all the sophisticated chemicals specifically designed to destroy it.

Then it hit her: where was her colleague, Ed Plant?

CHAPTER FORTY-THREE

Stacy had not been directly involved, but she'd read the reports about the outbreak of necrotizing fasciitis in a Lubbock, Texas, dialysis center a year ago. Caused by group A streptococcus, the disease ravaged chronic kidney patients. Invasive pneumonia struck rapidly and spread just as fast; victims suffered gangrenous flesh and muscle destruction, septic shock, and organ failure. Yet until nine patients had died a horrible death, the center failed to contact the CDC. The lesson: when in doubt, do not equivocate; call in the cavalry. And that's what Stacy had just done. She'd called her boss, who'd called his boss, who'd notified the director. Until fifteen minutes ago, Stacy had never spoken to the director of the CDC. Now she'd disrupted the woman's holiday weekend. Had she overreacted?

The Tampa City Hospital cases reminded Stacy in some ways of the catastrophe last year. High fever, myositis causing extreme pain in the extremities, and a necrotizing pneumonia. But Tampa ICU patients were spared the flesh-eating necrotizing fasciitis that had struck in the Lubbock center. The Texas epidemic was caused by a strep organism and Tampa's by a staph. Both were lethal—but neither as lethal as the staph that were incubating in the restricted section of her lab at the CDC. If her staph ever got out in a hospital like this, infected patients would already be dead, along with staff and anybody who'd come in contact with the patients, including visitors.

Visitors. Natalie. She needed to check on Laura's daughter the minute she'd finalized arrangements for the CDC's rapid-response Emergency Operation Implementation Program—EOIP. Stacy had been on the ICU clerk's phone with the CDC for almost an hour. Ever since Laura was called to the E.R.

Once the CDC program was in place, Tampa would receive all manner of federal support. Stacy would be gratified, but after the EOIP team arrived, she knew her role would be zip. She'd simply be a researcher who happened to stumble into this bio disaster.

Research. The cultures in her Atlanta lab. Stacy needed to get back there tomorrow. She should leave tonight, but if she could get in touch with Charles, maybe she could convince him to go to the lab and do the culture transfers. Certainly he wasn't too ill to cover her in an emergency scenario like this? Stacy wanted to stay to support Laura—and honestly, to observe the EOIP team in action.

On Stacy's advice, a communication center had been set up on the seventh floor at the opposite end of the building from the ICU. All patients other than those in the ICU had been moved from the seventh floor to a quarantined area in another wing of the hospital. As soon as Laura returned to the ICU, Stacy would suggest they check on Natalie.

She'd just hung up with the logistics director of the EOIP team when she spotted Laura rushing toward her.

"Stacy, I have bad news." Laura tried to catch her breath. "Maybe you know? We have two staff members presumably infected. One is my chief resident. What if—"

No, Stacy had not heard. This faulty communication would come to an end when the EOIP team arrived.

Laura's beeper went off and she dialed from the clerk's phone. Stacy watched her friend's face go pale.

"Thank you." She hung up. "Another patient, Norman Kantor, died in the ICU. Fulminating infection. Total organ shutdown. He was in here because of a pulmonary embolus following hip surgery."

"Norman Kantor? Was he a microbiologist?" Stacy repeated. Laura confirmed he had been. "How weird is that. I know him. I thought about calling him as a consultant. He was an NIH microbiologist who left and went to Keystone Pharma. Ironic, he's a world-class expert in staph, the developer of ticokellin."

"The wheels are in motion to get some down here. Not easy, cutting through the bureaucracy with a side effect like aplastic anemia. I think it'll happen, but probably not tonight. Tomorrow's more likely."

"Stacy, we need that drug. I know there have been cases of aplastic anemia, but what the patients need here, right now, is an antibiotic that will kill that staph. It's ironic and sad that Norman Kantor couldn't get the drug he invented."

"Laura, before you get all gowned up to go inside the ICU and before the CDC descends, let's go spend time with Natalie."

"I promised to check on her boyfriend," Laura said in a low voice. "But I got called to the E.R. Never even got to his chart."

"Natalie's boyfriend is one of the sicker ones," Stacy said. "I still can't imagine your little girl with a boyfriend."

"If he doesn't make it," Laura said, "Natalie will never get over it."

If she survives. Stacy hoped Laura couldn't read her mind.

CHAPTER FORTY-FOUR

The house was empty when Charles returned home from the Palace Hotel. Why wasn't Banks waiting with further instructions? He wondered whether there was something else he should be doing now. He and the chef had carefully plotted how they'd coordinate tomorrow's mission. The Palace Hotel restaurant would be closed to the public tomorrow to accommodate the *Atlantic Daily Reporter*'s celebratory banquet. For dessert, the banquet service would provide only the hotel's signature profiteroles.

Charles had first tasted profiteroles when he'd visited London with his parents. Since then, he'd always been on the lookout for them on dessert menus, but none had equaled the ones he'd devoured at tea in that London hotel. Never could he have imagined the wonderful puffs of chocolate and cream as the delivery vehicle for a bioweapon.

He'd only half listened when Collins explained how the shell was pâte-à-choux. Whatever the heck that was.

"Means the pastry for forming little cabbage shapes." Chef Lonnie continued, "First, I add the flour to boiled butter and water and beat till it forms a smooth ball of dough. Then I cool it to lukewarm, add eggs, beat, pipe the dough onto sheets, and bake."

"You can't overheat the bacteria," Charles warned. "The strain will resist stomach acid, but it can't withstand heat from cooking or baking." Could this be his 'sorry, it won't work' exit ploy?

Lonnie wasn't buying in. "Even I know that much," he said. "It's the cream phase where you'll do your thing."

"Oh, yeah. Told you, I'm no chef," he'd mumbled.

"After the pastry shells cool, I split them in half and fill them with my special cream. That's the trick, how I prepare my cream. I fill each round of choux pastry with enough cream so that when you place the top half of the pastry on it, the cream peeks out of the sides. The finishing touch is a drizzle of warm chocolate ganache."

Charles was about to ask what ganache was, but focused instead on the cream. The staph would go into the cream quite nicely. The smooth texture and the fatty nature of the cream would make the perfect carrier.

"We do the final assembly just before serving," Lonnie had continued, "so when dessert arrives, the chocolate sauce is still warm."

Lonnie had laid out all these steps methodically. Might as well have been coaching a sous chef, not plotting to kill hundreds of unsuspecting people.

Charles had tried to be equally matter of fact. Kept his thoughts on the task at hand, not straying from the logistical into the moral or ethical realm.

They came up with a good plan. Lonnie would thicken his cream, so that it would not overflow the shell and perhaps infect the kitchen or waitstaff. The profiteroles would be plated, and fifteen plates arranged on each large serving tray. Twenty-five trays. Just before Lonnie did his drizzle of chocolate sauce, Charles would introduce the bacteria into the creamy center of each of the plated profiteroles. Using a syringe, he would infect the creamy core of each dessert. The chef would control the flow of the trays. No one else would be allowed close enough to Charles to observe that he was injecting each dessert with an inoculum of staph no bigger than a speck. He would use gloves and sterile technique, as he did every day in his level P3 lab.

"Let's hope no waiter grabs one when I turn my back for two seconds," Lonnie had said with a shrug. "Happens all the time."

Charles had assured him that no trace of live bacteria would remain in the kitchen. Neither man could predict whether, nor how, their deadly recipe could be discovered. The victims would not fall ill until after they'd left the hotel, so for about twenty minutes or so

Lonnie would carefully monitor the dining room, collect any left-over whole profiteroles, or partly eaten, and put them immediately into the garbage disposal.

At loose ends, Charles retired to his bedroom. Too keyed up to read, he'd watch some mindless TV show. Would the plan work? Charles speculated as he stretched out on his leather sofa. When would Banks reappear to let him know where they'd arranged for him to start the next phase of his life. He was an excellent scientist and under normal circumstances would have no problem getting a job. But with a new identity? The Order would no doubt have figured out all of that. As for his parents, what would they be told?

"All in due time," Banks had answered when he'd raised the question. *What had he meant by that?*

Charles was trying without much success to relax when he heard a car pull up in the driveway. He waited for Banks to walk in the back door, but instead, he heard the front doorbell ring. Mystified, Charles hurried down the front stairway.

Too early for the motion detectors to turn on the porch light. Through the glass pane framed in the polished oak door, a familiar face. Stanley Proctor, his boss—until Stacy Jones's sudden promotion—stood on his doorstep.

Does he know about the cultures?

Charles slumped against the doorframe, trying to look composed, taking a deep breath to control his panic. Should he let Proctor in? What if he came to search for the cultures? But if that's what he wanted, why come alone? The bacteria were an extremely high security risk. The CDC should be sending the army, not a puny middle-aged scientist. Charles inched open the door, hesitating just long enough to glance up and down the street. No federal agents, no soldiers. He opened it wider to let his visitor enter.

"Stan?" Not only had his boss never before set foot in Charles's house, but he was disoriented by Proctor's sweatshirt and khakis. He'd never seen the man in anything other than a business suit or a starched lab coat. "Come in."

"Charles, I need to talk to you," Stan said as they traversed the spacious entry hall leading to his luxurious living room.

Charles stood silent as Stan gazed around the room, taking in the expensive artwork. All he said was, "Nice place."

Charles gestured for him to sit on one of the two matching love seats. "Can I get you something to drink?" He almost said, "My housekeeper left for the day," then he realized how pretentious his lifestyle must seem to Stan who he knew had grown up in a blue-collar family.

"No time," Stan said. "I understand you went home sick today."

Shit. He'd forgotten all about that ruse. Had that been only this morning?

"I had severe flu symptoms," Charles said. "Better now, but I haven't been able to keep down any food." Good thing he'd not taken him into the den where the telltale leftovers of his late lunch sat on a tray.

"There's an emergency, Charles, and I need your help."

How in the hell could he know that the cultures were gone? And he wants my help?

"What's going on? Sorry I didn't answer my phone today, I just felt too weak." They all thought he was a wimp anyway. Now Stan would go back and report, "Guess what he said? 'I was just too weak.'" So what? After tomorrow he'd never have to face Stan Proctor or anyone else at the lab again.

"There's a developing situation with a staphylococcal outbreak in Tampa, Florida. We're sending down an EOIP team."

What did that have to do with him and the cultures? Charles sat down in the nearest armchair.

As relief replaced panic, Charles's attention lapsed. When he tuned in again to whatever Stan was saying, he heard, "We want Stacy to stay in Tampa to support the team. She discovered it and—"

Stan continued talking without a pause as Charles tried to make sense of what he was saying. He'd told her that he was too ill to change out the cultures tomorrow. She said she'd come in to do it. And now—

"It started in the ICU," Stan's voice intruded once more. "Two dead there, and it's spreading to the staff. A medical resident—"

So the boss had come here about Stacy. The visit had nothing to do with Charles or his pilfered staph.

Relieved, yet angry, Charles worked to keep his tone neutral, "Stacy? How's she involved?"

"She got a call from an infectious disease doctor at Tampa City Hospital," Stan said. "Called her at home, and she responded. Not exactly protocol, but good thing she did. The bottom line is that she can't fly back now, so you need to replate the cultures, and you don't look too sick to do so."

Screw you, Charles wanted to respond. Instead, he inquired about the staph in Tampa, surprised that it was so virulent, resistant to all antibiotics, that it shared so many characteristics of the strain that they were developing at the CDC. How convenient, he said to himself, that Stacy was involved. Could she have had something to do with this? Could she have taken a culture, too? *That bitch.*

"Stan, from what you know, how similar is the infectious organism there to what we'd expect from our staph?"

"Confirmed staph; unidentifiable strain; either wild or experimental, we don't know; resistant to methicillin and vancomycin and everything else; site of inoculation unknown; rapid onset of shock and multiorgan shutdown, disseminated intravascular coagulation; the works."

"Skin lesions?" Charles held his breath as Stan responded. His bacteria had been engineered to cause necrotizing fasciitis. That's why they called it "flesh-eating."

"A mottled rash on the trunk, but no bullae or pustules."

So the staph is not the same. Where had it come from? A spontaneous mutation? How strange that the only connection between this epidemic in Tampa and what was about to happen in Atlanta tomorrow night was—Stacy Jones? A coincidence? Maybe not.

Charles certainly was not about to let Jones off the hook so she could go right on playing prima donna expert in Tampa. She'd have to come back to Atlanta and take care of business in the lab. Now, wouldn't it be too perfect if she could join her people at the Palace tomorrow night for dessert?

"No." Charles stood up. "I cannot make it into the lab tomorrow. I am too ill. Now, Stan, I must ask you to leave."

CHAPTER FORTY-FIVE

The shrill ring of the bedside phone jarred Victor out of a deep, delicious sleep. For a futile moment, he ignored the interruption, but knew that he'd not be able to recover the emotion-filled dream. He and Cindy and a little boy romped through a field of wild flowers, holding hands, and singing "Old MacDonald Had a Farm."

"Hello," he mumbled, resenting severance from the dream.

"Is this Dr. Victor Worth?" The voice sounded vaguely familiar.

"Yes, it is." Victor checked the clock. Almost three in the afternoon. He'd slept for three hours. He needed to get back to the hospital. He felt his chest contract, realizing that he'd have to tell the little boy in his dream that he would die of AIDS.

"Dr. Fred Minn. Keystone Pharma. We spoke briefly when you were here earlier this week."

"Yes." *You're the prick who blew me off.*

"I am calling with a rather urgent request."

How strange. Keystone Pharma calling me?

"I don't need your ticokellin," Victor said. "But I am disappointed that you refused to help me." He wanted to add, "And your company screwed up a drug that I was responsible for discovering."

With a sly smile he thought of Norman Kantor. Was that traitor still among the living?

"There's been an outbreak of a virulent staph infection at a hospital in Florida," Dr. Minn continued. "Resistant to methacillin and vancomycin. Two deaths already."

"Why are you telling me this?" Victor interrupted, feeling paranoid. Keystone Pharma knew that he'd wanted ticokellin sent to Tampa. *Could they think I'm somehow involved.*

Dr. Minn avoided his question. "Dr. Worth, your former colleague at the NIH, Dr. Norman Kantor, was one of the victims. You spoke of Dr. Kantor when you were here, as I recall."

"Norman's dead?" Victor tried to sound shocked.

"I'm afraid so. Full-blown staph sepsis. Poor guy." There was a momentary pause, then Minn said, "Happened at the same hospital where you wanted the ticokellin."

"Turns out I didn't need it," Victor said, needing to distance himself from the Tampa location.

"I'm glad. But with this outbreak, we have a new situation. We've gotten calls from the CDC and the FDA to release the drug on an emergency compassionate basis, but that's not why I'm calling."

Was this guy trying to connect the dots between Norman and Matthew?

Victor took a deep breath, held it, trying to think. Norman was dead; mission accomplished. And right now, Victor thanked God that he'd had the foresight to dismantle his lab and scour his basement of all traces of bacteria. Although he still had to make that trip to the landfill. "What does all this have to do with me? I've worked with staph, but my agency disbanded the staph research program."

"Your name came up today. Next to Dr. Kantor, who developed the kellin line of antibiotics, you know more about resistant strains of staph than anybody except the CDC and USAMRIID scientists. Now that we're facing a real problem, we need your expertise to pursue sister compounds to ticokellin."

"You may not know this, Dr. Minn, but it was I who developed the kellin line." *Have to watch it here.* "And the wrong chemical from the series was taken to the clinic. You should have gone with biskellin, not ticokellin. I warned Norman about the propensity for side effects with the ticokellin's binding profile, but he capitulated to management when the manufacturing costs for biskellin were deemed too high."

"Well, I can assure you, Dr. Worth, that manufacturing costs will no longer be an issue. We want to be back in the clinic with an effective kellin as soon as possible and we want you to lead the effort."

For a moment, Victor thought that he was hallucinating. After all the wheedling he'd done to try to land a research job at Keystone Pharma when Norman was there, he gets a bizarre phone call on a Friday afternoon. He sat down, speechless.

Minn waited for a response that did not come, then went on, "I know this is sudden, but the situation is urgent. Our CEO, Paul Parnell, has already cleared your hire with the NIH. Realize that he has top-level contacts ever since Keystone Pharma developed the antidote to that mutated adenovirus causing hemorrhagic fever in Africa. As you must know, he got the Nobel Peace Prize for that."

"You contacted my employer?" Norman asked, not knowing whether to be flattered or incensed.

"Just to clear the path. We'd like you to start immediately."

"I don't see how I can do that," Victor said. Even if I wanted to. And he did want to. He had to consider Matthew, who could be discharged on Monday.

"We'd like you to come in tomorrow, meet with the Human Resources vice president, get the paperwork cleared. We hope you can begin working on Monday, with the scientists on your team."

Victor had never led a team before and just the sound of it unleashed a surge of self-importance. Trying to decide what to say, Victor almost missed the next part.

"Dr. Worth, here's the offer. You accept the position of director of research, Infectious Disease. Your executive compensation pack includes a starting salary of two hundred ten thousand dollars, a year-end bonus, stock, and stock options. Full health care, the usual perks for directors. Human Resources will go over this with you tomorrow. Can you do this?"

"I believe I can—that is, if you really need me."

"We'll send the Keystone Pharma plane to pick you up tomorrow morning. And we have a spacious condo available for your immediate use in Philadelphia as well as a car. Of course, you'll have

access to our company planes and our apartments in Manhattan and
D.C. And all your moving expenses will be covered."

"I see," Victor said. Matthew could be moved to the company
condo. With that impressive compensation package, he could easily
hire around-the-clock care.

"Thank you, Dr. Worth. I must admit that we were planning on
bringing Dr. Kantor out of retirement until we heard that he was
one of those stricken. God bless his soul."

God damn the bastard's soul.

CHAPTER FORTY-SIX

She looked small against the mound of pillows, her skin an ashen white, her hair damp with sweat. Tim sat beside her bed, wearing the protective clothing now mandatory for all members of the hospital staff entering all patient rooms. He and Natalie both looked up as Laura walked in. Tim's eyes tired and droopy; Natalie's sunken, listless, and scared.

Tim jumped up holding out his arms, then letting them drop. Refrain from unnecessary touching to limit cross contamination. "Laura, are you okay?" he asked.

"I'm okay." Laura knew that she must look as awful as she felt. "How's Natalie?" She looked about for Natalie's chart, but then remembered that they'd removed all paperwork to the nursing station. She should have stopped there first.

"Mom, did you see Trey?" Natalie interrupted, her voice sounding stronger than Laura had expected. "Is he going to be okay?"

Laura wanted to take Natalie in her arms and hold her, to wipe away her tears, to tell her that her young man would be fine. But she had to maintain a physical distance, and, no, Trey was not okay.

"I need to see him, Mom," Natalie pleaded.

"I'm sorry, sweetie. There's an infection going on in the ICU and nobody is allowed inside."

"You mean Trey's all alone? Aren't his parents with him?"

Laura shook her head, no. "But I can still get inside. I'll tell him how badly you want to be with him."

"Trey is such a wonderful person, Mom. I'm so sorry I didn't bring him home to meet you. That lawsuit thing—I didn't want you not to like him because his father is going against you in court."

That wasn't exactly right; Laura was going against him. All that seemed so trivial now. "I'll talk to his parents if I can," she promised. "And let them know how concerned you are."

If Trey was still alive, Laura thought. She knew about the lab report indicating disseminated intravascular coagulopathy, an ominous indicator in patients with septic shock.

"Let's talk about you. How are you feeling?"

"My head hurts and they say I have a fever. I keep throwing up. And I'm getting this pink rash on my stomach. I sort of ache all over, too. Like a really bad flu."

"Tim?" Laura asked, needing an update on Natalie's clinical course.

"Natalie, do you mind if we talk doctor talk for a bit, about you and some of the other patients here?"

"No, but Mom, when you're done, I need to ask you a question."

Tim might be exhausted, but he was up on Natalie's medical details. "With regard to vital signs: temp's the same, B.P.'s stable, heart rate a hundred ten. Labs: high white count, lots of bands. Liver and coagulation factors okay. BUN is rising a bit."

"Azotemia." Laura said under her breath. Kidney failure. Her mind raced to compare this finding with the lab results of the deteriorating patients in the ICU. She'd examine their charts for kidney function trends as soon as she got back up there.

"Could just be she needs more fluids," Tim said, "but the creatinine is creeping up, just slightly above normal limits, so—"

"X-ray?" Laura asked.

"Her earlier one shows bilateral infiltrates, no consolidation. They've ordered a repeat, but now they're not taking any patient to radiology with infectious disease symptoms. I know they've requested a portable. With the staff down for the holiday and all the extra time spent gowning and ungowning, it'll probably be a while."

"Tim, you just have to keep pushing them."

"If I were in Philly, maybe. I've got no clout here, but—I mention your name and everybody jumps. Don't worry, Natalie's getting plenty of attention. Your friend Roxanne stopped by and lots of others. Right, kiddo?" he asked Natalie. "And Kellerman, the ID doctor. Said to make sure you knew that he was here."

"Nicole keeps calling," Natalie interrupted. "She wants to come and see me."

"Natalie, of course she does. I wish she could, but because of this infection, they're not letting anybody in. They might even close down the hospital—keep everybody who's here, but not let anybody else in."

"That bad?" Tim asked. "Guess I'm stuck here then. No leftover turkey."

Laura wished she knew more about infectious diseases. While well versed in post-op wound infections, she'd referred most of her infectious disease complications to the internists and deferred to their treatment plan. Now she needed to be sure that her daughter was getting the optimum care. Then she remembered. Of course, one of the world's top infectious disease experts was right here in this hospital. Stacy had been so inundated with ICU cases and protecting the hospital that she had not yet stopped by to see Natalie. Laura needed to find Stacy now and get her to check on her daughter. How had she not done that earlier? Where were her priorities?

"Mom, I still have a question," Natalie ended Laura's introspection.

"Yes, sweetie?"

"How old were you when you married Dad?"

Laura looked from Natalie to Tim, as his eyebrows lifted quizzically. She wanted to say, "Not now, Natalie; you're too sick. Later, once you and my patients are healthy again." The plaintive look in her daughter's green eyes, eyes the exact color of her own, persuaded her otherwise.

"Nineteen. I was a freshman at Michigan State and your dad was a sophomore."

"Not much older than me," Natalie said. "As soon as Trey gets better and I graduate, we're getting married."

"And look what happened to Steve and me," Laura wanted to say.

"You don't talk much about Dad," Natalie said. "Did you love him?"

"Yes," Laura said, not elaborating. She'd told the truth. She had loved him. They didn't need to know the rest.

"I don't remember too much about him," Natalie said.

This interrogation had to stop. "Natalie, when you get better, we'll reminisce about me and Dad. Anything you want to know. But, you're right, I never do talk about your father much and maybe that's not fair to you."

Laura thought she heard Tim say, "Or me either."

"Did you call the other kids?" Natalie asked, seeming fine with Laura's evasion.

No, Laura hadn't and she should. For all these years, she'd compartmentalized her life: either totally with family, or totally with patients. Now the two were intermixing, and she felt off kilter.

When a nurse came in to replenish Natalie's intravenous solution, Laura said goodbye to Natalie and Tim, and headed for the ICU, determined to stop on her way and call her mom and let the other four kids know that she would not see them soon.

CHAPTER FORTY-SEVEN

Waiting in line to pay his respects to Russell's wife, Charles realized he had to stop in front of the open casket, kneel for a minute, and move on to mingle with a crowd he didn't know. He couldn't remember Russell's wife's first name. Social graces were not his strong suit despite his mother having made him go to charm school. His social discomfort, added to the proximity of a corpse, made the bile rise in his throat.

But he needed to be there, Banks had insisted on that. Russell's wife would expect the man her husband "played cards with" on a regular basis to show up to mourn the loss of his buddy. Charles felt his knees start to quake. He was next in line to view the body. Russell was dead because he'd displeased The Order. Banks had been clear about that. Maybe that was why he made sure Charles came here tonight. To witness the fatal side effect of noncompliance.

Charles felt a nudge from the woman in back of him. "Your turn," she whispered over his shoulder.

He moved up to face the coffin, knelt, and felt the uncontrollable urge to reach out and touch Russell's hand. Russell looked as if he were asleep, not so much as a scab visible, despite the massive injuries he'd suffered when the pickup truck sent him flying. He let his hand linger on Russell's, fascinated by the coolness, the pallor, the waxy feel. Then he heard the whisper, "Sir, the whole line is waiting."

Charles rose from the kneeler and found himself on what he could have mistaken for a wedding reception line. He saw Russell's wife standing next to an older couple, perhaps Russell's parents. For a moment he pictured his parents if the body in the coffin was his. What would they say to these people? Then he noticed the two youngsters. Four and two years old. A boy and a girl. What was he supposed to say to them?

He felt her touch his arm before he'd formulated some words of condolence. "Charles, how could this have happened? He took a step off the curb and—"

"Accident. Best not to try to understand." He wanted to add: Don't start asking questions, just go on with your life, get through this safely with your children.

"Can I talk to you for a moment?" Russell's wife turned back toward the older couple holding the children's hands. "Russell's parents," she said. "They're devastated."

"How are the children?" Charles asked, relieved that he did not have to speak to them.

"They're the only reason I'm trying not to fall apart."

She led Charles to the far corner of the viewing room, and they sat on a low bench half hidden by an enormous potted plant. "Thanks for coming, Charles. Russell always respected you. That's why I want to share something with you. You and I know about The Order's vow of secrecy, but in our marriage nothing was secret. I knew what Russell was doing when he went to your place. Playing cards? Please, he hated card games. But what I want to tell you is, something important is about to happen."

Charles felt her red-rimmed eyes study him as she waited for a response. He never could manage a poker face and struggled not to flinch.

"Like what?" he asked, trying for innocent curiosity.

"Not nuclear unless they have somebody else Russell never mentioned. Maybe something to do with water contamination. Maybe an explosion. But a lot of people will be killed when this happens. Russell was worried about it, but he didn't know the details. I can't tell you, Charles, how much he wanted out of The Order after they became so violent. For him, I think having kids of his own helped him realize we are all human beings, anyone's kids are kids, all life is precious. I think if Russell knew more about The Order's plan, he might have gone to the police or the FBI."

"No, your husband was loyal," Charles said. But The Order had not trusted him. What if Russell had warned the authorities before his accident?

Charles needed to get out of the funeral parlor and think. Should he tell Banks about this conversation? But Banks had vanished. It was all on Charles now. No turning back. By tomorrow night, Atlanta would be burning, afire with his lethal staph.

CHAPTER FORTY-EIGHT

The Goode family had gathered at the restaurant off the lobby of the Palace Hotel. Counting her children, and grandchildren, twenty-nine of them sat around four tables near the piano bar. They chose their own seats, no place cards. Three generations, Emma, the matriarch and the closest living kin of the founder of *The Atlanta Daily Reporter*, rejoiced in the presence of every one of her direct descendants. Unaffected by all the big-name folks dining at neighboring tables, the family mood was as relaxed as it was festive; the children caught up with each other's lives, the grandchildren enjoyed their cousins. Emma sat back with a satisfied smile. She had done well. She'd kept the newspaper together during difficult times, and she'd raised seven productive, happy children.

Dignitaries in town for the Saturday night gala kept stopping at Emma's table to congratulate her. Some she knew well; others, among the political and civil rights crowd, she never had met personally. Hard to believe how many leaders of the civil rights movement had come to Atlanta to honor her. Amazing that Joe Frank Harris, the governor of Georgia, and Coretta Scott King had strolled over to chat. That Rosa Parks came by to introduce her boss, Congressman John Conyers from Michigan. With all the lovely interruptions, Emma hardly managed to eat a bite of the beautiful food. If only her Edward could be with her. And how proud her father would be of the newspaper he pioneered to give a voice to his people.

After that handsome Julian Bond had left her table, one of

Emma's daughters leaned in to say, "Ma, I see you're warming up to all this attention, but just you wait until the big party tomorrow night."

Finally, the family gathering broke up, her kids drifting off in different directions. Emma declined a cup of coffee, knowing that with all the excitement she'd have trouble enough sleeping. She'd skipped dessert, and tomorrow night she'd have her favorite—the house special, a heavenly profiterole.

She rose from the table as Karen came over to give her a hand with her chair.

"Grandma, do you know all those people who talked to you?"

Emma nodded. Most. Almost fifty years in journalism, you had to meet a lot of people.

"You better get some rest. Wait here and I'll get Dad to drive you home. You're going to need your sleep."

Emma smiled, ignoring the nagging pain in both knees. "I can manage," she said. "You run along with your cousins and have a wonderful evening together."

CHAPTER FORTY-NINE

Natalie hadn't realized that the phone had slipped from her hand, but when she woke, it was to a flurry of voices and bustling noises around her bed.

She must have drifted off while talking to Nicole. Her twin sister had been telling her about the family's day. Beach volleyball, teaching their little cousin to swim in Grandma's pool, leftover turkey for lunch, Mr. Bone's ribs for dinner.

"But everybody's worried about you, Nattie. Are you going to be okay?"

Natalie's head pounded and speaking was a struggle. Thump, thump—with every beat of her heart, racing now, so fast she didn't think that it would hold up. And she was hot and sweaty. Trying to cough, but too weak.

After a pause, Nicole asked, "How about Mom? Is she going to get out of that hospital and come back tonight?"

"I don't think so," Natalie said.

"Is she there right now?"

"No. She's in the ICU. That's where Trey is."

"Did you tell Mom?" Nicole asked. "That you're not really sick."

"I don't feel too good." Natalie's voice sounded like a moan.

"Uh-oh. Mom must have just come in," Nicole guessed. "Did you tell her about Trey? Just say yes or no."

Natalie just wanted to lie there and she wished Nicole would hang up. That must have been when she'd dropped the phone.

"I don't care how busy Laura is," she heard Tim saying. "Get her here. Now!"

"Mama," she heard herself groan. Her mouth was dry, her head a raging throb.

Another male voice, vaguely familiar. "Pressure's dropping, turn up the fluid volume. Electrolytes and blood gases STAT. I need a portable x-ray. STAT."

"Dr. Kellerman, Radiology is swamped. I'll try, but—" The female voice faded out.

"This is Laura Nelson's daughter," the male voice insisted. "Go find the tech and drag him up here. STAT."

Natalie had known that her mother was important in this hospital, but not until now had she realized that everybody was scared of her. She'd found that amusing and was anxious to tell the other kids. To them, Mom was Mom. Supposed to be there for them, and she usually was.

Every once in a while, one of her friend's mothers would make a remark, like, "it must be terrible for you that your mother gets called to the hospital so much." She figured those women were jealous of her mother. Her mom was pretty, had an important job, and often was even in the newspaper when people had medical questions. She and Nicole and her brothers often discussed Mom. They agreed that even if she was single, raising them on her own, she outperformed most of their friends' mothers. What was important to us that Mom has missed? Natalie and her twin occasionally had this discussion. Between them they came up with a dance recital—but they detested that dance studio, anyway. Their seventh grade school play, but that was because she was sick. There was the time Mom was in jail, but only for a couple of days. For some reason they'd never understood, their dad once had taken them to their other grandpa's in Traverse City in Michigan for a couple of weeks, and they'd really, really missed her. And after that, Dad had died and Mom was all they had, all five of them.

And now lying there, slipping in and out of consciousness, Natalie knew that her doctor mother would make sure that both she and Trey got better. *But what's wrong with me? And why isn't Mom with me?*

Tim said, "I'm going to get Laura. Stay with Natalie until I get back."

"Naturally," a voice she now recognized as Dr. Kellerman's said, "if Dr. Jones is with Laura, get her in here, too. She's trying to obtain ticokellin, and when it comes in, I want it for Natalie. But I'll need Laura's consent. I just hope the FDA didn't cut the eligibility at age eighteen."

Natalie heard Tim leave, just as they came to take more blood. She needed to stay awake until her mother got there. She had to know about Trey. But she could not hold off the darkness.

CHAPTER FIFTY

Victor had considered sneaking in a bottle of champagne so they could celebrate his job offer, but quickly realized the complicated cocktail of medications in his son's body would not mix with alcohol. Instead, he brought a bottle of carbonated white grape juice and two plastic champagne glasses.

Victor found Matthew sitting up in bed watching television, a tray of bland food on the folding table in front of him and an intravenous running in his left arm. He looked pensive, but seemed to cheer up when he read his father's expression of triumph. And triumph was right. He'd beat Norman at his own game. Hadn't Dr. Minn as good as said that Victor's compensation package would exceed what Norman had commanded? And most satisfying of all, Norman was among the dead.

The other patients in that ICU had been so sick, Victor convinced himself, they'd have died even without his intervention. They'd looked terrible and had been on life support with ventilators breathing for them. Why dwell on them now? What was done, was done.

Except, just before he'd left for the hospital, he had been unnerved by a call from Naomi Kantor. She said she wanted Victor to know that Norman had died of a certain staph infection, much like the type that he and Norman had worked on at the NIH. She'd caused him a moment of alarm when she added pointedly that Victor had been in the hospital where Norman died, and had actually visited and talked to her husband. Why, she'd wanted to know, had Victor happened to be at Tampa City Hospital?

Victor wasn't inclined to offer any explanation. But when she pressed, he'd said simply, "Visiting a friend." He had no intention of sharing anything with that pretentious bitch, much less his new paternity. But neither did he want her asking around about him.

Soon enough, she'd moved away from the dangerous subject to complain to Victor about her own plight—trouble contacting her children. Where were those ingrates when she needed them? Before hanging up, she'd actually thanked Victor for being there for her. *Wait until she finds out who has her husband's old job at Keystone Pharma.*

But now, here was Matthew, looking pinker and breathing on his own. Victor forgot all about Naomi Kantor. Matthew clicked off the TV set. Victor pulled the visitor chair close to the bedside and decided to tell Matthew the good news straight out. Pushing aside the tray of half-eaten food, he poured two glasses of juice.

"What's going on?" Matthew asked.

"Two news bulletins," Victor announced, raising his glass for a toast. "I've been offered a management job at Keystone Pharma, a big pharmaceutical company, and—"

"That's wonderful," Matthew said, lifting his glass. "Let's drink to that!"

They each took a sip of the sweet liquid, each trying to pretend that it was palatable.

"Sorry, I interrupted," Matthew said. "You said you had two bits of news. That one will be a hard act to follow."

"No, the next one is even better," Victor said, savoring this announcement. "The doctors said that I can take you home Monday. Only now it won't be my home in Bethesda, but my new condo in Philadelphia."

Matthew's reaction was not as warm as Victor had expected, nor did his son appear surprised. The doctors must already have told him that he would be discharged.

"Victor, it's not that I don't appreciate all you're doing."

Victor. Not Father.

"Without you, I'd have had no one in Tampa to get me though this difficult time, but—"

"I told you before, Matthew, that I will be here for you. Every step of the way. I know that AIDS is a tough diagnosis to accept, but there's a lot of research going on. As a big shot scientist at Keystone Pharma, I'll have access to all that research."

Matthew fixed soulful eyes on Victor. "I never had a father. And now, with the sacrifices that you've made for me these last few days, I feel that my most sacred prayer has come true."

This is what Victor had been waiting for, wanted more than anything else, sacred prayer. He closed his eyes, squeezing them tight for a moment before he felt them fill with tears.

Matthew reached for his hand. The touch was soft even though Matthew's hands were bony, the skin thin and still a little blotchy.

"Father," Matthew said, "my doctor came in and we talked. He said I could be released if I had home care to keep up the intravenous antibiotics for another two weeks. Then I can travel. I'll need to find an HIV specialist in San Francisco."

"San Francisco?" Victor must not have heard correctly.

"When Mom got so sick that she needed me with her in Florida, I left my friend—friends in San Francisco. I always intended to go back. After Mom died, I stayed in Florida to sell the house, settle all her affairs. But then I got sick, met you, and you rescued me."

"Don't go back," Victor heard himself plead. "I just found out I had a son. If I'd known, I'd have never left Cindy to deal with a child. I never even told her why—" Victor let his head slip into his hands. "I was so ashamed. I just couldn't tell her."

"Why ashamed?" Matthew asked gently. "Tell her what?"

"That I had testicular cancer. That I had to have a bilateral orchiectomy. They castrated me. Did a radical node dissection down there." Victor pointed to his crotch. "Radiation. Chemo. One of the drugs, cisplatin, did tubal damage to my kidneys. I was a wreck. I didn't want to put all that grief on Cindy. We both were graduating from the University of Florida. The diagnosis was my graduation present, and I left to live with my parents in Bethseda. Eventually,

I got my Ph.D. in D.C., lived with my parents until they died. Still do live in the same house."

"Geez, I never knew," Matthew said, gripping Victor's hand more tightly, tears starting in his own eyes.

"Your mother never knew," Victor said. "I never called her. She never called me."

"But she knew how to contact you," Matthew said. "Thank God that she sent you that letter."

"I tried to spare her pain and suffering," Victor said, looking up through tears, "and I never knew she was pregnant. If only I had, things would have been so different. So you see, Matthew, you need to come live with me. I can't lose you again."

His son looked so vulnerable, too fragile to live anywhere but with him. Maybe he did have friends, but Matthew was his biological son, a bond too powerful to ignore.

"Father, I have a special friend in San Francisco who needs me. We love each other and we want to spend the rest of our lives caring for each other. You see, he's HIV positive, too.

Victor had not even considered this. That Matthew was involved in an intimate relationship that would take precedence over their father-son relationship. Should he invite Matthew's friend to live in his condo, too? Matthew would have a companion. Lover, to be clear. Minn had said that the condo was spacious. Should he encourage this unusual arrangement?

"Bring him to Philadelphia. At least until you—"

"Father, San Francisco is the best place to be for HIV. They have more experience, more tolerance, than doctors anywhere else."

Victor nodded, knowing that AIDS was just making its way around the country. Washington D.C., New York City had cases, but Matthew was right about the concentration of cases and HIV care in the Bay Area.

"Come out and visit. Get to know my friend. How about that?"

Victor felt deflated. But lots of men had sons in different parts of the country—and with his new salary and access to Keystone's jets, he could visit Matthew regularly and bring Matthew to Philadelphia for visits. For a while, he'd be transitioning to corporate life at Keystone. Maybe this idea would work. He wouldn't even have to explain to anyone at work that he had a gay son with AIDS. The corporate world, like everywhere else, was full of ignorance and hate. Fear, too. Right now, he could concentrate on his new job, knowing his son had a support system in San Francisco.

"Son, I want what's best for you. But you'll need to spend a couple of weeks here until you're off the antibiotics. Why don't we talk about this later?" He welcomed the beginning of a smile he could see in Matthew's eyes. "I'll respect your decision and I can help with anything. Meantime, tomorrow they want me to spend all day at Keystone Pharma. They're expediting the hiring process so they can prioritize research. Because of some staph epidemic in Tampa at the same hospital where you were admitted. Thank God I got you out of there in time."

"In Tampa?" Matthew said, releasing Victor's hand. "I hope Dr. Nelson is okay, and that attractive resident who's always with her. Michelle Wallace. Those are two special women."

CHAPTER FIFTY-ONE

"Outstanding job, Stacy—you blew the whistle on what looks like a Class A disaster at Tampa City Hospital. But if you don't come and deal with our cultures here in Atlanta, well, I don't have to tell you—"

"Yes, Stan, I understand," Stacy told her boss. Rank had its privileges.

And she did understand: decades of research down the tubes. Charles Scarlett had to be the king of the pricks. He wouldn't be working for long at the CDC, Stan Proctor had as good as said. The boss had gone personally to Charles's house to convince him to show up at the lab tomorrow to replate the cultures. Charles, who had appeared the picture of health, had refused. Blatant insubordination, Stacy figured. But Stan—even at his management level—would have to contend with layers of bureaucracy to fire anybody from a government job.

The cultures were her problem now.

"So we'll send a plane to bring you back to Atlanta tonight. The plane will leave from the private terminal in Tampa at eleven p.m., so you won't get that much sleep tonight. At seven a.m., the director wants to see you in her office. She'll want to debrief you on exactly what you found in Tampa. She plans to go there herself, even though the rapid response team should have the situation under control. The media will be hounding her, so it'll be best if she's at the scene. Since staph is the culprit, I'm going down, too. Same plane you'll return on, so we'll cross paths in the airport. Be sure to go to the private terminal."

Stacy wondered whether she really was born for management. Disrupted plans; pressure from the media. But private jets sounded okay.

Members of the EOIP team were arriving in droves—she had no idea how many—doing what they do, responding rapidly. There were protocols for situations like this, and Stacy wanted desperately to see them in action, to observe and learn. But she was a good soldier and would be on that plane to Atlanta as ordered. Her first ride on a private jet.

Nine o'clock. Two hours till her flight. Tampa International was only a half hour from the hospital. And, tonight, no need to allow extra time for airport lines. She headed for the hospital's microbiology lab.

Soon after she'd arrived at Tampa City, Stacy had visited the hospital lab director to request special tests on the staph organisms growing out of the ICU victims' cultures. She also had asked him to sequester a small sample for her to transport to the CDC, where they had sophisticated testing equipment to characterize bacteria strains. She had just enough time now to collect her test results and pick up the sample.

Two uniformed men blocked Stacy's access to the lab. Their uniforms looked more like army than local police, but the men wore no identification.

"Ma'am, this area is off-limits." The shorter of the two guards held up his hand.

Stacy needed to get those cultures. A question was beginning to form in her mind. Something about this outbreak. She needed to see the sensitivity results for the ticokellin that Keystone Pharma had flown down for testing. "I'm Dr. Jones—CDC," she stated. "I need to see the lab director."

"Sorry, no exceptions," the man said. "There's a dangerous bacteria in there."

"Will you go in and let him know I'm here?" she asked. "It's vitally important."

The two men exchanged glances. Clearly, neither wanted to go anywhere near that laboratory door.

"I am from the CDC," she said again, trying to exude confidence. "I'm doing my job here." She presented her Center of Disease Control ID badge. Neither moved to touch it.

The two men nodded at each other. The burly one said, "Go ahead."

Stacy found the lab door locked, but when she knocked, she recognized the tech who opened it. She found a cluster of lab technicians grouped around a management type with a strident voice. "Nobody will leave the quarantined area until we give the clearance."

The announcement elicited a chorus of groans. Terrified at the prospect of quarantine, she bolted for the lab director's office. The door was closed. Without knocking, she opened it, finding him on the phone. "Honey, I don't know when I'll be home." Startled, he looked up to see her. "Yes, I'm okay, but I've got to go." A pause. "I love you, too."

"Do you—"

"Dr. Jones, I hope this helps. I have the test results you requested and the material. All securely wrapped, but be careful. I don't have to tell you about how contagious this is. Your CDC people are moving fast with the quarantine, too fast for me." He handed Stacy a wrapped package and a manila folder, and directed her to the exit on the opposite side of the hall. "Go. They haven't locked that one yet."

Good thing Stacy had taken time with the microbiology lab director yesterday to explain her concerns. Her extra care had been repaid, she thought, as she secured the package in her bulky shoulder bag. Once she got this culture back to the CDC labs, she'd be able to test her hypothesis. Should she share her idea with Laura? First, she had to find her. Eager to see for herself how Natalie was doing, she headed toward Natalie's room. Laura would be with her unless she was in the ICU.

Ignoring the quarantine sign and after a perfunctory knock, Stacy stepped inside. Several health care workers, wearing protective clothing surrounded a slim, blonde girl with skin the color of slate. The person at the head of the bed was inserting a nasotracheal tube into one of the girl's nostrils. A ventilator stood ready, a technician tweaking the settings.

Laura stood at the foot of the bed alongside a tall man in protective garb. Tim. Laura looked stricken and Stacy wanted to rush to her, but she backed up to reach for a pack of sterile clothing. Pulling her shoulder bag with the staph cultures down around her waist, she quickly donned the protective covering. Under her gown, the lethal bundle protruded as if she were a few months pregnant.

"Laura," Stacy spoke softly, not wanting to disrupt the intense focus of the team working on Natalie.

Laura looked up, tears streaming down her cheeks. Tim put an arm around her shoulders and pulled her closer.

"She started to get worse about two hours ago," Laura said. "Thank you, Stacy, for pushing Keystone and the FDA. The ticokellin just arrived at the Tampa airport. I have to sign the papers. I think it's her only hope."

Laura spoke through tears. "Natalie's course has followed the others', and now she's going into rapid decline. Septic shock. Pulmonary infiltrates. Azotemia. She needs that drug before all her organs fail. I just lost another patient in the ICU and her boyfriend is—"

"On life support," Tim finished Laura's sentence.

Stacy knew that Trey Standish would not make it. Even with the ticokellin. Once disseminated intravascular coagulation set in, you were out of options. In DIC, small blood clots form throughout the body and quickly consume all the coagulation proteins and the platelets in the blood so that internal and external bleeding is unstoppable. And the clots themselves cut off blood flow to the organs. She'd seen the boy's labs: prolonged bleeding time, no platelets. And she'd seen the boy, literally hemorrhaging from every organ in his body. No wonder DIC also stands for "death is coming."

"I don't think he's going to make it," Stacy said, "but, Laura, I came to tell you that I have to go back to Atlanta. My boss called and they need me. They're even sending a private plane to get me. Believe that?" Stacy wasn't sure she was getting through to Laura, but she needed to say goodbye. "The CDC is on the way, mustering all its resources. Before I go, I'll make sure that the senior clinician checks on Natalie."

"I understand," Laura said, "and thanks so much for getting the ticokellin released to us. If Natalie gets it in time—"

Stacy turned to leave, wishing that she could hug her friend, but touching was prohibited in that environment.

"One more thing," Laura said.

Stacy turned. The ventilator was hooked up now, filling Natalie's lungs with oxygen-enriched gases.

"Will you promise to make sure that Natalie gets the ticokellin? Please?"

CHAPTER FIFTY-TWO

Natalie, seemingly lifeless except for the rising and falling of her chest, tore at Laura's heart. She sat slumped forward in the bedside chair next to Tim. Keeping vigil, praying. Of her five kids, Natalie and Nicole claimed the softest spot in her emotional core. Still, she believed she loved all five of her children equally. All five had such different personalities, but she'd always felt more protective of the girls. These days she rarely thought about Steve, their father. Whereas most fathers would have cherished the adorable little twins, Steve had barely tolerated them. On the other hand, he'd been a good father to the boys. Had Natalie and Nicole's emotional development been damaged by Steve's attitude? Is that why they had such disparate personalities? Nicole, outgoing and aggressive; Natalie, sweet and compassionate? No way to know, but Laura blamed herself. She'd let Steve get away with it, too busy with her career to intervene.

Why was she thinking about the past? The present needed every morsel of her attention. Laura decided to do a checklist, an exercise that always helped her cope. To-do: first, make sure Natalie gets ticokellin. She'd signed the informed consent, cringing as she read about the side effects, the most dangerous of which was aplastic anemia, a rare lethal condition that wipes out the bone marrow. There'd been three cases in the clinical trials. Perhaps simply by chance, perhaps drug toxicity, but too many for the FDA to approve the antibiotic. One case in every five hundred patients treated. Next on the list:—

The phone rang and Tim got up to answer it, mumbled a few words, hung up the phone, and sat back down beside her.

"Trey Standish died," he said. "Poor Natalie. She poured out her heart today, Laura. Made me feel so much like a father. She's so young, but she's in love. Remember that song by Paul Anka, I think. 'They say it's puppy love' or something like that."

"That's where Natalie got this staph, Tim, from Trey Standish."

"The clerk in the ICU said the parents asked to talk to you," Tim said, "before they were escorted to the quarantine section."

Laura looked at Tim. In only one day, he'd come to know more about Natalie's life than she did. "Tim, I feel so conflicted. I have to be here with Natalie and I have to care for the ICU patients. The CDC is sending in doctors who don't have Florida medical licenses and most of the Tampa doctors are staying as far away as possible. How can I be with Natalie and still do my job? And now with the CDC decontamination protocol, each time we move out of a patient room, we have to go through a twenty-minute process."

"I'll be here with Natalie," Tim said. "You can rotate between here and the ICU. It's the only logical solution."

"You've done so much already, Tim. You need sleep. We've been up for how long?"

"Forty hours. But it's you I'm worried about, Laura."

Before she could answer, they heard a knock on the door. An apparition clothed in full-body cover: tangerine-colored, hooded jumpsuit, helmet, and face protector. So this was the new dress code.

"Natalie Nelson. You're her parents?" A female voice issued from under the gear. Your daughter is on the list to get ticokellin if you've signed the release."

"I'm her mother," Laura said. "And yes, I signed the informed consent." Without another word, Laura handed the document to the figure. A gloved hand reached out, took the form, and the figure turned to go.

"When?" Laura asked.

"We'll see where she fits on the priority list," the muffled voice said.

Laura had always thought of Tampa City as her own hospital,

her domain. Now, at her moment of greatest need, the Feds relegated her family to a priority list. Stand in line like everybody else. Natalie would have to wait her turn. For an instant, she remembered the grief in Dr. Victor Worth's eyes when he failed to get ticokellin for his son. Now they had a supply, and she prayed the pharmaceutical company had sent enough.

The clock on the wall said it was almost midnight. Tim would watch over her comatose daughter. Laura knew she could not abandon her patients. She spent the rest of the night rotating, just as Tim had suggested, between her daughter's room on the pediatric floor and the ICU on the seventh. The ICU was fully staffed now with medical personnel on call from the CDC. The CDC team took charge and Laura was impressed by their competence. But they still needed her as a licensed local doctor with hospital staff privileges here, to write orders. She thought of Ed Plant, where was he? He had looked terrible the last time she'd seen him. And he wasn't the type to walk out in a crisis. She needed to find out if he was okay. She felt responsible for him, too. As well as Michelle, and Bunnie, and the others. She'd have to drag herself back to the ICU.

Every time she changed floors, she had to go through the time-consuming decontamination process. A total antiseptic scrub, a complete change of garb from head to toe.

On her first two tours of Natalie's room, she found her daughter unchanged, still febrile with a rapid heart rate, still poor oxygenation, respiration controlled by the machine.

On each of her tours of the ICU, she'd found death. The first, Tom Mancini, the patient she'd operated on for beryllium-induced lung cancer, a victim of the toxic mineral in Standish's factory environment. The irony, the Standish son and Mancini in the same hospital unit. Then she'd learned that the middle-aged nurse who'd had complications following a hysterectomy had died.

Now as Laura left for the ICU, she wondered whether she should try to contact Trey Standish's parents. Wouldn't Natalie expect her to? But what could she say or do? Their son was dead. Ultimately, the decision was made for her when she inquired about the Standish parents' location. A CDC responder fielded her call, explaining the strict isolation mode in force in the hospital. Those patients and personnel not exposed were quarantined in a clean area, monitored carefully. Those who'd had any exposure—which included Standish's parents—were sent to a private room with total isolation until forty-eight hours passed with no evidence of infection and confirmed negative cultures. Laura was spared what would be a most uncomfortable encounter with Trey's parents.

In the meantime, the E.R. had transitioned into a dirty zone. Ambulances were redirected to the closest regional hospital.

Tampa health care was under siege. Under the direction of the CDC, all hospitals within a sixty-mile radius had initiated cultures on all patient admissions and all staff. No visitors, except parents of small children. Laura realized that it had been Stacy who had wisely instituted these precautions. As horrible as the situation was, how much worse if this staph ran rampant in the community. She wished that Stacy had not been called back to Atlanta. She was the real hero in this tragedy and the only person Laura could trust to ensure that Natalie got ticokellin. Tomorrow the CDC big shots would arrive, causing a media circus, which Laura worried could shift the focus away from patient care.

Rotating every two hours between visits to Natalie and to the ICU, Laura had not been to visit the additional intensive care units set up to handle secondary cases, starting with her chief resident, Michelle, and the ICU cleaning lady, Bunnie, whom she'd seen in the E.R. When she inquired, she was told that Michelle had been given ticokellin. Only two days ago, she'd asked Michelle to report back to her about ticokellin, the investigational drug Matthew Mercer's father had so desperately wanted for his son. Thankfully, Mercer improved without it, and he'd been medevaced out of Tampa City in the nick of time. An HIV victim would not survive this aggressive staph organism, ticokellin or not.

Bunnie wasn't doing well, Laura was told. A woman of her age with a temperature of 104.8 degrees, delusional and hallucinating and showing signs of DIC wasn't going to make it. Laura had wanted to follow up on whatever it was Bunnie had been trying to tell her in the E.R. Something like "a man doin' sumthin' to the patients like feedin' them somethin'." Had she said the man was a new doctor? Laura was too exhausted to remember, and now it could be too late to ask Bunnie for clarification.

At six a.m., with only two of yesterday morning's seven ICU patients surviving, Laura headed for Natalie's floor. She managed to change into fresh isolation garb before she all but fell onto the closest of two cots crammed into the small room. Tim snored on the other cot, loudly, through the protective mask. Before Laura could even inquire about the ticokellin for her daughter, she'd fallen fast asleep.

And, again, she'd neglected to inquire about her colleague, Ed Plant.

CHAPTER FIFTY-THREE

When Stacy entered the stark lobby of the CDC, she found Director Madeleine Cox chatting with the receptionist. The director, always polished and professional, looked ready to travel, briefcase in hand, a forest-green pull-along suitcase by her side. Dr. Cox was in her late fifties with steel-gray hair cut just above shoulder length, slim with broad shoulders and in three-inch heels, taller than Stacy by half a head.

"Stacy, I've been waiting for you," she said, checking her watch. "I'm on my way to Tampa to see for myself what you've discovered there. I wanted to ask you some questions before I go."

"Of course, Dr. Cox," Stacy said, pulling her shoulder bag closer. Inside, wrapped in layers of protective insulation, was the culture she'd taken from Tampa. Unauthorized. Against every protocol. Had the director found out?

"I don't have much time, so let's talk over there." Cox pointed to two chairs in a far corner of the lobby.

"Nobody's here but us at this hour." The director's trim suitcase rolled efficiently, her heels clicked against the polished marble floor. Stacy followed.

"I'm most curious about how you got involved with this staph strain attacking Tampa?" Cox asked as soon as they were out of earshot of the receptionist.

"Serendipity," Stacy said. The two women settled into matching upholstered chairs, facing one another. "A friend in Tampa called me for advice on a HIV patient, the first in the Tampa area, we think. She wanted to put me in touch with the infectious disease specialist there, Dr. Duncan Kellerman. He did track me down in Detroit, where I was visiting my mom for Thanksgiving. Only he wasn't calling me about HIV. By then, the Tampa City ICU had several patients with a virulent, resistant staph."

"Who is this friend?" the director asked.

"Dr. Laura Nelson. She's a thoracic surgeon. Chief of surgery at the University of South Florida and Tampa City Hospital. I consider her my mentor. We've known each other since she was a medical student in Detroit and I was in high school." Stacy still flinched when she remembered those bad days in Detroit, how close she'd come to a life of drugs and despair.

"So this Dr. Kellerman calls you and you drop everything and head for Tampa? Stacy, I know you earned a medical degree, but your focus now is research. Research relating to virulent, infectious staph. Doesn't that seem like quite a coincidence?"

Where was the woman going with this? Yes, it was quite a coincidence. But coincidences do happen.

"There was something else, Dr. Cox," Stacy said, starting to sweat in the small of her back.

She must have found out that I took the staph, Stacy feared. Can I make her understand that I need to test it myself? To see whether the specific strain in Tampa is related to the strain developed initially at the NIH. Why should it be? Her thoughts raced. That research was closed down several years ago. But a crazy idea had occurred to her when she heard a Dr. Norman Kantor, a NIH scientist, was one of the infected Tampa patients. Talk about coincidences. Could he somehow have infected the hospital? But how? And why?

"Yes?" Cox was staring at her now, a curious stare.

"My friend, Laura—Dr. Nelson—called me back, too. She wasn't at the hospital when the infection started; she was out of town with her family for Thanksgiving. But Dr. Kellerman called her in. She found out her teenaged daughter Natalie had been admitted to Tampa City Hospital."

"I'm confused. She's out of town with her family. But her daughter's in Tampa?"

"Yes. Laura was worried. The daughter is seventeen and hadn't gone away with the rest. Laura has five kids." Stacy paused in mid-ramble. What did the director care about Laura's family? Madeleine Cox had no kids, wasn't married; word had it she didn't believe a woman could be both a professional and a mother.

"You lost me, Stacy. I don't understand how you got yourself in the middle of this—although I'm glad you did. Because you acted fast, we had our rapid-response team already in place last night. Tampa City Hospital is in lockdown. We should have this bug contained. Next, we'll have to characterize it. That'll be your lab's job. Run every bio and genetic screen that you can get your hands on. We'll get culture material to you by mid-afternoon. In the meantime, get everything set up."

By mid-afternoon? Stacy let out her breath. Cox had no idea after all about the purloined culture. Stacy could start the biogenetic profile on the culture she'd taken from Tampa right away. Once she got the official culture via the CDC, she'd be well into characterizing the staph stain. And if her hunch was right, what would she do next?

"Stan Proctor told me that you wanted to stay in Tampa to watch how all this plays out," Cox was saying, "but I told him you're needed here. You have talent, Stacy. I'm pleased about your promotion. Stan went to bat for you with some powers-that-be who pushed for Charles Scarlett. I'm sure we made the right choice."

Cox rose from her chair, again checked her watch, "I really have to go."

"Please, Dr. Cox," Stacy said, almost reaching for her sleeve so she wouldn't leave yet. "Can I make a request?"

"Of course."

"Dr. Nelson's daughter, Natalie Nelson. Will you check personally, please, that she's doing okay?"

"I'm going to be very tied up," Cox said. "The media, you know. I'll be prepped on the flight to Tampa, so—"

"She has the staph," Stacy blurted. "Her boyfriend was one of the ICU patients. Before anyone knew what was going around the unit, she had physical contact with him."

"My lord. Yes, Stacy, of course I will. I didn't realize. Of course you didn't want to leave your friend and her daughter. How is the boyfriend?"

"He died. Natalie's condition is worse. Last I heard, waiting on ticokellin. I hope you will look in on her as soon as you get there. We were able to get a limited supply of ticokellin, but I'm not sure how they're allocating it."

"I will. And we appreciate how you worked with Keystone Pharma and the FDA to bring in the drug so expeditiously. Dr. Jones, you're not only a world-class scientist, but you've got the makings of an administrator, too."

"Thank you, Dr. Cox." Stacy reeled from the praise. Madeleine Cox, director of the CDC, was not given to compliments.

Cox gathered up her purse and hefted her leather briefcase over her shoulder. Reaching for her rolling case, she suddenly paused. "Oh, I almost forgot. I have something for you. An invitation. For tonight. A posh affair at the Palace Hotel. Cocktails, dinner, dancing, the works. Just one problem. I have only one ticket so you can't bring a date."

"I don't think I'll have time to go, but thanks," Stacy said, knowing she'd be working into the night on the Tampa staph.

Cox ignored her response, set down her briefcase, and reached into her purse for an ivory-colored envelope, one of those expensive ones, heavy paper, elaborate calligraphy. She handed it to Stacy. "High priority," Cox said. "The *Atlantic Daily Reporter* banquet tonight—in honor of Emma Goode. You do know who she is?"

In the African American community who did not know the name Emma Goode?

CHAPTER FIFTY-FOUR

Victor had been miffed when Keystone Pharma called to say no planes were available. How can that be? he'd asked. After all, he was giving up a weekend to get them out of a jam. He was told the company's private jets had to be diverted to Tampa because of an emergency there. But he cheered up at the offer to have a limo pick him up at the airport and drive him to corporate headquarters. Quite a change of attitude from his last trip to Keystone, he mused.

On his way to Washington National Airport, Victor had stopped at the hospital to check on Matthew, to tell him that he'd be back too late that night to see him, but that he'd be there first thing in the morning. He found Matthew breathing easier, his skin less mottled, and his attitude cheerful. They'd talk tomorrow about arrangements for Matthew's discharge on Monday and his subsequent transfer to California.

During the flight, Victor pondered a professional problem. In his anxiety to rid his home of all traces of the experimental staph, he had destroyed years of his clandestine research. Now, when called upon to lead Keystone Pharma's new drug program, he no longer had the data that would propel them into the future. A short-term solution would be to go with the biskellin analog rather than the more toxic, but cheaper ticokellin—but in his basement he'd been developing a whole new generation of antibiotics. How could he not have kept a backup copy of his results in a secret, safe place?

The flight turned turbulent, and Victor was the last passenger to be served before the attendants were told to take their seats. As

Victor reached for his coffee, the plane bounced, splashing the hot, brown liquid all over his white dress shirt and pale-blue tie. "Soda water," he called. He thought he heard a hollow, "Sorry, sir."

So, shaken by the bumpy flight, coffee-stained, he showed up at Keystone determined to drive a hard bargain, not to be bested by the corporate honchos.

Dr. Minn greeted Victor and introduced him to the vice president of Human Resources, Al Mills. They drank coffee in the H.R. conference room this time, served in china cups with matching saucers. Yes, he had vaulted up the food chain.

CHAPTER FIFTY-FIVE

Charles took great pride in his home, built in the French Normandy style in 1945 on three wooded acres. Bountiful clusters of midnight-blue rhododendron surrounded the white mansion and lined the drive leading from the road. Everyone commented on the rhododendron. Not that he was into gardening; the huge blue-flowering plants had been there when he purchased the place three years ago.

Stan Proctor's reaction yesterday had been typical. Not many thirty-three-year-olds boasted a six-bedroom house, custom-designed pool complete with gazebo, three-car garage, and lush gardens. But isn't that what trust funds were for?

This morning he walked outside, noting that the pool cover was sagging and that the gardener had failed to remove a ladder leaning against the trellis. Mental note: call the lazy Negro. Even in his mind, he did not use the other *N* word lest it slip from his lips as the wrong moment. When you work for the government these days, you had to be careful. Civil rights advocates had infiltrated every agency. He thought about Stacy Jones. Never could he have endured being subordinate to her. Nor would he be. Instead he'd infect the whole lot of partying African Americans and any whites who chose to party with them. He'd been chosen to execute the preemptive strike.

Charles had two concerns. He had been mulling over what Russell's wife had told him. She thought that The Order was planning an explosion or water contamination. She'd shared her fears with him. Had she shared them with anyone else? Could Russell have gone to the police before The Order took him out? If he had, they'd know Charles's name. Would they put him on a watch list? Could they be following him? He couldn't help feeling smug. He'd done nothing to arouse suspicion. He'd gone to work yesterday, come home sick, had a visit from his boss, stopped by the Palace Hotel, but what of it? Then he'd gone to his friend's viewing and back home.

The second concern was more worrisome. After the profiteroles had been served tonight, it would take at least an hour for people to start getting sick. Charles had to hand it to Will Banks and The Order for choosing the dessert course. The victims would go home, start feeling ill during the night with fever and muscle pain. By morning they'd have difficulty breathing, high fever, extreme muscle pain, and horrible sores all over their body. They'd then start pouring into area hospitals. By mid-afternoon, panic will have set in, and by evening, the staph would have invaded body tissue. External lesions eating through skin and muscle. Internal organs under attack and susceptible to failure. This was the nature of the staph they were engineering at the CDC. Bioterrorism, masquerading as biomedical research. No wonder USAMRIID brass at Fort Detrick threatened to shut down this program just as they had a parallel effort several years ago at the NIH. In 1969, the United States outlawed organisms for bioterrorism, and in 1970, toxins.

Of course, he couldn't be sure of the timing of symptoms since his staph had only been tested in vitro—test tubes, petri dishes, not in vivo—people or even animals. But Charles was still uncertain as to what would happen to him. Why hadn't he been instructed what to do or where to go after dessert had been served? Was someone from The Order going to whisk him out of the Palace? Banks, perhaps? By tonight would he be in one of The Order's safe houses? Somewhere in North America or overseas? Maybe Canada, The Order liked to hang out in Canada. Or the Caribbean. Maybe the South of France—he'd mentioned Nice to Will. There was an excellent biotech lab there. Perfect for someone with his skills.

Charles walked the perimeter of his property and when he'd come full circle he checked his watch. Ten o'clock. The sky was blue, the sun promising to take the chill out of the air. All was serene among the rhododendrons and Charles promised himself that wherever he ended up, he'd plant lush beds of the spectacular plant. He'd read that the genus rhododendron, which includes azaleas, grew almost anywhere in the world.

He'd gone outside without a jacket and it was time for him to say goodbye to his grounds.

Entering the warmth of his home, his mind drifted to his lab at the CDC. Had he left any trace yesterday? When Stacy got there, would she find anything out of order? She was a suspicious, small-minded woman, always looking to find something that he'd done wrong.

And how long would it take the CDC to track the Palace outbreak to him? But so what? He'd be far away from Atlanta, with a whole new identity. And the pride of his parents.

According to the plan, Charles had two hours before he was scheduled to enrich the media for his cultures. He strolled through his house to the front door and out to the porch to pick up his copy of the *Atlanta Constitution*. As he turned to go indoors, he opened the paper and scanned a front-page headline, "Fatal Staph Infection Rampant at Tampa Hospital."

Was it possible that Stacy had something to do with this? Could she, too, be trying to commit mass murder with the staph strain from the CDC lab? Impossible.

CHAPTER FIFTY-SIX

Laura slept until Tim tapped her on the shoulder at nine thirty on Saturday morning. Three and a half hours of sleep since the alarm had awakened her on Thanksgiving morning, fifty hours ago. Like the old days when she'd been a resident, only she'd been younger then.

"I thought you'd want to wake up, but I hated to—"

"Of course, Tim." Laura sat up. "How is Natalie?"

"I just checked." Tim sat down next to her on her cot. "Her heart rate is rapid, her PO2 is low despite optimal ventilation, her temp's at 104.8."

She leaned in to him as close as she could in their bulky isolation suits, feeling the tears start to trickle down her cheeks. "So high, even with the icepacks," she said, her voice shaky.

"Ma'am, I'm a nurse with the CDC, with the experimental drug," a voice announced. Laura had never been called ma'am in this hospital.

Laura looked to the tangerine polyester garbed person, a man this time, judging by the bass voice.

"You already signed, waiving all liability, so I just have to confirm the patient's identity." He walked over to Natalie, picked up her hand in his gloved one, and checked her wrist bracelet. "Natalie Nelson. Yes." Then he looked at Laura. "Ma'am, are you Dr. Nelson?"

"Yes," Laura said. Not wanting chitchat. Just wanting that drug flowing through Natalie's veins.

"This is the last dose we have in house," the nurse said, holding up the vial of amber-colored liquid. "I was told to get it to this room. I've heard lots of people talking about you tonight. My CDC colleagues and the nurses here. They are real grateful for you being there for your patients, but honest to God, I didn't know that your own daughter was one of the infected ones. God bless her, ma'am— I mean, doctor—and you, too." Then he turned to Tim, "And her father—? God bless you, too."

"Thank you," Laura managed to answer, as she watched the drug finally flow from the disposable syringe into the plastic tube inserted into Natalie's arm.

"Please, God," she said aloud, followed by a silent prayer, the Memorare, "Remember, most gracious Virgin Mother, that never—"

When the nurse left, Laura sat on the cot beside Tim, both watching the rhythmic rise and fall of Natalie's chest.

Tim held her hand until someone wearing a gown, mask, and the rest of the mandatory garb, opened the door to announce that he had breakfast, but they'd have to leave the patient's room to eat. "Bacon and eggs and toast, orange juice, and a pot of coffee."

Laura was about to decline when Tim said, "You need your strength. We're going out there. You are going to eat something."

She did. The coffee perked her up.

Laura went to check on the remaining patients in the ICU. When she'd left them three and a half hours ago, two still had been alive, the younger woman with the colectomy for ulcerative colitis and an older man. They were infected with the staph, but their infection had started several hours after the first cases and so far had not been as severe. Why? she wondered. Especially the older man with heart disease.

This time, while away from Natalie's room, she wanted to personally check on her chief resident Michelle, on Bunnie the cleaning lady, and the other patients in the makeshift ICU. This was the second of seven rapidly assembled ICUs, Laura had been told. The number of staph disease cases continued to escalate.

Laura really didn't want to know the latest count, the CDC was tracking the epidemiology. But what had Bunnie tried to tell her in the E.R.? Less than twenty-four hours ago? Felt like a lifetime. The cleaning woman's words haunted her. What had she seen? Something that might shed light on the disaster in the ICU? Was Bunnie still alive?

Hampered by a sky-blue suit and the rest of the protective gear the CDC had provided, Laura made her way down the near-empty corridors. She thought about Tim. How she was leaning on him. How willing he'd been to step in, almost as a surrogate father. For all these years she'd been fiercely independent, but did she need somebody? Did her children deserve somebody, a man in their lives?

CHAPTER FIFTY-SEVEN

Alone in her P3 lab in the early hours of Saturday morning, among banks of sophisticated state-of-the-art gene sequencers and gas chromatograph-mass spectrometers and low-tech incubation baths and autoclaves, Stacy was free to experiment. On her own, unsupervised.

However reluctant she'd been to leave the epidemiology drama in Tampa, now back in her lab, she was in her element. The only thing she hated about her lab was the fastidious entry-exit process and the cumbersome garb. She might as well be experimenting in outer space, contending with the full-body cover and controlled airflow through a mask that she'd never get used to.

Today, seclusion was her ally as she went about collecting a series of samples from the CDC's staphylococcal culture bank. She had set the Tampa culture to run on autopilot while she gathered cultures that she hypothesized should show similar characteristics to Tampa's. Stacy selected six specimens from the archived culture bank; two from the NIH's discontinued research—one dating from earlier in their program and one from just before the program had been discontinued. And to the chagrin of the NIH, the research had been transferred to the CDC. If she recalled correctly, that was about the same time that Keystone Pharma had hired Norman Kantor. The other four specimens, she chose at random.

And the CDC had taken NIH's staph research further, as Stacy well knew. Her staph cultures were indeed resistant and more virulent. If her strain ever got into the population, by the time those infected were able to get to medical treatment, their organs would already be liquefying—and Keystone Pharma's ticokellin would be completely useless. The thought made Stacy shudder. She loved her work and though she realized the endgame for developing such potent strains was to facilitate the development of new families of antibiotics, in her heart of hearts, she believed that such lethal research should be conducted exclusively by USAMRIID at Fort Detrick, Maryland, where biodefense was the mission and where security was ironclad.

Once Stacy had her selected cultures all set up on automated equipment, she thought about calling home. She should be sitting around Mom's living room gabbing with her sisters. That prick Charles Scarlett had been scheduled to work today. She'd counted on the four-day holiday weekend off. Too bad she'd had to leave so abruptly. Mom had wanted her to talk to her youngest sister Katie about her boyfriend. What had that been about? Stacy thought about calling home, but she knew that as soon as she got into the family chitchat, an alarm would go off and she'd have to attend to one of her machines.

Besides, there were only fifteen minutes left for the Tampa culture. And then she could plug the data into her computer program and get an early idea of comparative results. Don't forget to delete the results, she reminded herself. The culture that she was testing had not officially arrived in Atlanta yet.

In the meantime, she did have time to go into the CDC culture database and prep everything in advance of replating her own, routine cultures. As things worked out, Charles's absence today meant she had the lab to herself and could test the covert Tampa culture unobserved. Had Stan Proctor actually said he intended to fire Charles? An appropriate step, but would he be able to? Charles was a government employee. And he did know the lab backward and forward. The thought of training a replacement made Stacy groan.

Stacy hated wasting time, and though she had to wait for the equipment to finish running her clandestine experiment before she went into the incubators, she logged into the tracking program that she and Charles shared. Immediately, she noticed that the timing seemed odd. Yesterday, Charles had been in that incubator longer than usual. Stacy idly wondered why.

Nothing she could do now but wait. Wait for her experimental results. Wait to get into the incubator. Then she remembered—that banquet tonight. No way would she would finish here in time to attend. And thank goodness for that. Her hair and nails were a disaster. She had nothing to wear. She was dead tired, too.

CHAPTER FIFTY-EIGHT

"Dr. Nelson, is that you under the moonwalker disguise?" Michelle Wallace asked, her voice low and hoarse from the endotracheal tube, now removed. "Everybody looks like they're from outer space."

Laura found Michelle alone in a room with four beds, two empty. Her chief resident sat propped up, a tray of clear liquids in front of her: orange Jello, brownish broth, a mug of tea. An IV bag hung over her bed, she still had a Foley catheter draining her urine, and nasal prongs clamped under her nostrils.

"Michelle," Laura could hear the relief in her own voice. "You're going to be okay."

"I think so. I was the first to get the antibiotic. I told them I knew the risks, I had just researched the drug for you. If you hadn't given me that assignment, I don't know what I would have done."

"The ticokellin worked. Thank God," Laura said, thinking as much about Natalie as Michelle. But had Natalie gotten the drug in time? She'd been given the last available dose, but what about all the other patients? Keystone Pharma had to send more.

"From what they say, it starts working within the first four hours. I just wish Bunnie—" Michelle glanced to the empty bed next to hers. "She was too sick to give informed consent and her family was too scared of the side effects and she— They took her away a few minutes ago. And the lady in the other bed, she died too. You know her. She was the ICU clerk on duty when the patients in there started getting sick."

Laura felt her heart plunge. The amiable desk clerk—the one she'd warned not to eat the apple—dead, too. And she never would get any more information from Bunnie.

"Michelle, do you remember when I came down to the E.R. just after you and Bunnie got there?"

"No, they said I was delirious. They told me you were there, though. I've been so worried about you, Dr. Nelson. You were there from the beginning, too. We all were so vulnerable. Even the woman who found Bunnie and brought her to the E.R. has it. They said she's still waiting for ticokellin. But I don't know; there are so many rumors. I can't tell you how glad I am that you didn't get it. And thankful that I got ticokellin in time. Now I just hope I don't get aplastic anemia."

"Michelle, you're doing fine, and we'll be back in the operating room soon," Laura said. "But we have to find out what happened here. Do you have any idea how a staph like this could take over the ICU? Any idea at all?"

"No, Dr. Nelson, we've had a stellar infection control record. We were worried about AIDS since we'd not seen it in Tampa. So little is known about how the virus is transmitted, how to test for it, but staph—"

"There's just one connection that I can think of, but it's so bizarre." Laura decided that Michelle was alert and oriented enough to bring this up. "Matthew Mercer, our AIDS patient. His father—different last name—comes charging in here, demanding that we get ticokellin, claims it's his drug, from his friend at Keystone Pharma. He was not successful, nor was I when I tried. Reasonable, since the trials had just been terminated." Laura suppressed a chill—her daughter and Michelle had been subjected to this unsafe investigational drug.

"But Matthew responded to the usual antibiotics for staph, didn't he?" Michelle asked.

"Yes. And Victor Worth took Matthew home in a medical jet on Thanksgiving afternoon."

"Good thing," Michelle said, "with his compromised immune

system, he'd be dead for sure. I really liked Matthew, but I dread what's in his future."

"There's one more thing," Laura said. "I've been so distracted that I haven't given it any thought. But that friend of Worth's at Keystone Pharma. Turns out he had retired, and he was a patient in the ICU. Not our patient, but an overflow patient from the medical service. They were treating him for arrhythmias triggered by a pulmonary embolus. Name was Norman Kantor."

"I remember him," Michelle volunteered. "A bit of a jerk, and his wife was a super bitch. What happened to him?"

"A victim," Laura said. "He's dead."

"Holy shit. I mean, don't you think that's strange? Dying of a staph infection when that's been your life's work?"

"Even stranger, with his former staph researcher colleague on-site?"

Then Laura told Michelle that Natalie had been infected and that she was about to go back to her, check on whether the tico-kellin was working.

"I had no idea," Michelle said. "The rumor mill isn't perfect. This must be so difficult for you, don't spend another minute here."

"Her boyfriend, Trey Standish, is dead, and I have to tell her. Michelle, that terrifies me, having to tell her."

"Oh my God, I had no idea—about him and your daughter. He seemed like a good kid. Nice parents, too. I spoke to them a couple of times, but I never saw your daughter with him."

"Long story," said Laura. "On my way to Natalie's room, I'm going to stop by the ICU to check on the two patients there. I keep wondering why they survived and the other five did not." Could their cases help explain what had started this horrible epidemic?

"Dr. Nelson, please get some rest. You look so tired. Almost as bad as I do, and I've been in a coma."

"Time for your lunch," Laura said. "Too bad they didn't give you the cherry flavored Jello."

"Thank you, Dr. Nelson, and thanks for coming to see me in the E.R. even if I can't remember. All I remember about that night was Bunnie—hallucinating about some ghost doctor feeding all the patients in the ICU. 'Evil doctor,' she kept raving.

Laura shook her head. She couldn't ask what "evil doctor" had crossed paths with the cleaning lady in the E.R. Or, know for sure whether Bunnie had been hallucinating on her deathbed.

"Excuse me, ladies." A voice from the bed across the room, weak but familiar. "Have you forgotten about me?"

Laura turned about, then bolted across the room, stopping at the edge of the bed. "Oh, Ed," she cried. "Thank God. I was so worried. I hadn't heard. I am so, so glad to see you. You're going to be okay?"

"I tried, Laura. How many dead?"

"I don't know, Ed, but you are the real hero here—"

CHAPTER FIFTY-NINE

Charles had heard nothing from Banks. He liked the idea of leaving his parents a puzzle-type clue as to where he'd be, but without a hint of where he would end up, he was helpless. Banks was smart, Charles knew, and would try to protect The Order from just such a leak. Banks was ruthless, too. *What were The Order's plans for Charles?*

Nothing to do but wait. Just wait until three o'clock when he'd leave for the Palace. He'd been told specifically to leave at three. So he would. Until then he'd pace, too keyed up to read or to eat or to think or to do anything but breathe in and breathe out.

Practical person that he was, Charles had written a last will and testament when he turned twenty-one. His only heirs: his parents. His trust fund, his estate, his art collection, his fleet of cars, all would revert to Chas and Rosabelle Scarlett. Not that they needed the money. They epitomized wealth. He had no one else, no other heirs. Should anything happen to him, when would they find out? How? Would Will Banks make good on his promise to let them know about their son's heroic sacrifice? Would his mother turn his mansion into a shrine?

All for you, Dad, to make you proud. Finally.

CHAPTER SIXTY

Every process executed in the incubator was monitored and recorded. Every moment of the undertaking was accounted for. Start inoculation. Complete inoculation. That sort of thing. And under the watchful eyes of sophisticated security cameras.

Stacy worked in the claustrophobic space, garbed as required in full-body cover and breathing through a respirator. God forbid even one of these ultra-virulent microorganisms escaped. She forced herself to focus on her chore, a routine replating of each series of cultures from one nutritionally depleted petri dish to another filled with fresh nourishing media. This task had to be repeated every twenty-four hours and certain procedures and tests and documentation had to be completed.

After her observation that Charles's last foray into the incubator on Thursday clocked longer than usual, Stacy continued to wonder why. With every procedural step accounted for, why had he stayed forty-eight minutes inside rather than the usual forty-three?

While she waited for her Tampa culture experiment to complete the autopilot stage, she investigated the incubator research log. Charles's and hers. The historical range had been forty-one to forty-five minutes. Never forty-eight minutes. She wondered why he'd been in there so long. Then she realized, that the guy had been sick. When you're not feeling well, everything takes longer. Right?

When she thought about it, this small aberration no longer seemed important.

Stacy's mind drifted back to the culture that she'd snuck in from Tampa, the purloined culture. What if it did match the cultures that the NIH had developed toward the end of their staph research tenure in Bethesda? What would that mean? Coincidence? Possibly. And what had Laura said about the two men working on this staph at the final phase? Norman Kantor, who had headed up the infectious disease research at Keystone Pharma after leaving NIH, and his junior colleague Victor Worth, who stayed at NIH but was reassigned to a project on fungi. Kantor had died of the Tampa staph, Laura had pointed out, and Worth had been there about the same time, visiting a relative. How weird was that?

That connection stuck in Stacy's mind as she moved the bacterial material from plate to plate, watching the clock on the program monitor. She finished at forty-four minutes. A minute longer than her usual time, but she'd been so distracted, mostly thinking about the Tampa staph.

Charles had set a record for slow: forty-eight minutes. The oppressive heat of the incubator started to get to her—then came the realization that, if Charles had been febrile, as he'd claimed, he'd have rushed through the culture plating. With all the gear they had to wear, the temperature in the incubator was oppressive, marginally tolerable under normal circumstances, but with a high fever? He'd have rushed through the tasks, needing to cool down. Maybe her instincts had been right, and Charles had been up to something Thursday.

Stacy stepped away from the computer input panel and gazed about the ceiling, noting the familiar cameras, lights flicking as usual. No doubt that would raise the suspicion of any attentive security guard. Like, why is Dr. Jones checking out the cameras?

Nevertheless, Stacy traced the perimeter of the room. The cameras seemed to cover every square inch, following her. Then she saw it. In the far corner, an area maybe a square foot of a lab bench was off-camera. She stepped to the space, looked upward, and dramatically waved. If this area was under surveillance, she'd have a visit from security the moment she reached her office. But she wanted to make sure. Before leaving, she bent down, closely inspecting the bench and the flooring beneath. She saw nothing but a bare surface. Why was she wasting her time in here?

Time to check out. After passing through the complex decontamination process, Stacy headed down the hall and around the corner to her office. With the cultures replated for this go-round, she was fascinated to find out whether security would show up to check her out. What would she tell them? Why had she been wildly waving at the camera? She found her office empty, poured herself a cup of coffee, then waited for the buzzer letting her know that the Tampa culture experiment was ready to read—the Tampa culture not yet officially in her possession.

CHAPTER SIXTY-ONE

Emma had never been a "lady who lunched." Certainly, she'd had her share of business lunches, mostly tedious, none social. She had few close female friends and of those, most were married to rich and successful men. They shopped and gossiped and had their hair and nails done. Whereas Emma had worked fifteen-hour days, managed to raise seven children, and get a newspaper out.

But today being the first official day of her retirement, she accepted an invitation to a celebratory lunch at the Atlanta Press Club. Women only, a group of forty of her closest work associates, her small circle of friends, and her female children and grandchildren. A "dress-up" affair her own mother would have called it, and Emma would have given anything if her mother and her four sisters, now all deceased, could be there to share this special day. She was the last living sibling of the founding Goode family, all of whom had worked at the paper in one capacity or another. She missed them all.

But to look on the bright side, seated at the tables surrounding her were her own daughters, Patricia, Deborah, Maxine, and Caroline, her two daughters-in-law, and her youngest son's fiancée. Even better, five of her precious granddaughters. She had eight, but the younger three needed a nap to get them through the evening festivities.

The ladies talked of everything and nothing, bouncing from civil rights to Howard Stern's radio program. From the terrorist dubbed the Unabomber to the first AIDS-themed TV movie, *An*

Early Frost. From the new world chess champion to the latest Challenger mission. From Paul McCartney's *Spies Like Us* to Egyptian commandoes storming Malta to reclaim their hijacked jet.

Women who knew their current affairs. They had to; many were in the news business.

As dessert was served, a New York-style cheesecake surrounded by blueberries, the mood turned nostalgic as one after another of Emma's cherished family and friends spontaneously shared a favorite memory.

"I don't know how much of this I can take," Emma said with a broad smile. "I signed on for tonight, knowing that there'd be speeches, but I thought you girls would give me a break."

As the event came to an end, Emma, never one to waste food, told her daughters-in-law to take the extra cheesecake back for the "boys."

"Grandma," Karen, her eldest granddaughter, said, "they're not going to need it with the dinner we have planned tonight. And guess what I heard just before we left to come here. John Kennedy Jr. is going to be here. He's flying in to represent the Kennedys. You know how supportive they've always been to us. I had wanted to sit next to Eddie Murphy, but now—"

That announcement kicked off a new level of buzz, and amidst it, Emma was able to slip away with her granddaughter as her chauffeur.

CHAPTER SIXTY-TWO

There could be no mistake. Shaken, Stacy stood up and went to look out her office window, but retained nothing of what she'd just seen in the familiar hustle-bustle below. She returned to her desk, sat down, took a breath, and went over the data one more time. Her hunch had been right. The Tampa culture results and the 1977 experimental bacteria out of the NIH lab were too close to attribute to chance. Not precisely superimposable, but much closer than she'd had any right to imagine when she had the harebrained idea to secure a sample of the Tampa culture.

She now had a dilemma. The legitimate sample coming via CDC courier still had not arrived. And she had uncovered vital information. She had confirmed the connection between the staph ravaging Tampa and the staph grown by the NIH in Bethesda, preserved here in the CDC Atlanta archives. She knew of the professional connection between Norman Kantor and Victor Worth, and she knew both were in Tampa. One a victim of the staph; the other the father of a patient. How did these connections add up? Could she afford to wait for the arrival of the Tampa culture, redo the testing, report the results all in due course? She decided to call Laura.

Whoever answered at the hospital reported that Dr. Nelson was under quarantine.

"I'm from the CDC," Stacy insisted. "Put me through. If she's in quarantine, the EOIP team will know exactly where she is."

The individual manning the phones did not know what to do.

Not good, Stacy noted. In an emergency such as this epidemic, incoming communications must be triaged with confidence. She asked to be transferred to Natalie Nelson's room.

Tim answered, telling her that Laura was expected back at any moment from checking the ICU patients. Laura's mobility, along with anyone who circulated in the hospital, was severely hampered by the bulky equipment they had to wear. "But you'd know all about that since it's your agency calling the shots."

"I have to talk to her," Stacy said. "I've directly connected the bacteria that's killing patients in Tampa to the bacteria developed in the Bethesda NIH lab."

"I'm too tired to think. What does that mean?"

"I don't know, but—"

"Hold on, Stacy, Laura's getting suited up to come in, and she has somebody with her. Somebody I recognize from seeing her on TV. Your big boss, Dr. Madeleine Cox, the director herself."

"Good," Stacy said, "I'd asked her to personally check on Natalie. Do you mind if I hold on? I may need to talk to her, too."

Stacy felt sweat in the small of her back. Should she tell Director Cox, or should she hold off for now? Protect herself—and the Tampa City lab director who'd provided the staph sample? She had a few moments to temporize while Laura and Dr. Cox conferred in Natalie's room.

"Dr. Cox," Laura said, "I so appreciate your taking time to check on Natalie."

"I understand she got the ticokellin infusion. You have your friend Dr. Jones to thank for that. She put two and two together pretty quickly. If not for her, I don't know how long it would have taken to convince me to send our EOIP team down here."

"Yes, I know," Laura said, already at Natalie's side, looking reassured by the steady beep-beep of the heart monitor, then dismayed by the pallor of her still unconscious child.

The director of the CDC consulted her notebook. "Your daughter was injected almost four hours ago. She should be showing signs of improvement."

"Tim," Laura said, "about Natalie?" Before he could answer, she recovered her etiquette, "Oh, I'm so sorry, Dr. Cox, let me introduce you to my friend, a peds surgeon from Children's in Philadelphia, Dr. Tim Robinson. He's been here the entire time with Natalie, while I've been shuttling between my patients and my daughter. "

"Holding her own," Tim said, the telephone receiver still in his hand. "Not worse. Not much better. Since you went upstairs, Laura, she has not stirred. To be expected, since she's sedated." He nodded to Dr. Cox, "It's good of you to be here. And good timing, Dr. Jones is calling." He held out the phone midway between the two women. "I believe she wants to talk to both of you."

"I'll take it," said Dr. Cox.

Laura watched as the director listened to whatever Stacy had to say. She shot a questioning look at Tim, who only shrugged.

Laura and Tim heard the rhythmic heave of Natalie's respirator.

"Stacy, I don't know what to say." Dr. Cox's back was to them, as she hunched over the phone.

"You put me in a precarious position." Another pause, then a huge sigh. "All right. I'll act on it, but you'd better jump on those cultures. The courier should be there any minute."

Dr. Cox tapped her foot as she listened to more from Stacy.

"I have to get on this now. I'll go over the details on this end with Dr. Nelson. And, no, you can't decline the party tonight. You must be there. As appropriate, make my apologies. Make sure that everyone knows how serious the situation is in Tampa—why I'm not at the banquet. Etcetera. By the way, you'll be seated at the table headed by Congressman John Conyers of Michigan, and his assistant, Rosa Parks."

What was that all about, Laura wondered. A Michigan native, she knew all about Representative Conyers. He'd stood on top of a car during the Detroit riots, trying to quell the looting and the burning and the sniping. And Rosa Parks, the first lady of civil rights, sitting at the table with Stacy? And what had the CDC director heard from Stacy that involved *details* she had to go over with Laura? Dr. Cox had just hung up the phone.

"Okay, Dr. Nelson, I need to take you into my confidence, and Dr. Robinson. Are you both okay with confidentiality?"

"Yes," Laura and Tim said as one.

"Before Stacy left the Tampa City Hospital, she was able to get her hands on a culture of the staph we're dealing with—a sample the CDC did not authorize, I'm afraid. But back in our Atlanta lab, she did some tests. She's determined that the Tampa staph strain is almost identical to that developed about nine years ago at the NIH by Dr. Norman Kantor and Dr. Victor Worth. Now Dr. Kantor, a patient in your ICU is dead, and Dr. Worth, who was visiting a patient here, has returned to Bethesda. Talk to me, what's the connection?"

Tim kept silent, looking at Laura, deferring to her.

"Tim's from Philadelphia," Laura explained. "Since arriving at Tampa City, he's never left Natalie's side. He's had no interaction with either Kantor or Worth."

Tim simply nodded, a silent assent.

"Let me tell you all I know." Laura related to Dr. Cox the story of her recent Tampa City patient, Matthew Mercer, and his father, Victor Worth, and Dr. Worth's link to deceased Tampa City patient, Dr. Norman Kantor, retired research head of Keystone Pharma. "Having an AIDS patient in the ICU, even though he was in isolation, spooked a lot of the staff, and we started out short staffed that day, Thanksgiving, when the breakout happened."

Dr. Cox listened, asking questions about Victor Worth: exactly when he arrived, exactly how he arranged for the discharge of his son.

Laura answered to the best of her knowledge.

"I need to call the FBI," Dr. Cox concluded with another sigh. "You'll be asked more questions, I'm sure. Again, our discussion is confidential, please. This all may come to nothing more than a horrible coincidence. In the meantime, my most sincere wishes for your daughter's recovery."

The director turned to leave, about to start the decontamination and regowning process.

Laura absorbed Dr. Cox's revelations. Had Victor Worth inadvertently brought the staph into Tampa City? But didn't he tell her he now works in mycology? Then she remembered what Bunnie had said.

"Dr. Cox," she called.

The director turned.

"This may mean nothing, but one of the Tampa City staph victims, ICU housekeeper Bunnie Miller, said she saw someone doing something to the patients as would a doctor. But Bunnie didn't recover. Maybe someone else saw something."

After Dr. Cox left, Laura called her mother, talked to each of her children, tried her best to reassure them. If Natalie was no better by tomorrow, she didn't know what she'd tell them.

Laura gently hung up the receiver. She then took Tim's arm and led him from his vigil at the bedside chair to the cot, where she coaxed him to lie back against the lone pillow. When he'd closed his eyes, she covered him with a light blanket. Her only wish now was to sit in the chair by the bed and hold Natalie's hand.

CHAPTER SIXTY-THREE

Charles changed from khaki pants and pale-yellow golf shirt to jeans and a black tee shirt to a navy-blue suit with a crisp white shirt and a striped blue tie to black dress pants and a blue button-down shirt, no tie. Just how was an assistant pastry chef with murder on his mind supposed to dress?

No reason he'd attract attention on his way into the hotel, and once in the kitchen, he'd be wearing a chef's white coat and checkered pants. He was more worried about his exit from the Palace that night, trying to foresee glitches in the scenario.

Would the profiteroles be injected as they sat on baking sheets? Or as they were transferred from the sheets to the individual dessert plates? Or would he do it once they sat on the individual plates? He'd not been paying close enough attention to instructions. He'd have plenty of time to work it out with Collins. Based on the classy banquets he'd attended, dessert would be served as the speakers began their accolades, honoring this one or that.

He hadn't thought much about tonight's honoree, a seventy-year-old black woman from a family, who through their newspaper, had promulgated so much injustice and propaganda that The Order had chosen her as a worthy target. Did it bother him that the woman was seventy? Not really. She was just an excuse to wipe out three generations of blacks at one sitting. Yes, there would be whites, too. He accepted that. Whites who associated with blacks were not worth worrying about, just as Banks had said.

Once dessert had been served, the guests would finish their coffee, wait politely for the speeches to end, and begin to leave. Would they feel ill by then? Charles didn't think so. He estimated that it would take a good two hours for the staph to flare up in the body, depositing its toxin throughout the organs. This strain had never been in humans, so he couldn't be too sure of the timing, but before anyone suspected an epidemic, he'd be long gone.

In jeans and an ordinary shirt, he'd be any fairly young guy leaving the hotel. That reminded him: what car to drive? He'd half expected that The Order would send a car for him. That way his own car wouldn't be left in the Palace Hotel garage. But it was time to leave and no sign of transportation courtesy of The Order. He'd certainly expected another communication from Banks, but all quiet on that front, too.

Three o'clock p.m., Charles walked out of his home, turned on the security code, and locked his door. He carried with him a basic overnight bag. In it were the usual toiletries, a change of clothes, and a selection of family photos. After tonight, he'd be starting anew. He just wished he knew where.

Standing in his pristine garage, Charles looked from his Porsche sports car to his elegant Cadillac sedan. Then he jerked open the door to the Porsche and slid in.

What did it matter? By the end of this day, The Order already would have whisked him away to parts unknown.

CHAPTER SIXTY-FOUR

When Special Agent Something introduced himself, Stacy had a moment of terror. *Had they come for her?* But the handsome young black agent appeared deferential, if poker faced. He made sure nothing in his expression hinted he could be surprised to meet an African American female researcher qualified to handle top-priority and top-security biological samples. His stay on the CDC campus was brief, however. Not even macho FBI men courted unnecessary proximity to a container of deadly staph cultures. For her part, Stacy could not allow lethal bacteria to scare her. She knew the biology cold, took all the prescribed precautions, never cut corners, and never had contracted so much as a sore throat.

She asked whether he was returning to Tampa tonight.

"No, I work in Atlanta. Heading home now." He eyed the package she'd just signed for and then carefully placed on her desk. "Looking forward to a very long, very hot shower. With Lava soap if I can find any."

Stacy wished she could prolong the conversation. The guy was genuine flirt material. Stud city. But, of course, she had other urgent priorities. She had carefully explained to Director Cox why she'd transported the Tampa cultures. Now she'd better replicate her work on the purloined—better word than filched—cultures, if she were to keep her neck from the chopping block. The test results would be identical, she reasoned. But what if they weren't?

Nice escort for a black tie dinner, she thought as the agent retreated, clearly wanting out of there.

"Oh, leave a card, please?" she suggested, all business. What would her sisters say if she showed up next Thanksgiving with this hunk?

"Sure." Special Agent Hunk extended a worn leather case so she could take one of the cards emblazoned with the dark gold-and-blue insignia.

She nodded as he closed the door behind him. Obstructing justice? Violating CDC rules? Whatever her crime, he should be her arresting agent.

Pulling herself together, Stacy proceeded to the P3 lab to unwrap the package. She had all the machines up and running, having been through the drill earlier in the day. No reason for the test per se to take more than ninety minutes. Then she'd have to call and assure Director Cox that the results of this test matched those she'd obtained with the Tampa culture. Then she'd have to rush home to get ready for the Palace event. Nothing much she could do with her hair other than pile it up on top of her head and stick in some rhinestone pins to secure it. Her nails were a mess, but maybe, just maybe, she'd have time to redo them. The dress—maybe she'd pull out that black satin number she'd worn as her sister's maid of honor. Thank God it was black and just enough off the shoulder. With black stiletto heels, she'd be presentable, just barely.

As her experiments perked, Stacy started thinking of what questions she wanted to ask Rosa Parks. She knew Rosa was born in Tuskegee, Alabama; her grandparents were former slaves. She'd attended segregated schools but then one day, when the segregated rows of seats on the bus were pushed farther back to accommodate white passengers, in a singular act of courage, she had refused to give up her seat. Media reports of her arrest triggered the historic boycott and legal actions so pivotal to the civil rights movement.

Stacy wondered if she'd mind being asked questions about what gave her that courage. What had prompted her move from Tuskegee to Detroit? What could she, Stacy Jones, do to carry on Rosa's legacy?

"Ding!" Testing complete. Results to be read and interpreted.

CHAPTER SIXTY-FIVE

Natalie still had not stirred, but her blood tests had improved. Kidney function, electrolytes, and white blood count, all abnormal, but getting better. The ticokellin was working. If Victor Worth had anything to do with the development of the drug, as he had claimed, Laura wanted to hug him. His research would save Natalie's life. Thank God.

Director Madeleine Cox requested a meeting in the ICU. Laura hated to leave Natalie yet again, but if she could help Stacy out of a bind, she knew she should. What was Director Cox up to? Laura hadn't managed to concentrate on what Cox had said in Natalie's room after Stacy's call. But Victor Worth finally should be recognized by Cox's agency for developing a drug effective against methicillin and vancomycin resistant staph. She wondered how his pleasant son Matthew was doing. Well, she hoped. Miraculous that he'd left the hospital before the epidemic would have ended his life. Lucky for him, his staph infection was susceptible to methicillin.

Ticokellin doses, now in short supply, were under the CDC control and Natalie might need additional doses. Another reason Laura was on her way to the ICU to meet Cox. But the specter of the deadly side effect, aplastic anemia, still lingered.

As she approached the ICU, Laura slowed, anticipating security control and the isolation protocol. At last count, only two of the original seven patients survived. So far. The fatalities: the two patients she'd operated on five days ago, the good guys, Bart Kelly and Tom Mancini; and the forty-eight-year-old nurse with complications after a hysterectomy; Dr. Worth's colleague, Norman Kantor, former Keystone Pharma research director, in the ICU for complications following hip surgery; and Natalie's love, Trey Standish, a healthy adolescent boy, who should have been the most resistant.

Still alive in the unit: Markus Riedenberg, an eighty-two-year-old man admitted after an observed cardiac arrest in a department store, and Holly Knight, age thirty-three, who'd had a colectomy for ulcerative colitis. In each of these staph-infected patients, symptoms showed up about fifteen hours later than in the five patients who already had died. Each of the surviving two had been treated with ticokellin, and Laura would learn soon whether they'd responded.

Director Cox met Laura just outside the ICU.

"I'd like you to listen to what Ms. Knight has to say," Director Cox got down to business. "Come over here."

Cox introduced Laura to two men wearing protective gear; the pair of FBI agents stood as far as they could from the patient's bedside.

Laura had not been Holly Knight's attending physician, but she had rounded on her with the students and house staff on Wednesday. She remembered Chief Resident Michelle Wallace had pointed out the high risk of colon cancer with the patient's ulcerative colitis, and that Holly had a strong family history of cancer as well as a history of severe bleeding. So at thirty-three, she'd opted for a procedure that would mean wearing a colostomy bag for the rest of her life. What she had not bargained for was a postoperative course to include massive blood loss, followed by a severe transfusion reaction that landed her in the ICU—where she would catch a raging staph infection.

"Thank you, Dr. Nelson," Holly said. "All of the patients and nurses have talked about how when everyone started getting terribly sick, you were the one here for us." She hesitated, looking away from her visitors toward the empty bed next to hers. "The patient next to me was a nurse and knew you, but she died."

Laura wanted to say something, something appropriate, but no words came.

The male agents seemed to shuffle, impatient, Laura suspected, to leave this hotbed of infection.

Director Cox moved in a little closer and said, "Holly, you are one of the lucky ones. Your symptoms started much later than all the others, except for Mr. Riedenberg." Cox gestured to the elderly gentleman across the room, his head hidden under an oxygen tent. "You told the FBI agents that the cleaning lady saw something strange and that she told the patient next to you, the nurse?"

"I did hear her," Holly's eyes widened. "She said to the nurse, 'You saw that new doctor? I've never seen him here.'

"I heard the nurse say, 'No, but I've been so drugged up, I wouldn't know my own physician.'

"'Well, he gave you some kind of a treatment, and the others, too,' the cleaning lady said. 'Not everybody. He didn't go to every bed.'

"The nurse said, 'I've had so many doctors probing me and sticking me with needles, I couldn't tell you, Bunnie. You know with all the students and residents and technicians, there's always somebody new.'"

"Bunnie," Laura said. "The woman who was trying to tell me something in the E.R. About a man doing something to the patients. Was the man she saw Victor Worth?"

"I've been trying to remember," Holly volunteered. "I think I saw him, too. I was groggy; he didn't stop at my bed."

You are one lucky woman, Laura thought.

Cox turned to the FBI agents. "This could be Victor Worth. He's the one we need to focus on. That's what I wanted you to hear."

One agent wrote in a notebook, but both eyed the ICU door.

Cox led Laura and the agents across the room to a quiet space. "According to the patient, a man apparently was seen in this unit, someone whom we think may have a link to this particular lethal bacteria strain. My labs in Atlanta are testing for this connection right now, and if it's confirmed, maybe we're looking at homicide. This 'doctor' may have got a hold of the toxic staph and purposefully infected the ICU."

"What if it was not purposeful, but accidental?" Laura dearly wanted to exclude the possibility of such evil afflicting her hospital.

"I realize that this is not an official investigation yet, gentlemen, but we need to show the patients and any staff Victor Worth's photo," Cox said. "Start with Holly. Find out exactly what she observed. And Mr. Riedenberg, he's having some lucid moments. Maybe he saw something that could connect Victor Worth to the infected patients."

"Worth was here visiting his son," Laura said. "His son was in isolation for HIV. Worth shouldn't have been in the main ICU."

Laura noticed the agents shift back even farther at the mention of HIV.

"Except," she continued, "that he knew a patient in the ICU, Norman Kantor. They'd worked together at the NIH. In the same staph program."

"How quickly can we get a photo of Victor Worth, circulate it? See if anyone saw him in the room?" Cox pointed to the agents. "Start with Holly Knight."

"And contact Kantor's family for background on the two men," Cox said, then added, "Please. And will you find out if Worth visited anyone in the ICU? This is where epidemiology and criminology intersect. If ever there's a time to cooperate, it'd be now."

Laura wasn't sure if the agents agreed, but she figured that until the CDC director got word from Stacy about the "official" cultures, Cox couldn't press too hard.

CHAPTER SIXTY-SIX

Charles found his chef's outfit waiting for him in Lonnie Collins's office. The white jacket large enough to slip over his shirt, and the baggy checkered pants that would fit over his jeans. He'd worn black sneakers that he figured would blend in with all the other kitchen workers' footwear.

"You just wait in here until I tell you," Lonnie instructed him. "You come out too soon and it won't take long for my team to figure out you don't know shit."

Charles looked at his watch. If dessert was served about nine, he had almost five hours to cool his heels.

"You got the nasty bacteria?" Lonnie asked. "I don't want any part of that. I'm going to step back and let you do your thing. I'm not touchin' that shit. I'm doing what I'm told to get my daughter back. That's it."

"You won't have to touch a thing," Charles said. "My delivery system is secure." And it was, too. Charles had secured a syringe that could efficiently deliver small aliquots of the staph-infested media. Just a simple tap. Tap, tap, tap, profiterole after profiterole. Lonnie had explained that there'd be fifteen plates per tray, pastries already on the individual plates. Shouldn't take more than fifteen to twenty seconds to complete a tray. Twenty-five trays of fifteen. Done. Mission accomplished.

"I gotta go out and set up," Collins said. "On my way out, I'm locking the door. You don't answer for anybody. Not the phone. Nothin'." Lonnie reached over and pulled a book off the shelf.

Here, you can read this. Take your mind off what's on the menu tonight." Lonnie tossed him a hardcover book with a cover illustration of a gorilla. "Skeleton Crew," he said. "Bunch of short stories. Stephen King. Scare the shit out of you."

Charles restricted his reading to nonfiction: biographies, mostly of American heroes. Short stories by Stephen King? He looked around the office for other books. There were none.

CHAPTER SIXTY-SEVEN

Now that Natalie was regaining consciousness, Laura could put it off no longer. She needed to tell Natalie about Trey. Seven years ago, she'd had to tell her children that their father was dead. Each one had taken it so differently. Natalie had been only ten years old then; now she had to tell that same child that someone she so held so dear had died. Natalie was now seventeen, and Trey had meant so much more to her than Laura ever could have imagined. And Laura felt profound guilt and a powerful sadness. Had she acted differently, could she have saved Trey Standish? Now she had to be the bearer of tragic news.

To prepare herself, Laura had called home. Her kids all had come back to the Tampa house, wanting to feel close to Natalie even though they knew they couldn't go to the hospital to see her. The grandparents were with the kids and Laura's housekeeper, Marcy Whitman, had come home, too. Her sister and brother remained at her parents' place on Anna Maria Island. The phone lines were kept burning back and forth.

Several times during the day, she'd talked to the kids—giving them updates on their sister, hearing the fear in their voices. Stories about the deadly staph epidemic at Tampa City dominated the local news, and with the arrival of the director of the CDC, now had gone national. Director Cox's appearance on the scene effectively marshaled resources, but also intensified the media hype. The reality was bad enough, the headlines way off the reality charts: Toxic Staph Annihilates Major U.S. City; Florida Quarantined; Scourge

Infecting Thousands With No Cure In Sight; Tourists Leaving The West Coast Of Florida In Droves.

Laura reviewed the events of the last six days. Because of her AIDS patient, she'd consulted Stacy, and mentioned her to Dr. Kellerman, who'd called Stacy at her mother's; with Natalie in grave condition, Stacy responded. By this fortunate chance, Stacy was present and had the authority to call in the CDC rapid-response team. She had such a reassuring effect on Laura—if Stacy could only have stayed in Tampa. And how ridiculous for her to have to fly back to Atlanta just because an insubordinate employee claimed to be ill. Stacy had predicted that he'd be fired, and Laura, too, hoped he would be.

Now as she dialed her home phone number, she knew she needed advice from Natalie's twin sister, Nicole. The girls were dramatically different in personality—but they shared everything. Laura remembered the birth control pills falling out of Nicole's purse. They must have been Natalie's. And she'd blamed Nicole.

Laura's mother answered the phone. "How is Natalie?" she asked, before Laura could get out a word.

"Better, Mom, she's responding to that investigational drug. Thank God."

"I've been praying so hard. We all just said the Rosary. All the kids and your dad."

"Thanks, Mom, for being there for me and the kids. Dad, too."

"All we've done is huddle together, trying to keep up each other's spirits. And, you—we've been worried about you, too. All that TV coverage about how fast the infection is spreading and how dangerous it is. You've been there the whole time. Honey, are you okay?"

"Yes." Yes, surprisingly. Once she realized that she faced an infectious disease out of control, she'd taken precautions, but being in such close contact with Natalie and being so exhausted, Laura knew she must have a solid immune system to thank for her health. Look at her colleague Ed Plant and her young resident, Michelle, not so lucky, but both had taken a dramatic turn for the better with the ticokellin. And Natalie was responding, too.

"Laura, how is Natalie's boyfriend. Trey? Nicole told me all about him. Everything, including the birth control pills you discovered."

"Mom, he died."

Laura heard a gasp, then silence. Finally, her mother said, "Maybe you should talk to Nicole."

But she hadn't yet talked to Natalie. "The boys? I never had much chance to see Mike and Kevin. They'll go back to school tomorrow and—"

"They won't go back until Natalie is okay. Neither of them."

"I think she's going to be okay, Mom. She's in and out of delirium, but when she wakes up, she'll want to know about Trey. What should I do? Should I tell her right off or wait until she's stronger?"

"Talk to Nicole," her mother repeated. "She'll know. Natalie and Nicole have always had a secret language, some kind of unique communication."

A brief silence on the other end before Laura heard her other twin daughter's urgent tone. "What did you tell Grandma about Trey?"

"Honey, he didn't make it. He died of the staph bacteria. He was one of the first infected, too many days before we got the new antibiotic."

Nicole burst into a breathy sob. "Mom, Natalie will not be okay without Trey. They loved each other. I mean, deep love. We're young, but Natalie loved him so much. She wanted to tell you, but—"

"Nicole, she did tell me before she fell into the coma. And I am so sorry that I accused you—"

"That doesn't matter," Nicole said between sobs. "Why didn't you tell me that she was in a coma?"

"That happened before she got the drug, but now she's coming out. What am I going to tell her about Trey?"

"You're sure that she's not going to die, Mom? You're *sure*?"

"All I can say, honey, is that she's rallying. Her vital signs are better, temperature not so high. She's starting to wake up, ask about Trey, then slip back to sleep."

"Because if you think she's going to die, don't tell her. Just say that he's getting better, but that she can't see him yet. But, Mom, if you think that Natalie will get well, she'll never forgive you if you don't tell her the truth. That's what you've always taught us. Even though we may not always have been one hundred percent honest with you. Natalie and I talk about this a lot. We need to know the truth."

"I'll tell her as soon as she seems stable enough. Maybe this evening, but I feel so inadequate." Laura had told so many people of all ages and all races and all religions that their loved ones had died. But how could she impose this agony on her own daughter? For an instant she wondered if she was the right one or Tim or another doctor, Kellerman maybe.

"You have to do it, Mom. She needs to hear it from you. Even if you're going to court against his dad. That really scared Natalie. That she and Trey would be like Romeo and Juliet, the families hating each other."

"I wish she'd told me," Laura said. "The beryllium case involving Mr. Standish is not personal. But—"

Nicole finished her sentence, "But, you'd have read her the riot act about being too young. Even though you and Dad met when you were only eighteen."

"I do understand, Nicole. She loves him."

"Mom, when you tell her. She'll be devastated. More than you know. Promise me you will stay with her. I mean, totally. Do not go off to see the other patients. No matter if she tells you to go ahead. Stay with her and don't leave her alone, not even with Uncle Tim."

CHAPTER SIXTY-EIGHT

Stacy called Dr. Cox on the director's secure, private line. "Identical results," she announced, "to the culture I took from the Tampa City Hospital lab. Technically, not identical, but close enough."

Stacy could hear Cox exhale. "My God. That means that the staph strain we're fighting in Tampa is based on the same one the NIH transferred to the CDC bank just before the NIH shut down their staph research program. The strain Victor Worth and Norman Kantor developed at the NIH when they worked there together."

"And both of those two were in Tampa City Hospital at the time of the outbreak." Stacy tried to sound professional, but she couldn't quite keep the excitement out of her voice.

"We've confirmed that Worth did visit Kantor in the ICU."

"Coincidence?" Stacy asked. "Or planned?"

"Norman Kantor's wife claims she was surprised to run into Worth that afternoon in the hospital cafeteria, told Worth about her husband's medical problems, brought him into the ICU to see Kantor."

"And?" Stacy prompted.

"The wife didn't stay. Kantor sent her out. When she got back, she asked her husband how it went. Kantor told her, 'Worth has a knack for making himself a pain in the ass.' That was it. End of discussion. Never again mentioned the name Victor Worth."

"So—"

"But," Dr. Cox said. "Thursday morning during a shift change, Worth was seen again in the main ICU. He had no reason to be in there. Wasn't on any patient's visitor list. His son was still a patient—but in the isolation room. A surviving ICU patient said that she can identify Worth as being in the ICU that morning. She'd assumed he was a staff doctor. He skipped two beds, hers and the one next to hers. Those two are the only patients in the ICU who survive. Agents are headed to Worth's house in Bethesda now, with a warrant."

"This was—murder?" Stacy asked, horrified. "He deliberately infected helpless patients? Why?"

"We don't know why," Cox said. "His only connection is to Dr. Kantor. Why the others? We don't know. Maybe we will soon when he's apprehended."

"They have enough to arrest him?" Stacy asked, doubting herself for the first time. Had she done the right thing? Victor Worth is a fellow scientist. What if she'd made a mistake? Verified the wrong premise?

"The FBI team has his address," Cox said, "We'll see. And meantime, you'd better scurry home and get dressed up for the gala tonight. You'll be surprised at who all is there, Stacy. Oh, and by the way, Dr. Nelson's daughter is improving. I know you're glad to hear that."

Stacy was. If only she could skip that dinner tonight and crash into bed. But Director Cox had left her no out, so Stacy left the CDC thinking about her nail polish color choice.

CHAPTER SIXTY-NINE

Stephen King's *Skeleton Crew* held no interest for Charles, so he tossed the book aside and slouched in the lone chair facing Lonnie Collins's desk.

He watched the clock tick by. Five o'clock came and went. No Lonnie. Nobody interrupted his solitude until he heard a key turn in the door.

Turning in his chair, he faced a stranger.

"Don't recognize me, hey?"

He knew the voice, all right. Nothing else about Will Banks was familiar. Unremarkable suit and tie, shiny buffed-leather shoes, and what must be makeup. Or a mask. Bank's pasty, lean face was bulked up and tan. His hair, normally a dull brown, was a sandy blond, with sideburns you could call stylish.

Before Charles could speak, Banks said, "I'm here as a guest tonight, Chuckie."

Charles watched Banks crack a wide smile, "Think I'll pass on the dessert, though."

"Thank God you showed up," Charles said, still looking his handler up and down, shocked by the drastic change in his appearance. "I've got to know where to go once the—" He found that he couldn't say the words.

"Once that you've infected a roomful of degenerates with flesh-eating bacteria?"

"You need to tell me what to do, where to go."

"Chuckie, I don't got to tell you anything. Show me where the bacteria are now. Lonnie's getting close. He's got the pastry shell shit all lined up. All the ingredients for the creamy filling. Yummy. I want to see your shit now."

Charles stood and bent to pick up his satchel. "It's in here," he said, "in test tubes. I'm going to use this special syringe." He pointed to the cylindrical object in the bag. "Hook up a needle, and start injecting the fillings of the profiteroles, one by one." He pressed down his right thumb, as if on a plunger.

"Why not just dump the nasty little bugs in a big mixing bowl?" Banks asked.

"Too dangerous. No reason to contaminate the kitchen. I don't want innocent people hurt. Just the banquet attendees."

"Okay by me," Banks said. "So you're good with this?"

"My duty to The Order," Charles saluted, right hand to heart. "I want to make my parents proud. Get to a safe place. Start all over. You will let my mother and father know, won't you? Where to contact me?" Charles already savored their praise. They'd not expect him to do something so potent, so brave.

"Of course," Banks said, "once you're settled."

"And that will be where?"

"I'll be back for you once the guests are enjoying dessert. Look for me in a busboy getup. I'm your master of disguises, so don't be scared. I'll get you out of here. And I'll make sure Mama and Papa are proud of their Chuckie."

"Will, I told you to call me Charles. I think I deserve more respect. Okay?"

"You just be ready when Collins comes to get you. Do your thing. I'll take care of the rest, *Chuckie*."

CHAPTER SEVENTY

The evening news played on Stacy's bedroom TV as she flipped through clothes in her closet looking for the most appropriate attire. She imagined the ladies arriving, coiffed, gowned, and bejeweled. The Goode family ladies especially. Stacy had seen the daughters' and daughters-in-law's photos often enough, in coverage of fashionable Atlanta political and social events. *The Atlanta Daily Reporter* had been as financially successful as it had been politically influential.

She had lots of classy business suits, but precious few cocktail dresses and nothing that qualified for the label, gown. She had laid out on her bed a dress with an embroidered tunic over a short white pleated skirt. Next to it, she placed the black satin bridesmaid number, knee length, straight skirt, scooped top. She wasn't thrilled with that one either, but figured November called for a darker outfit. She was about to replace the white dress on its hanger in the closet when she heard the evening news anchor introduce the next news story.

> In Philadelphia, Keystone Pharma today announced that Dr. Victor Worth has joined the company as director of Infectious Disease Research. In a late-breaking press release, respected Keystone CEO Paul Parnell, made the disclosure, noting that while at the National Institute of Health, Dr. Worth was instrumental in the discovery of a new class of antibiotic drugs effective in treating resistant staph. Today

the tragic bacterial epidemic threatening the Florida's west coast has—

Stacy stared at the news footage of a man identified as Victor Worth, shaking hands with the Nobel Laureate Paul Parnell renowned for developing the cure for a lethal adenovirus prevalent in Africa.

Stacy wondered if Director Cox knew about Worth's new post at the pharma giant. Would that make the FBI think twice about taking action against him for his suspected criminal role in causing the Tampa infections? She looked at the clock. No time now to speculate. Once again, she cursed Charles Scarlett. If not for him, she'd be in Tampa tonight with Director Cox, instead of trying to make herself glamorous enough to step out into Atlanta society. Just the thought of those four-inch heels was painful, but she could not delay much longer the moment when she'd have to slip her feet into the pumps. She zipped up the bridesmaid number, feeling the black satin soft against her skin. The soothing instant passed, and something in the back of her mind kept her off kilter—Charles Scarlett? What about the incubator log? No time now, she had to be out of the door. With reasonable traffic, she had just enough margin to arrive at the Palace fashionably late.

CHAPTER SEVENTY-ONE

The Keystone Pharma jet en route to Tampa with a ticokellin shipment for the hospital dropped Victor off at National Airport in D.C. For him, the day had been wildly successful. He'd signed the employment agreement and the confidentiality and noncompete agreements in the presence of Dr. Minn, his new boss, and the vice president of Human Resources. Then they showed him to the palatial executive suite of the CEO, the illustrious Paul Parnell. Norman Kantor had boasted of traveling to Stockholm with the wealthy gentleman for the Nobel Prize ceremony. Well, Norman, it'll now be me basking in Parnell's benevolent presence.

And to his astonishment and unadulterated delight, Paul Parnell asked if he'd be willing to participate in a press conference announcing his joining the research staff. Paul explained how important it was to try to reassure the public that all possible resources were being focused on a cure for the deadly staph now invading Tampa. Clearly, Dr. Minn had briefed the CEO on Victor's claim that he had the antibiotic drug that would prove effective against the staph: ticokellin's sister compound, biskellin—a compound without the risk of aplastic anemia. Victor's chest puffed up with pride, knowing that he would be seen across the country on tonight's evening news.

Now on his way from the airport to George Washington University Hospital, Victor felt exhilarated. Light traffic so far; chances were good he'd reach Matthew's room in time for the evening news. How proud his son would be. And for Matthew, the medical benefits would be incalculable. Access to top care through Keystone Pharma's connections. In Victor's position as head of all infectious disease research, he could handpick the most promising HIV cures, authorize clinical trials, provide access to antiviral medications currently under development by research institutes throughout the world.

But when Victor reached Matthew's room, his son was not alone. A young man looking about the same age as Matthew, with dark-brown hair, dark brooding eyes, and a neatly trimmed moustache sat on Matthew's bed, holding Matthew's hand, leaning in close as if to hear Matthew's every breath.

Victor had planned to try again to convince Matthew to remain with him in Philadelphia, not to return to San Francisco. But as he watched the two men together, Victor felt his hopes slipping away.

"Father, this is Vern," Matthew said. "I told you about him. We live together in San Francisco."

CHAPTER SEVENTY-TWO

Emma knew the preparation had been elaborate, but she had not anticipated the detail planners would lavish on her special night. The *Atlantic Daily Reporter* logo decorated every tablecloth; the Palace ballroom walls all had been papered with oversized photos of the early days, dating back to before her birth, through the years of her father's tenure, through the years of hers, and right up to two days ago, with wide-angle color shots of the paper's Thanksgiving dinner for the homeless. If only her siblings were here. She was the last survivor of her generation.

"Look, Grandma, that's you," the younger grandchildren squealed as the huge screen that dominated the stage started rolling a slide show of Emma's life.

And then the parade of well-wishers. Most she knew. Some she did not. Many were famous. Some were civil rights leaders. Some, popular entertainers. Most were black. Many were white. A few were Asian. Even fewer were Hispanic. Tonight, Americans of African descent were the majority. Her own fifteen grandchildren were the only kids in the ballroom—and not all of them kids anymore, she reminded herself, with one granddaughter in medical school.

As Emma stood, draped in the satin of an emerald-green designer gown that defined to perfection her slim, almost youthful figure, she felt blessed, yes. But she couldn't fend off nostalgic feelings as her life floated in front of her on the big screen. She missed Edward as well as her parents and siblings. They would never have believed this fairy-tale evening at the Palace Hotel.

Soon it would be time to go in to dinner, Emma thought. Would there be time to greet all the guests? She hoped so. It was the least she could do, considering that they'd come to honor her. Still hard for her to believe.

Stacy arrived at the Palace Hotel, just a few minutes before dinner was to be served. Traffic had been unreasonable, even for a Saturday night in Atlanta. She valet parked and made her way to the grand ballroom where she stood in a receiving line to meet the regal lady, who stood erect in her emerald-green gown. Emma Goode was seventy, but if it hadn't been for the gray that streaked her pulled-back hair, she couldn't get a senior citizen movie ticket.

Looking around the elegant room, Stacy saw no one she knew. If Madeleine Cox had been able to attend, Stacy knew Cox would be hobnobbing all over the room. Didn't that go with the territory of her status as director of the CDC. But she did recognize the gentlemen in the tuxes conferring near the bar: Maynard Jackson and Andrew Young. And joining them, Julian Bond. If only her mother were here. Lucy Jones loved Julian Bond. And out of the corner of her eye, she saw another of her mother's favorites. John F. Kennedy Jr. Mom remembered him as the little boy saluting his father's casket. A sad memory, but after losing two sons of her own, Mom seemed to cherish sad memories.

Stacy couldn't even imagine being in a room with so many important black people. People who had made a difference in so many lives, hers included, she thought. Stacy's father had died when she was ten years old. Standing here, about to say happy birthday to Emma Goode, she thought how proud he'd have been, the same feeling that she'd had when she graduated from Harvard. Her dad and mom had not had the opportunities that she had, thanks in large part to people in this room, people of both races.

She moved ahead in the line, still thinking about her dad—how deeply Dad had valued education. When Stacy reached the guest of honor, she extended her hand to introduce herself, careful not to squeeze Emma's delicate hand too hard.

"At the CDC," Emma commented. "They only hire the brilliant ones. I've interviewed Madeleine Cox and know how demanding she is of her scientists."

"She sends her regards," Stacy said, "but she had to stay on in Tampa, where we have teams trying to control an outbreak of serious infection."

"I'm glad Dr. Cox sent you, young lady. They told me you'd be here, and I know you grew up in Detroit. So you'll be seated next to John Conyers and Rosa Parks. She works with him, you know."

Stacy was astounded that Emma knew where she came from and that she'd be privileged to sit at the same table as the brave woman who'd refused to move to the back of the bus. If only her mother were here. Lucy idolized Rosa.

At that moment, a gong signaled guests to stroll from the cocktail party into the dining room. Stacy stepped back as three tall, tuxedo-clad men approached Emma.

"Time to go inside, Mom," one said.

"Escorted to dinner by my three sons, now that's a mother's dream." Emma gave Stacy a little wave as two of them offered her an arm and the third followed protectively.

I wonder if I'll ever have kids of my own. Stacy knew that Emma had had her first child when she was twenty-three and Stacy was already thirty-two.

As an usher showed Stacy to her table toward the front of the enormous ballroom, she kept an eye out for Emma's one bachelor son. But her fledgling hopes were dashed when Emma's youngest son veered off to join an equally tall white woman.

CHAPTER SEVENTY-THREE

"Time to suit up, pal." Lonnie handed Charles the creased white jacket and baggy checkered pants, along with a white baseball cap with no logo. "I don't like doin' this one bit, but they have my daughter. Will Banks swore they'll torture her, kill her, and dump her on my lawn. What happened to Russell Robertson doesn't leave much doubt as to how far Banks will go. Hell, he's got guys like us, active members of The Order, scattered all over the South. All he's gotta do is put out the word, know what I mean?"

Charles cringed. Yes, he did know. He accepted the bundle of clothing without a word and pulled the loose-fitting outfit over his clothes.

"You saw the menu?" Collins asked. "Lobster and filet mignon, surf and turf, only the best for this group. I took a peek in the dining room—JFK's son's supposed to be here. Didn't see him. Couldn't believe all the white people out there. Now what's the deal there? Shit, man, what if JFK Jr. eats dessert?"

The Kennedy family's civil rights stance had never endeared them to the Scarlett family. Charles thought of this year's conversation around the Thanksgiving dinner table. The typical race-bashing talk. What makes whites feel that they had to kowtow, and on and on. Dad's face had turned an angry shade of red when he fumed that even partners in his own firm were insisting that he had to appear more tolerant, kiss up to Atlanta's black mayor. Charles couldn't imagine his dad kissing up to anyone who wasn't white.

"You just keep your mouth shut," Collins said as he opened the door leading to the kitchen. "I've got the profiteroles all ready. All you have to do is inject them. One at a time. On the tray. I was careful not to overfill them so the cream won't leak onto the tray and contaminate the whole kitchen. I'll keep the other kitchen dudes out of your way. The trays are all lined up ready to parade out in style, the way the dining room manager likes it. 'Flashy elegant,' is how he always puts it."

Charles thought about tomorrow. When he would be far away in a safe place, so secret that Will Banks had not even told him. As for the diners sitting out there, who'd be oohing and ahhing about the delicate profiteroles? By this time tomorrow night, their skin would be peeling off as the staphylococcus organisms penetrated ever deeper, destroying one organ after another. The staph would move fast and relentlessly, multiplying as they go. No antibiotic could stop them. The Defense Advanced Research Projects Agency, known as DARPA, had been worried about something just like this and had been determined to terminate the CDC program, citing the potential for bioterrorism. They were worried, Charles thought, about the crazies in the Middle East or the remnants of Communism, never even dreaming of the possibility of homegrown terror inflicted by The Order. But DARPA was too late. The Order was on the move. The Order would prevail. Charles Scarlett was leading the cause. Chas and Rosabelle Scarlett would be so proud.

Charles followed Lonnie as they made their way into the large section of the kitchen dedicated to pastry preparation. All the walls were white, the machinery stainless steel, as were the mixing bowls and implements. Pretend you're in your lab, Charles told himself.

Charles found the trays of profiteroles all lined up as promised. Tasty-looking morsels of puff pastry filled with a creamy substance. "The chocolate drizzle?" he whispered to Lonnie. "When did you say that happens?"

"Has to go on at the very last minute, so it's still warm," Lonnie responded in a low voice. "And don't whisper. Other dudes will think it odd. Just keep your mouth shut. You can start right there." Lonnie pointed to the farthest tray. "Just do your thing. I'll casually hang back so nobody sneaks one. These things are so damn delicious. The staff's always pilfering them."

Charles hadn't eaten much for lunch and the aroma of the baked delicacies was overpowering as he shifted from foot to foot, anxious to complete his part of this massacre.

"I'm worried about the timing," Charles said, trying to keep his voice low while not wanting to attract attention by whispering to Lonnie. "These bacteria grow fast, and we don't want an odd taste." Charles assumed the bugs would be tasteless, but, of course, no one ever had ingested them. The meticulous safety precautions in the CDC labs had proved successful and so had the security systems. Until now.

Charles saw Lonnie look at the big clock hanging on the white wall. Eight twenty eight. Then he checked the clipboard hanging on a cabinet door.

"The schedule says eight thirty, but I need to wait for confirmation. They're collecting the dinner plates. I'll get word very soon that the first tables are ready for the dessert course. The trays go out two at a time. Fifteen plates on a tray."

Charles counted. Rows of twenty-five trays lined up on the counter closest to the door leading to the dining room. Plenty of room for him to inject the center of each. Pretty much as he'd visualized. Should work well as long as there was no one close enough to see what he was doing. Lonnie would be the barrier.

"There's always a few who'll pass on dessert," Lonnie said. "Though with my profiteroles, that's rare. If a server has extras on a tray, they are to bring them back, leave them on the tray, and put down the tray over there." He pointed to a cart with shelves that would hold several trays. "I'll keep that cart next to me. I'll watch it for pilfering. But I won't be able to control the profiteroles as they are carried back from the dining room to the kitchen. Anyone who sneaks one will—"

"Yes," Charles said, not wanting to dwell on that particular possibility. He'd made it a point earlier to call Bank's attention to this likely occurrence. Banks had shrugged. "Collateral damage, Chuckie," he'd said. "Can't be helped in war."

"You want me to start now?" Charles asked Lonnie, anxious to get the profiteroles injected and to get as far away from the Palace Hotel as possible.

"I'll take a look out there." Lonnie left Charles's side to peer out into the dining room.

Charles had gawked at the room before the guests were seated. He'd been to formal banquets with his parents, but the lavish appointments at this affair amazed him. And all for a black woman. Hard to comprehend. His dad would be outraged to see how far off-track America had veered. But, Dad would be so proud when he learned that his son, Charles Jr., was the instrument chosen to put America back on course. With that, Charles reached into his satchel, carefully, so gently, extracting the first of three test tubes. He already had unwrapped the syringes. Sterile technique must be meticulous to protect him against even one errant microbe—but that was his job, and he'd always done it well. Would it be his job ever again? Would this be his last act as a microbiologist? No more time now to try to foresee his future.

When Lonnie returned, he gave Charles the thumbs up, and Charles moved to the first tray. His back to the waiters and ancillary kitchen workers milling about, paying him no mind, he slipped on rubber gloves and worked quickly, injecting a tiny aliquot of the staph into each pastry center. The process took almost no time; he already had finished a whole tray of fifteen.

"Next tray," Lonnie said in a voice so low that Charles could hardly hear.

Charles saw that Lonnie, too, wore rubber gloves as he expertly tipped a spoon, drizzling warm chocolate sauce over the injected profiteroles.

They repeated the process for the next tray, and as Lonnie completed this final touch, he nodded for the server to pick up the trays for delivery to the dining room. As always, the first tray would go to the guest of honor's table.

CHAPTER SEVENTY-FOUR

Victor's head buzzed with the reality of his new, vaunted executive position and the notoriety that it had already attracted. But his heart, bruised by the reality that Matthew's relationship with this Vern would take his son away, put him in a funk.

He had arrived at the hospital in time for the seven o'clock news. With Matthew and Vern, he watched his appearance with Paul Parnell. Matthew had congratulated him, enthusiastically sharing his pride of accomplishment. Vern, however, didn't comment. He seemed not to acknowledge the magnitude of Victor's new position as lead researcher in the big pharmaceutical company. Apparently, Victor's expertise didn't impress Matthew's boyfriend. Expertise now critical to stopping an epidemic in Tampa and, perhaps, about to spread elsewhere.

Vern, as it turned out, was himself a researcher. He was an associate professor in the department of physiology at Stanford University in Palo Alto. Victor sensed that publicity like this didn't impress him. Arrogant, Victor thought, like someone who was accustomed to notoriety and wealth. When Victor had enumerated the elements of his compensation package, Vern all but sneered.

Victor understood why when Matthew later informed him that Vern's father was an investment banker who had made millions in health care start-ups. Victor wondered if Vern's old man knew that Vern was gay and was infected with HIV.

Before Victor could phrase the question, Matthew cleared up the matter. Vern's father had, in fact, become an AIDS activist in

San Francisco. What could be more appropriate than for him to oversee medical care for Vern and Matthew as they faced a future with AIDS? Did this mean Victor would have no say in his own son's care?

Exhausted as he was from his exhilarating yet demanding day, Victor still tried to out wait the boyfriend and get some time alone with Matthew. But Vern made no move to leave. Victor's plan was to delay until visiting hours ended, diplomatically suggest that Vern say goodnight, and then talk to Matthew about his discharge. Maybe when they talked alone, Matthew would agree after all to move to Philadelphia with his dad. On the way back from Keystone, Victor had concluded that prestige, money, and fame would not fully satisfy him. He needed to be close to his son, to compensate for all the years that they'd missed together. He felt compelled to be with Matthew.

Barely hiding his agitation, Victor waited for the nine o'clock announcement that would end visiting hours, as Vern clung protectively, intimately, to Matthew. Soon the two of them talked only to each other, excluding Victor, marginalizing him.

Victor began to wish he had not destroyed every trace of the staph he'd cultivated in his basement lab. All the official cultures had gone to the CDC. Would it be possible to get his hands on another culture? Once all the Tampa fuss blew over? In time to infect just one more person: Vern.

The door to Matthew's hospital room flew open and two men entered. One white. One black. Both wore suits.

"FBI," the white guy announced, extending a badge for Victor's examination.

The black agent, his hand on the large gun strapped to his waist, spoke clearly but in a normal voice. "Dr. Victor Worth, you are under arrest."

"What?" Matthew sat bolt upright in his bed, shaking off Vern's protective hand. "That's my father. He's a well-respected scientist. He was just on the evening news. Officers, you've made a grave mistake."

Stunned, Victor could manage only a proud smile as his son came to his defense.

"What's all this about?" Vern asked, standing up to inspect the proffered badge.

Pocketing his badge, the white agent produced handcuffs and approached Victor; his partner kept his hand on the gun, eyes roving from Vern and Matthew to Victor. "You're coming with us," he said, gesturing for Victor to show his wrists. "And you," he said, pointing at Vern. "I don't want any interference. Who are you? Let me see some identification."

"Why are you doing this?" Matthew asked, sitting upright, his eyes starting to tear.

As Vern started to reach into his pocket, the second agent, the one with the gun, said, "Carefully, sir."

"I know who you are," the agent said to Matthew. "We need to question you, too. We will be back. Right now, we have a warrant for Victor Worth. Interesting, what we found in your basement, Dr. Worth."

Victor's heart plunged. He hadn't taken the time to get rid of the broken shards of glass or to dispose of the autoclave. But with no live bacteria, so what? Big deal, so a microbiologist has outcast lab equipment in his basement.

"We're going to read you're your rights, sir," an agent said.

"Not necessary," Victor said, choking back panic. No Miranda warning. Not in front of his son.

The agent read it anyway.

Vern showed his driver's license, standing stiffly, glancing at the door as if he might bolt.

"Vern Lutz. Have to run your name."

"Matthew, what's going on?" Vern asked. "Are you in trouble?"

"Keep Matthew out of this," Victor said, his voice sounding old and weak. *Had they found active staph growth in the basement?*

"Officers, please, Dr. Worth is my father. He's a famous scientist. He was just on the news. He's going to produce a new antibiotic that will be effective in resistant infections. Like the one in Tampa."

"That so?" an agent said, securing Victor's wrists with cuffs, pulling them painfully tight. "I suggest you watch tomorrow's news for an update on your old man."

"Matthew, what did he mean by that?" Vern asked.

Victor twisted to face Matthew. He wanted to say something. But what?

"I don't know," Matthew said, his eyes wide, staring at Victor, pleading for him to say something.

"Let's go, Worth," an agent said, elbowing Victor toward the door.

On his way out the door, Victor heard Vern say, "I told you to not to get involved with that loser. But no, you didn't listen."

What could the Feds prove? Nothing.

Victor would not say one word until he had an attorney. Would Keystone Pharma provide one?

CHAPTER SEVENTY-FIVE

Luckily, in that simple kiss on Trey's lips, the bacterial load had not been nearly as high as if Natalie had received an injection of the staph. As grateful as Laura was for Victor Worth's role in discovering ticokellin, Laura was certain in her own mind that Worth had been the vector of death in the ICU. While the pulmonary technician disassembled the respirator, Laura sat in the chair by her daughter's bedside. Natalie still would be on oxygen, but her lungs were clearing and her blood gases good enough for her to come off the machine. Not out of the woods, Laura knew, but definitely getting better.

Natalie's face was averted. Could she have an inkling of what was to come? Laura was sure that she and Tim had not discussed Trey's death, yet somehow Natalie seemed to know.

"Okay, Natalie," the technician said, hands gently turning her head forward so her neck was aligned. "This tube will come out. It won't hurt, but it'll be uncomfortable. You might gag a little so I'm going to prop you up just a bit. Okay?"

A weak nod of her head, as Natalie listlessly watched the man deflate the rim holding the tube in place.

"Here goes," he said, slipping the plastic tube out of her throat. "Your throat will be sore, and your voice will be hoarse for a while." He helped ease her back against her pillow. "Doing okay?"

Again a weak nod of her head.

Laura looked to the hospital cot across the room. Tim was a

sound sleeper. You had to be to survive as a pediatric heart surgeon. Tim would not be able to help her through this.

Laura took a deep breath.

"Mom?" Natalie's voice was low and scratchy. "My throat does hurt. Especially when I talk. But—"

"Let me get you some Tylenol," Laura said. "The nurse left a dose for you. Liquid so it won't hurt your throat."

Natalie stared at Laura as she poured the red liquid into a dosing cup and brought it to her.

"Why is everyone wearing that?"

The isolation gear that looked like a space suit, worn by all hospital personnel.

"We have a terrible infection going on in the hospital. That's why you were so sick. But you got a special antibiotic and you're going to be okay."

Laura marveled at the effectiveness of ticokellin and mentally thanked Stacy for making it available to Natalie and the others. But she still worried about Natalie getting the rare but fatal side effect, aplastic anemia. Worry later, she told herself; be here, in the moment, for Natalie.

"Is everybody going to be okay?" Natalie rasped.

"No, not everybody got the antibiotic in time, sweetie."

Laura leaned in close to Natalie. Should she go ahead, or wait for Natalie to ask?

"Natalie, honey, about Trey—"

"Can I see him, Mom, can he come here or can I go to the ICU? Is he still in the ICU?"

The hurt, as Natalie tried to get the words out of her bruised throat, cut through Laura's resolve. What had Nicole said: tell Natalie the truth.

"Natalie, sweetie, I am so sorry, but Trey—he didn't make it." Laura stroked Natalie's uncombed, soggy blonde hair. "He died, sweetie. I'm so, so sorry."

Natalie's body began to shake, her chest heaved so deeply that Laura thought that she risked a convulsion. A croaky sob woke Tim.

"What's wrong?" he called, jolting to his feet, blanket dragging, and rushing to Laura's side.

Laura sat on the bed, taking Natalie in her arms, no longer caring if she ignored isolation protocol. In Laura's head, she heard the clunk as the dial pack of birth control pills hit the floor. How could she have been so insensitive?

"No, not dead." Natalie moaned through the sobs. "We are going to spend our lives together. Me and Trey. Please, Mom. Will you go check? Maybe there's been a mistake. Maybe he's just in a coma. Please make him wake up. I want to see him. Now." Still tethered to the bed by an intravenous line, Natalie struggled to pull herself up.

The bedside cardiac monitor started to beep and a nurse hurried into the room to check her patient's vital signs.

Natalie pulled with one arm to get up. "I have to go to him," she rasped.

"Sedation," the nurse said, and Laura stepped back so the nurse could inject the IV tubing.

Tim held Laura close as they watched Natalie drift off into sleep. Seventeen years old and her daughter feels, deeply feels, that her life is over. I know, Laura thought. *When I was nineteen, if anything had happened to Steve—*

CHAPTER SEVENTY-SIX

The next tray would be the last and Charles had to wait a few seconds for Lonnie to finish the chocolate drizzle before he could start to inject the next pastry. Only one more tray of profiteroles. Charles began to breathe more easily. His assignment had gone without a hitch. Lonnie had either dismissed his kitchen helpers or they were busy somewhere else. No one had paid him the least attention. He wasn't in the slightest worried about the process, this was so much like his everyday job, handling lethal organisms. Using a syringe designed with the latest in isolation technology, he methodically injected one plated profiterole after another. No problem.

He was curious as to whether the victims had started eating dessert, and as the door to the dining room swung open, he peered out. More white faces than he'd expected. What was wrong with those people? Was it political, because Atlanta had a black mayor?

Charles had thought that he'd feel a modicum of guilt for infecting so many unsuspecting people, with a flesh-eating death, but strangely, he didn't. He felt a surge of power and pride.

The swinging door had stayed open, and Charles continued to peer out, refocusing his attention on Lonnie, who warned, "When you're done, you take your shit and get out."

"Yes," Charles said, waiting for Lonnie to paint the last profiterole on that tray with warm chocolate sauce. "I'm taking all evidence and burning it." Until now he hadn't given much thought to how he would destroy the staph, but he hadn't been worried. Since there were no spores involved, he could simply boil the vials and syringes to kill the organisms. There would be staph organisms left on the plates, no doubt, but without the proper culture media, they'd die out fast. Strain AZ3510 was designed to strike fast in human flesh, but die quickly in ambient environments.

"That leaves me to stick around here and destroy any leftover profiteroles," Lonnie said.

Charles noted that a waiter had returned through the open door with an empty tray. He wondered when Banks would show up to disclose the next step, Charles's final destination. Time was getting short.

Charles knew that Banks was out there among the diners, posing as a busboy, watching the victims eat their dessert. But when he looked more closely, he saw that the diners were silent. Through the open door Charles craned his neck for a view of the podium.

A rotund, balding man of medium stature stood, his arm extended to the sky. "And joining me to lead the prayer is Coretta Scott King, widow of Dr. Martin Luther King Jr, who, himself, would rejoice in an evening like this."

Charles watched as the statuesque black woman, a familiar figure in the South, and if Charles was honest with himself, all over the world, walked to the stage. Dr. Martin Luther King, now that was a name that his father despised.

"Didn't we plan—" Lonnie repeated, retrieving Charles's attention, "to put any uneaten ones in the disposal with all the other garbage."

"Yes," Charles said. And they had, but he wasn't sure that the sanitation system was adequate to prevent any of the toxic staph from infiltrating the water system. Too many unknowns and Charles was not a sanitation expert. He thought that the bacteria would die off in a hostile environment, but he wasn't sure. He had a moment of panic. His parents, he'd need to tell them to use bottled water for the next few days. But then, they always used bottled water.

"I'm trying to locate Will out there. He should be back in here by now," Charles said.

"Not before you finish this last tray," Lonnie said, pausing as another waiter came through the open door with a tray containing two profiteroles. Lonnie deftly intercepted the tray just as the waiter reached for one of the pastries.

"Give me that," Lonnie said. "Don't eat that shit." Lonnie had on rubber gloves, and Charles made a mental note to put them in his satchel when they finished the last tray.

CHAPTER SEVENTY-SEVEN

At Emma's request she had been seated, not among the dignitaries, but with her grandchildren. Her eldest, Karen, sat at her right, and her youngest whom she considered her namesake, Emeril, a chubby four-year-old, sat on her left. The other kids ranged around the rectangular head table of sixteen.

Emma had been strict with her own children, but she never tried to discipline the grandkids, even if she found fault, as she occasionally she did, with their parents' child-rearing practices. Case in point; Emeril, reaching in front of her to grab a dessert.

"Emeril," she said, "didn't you hear the preacher? Everyone has to say a prayer first."

The child's arm remained extended, hand almost reaching the plate with the pastry. Emma looked to the nearby table where the boy's mother sat, eyes focused on the podium where Coretta King now stood. An only child, Emeril had been known to throw quite a fit when he was crossed; Emma wanted to avoid anything like that at this exact moment.

"I want one now," Emeril insisted.

Coretta King joined her pastor in prayer. Emma sighed. Now was not the time to correct a spoiled child.

Stacy had woofed down her shrimp cocktail—she'd eaten not a bite since a breakfast bar early that morning. But by the time the lobster and filet mignon were served, she was deep in conversation. Her plate sat untouched as she listened to John Conyers, Michigan's longtime U.S. Congressional Representative from Detroit and his heroic and celebrated assistant, Rosa Parks. Stacy found herself spellbound by Conyers's account of the Detroit riots of 1967, in which he'd prominently played a conciliator role. Stacy had lost two brothers to those riots. Those five nights when Detroit burned amidst looting and sniping would always stay with her. She could never forget. And what happened afterward. She could never forget that, either.

When the profiteroles were served on the fine china plates, Stacy promptly salivated. She felt the childish impulse to just pop a quick spoonful into her mouth. But, of course, she refrained. She'd sit politely though another moment of solemn prayer. They had prayed before each course. Stacy was Catholic, but the Goodes were Baptists. The Catholics prayed once, and that was it. Now she folded her hands on the cloth napkin and waited for Emma Goode's pastor and Dr. King's widow to finish what unquestionably was a record-setting lengthy prayer.

CHAPTER SEVENTY-EIGHT

Charles stared out across the tables. Even in subdued lighting, he could make out the shade of everybody's skin. Skin coloring had been important to his parents and thus to him. He'd learned that lesson after school in the fifth grade, the first and only time he'd invited home a kid with darkish-colored skin. He'd known not to associate with Negroes, of course, but this kid's skin was just a bit darker than the other kids'. A really great tan, Charles thought. But his mother had been quick to usher the kid out of the house and out of the neighborhood. She'd sat down with Charles and explained about skin color.

Absorbed by the mix of races, appalled by how this had come about, Charles jerked to attention as Lonnie interrupted, "Get the fuck over here and finish the last tray. What the fuck you lookin' at out there?"

One last glance from table to table as the preacher and Coretta King led the diners in prayer. So many different tones of skin color. Many quite dark and lots lily-white, too. Then his eyes fell on two white people. A man and a woman. Sitting among whites-only at a round table.

His hand opened, the syringe clacked onto the final tray of to-be-injected profiteroles, and he bolted through the door into the dining room.

The table compelling his interest was on the far side of the banquet room, so he had to run past several tables to get there. Most of the diners had their eyes reverently cast down so he didn't attract that much attention, but as he passed one table, he found himself staring into the eyes of Stacy Jones. He almost didn't recognize her in the scooped neck black dress, her hair up, pinned with a cluster of jewels. Fake, obviously.

"What the heck are you—" Stacy said.

Charles barely hesitated, then propelled himself toward the back table. Still, the diners focused on the podium.

Charles reached one of two all-white tables toward the back. Twelve people, exquisitely dressed, expensive jewelry. No fakes here. They looked out of place, their eyes wandering as Mrs. King recited what must be the last verse before her final amen.

The animated woman reached for her knife and cut into the dessert, smiled to her dinner partner, and with a fork scooped a generous helping of the cream from inside the profiterole.

"Mother, don't!" Charles yelled, diving toward the table, jerking the tablecloth off, sending everything on the table crashing to the floor, including the tainted profiteroles.

The fork had reached his mother's mouth, when his father stood. "Charles, my word, boy, what are you doing here? Why are you wearing—those clothes?"

"Put it down, Mother!" Charles shouted again, louder. "Don't eat that profiterole!"

Rosabelle Scarlett looked dazed as her hand continued toward her mouth.

"Dad, stop her, they're poisoned," Charles warned.

Charles, now at his mother's side, tried to slap aside the forkful of pastry, but tripped on a small, heavy handbag on the floor in front of him, and instead shoved the profiterole against her open mouth.

His father stood, grabbed Charles's arm, and yanked him back. "What's gotten into you, son?"

"Mother!" Charles's cry of anguish could be heard above the resuming chatter.

In an agonizing instant, Charles realized what he had done. Eyes wild, he looked around at all the black faces. All their fault. I have to stay calm. Let them eat their dessert. But his mother—

Out of the corner of his eye, Charles saw a busboy approach, stepping quickly. Will Banks in the promised disguise, his auburn hair in a ponytail. His coal-black eyes blazing with menace.

"Charles, look what you've done to my dress, it's ruined," Mother said, wiping away the creamy white filling with her napkin. "Have you gone mad? And what in Hades are you doing here?"

Will now stood next to him. "They need you in the kitchen," he told Charles, as if he'd been sent to fetch an errant kitchen worker.

"Charles, what is this all about?" his father asked, scrutinizing his checkered pants. "And you," he said to Banks, "get some soda water for my wife's dress."

"To the kitchen," busboy Banks reiterated, with a shove to Charles's shoulder.

Charles had no choice: leave Mother, obey Will Banks, return to the kitchen. His father would expect him to complete his assignment from The Order.

CHAPTER SEVENTY-NINE

Stacy shoved back her chair and chased after Charles. What was he doing here? A racist like him never would show his face at an event like this. And why was he tearing across the room and yelling? Dressed like a kitchen worker? No chef's hat but in a white coat and baggy pants. Moonlighting? Hardly. A trust fund kid who lived in a Buckhead mansion?

She caught up with him quite fast, considering her four-inch heels. She heard a yell, "Put it down, Mother." His parents? Stacy had always suspected they were old-school Klan. Attending an event honoring Emma Goode?

Only an instant. Less than an instant. Factoids converged. Charles's so-called sickness. Her suspicion that something may have been tampered with in the P3 lab. Oh, no! A terrible long shot. But what if— I have to stop it *now*.

She'd been close enough to hear the shout, "Dad, stop her. They're poisoned."

The man who must be "Dad" held onto one of Charles's arms. Stacy grabbed the other, pushing away a ponytailed busboy who seemed to be trying to intervene. What was Charles doing here? What were his parents doing here?

By now everyone was gaping in their direction. Stacy knew that she had to act. She hesitated for a fraction of a second, distracted when she heard the busboy order Charles to the kitchen. A Scarlett taking orders from a busboy? No time to ponder that. She had to act now. Not a millisecond later.

Summoning all her courage, Stacy took a deep breath and yelled as loud as she could, "Everybody! Stop eating! Now!" She could hear the "now" come out as a hysterical screech. The diners would think she was mad, a natural reaction to this outlandish behavior, yet she had to do something immediately. Letting go of Charles's arm, Stacy kicked off her shoes, and climbed onto an empty chair. She yelled again, this time trying to sound authoritative, like somebody in control, "Attention, everybody in this room!"

Now the diners gawked and silence evolved to a buzz, making her warning harder to hear. She heard a voice at the next table say, "Somebody call the cops!" She heard the busboy yell, "Get the fuck out of here!"

What Stacy did not see was a wave of profiteroles going into mouths. Good.

"I am Dr. Jones," she continued, trying her best to lower her voice an octave without sacrificing volume. "This is an emergency. I'm from the Center for Disease Control. I repeat. Stop eating. Do not touch the food. Do not eat the dessert. It may be contaminated."

"Get down from there, young lady," the distinguished-looking white man, whom she now knew was Charles's father, ordered.

She felt a yank on her dress, a rough arm go around her legs, the busboy's. She was about to repeat, "Do not eat the dessert," when her knees buckled and she tumbled off the chair onto the industrial-grade carpet.

Stacy pulled herself up, knowing that she had to repeat her message, reiterate her credentials, and stop everybody from eating. Based on Charles's warning to his mother, he must have contaminated the profiteroles. The creamy filling would be an ideal delivery form. Based on the creamy residue on Mrs. Scarlett's face, Stacy could predict the scourge that would be the sophisticated socialite's final hours.

"Let's go," the busboy said, yanking Charles by the arm, and dragging him away.

By then security, both uniformed and in tuxes, started to surround the table of chaos. Stacy could hear them talking into their radios: "unstable situation," "send backup," "get your people out," "unknown."

How could she make them believe her?

The first, a burly white man stuffed in a tux, reached her just as she'd shouted out again. "Do not eat anything. I'm a doctor. The food may be poisoned. I'm from the CDC. Don't touch—"

"Ma'am, what are you talking about?" He started to grab her wrists, but she yanked them behind her.

"Table eighteen," she said, "next to my chair. My purse. My credentials. This is an emergency. You have to quarantine everybody in the dining room and kitchen. We have a deadly bacteria. A flesh-eating bacteria. You have to stop everybody from leaving. We can't let the lethal bacteria out. We have to contain it in the hotel."

Stacy watched the big man recoil. A uniformed officer ran to her table and burrowed under it to locate her small purse and extracted her ID card. He rushed back to the growing group surrounding her. "Yeah, she's a doctor. Works for the CDC."

"I have to talk to Dr. Madeleine Cox, it's urgent. She's the CDC director. She needs to know this so she can tell you what to do. There's a number in my purse, her emergency line. She's in Tampa. Call it now. Hurry. Meantime," Stacy gestured to the officers, "do as I say and don't let anybody leave the hotel. We have a biocontamination emergency. Go! If you hurry, you can save lives. Please. Go. Now!"

Among the throng of officers, no one seemed to take charge. "Now," Stacy ordered. "Stop everybody from eating anything. Stop them from leaving the hotel. Everybody. From the head table to the serving staff." She spoke as loudly as she could. "We have a flesh-eating staph in this room, and it's resistant to all antibiotics. If you don't act, people will die a horrible death."

Finally, a tall, fit man appearing to be in his fifties stepped forward. "I'm taking charge, miss. God help me if this is not for real."

Stacy heard a male voice boom from the loudspeaker, reiterating her orders. Good.

But was she right? Or was she screaming about nothing at all?

Were the profiteroles safe and delicious after all? Could Charles be innocent of any wrongdoing?

As much as she did not want to be proved wrong and ruin her blossoming career, she hoped she was wrong. Maybe she had sounded a crazy false alarm. She hoped everyone who'd tasted a profiterole, including Charles's mother, would be just fine. Then she remembered Emma Goode's grandchildren. The horror if her theory were right and what if one of those cute little kids sitting around Emma—

The circle of police and security grew as even more officers converged on the Palace ballroom to enforce her quarantine orders. Having observed the quarantine procedure on-site in Tampa earlier that week, Stacy felt confident that what she was doing was right. If the AZ3510 strain from her lab was involved—

But what if not? She was in way over her head. Earlier in the day, she'd made a discovery that implicated Victor Worth in the staph outbreak in Tampa; this disaster was on a whole other level. With no solid basis.

Stacy had started to hyperventilate. She felt a tingling numbness and began to go lightheaded. She felt she might pass out, but rallied when a gentleman in a business suit showed her a badge, and escorted her over to a house phone.

"Director Cox, for you, Dr. Jones."

She took the receiver and began to brief the director on why she feared an AZ3510 incident could be an immediate threat to Atlanta.

CHAPTER EIGHTY

"Mother—" Charles called, sobbing as Banks pulled him into the kitchen.

"You fucked it up," Will spat into his ear. "You fucked it up before they ate all the killer germs."

"I can't leave my mother," Charles protested. "The cream must have gone into her mouth. Even if it's only on her skin, she'll be infected."

"Then she's a goner. Too bad. Collateral damage. Only you didn't think it'd be Mommie, did you, Chuckie. Now, you tell me, what the fuck were your parents doing at an affair for black people? You tell me that."

Charles had wondered. His father had mentioned that certain niceties were being expected what with so many blacks with money and in high places. But his parents? Descendants of the Klan? It didn't make sense.

Except for Lonnie Collins, the kitchen was empty. All the trays had been returned and stacked on the cart.

"I doused the trays with alcohol, just to be sure," Lonnie said, following Charles's gaze, "except the last one, the one you didn't do, but what the hell is going on out there? I sent my help home early so I could clean up the way you told me, then all hell started breaking loose. Two security guards started checkin' out the kitchen. Must not have found anything because they left right off. What's going on?"

Banks gripped Charles's arm tightly with his left hand, while in his right, he held a gun. Charles didn't know guns, but this looked big for a pistol—or maybe a revolver—and it had an extension. A silencer, he guessed.

Charles tried to pull away, but Banks held tight and pointed the gun at Lonnie's chest, and pulled the trigger. A clapping sound. Not very loud.

Before Lonnie hit the floor, Charles knew with absolute certainty that Banks would kill him, too.

Charles was left handed, and with his dominant hand, he picked up the syringe he'd dropped on the last tray of profiteroles. With one forceful jab, he discharged the contents into Banks's left side. Right into the flank, aiming for the kidney.

There was still enough staph in that syringe to down a roomful. Banks's hours would be numbered.

But what about his own hours? Lonnie dead on the floor. Banks staggering around, flailing.

Charles, syringe in hand, headed back into the dining room to find his mother. He had to tell her how sorry he was. How sorry he was to have killed her. Just like when he'd disappointed her when he was a little boy. "I'm sorry, Mommie, I killed you."

At first, no one noticed him amid the pandemonium as he calmly strode to his parents' table. Again, Stacy Jones stood in his way. His eyes met hers as she turned in his direction with a phone receiver in her hand. For a moment she stopped talking. Then said to a man right next to her, her voice audible but not loud: "Watch it, Officer—" a bit louder. "Behind you, Charles Scarlett. He's holding a syringe with enough lethal bacteria to kill us all."

That bitch, what the fuck. Without hesitation, Charles lunged toward Stacy, syringe poised. If he couldn't get in close enough, he'd launch it like a dart. She was responsible for all this. If she hadn't manipulated Stan Proctor to get that promotion, none of this ever would've happened.

Not far behind Stacy, he could see his parents. His father's face etched in anger, red, stern. His mother's face flaccid, pale, her eyes looking vacant. But he must focus on Stacy. Out of the corner of his eye, he saw his father rise up, move toward him. Is he going to strike me? Stacy had to pay. He took a step closer.

Charles felt pressure in his chest, like a refrigerator crashing into him. He tried to twist, to see through the door to the kitchen. Banks had a gun; he'd shot Lonnie. Had Banks also shot him? He never would know. The light went out of his eyes before he even saw the bright-red blood saturating his white jacket.

Stacy stood transfixed, the noise of the weapon discharging echoed painfully in her ears. Charles had been coming at her with a syringe, and she knew what was in it. A large tuxedoed man, a black man—FBI? Cop? Private security?—had fired at close range. Charles was down, lots of blood pouring out of his chest.

At first too stunned to think, she hesitated. Then clarity. What should she be doing? Chaos broke out after the shot. People were getting up, some running toward the exits, some throwing themselves on the floor, clambering under the tables. How could she be most effective?

Barefoot, Stacy maneuvered toward the stage, grabbing the microphone from the podium. The same podium where Coretta Scott King had just stood, reading a prayer.

"Everyone, I need your attention," she shouted, her tone urgent, but not panicky. "First, do not eat any of the food, but most important," she drew the microphone closer to her mouth hoping for more volume, "Do not eat the profiteroles, the dessert course. Do not even touch the profiteroles." Not confident that her voice could be heard over the pandemonium, she repeated the words, three times. "I am from the CDC. Dessert may be contaminated. Poisoned." She'd heard Charles yell to his mother, "It's poisoned!"

The tuxedoed black man, who said he was the Atlanta deputy police commander, took the microphone, introduced himself, and repeated Stacy's message. The only difference was that his voice thundered throughout the room. Several other men came up onto the stage and the big voice explained in no uncertain terms that no one would leave the ballroom. Quarantine procedures were being put in place. No one comes in. No one leaves. No exceptions.

Satisfied that law enforcement had things under control, Stacy left the podium and the stage. She needed to do one more thing before someone thought they'd better interrogate her. Had she been justified causing this terrifying chaos? Had she saved hundreds of lives tonight? Or not? She simply didn't know. What she did know: Charles was dead. What had he been trying to accomplish?

Stacy hurried toward the head table.

CHAPTER EIGHTY-ONE

Emma clung to the hand of her youngest grandchild, Emeril. The same hand she'd slapped just moments before. The hand that had reached for the profiterole while Dr. King's wife was speaking.

"Emeril," she had whispered, "that's not polite. We have to wait until the prayer is finished."

"No," her daughter Maxine's only child had declared. "I want one now."

This attitude was new to Emma. His cousins all were deferential, at least to her.

Torn between not wanting Emeril to fuss and letting him disrespect her, Mrs. King, and God, Emma made a choice. For the first time in her twenty-two years of grandparenting, she struck a child. Not really struck, just a modest slap on the hand. The result had been embarrassing. Emeril hissed, "You're not allowed to hit me." Result: stifled snickers from Emeril's fourteen older cousins.

Most important result: Emeril had not touched the profiterole. God, once again, had provided guidance, Emma realized.

And now, Dr. Stacy Jones, who was at the epicenter of whatever was happening, approached under the suspicious gaze of the bodyguards who'd showed up around her table and the tables of all her children.

"Mrs. Goode, I want you to know that I did what in my judgment was necessary," Stacy said. "For safety. I am so sorry that I ruined your retirement party. I was having such a good time until I saw my colleague acting suspicious. I believed, though I couldn't be absolutely sure, still am not, that he was trying to poison all of us, infect us with a deadly bacteria. I had to act. If I am right, anybody who ate those," Stacy pointed at the pastries oozing with cream, drizzled with chocolate, "would die a very painful death."

Emma tried to scan the surrounding tables for any empty dessert plates, but she couldn't see past the growing contingent of law enforcement and private security people. Her beloved husband, Edward, had told her never to skimp on security. "There are those who don't want to see us succeed," he'd warned.

Emma pulled Emeril onto her lap. He still sulked but gave in and cuddled when she held him. She gazed the length of her table: all the profiteroles looked uneaten and untouched.

"I just wanted to explain," Stacy said. "Now I have to make sure that these dessert plates are removed with sterile technique, stored, and secured. Director Cox will be in tonight, and I know she'll give you an update. I hope I was wrong and that this turns out to be a horrific false alarm. I really do."

"So do I, Dr. Jones, and thank you. You did what you had to do. You were brave. No matter how this turns out." With a sigh of profound despair, Emma acknowledged her fear that Edward had been right. *They don't want us to succeed.*

CHAPTER EIGHTY-TWO

Following Stacy's urgent call, Director Madeleine Cox left Tampa City Hospital a little before midnight. She'd commandeered an Air Force jet to fly her and Stan Proctor to Atlanta, where police met them and escorted them to the Palace Hotel.

She'd called Stacy from the air, confirming that she'd endorsed Stacy's initial quarantine orders, locking down the hotel, no exceptions. Not a pleasant task with all the dignitaries in attendance. But security was heavy at the gala, and the Atlanta police commander was a guest. Because Dr. Jones moved quickly to sound a public health alarm and to issue clear directives, the commander said, no one had left the building. One exception the cops knew about: a white male in his late twenties or early thirties, dressed like a Palace busboy, had been seen speeding away from the hotel in a white panel truck. Hotel security had observed the same truck earlier in the evening, parked in the employee lot near the service road exit. Atlanta police said the male driving the white truck resembled Dr. Jones's description of a busboy who scuffled with Charles at the elder Scarletts' table, and soon after, assaulted Dr. Jones herself. When she stood on a chair to warn everybody to stop eating, the busboy pushed her to the floor. After that, he managed to flee the scene.

Stacy had been relieved to see her boss, Stan Proctor, walk into the security director's office of the Palace Hotel. She was ready to transfer some of the tremendous weight of the evening's events to his hefty shoulders. But Stan, geared up in the hazmat suit looked ashen and withdrawn. He already bore too much weight. The toxic staphylococcal organism meant to infect hundreds of people came from his supposedly secure labs, carried by his supposedly sane scientist—who also held top-secret clearance. Stan's CDC program, already in DARPA's crosshairs, didn't stand a chance of survival now. Neither, probably, did his career.

The security suite of the luxury hotel had its quota of leather armchairs. Stacy had collapsed into a burgundy-toned one and stayed there, surrounded by FBI agents, recording devices, and radio receivers. She still was in her party dress, not yet having undergone the decontamination process the CDC had set up for everyone who'd come anywhere near the Goode banquet.

She answered the agents' questions as best she could. About the bacteria. About Charles. About herself. But the investigators took turns quizzing her, and she could no longer mask her fatigue. At first, the authorities had praised her fast action, but now they had more questions than kind words. Were they starting to look at her from a different angle? For a moment, she wondered if she needed a lawyer.

Director Cox's entrance created a diversion. Stacy got up from her comfortable chair and greeted her big boss. "I need a moment with Dr. Jones," Cox said, dismissing the cadre of agents.

"Sit down, Stacy," Cox said, looking odd in the bulky protective suit. "You've had a remarkable evening. How'd you get that tear in your dress? Hair looks good, though. I've never seen it pulled up like that at work."

The FBI had been harassing and haranguing her, and Madeleine Cox is talking about her hair?

"On our way in," Dr. Cox said, "Stan confirmed that the creamy centers of the profiteroles already on the tables were teeming with staphylococci. Our AZ3510 staph, the flesh-eating, resistant one. Lucky we have that rapid ID test. Your idea, as I recall."

Until that moment, Stacy had not known for sure what she had so strongly suspected. Charles's extra incubator minutes—Charles wanted to kill her and her people. The vile, despicable worm.

"Resistant to all known antibiotics," Cox continued. "Unlike the Tampa staph that's responding nicely to ticokellin."

"Victor Worth's ticokellin?" Stacy asked, reminded that she'd set up the experiments to confirm he was implicated in the Tampa toxic staph.

"Worth had a good day and a bad day," Cox said.

"Good?" Stacy could not imagine what about Worth's day could have gone well.

"He got a big job at Keystone Pharma, big comp package, lots of perks."

"He—?" Then Stacy remembered she had caught that on the seven o'clock news while she dressed for the gala at the Palace. She was so exhausted now, she'd blanked it out.

"Later, the FBI picked him up and put him in a cell. Next voice he hears will be the U.S. Attorney's. Intentionally infecting sick, innocent patients. Premeditated. Serial murder. How do you feel about the death penalty?"

Stacy always had been against capital punishment. But now? She was too tired to think straight, her brain a jumble of ghosts— Natalie Nelson's boyfriend and the others. Now, she couldn't be so sure.

CHAPTER EIGHTY-THREE

The quarantine lasted seventy-two hours. Emma's whole family—all twenty-nine of them—sojourned with her in the large meeting room allocated to them. Each was enveloped by an isolation cocoon, no physical contact, but they could communicate through the high-tech microphone embedded in each of their space suit-like getups. The kids loved it.

Early in their confinement, Emma had been despondent, appalled by the evil that was Charles Scarlett. She needed Edward to help her understand the depth of the hate and contempt that one human element imposes on another. Of course, Edward wasn't there, but Emma did feel his spirit reach down, cajoling her, as he always had, to move forward, to leave the past behind, and make a better world. So she'd shaken off her melancholy, encouraged each of her seven children to follow Dr. King's dream and their father's road of optimism. Each time her little Emeril strutted into view, a little brat compared to his fourteen older cousins, she thanked God. That child had come so close to the most horrible of deaths. Emma also thanked Coretta Scott King for the prolonged prayer that had kept them all waiting to eat their dessert.

On Emma's advice, the family watched one hour of news coverage a day. One hour and they turned it off.

What they learned: Thirteen known victims in metro Atlanta, of the virulent and disfiguring staph. The Goode family knew three of them: a pleasant white neighbor and a former college roommate of one of Emma's daughters, along with her husband. Also, three security detail, four banquet waitstaff, a member of the mayor's staff, John F. Kennedy Jr.'s bodyguard, and Charles Scarlett's mother. All dead within thirty hours of ingesting the tainted profiteroles.

The Goodes and the rest of the world learned more than they wanted to know about the hate groups out there. And there were many, too many. With the segregation battle lost, descendants of the Klan organized the Council of Conservative Citizens. Well-funded and politically connected, these rabid extremists united not only against blacks, but gays and Jews, as well. The council screened its members, who commonly stockpiled arms. They worked alone, lone wolf; or in small cells, strong packs. Speculation was rampant on the airwaves, but the consensus among experts interviewed on the news was that Charles must have been a member of a small cell that had recruited him specifically to discharge the bioweapon-grade staph. But no one knew conclusively. His mother was dead. His father refused all interviews.

On the last quarantine day, Emma had allowed an exception to the one-hour television rule. They'd be going home the next morning, all healthy, no bacterial growth on the myriad of cultures done on every accessible body fluid and tissue. Local news interrupted normal programming to announce that police had found a body in the driver's seat of a panel truck pulled off a side road leading to the Middle Georgia Regional Airport near Macon.

An off-duty flight attendant had noticed the van both coming and going on his commute on two consecutive days. He decided to take a look and persevered despite the intense odor emanating from the truck. Inside he saw a grotesque, melting body. He did not touch the truck; alerted, like everyone, by round-the-clock news about the deadly, flesh-eating staph. He'd pooh-poohed the coverage as hype, but now, he told reporters, it might have saved his life. On camera, the flight attendant described the body. In fact, the staph had liquefied all flesh and muscle, exposing elements of a slimy skeleton.

Later, the body was identified as William Matthews aka Will

Banks. Age thirty-one. A known white supremacist, member of the Council of Conservative Citizens, wanted by the FBI for questioning in a rash of hate crimes throughout the South.

Emma turned off the television and gathered her family in prayer.

EPILOGUE

THREE MONTHS LATER
FEBRUARY 1986

Laura and Stacy savored a cup of tea and a croissant in an airport coffee shop. During a random phone call, they'd discovered that their paths would cross in Atlanta. Stacy heading to San Francisco, Laura changing planes on a flight to Philadelphia.

"First flight I've been on since the epidemics," Laura said. "The hospital's back on course, busy as ever. The kids are in school. And I'm on my way to Tim Robinson's surprise birthday bash."

"How old is he and what's going on with you two?" Stacy asked.

"Tim's turning forty-five. I got an invite from the Pediatric Surgery Department at Children's Hospital. I got to know a lot of the doctors back when Patrick had his surgery there seven years ago. Tim'll be surprised to see me, in a good way, I hope."

"I'm impressed that you're going that far, leaving the twins and Patrick at home. No more significant motivation here than a surprise party?"

"No, Stacy, I don't think so. Tim's been there for me, albeit long distance since Steve died, but—"

"We'll see after this weekend," Stacy said, gulping her tepid tea. "Tell me about Natalie. You were worried about her the last time we talked."

"At first, she was reclusive, refused to talk to anyone except Nicole. She was angry, she told her sister; angry that I'd let Trey die. She believed that I could have gotten him ticokellin in time to save him. With time, she's improved. You know what helped?

Spending time with Trey's parents. I reached out to them, despite our legal entanglements, which, by the way, have gone away with a settlement to workers. The Standishes have literally put their arms around Natalie and, more than anyone else, have gone a long way toward convincing her that Trey did not have a chance."

"So she'll be okay," Stacy concluded.

"I think so," Laura said. "I hope so."

Both women checked their watches, smiled, and rose from the table. An elderly couple at the next table turned to gape.

"They're looking at you, Stacy," Laura said. "You're that famous scientist now."

"Hey, girlfriend, have a great party. I'll be thinking about you." Stacy leaned in to hug Laura. "And guess what? When I get back, I've got a date with that special agent who delivered the Tampa staph culture to my lab. Stay tuned!"

AUTHOR'S NOTE

While *Weapon of Choice* is a novel, with fictional characters, places, and events, the era circa 1985 was embroiled in the emergence of the biggest health care concern in modern history. Four years earlier in 1981 an outbreak of Kaposi sarcoma and pneumocystis among gay men in New York and California became known as GRID—gay-related immune deficiency. But soon the disease spread to heterosexuals, intravenous drug addicts, and patients receiving blood transfusions. In 1983, a virus was found to be the cause of the disease, and the outbreak became known as HIV/AIDS (human immunodeficiency virus/acquired immunodeficiency syndrome).

By 1985 a test was approved by the FDA for use in blood transfusions. In the meantime the virus was spreading throughout the country and there was no known cure. Thus the scenario in Tampa—the city's first known case of HIV/AIDS—typifies the reaction of communities all over the country as they grappled with the frightening epidemic shrouded in misinformation and controversy. In 1987, an antiviral drug, AZT, was approved by the FDA. That was the year President Reagan first publicly acknowledged the HIV/AIDS problem and used "AIDS" in a speech. Now, over twenty-five years later, we have dozens of drugs approved to fight HIV, but the disease is still a global plague.

Flesh-eating bacteria, as well as bacteria causing necrotizing fasciitis, are real and are usually due to either a group A Streptococcus or a resistant strain of Staphylococcus. Both are highly lethal. In *Weapon of Choice*, the research scenario in the NIH and the CDC is fictional, but judging from what we know about the government's experiences with anthrax, not unrealistic. In 1985, Iraq began an offensive biological weapons program producing anthrax, botulism toxin, and aflatoxin. In 1985, what was the United States' secret biodefense program focusing on?

We do know that in 1984, the American Biological Safety Association (ABSA) was officially established and biocontainment requirements were set and classified so that researchers like those in *Weapon of Choice* would have protection against biological hazards in their BSL3 (P3) laboratories.

As encountered in *Weapon of Choice*, the element beryllium is an industrial problem. Because of its stiffness, light weight, and stability over a wide temperature range, it is used extensively in the defense and aerospace industries as well as in the production of precision optical instruments, meteorological satellites, MRI scanners, and other sophisticated equipment. But beryllium is a Category 1 carcinogen and causes pulmonary and systemic granulomatous disease. The element can be handled safely as long as appropriate procedures are used. However, some individuals are hypersensitive to beryllium and if they inhale dust are susceptible to chronic beryllium disease, an immune disease that requires aggressive treatment.

In 1985, the Council of Conservative Citizens (CCC) was founded on the premise of white nationalism, and is now headquartered in St. Louis. The CCC was the 1980's reincarnation of the White Citizens' Council (WCC), which had been formed in the 1950s and kept active in the 1960s by remnants of the KKK in order to combat school desegregation.

The CCC is made up of local chapters, the agenda is unabashedly racist, and the meetings regularly feature politicians as keynote speakers. And like the KKK and the WCC, rabid extremism is never far from the surface at the CCC chapter meetings.

Circa 1985, white supremacy groups were active throughout the country. The Order, a radical extremist group, is real. Founded in 1983 by factions from the Aryan Nations and the National Alliance, the group funded their terror tactics by armed robbery, counterfeiting, and other violent operations until forced underground when the leadership was apprehended by the FBI in 1984.

Sadly, despite hate crime legislation, hate groups are active across America today. In 2010, The Southern Poverty Law Center had documented a staggering 1,002 active hate groups in the United States—a more than 65 percent increase since 2000.